Beckon

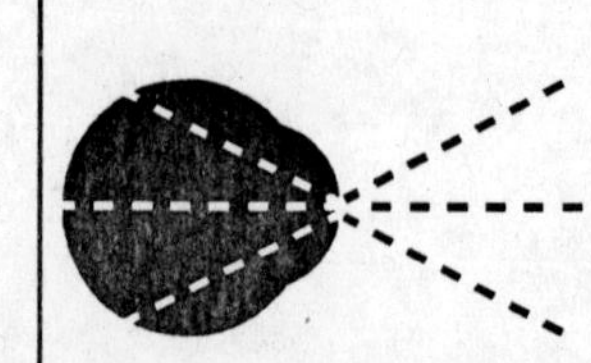

This Large Print Book carries the Seal of Approval of N.A.V.H.

Beckon

Tom Pawlik

THORNDIKE PRESS
A part of Gale, Cengage Learning

Detroit • New York • San Francisco • New Haven, Conn • Waterville, Maine • London

Scripture quotations are taken from the *Holy Bible,* King James Version.
Thorndike Press, a part of Gale, Cengage Learning.

This novel is a work of fiction. Names, characters, places, and incidents either are the product of the author's imagination or are used fictitiously. Any resemblance to actual events, locales, organizations, or persons, living or dead, is entirely coincidental and beyond the intent of either of either the author or the publisher.
Thorndike Press® Large Print Christian Mystery.
The text of this Large Print edition is unabridged.
Other aspects of the book may vary from the original edition.
Set in 16 pt. Plantin.

LIBRARY OF CONGRESS CATALOGING-IN-PUBLICATION DATA

Pawlik, Tom, 1965–
Beckon / by Tom Pawlik.
pages ; cm. — (Thorndike Press large print Christian mystery)
ISBN 978-1-4104-4981-8 (hardcover) — ISBN 1-4104-4981-5 (hardcover)
1. College students—Fiction. 2. College teachers—Fiction.
3. Businessmen—Fiction. 4. Small cities—Fiction. 5. Large type books.
I. Title.
PS3616.A9573B43 2012b
813'.6—dc23 2012014520

Published in 2012 by arrangement with Tyndale House Publishers, Inc.

Printed in Mexico
1 2 3 4 5 6 7 16 15 14 13 12

For Andrew, my firstborn.

ACKNOWLEDGMENTS

To my beloved wife and best friend, Colette: What a blessing you are to me. Your support and encouragement continue to inspire me. I thank God for that day you walked up the driveway and I said you had the wrong house and you told me to shut up . . . and we've been in love ever since. Though, all things considered, I have by far gotten the better end of the deal.

To my Pentebrood — Andrew, Aryn, Jordan, John, and Jessi: You have subtly transformed my passion for writing into a necessity. But I wouldn't change a thing. You'll never know how much I love you until you have children of your own someday.

To my agent, Les Stobbe: Thank you for all your prayers, counsel, and efforts on my behalf.

To Dan and Dr. Rachael Romain: Thank you for the enthusiastic support and for lending your expert scientific consultation to this endeavor. And especially for cool-sounding terms like *oxidative phosphorylation.*

To the great team at Tyndale:

Stephanie Broene — thank you for your continued input, patience, and encouragement. It was a long and arduous road but hopefully a worthwhile one.

Sarah Mason — once again it was a distinct pleasure working with you on this project. Thank you for all the spackling, sanding, painting, varnishing, and polishing that this book needed. You should have your own editorial reality show.

Dean Renninger — thank you for your inspired work on the cover design. Once again you've captured the mood of the book perfectly and hit the three c's: cool, creepy, and compelling.

Babette Rea, Andrea Martin, and the whole sales and marketing team — thank you for all your ongoing efforts to make this project successful.

And last but not least, to Jerry Jenkins and your excellent staff at the Christian Writers Guild: May God continue to bless your service for Him.

And the Lord God formed man of the dust of the ground, and breathed into his nostrils the breath of life; and man became a living soul.

GENESIS 2:7

■ ■ ■ ■

Part I
Jack

■ ■ ■ ■

Of all the animals, man is the only one that is cruel.

MARK TWAIN,
LETTERS FROM THE EARTH

Chapter 01

Chicago, Illinois

The last time he saw his father alive, Jackson David Kendrick was only nine years old.

The gray light of dawn was seeping in between his bedroom curtains when Jack woke to find him standing in the doorway. Dr. David Kendrick was a willowy, spectacled anthropologist at the University of Chicago. His black skin and wide brown eyes gave him a youthful appearance, but the flecks of silver frosting the edges of his hair made him look more distinguished and professorial. So people who didn't know him could never tell if he was twenty-nine or forty. But this morning, his normally thoughtful eyes looked weary as he sat on the edge of Jack's bed.

"Sorry to wake you so early, but my flight leaves at seven thirty."

"Where are you going this time?" Jack sat up and asked through a husky yawn.

"Out west," his father said. "Some field research on an old Indian legend."

His father had often explained the kind of work anthropologists did, but all Jack really knew was that he was gone more often than not. Always traveling around the world to study some obscure ancient culture. He said he was trying to learn more about them — who they were, where they had come from, and why they had disappeared. But Jack had always felt there was something in particular he was searching for. Something that continued to elude him. Most of the time he would come home from his trips looking tired and disappointed.

"What kind of legend?" Jack persisted, figuring that if he kept peppering his father with questions, he could keep him from leaving as long as possible.

His dad stared out the window for a moment. In the shadows, Jack thought he saw hesitation in his eyes, as if he was pondering exactly what to say. "One about a very *old* civilization that I believe actually existed out there. A long time ago, before most of the other tribes had even migrated to this continent."

"Who were they?"

"Well, that's just it — nobody knows for sure. One legend says they built a whole subterranean city under a mountain somewhere. And that they may have been very advanced . . . maybe even more advanced than the Egyptians."

"That's cool."

"Very cool." His dad grinned. "Anyway, it's kind of a mystery I've been working on for a few years now. So if I can find some proof that they actually *did* exist . . . well, it could change most of what we know about human history."

"Change it how?"

His father laughed and rubbed Jack's hair. "I'm on to you, kiddo. I'm running late, so we can talk more about it when I get home."

"Fine," Jack huffed. "Are you gonna be back for my soccer game on Saturday?"

"I'll try, but Aunt Doreen's bringing her video camera just in case."

Jack's shoulders drooped. His father's sister had moved in with them after Jack's mother died in a car wreck six years earlier. It wasn't that he disliked his aunt — indeed, she was the closest thing to a mother Jack could remember. It was just that his father had missed five of his last seven games, and watching Aunt Doreen's shaky video footage wasn't the same.

His father stood to leave, but Jack clutched

his wrist. "When can I start going with you?"

His father looked down and sighed. "Maybe when you're a little older."

Jack groaned and lay back on his pillow. "You always say that. But you never say how much older."

His father gave a soft chuckle. "Just a little more than you are now."

He kissed Jack on the forehead and slipped out of the room. Jack listened as he collected his bags from the hallway and carried them out to the car. A minute later the engine chugged to life, and Jack ran to the living room window as the car backed out of the garage. He watched his father drive off down the street, turn the corner, and disappear.

Chapter 02

Chicago, Illinois
Twelve Years Later

"Jack . . . you haven't gotten any further."

Jack Kendrick looked up from behind his father's old mahogany desk as Rudy finally returned with the pizza. "Because I've been too weak from hunger. What took you so long?"

Rudy shrugged. "It's Friday night. The place was packed."

Jack had spent most of the day sorting through the contents of his house, trying to get it ready for the estate sale. He'd been making great progress until he got to his father's study. In that room Jack felt more like he was emptying memories out of his own head, dredging up a strange concoction of old emotions.

Rudy set the pizza on a stack of boxes. "You've been stuck in here for the last three hours. What's up with that?"

Jack sighed and shook his head. "I guess I just put it off too long."

Jack and Rudy had been best friends since their sophomore year in high school, when Rudy's parents relocated from New York. Jack had first seen the scrawny white kid getting harassed by a gang of juniors and couldn't help but feel sorry for him. He had intervened on Rudy's behalf and wound up getting suspended for the ensuing fistfight — just one of many during his teenage years. His aunt Doreen had grounded him for a week, but he had won a loyal friend in Rudy Peterson.

Jack took a slice of pizza and looked around the room. "He never even let me in here when I was a kid. Dad was always pretty guarded about his work."

"I guess." Rudy chuckled. "So, what? You got this psychological never-measured-up-to-my-old-man's-expectations-and-now-I'm-all-filled-with-regret thing going on?"

"No, it's just that there's so much stuff," Jack said through a mouthful of pizza. "He never threw anything away. I guess he was a more meticulous researcher than I remember."

"Y'know, Jack, no offense, but some people call that being obsessed."

Jack stared at the stacks of boxes filled

with files and books and a host of obscure artifacts his father had collected from all over the world. The man had apparently not been able to part with any of them. And neither had Jack.

The last twelve years had been filled with regret. A day hadn't gone by that Jack didn't wish he could travel back in time and beg his father not to go on that trip. But research had been the man's sole passion in life.

He'd written several papers on his theories about the lost pre-Columbian civilization, none of which were very well received by his peers in the anthropological community. In fact, they had largely repudiated them. After his disappearance, one had even written an article for the *American Journal of Archaeology* titled "David Kendrick's Fatal Obsession."

The scurrilous piece had been intended to lay his father's crackpot ideas to rest once and for all, but it had only served to strengthen Jack's resolve, and he promised himself that someday he would make them eat their words.

So when he finally arrived at the U of Chicago, Jack pursued his degree in anthropology with the goal of salvaging his father's reputation and following in his research. It had been no easy task enduring the insufferable arrogance and condescension of his father's former colleagues. Yet for Jack, rehabilitating his father's legacy had now become *his* life's expedition. *His* odyssey.

His obsession.

After graduation, Jack was set to start working on his PhD and decided it was time to finally sell the old house to help finance this new stage in his life. And part of him was well ready to be rid of it. The place had become a brooding mausoleum of sorts, haunted by the ghosts of a father he had barely known and a mother he couldn't remember.

It had only been on the market for two weeks when he'd gotten an offer, and now he was in a rush to clean it out. Aunt Doreen and his other relatives had already divided up most of the furniture, and Jack was going to box up the files and artifacts from his father's office to go into storage. Everything else was slated for the estate sale. Jack would've loved to bring the massive, ornate desk with him, but he knew it wouldn't fit in his apartment. He just hoped it would go to a good home. A doctor or a lawyer perhaps. Or maybe another teacher.

They polished off the pizza, and Rudy started hauling boxes to the garage while Jack finished cleaning out the desk. He pulled the drawers out one by one to wipe the insides with a damp rag. Years of dust and moisture and more dust had built up a mucky residue.

Jack was stacking the drawers in a clear spot on the floor when he noticed something strange. One of the drawers was a little shorter than the rest. And the back panel looked like it had been glued together with considerably less craftsmanship than the others . . . as if someone had lopped four inches off the drawer's length to make room for something inside the desk itself.

Jack peered in and saw a crude wooden box mounted to the back with something wedged inside. His heart was pounding as he pulled out a large yellow envelope and tore it open. Inside was a brown folder.

Rudy returned for more boxes, and Jack showed him what he had found. Rudy's eyebrows curled into a frown. "What is it?"

"I don't know," Jack said, almost too excited to talk.

The folder contained several loose pages, and Jack laid them out on the desk. One of them looked like a copy of some kind of official document. Large portions had been blacked out, but it appeared to be a journal entry or maybe part of a report. The date in the corner was four months before his father had disappeared.

> . . . suggests similarities to original piece found in . . . pre-Columbian engravings, even though the peripheral markings point to a later dating; the design and construction are definitely Bronze Age or earlier. . . .
> Access to the original data is extremely limited. . . . has been kept under tight security at . . . The first artifact discovered in . . . and the next stage is to determine location of second site . . . hopes to find the second piece at that location.

There were also several photocopied pages from an old *National Geographic* article titled "Diminishing Caieche Population Raises Concerns among Anthropologists."

The body of the article largely discussed the plight of an obscure American Indian tribe in western Wyoming called the Caieche. Anthropologists worried that the decline of the enigmatic tribe could lead to a total loss of their history, still relatively unknown. But there was no mention of an artifact or anything else related to the first document.

The final page contained what appeared to be a hand-drawn depiction of a circular emblem with various figures scattered

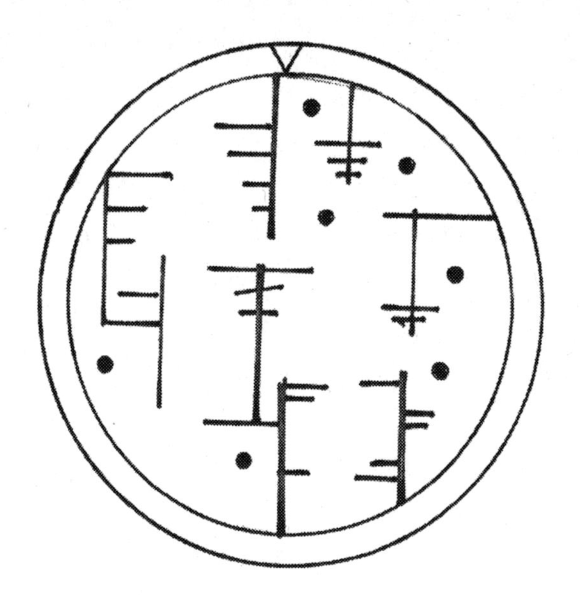

around the interior.

There was some text in the lower corner of the page that had been blacked out completely. Everything except a string of numbers: 520712.

Rudy peered over his shoulder. "What is that thing?"

Jack could barely contain himself as he paced the study. "I'm guessing it's a drawing of the artifact the report mentions."

"Yeah, but what *kind* of artifact?"

Jack shook his head. That was the million-dollar question. The mystery only seemed to deepen. He had spent the better part of the last twelve years looking for an answer to his father's disappearance. The FBI had searched for months but found no trace of him. No clothing, no equipment, not even his rental car. Yet after all these years, these documents had to hold some significance. Some clue to what had happened.

Rudy continued, "Why would he hide these in here?"

"And who was he hiding them from?" Jack muttered, lost in thought. Then he perked up. "I need a map of Wyoming. I have to find this reservation from the article."

They went to the kitchen, where Rudy had his laptop sitting on the table. He booted it up and typed *Caieche* and *Wyoming* into the Internet search engine.

"Not much here on the Caieche," Rudy said. "But it mentions the small reservation in Wyoming. Eagle Creek."

"That's got to be where my dad went. I bet someone there talked to him. They might even remember him."

"Jack, look —" Rudy held up his hands — "I don't mean to rain on your parade, but that was twelve years ago. And you don't even know if that's where your dad actually went."

"It's got to be. The only clue the FBI had to where he went was his plane ticket to Salt Lake City. And this Eagle Creek reservation is only a few hours' drive from there."

Rudy snorted. "And a much longer drive

from Illinois."

"I know." Jack grinned at him. "That's why you're coming with me."

Rudy shook his head and laughed. "Uhh . . . no, I'm not. I've got a research internship lined up for the summer, remember?"

"C'mon, Rudy, all I need is a week," Jack persisted. "Two, tops. We can take my dad's old Winnebago and make a whole road trip out of it. It'll be fun."

"Dude . . ." Rudy rubbed his eyes. "I'm telling you, I am *not* going to Wyoming. Especially in that ratty old RV. Does that thing even run?"

"Of course it runs. It runs just fine." Jack tried to sound confident, though he hadn't had the vehicle running in over a year. "I've just . . . never actually taken it that far before."

"Which is another reason why I'm not going with you."

Jack grew serious. "Look, this is the first real clue to finding out what happened to my dad. Do you have any idea what that means to me?"

"That's exactly my point. You're not thinking straight. Your dad disappeared out there somewhere, and now you want to go after him? You don't think that's a little dumb?

Not to mention dangerous?"

"That's because he was alone. He didn't have anyone to watch his back. I'm not going to make that same mistake."

"No, you're going to make a whole new one."

"That's why I need *you,*" Jack said. "I need your expertise."

"Really? I have a molecular biology degree. How much good will that do you?"

"Come on. You've forgotten more about science than I'll ever know. Plus, you're the only person I really trust on this." Jack sighed, and his voice softened. "I'm asking you . . . *please.* You're my best friend. I need your help."

Rudy stared at him for a moment. A long, painful moment. At length he rolled his eyes and took a breath. "Fine. Two weeks. Just don't get all sappy on me."

"Great." Jack grinned and slapped Rudy's shoulder. "I knew I could depend on you."

Chapter 03

Eagle Creek Indian Reservation,
Western Wyoming

Rain fell in raucous volleys, drumming down on the ramshackle 1978 Winnebago as it crept along a gravel road. Jack gripped the wheel with the resolve of a grizzled sea captain. A metaphor, he decided, that at present was not so far off the mark. Beside him, Rudy was slouched in the passenger seat, baseball cap pulled down over his eyes. Snoring.

Jack had begun planning for this expedition immediately after the estate sale two weeks earlier. He bought all the gear he thought he might need for the trip and packed up his father's old RV. Then the two of them set out four days ago, making the road trip from Chicago to Wyoming. Rudy had come along as Jack's science expert, to document the trip on video, and for general moral support.

They lurched through water-filled potholes in the road, some of which looked big enough to have their own lifeguards. The tattered wiper blades swish-swashed valiantly in a hopeless struggle against the barrage of raindrops pelting the windshield like an angry mob lobbing water balloons. Jack knew they could get mired in one of the massive puddles at any second, but he had to keep going. Sheer anticipation was driving him now.

After all these years, he was finally on the cusp of finding some answers.

He could see the A-frame visitor center ahead through the rain and pulled into the small parking lot. The place was empty with the exception of the guy managing the gift shop. He was a burly, middle-aged Caieche with a name badge that read *Ben Graywolf* and a thick mane of gray-streaked hair pulled back in a braid.

Jack explained that he was an anthropologist curious about Native American myths and legends. "My father was doing research a while back on a lost civilization that he believed may have existed out here a long time ago. And he seemed to think the Caieche might have some stories about one."

"Lost civilization?" Ben frowned. "You

mean like the Shadow People?"

"Shadow People?" Rudy snorted. "Yeah, that sounds innocuous."

But Jack ignored him. "What can you tell me about them?"

Ben shrugged. "Well, they're just a bunch of old ghost stories, really. The N'watu, they're called. The Shadow People. The legends say they lived inside caves somewhere in the mountains."

"What mountains? Someplace nearby?"

"No one knows for sure," Ben said. "Like I said, these were mostly stories we heard as children. But if you really want to know more, you should probably go talk to Running Bear."

"Running Bear?" Jack said, looking around. "Great. How do I find him?"

"He's the oldest man on the reservation." Ben gestured out the window. "He lives in a little shack up in the hills. I close up in a half hour. I can take you past his place if you don't mind waiting."

Forty-five minutes later, Jack and Rudy were following Ben's battered white pickup along the gravel road deeper into the wilderness. They arrived at a dilapidated log cabin perched alone on the crest of a rocky knoll jutting out of the forest and sloshed through the mud onto the sagging front porch, where Ben knocked on the door.

"I can stick around if you want," he said. "You'll probably need me to translate anyway."

"He doesn't speak English?" Jack said.

Ben chuckled. "Oh, he speaks it okay. He just doesn't always *want* to. He can be a bit stubborn that way."

After several long moments the door finally opened, and Jack immediately understood why it had taken so long. Peeking out from inside was a shriveled old man. His face was gaunt and leathery and stippled by enormous moles and liver spots. Had Jack not witnessed him moving under his own power, he'd have sworn the little guy was just some mummified museum exhibit.

Ben gave the old man a greeting in the Caieche language and then introduced Jack and Rudy. Running Bear nodded brusquely with his pale eyes sparkling and waved them inside. The one-room hovel was quite warm and smoky with a fire crackling in a small stone fireplace. He motioned for them to sit down, and since there was only one chair in the place, they all took a seat on the dusty wooden floor near the fire.

The rain continued to drum softly on the roof in a mesmerizing rhythm as Ben asked

Running Bear to give a brief history of the Shadow People legends.

The old man sucked in a raspy breath and spoke in the Caieche language with a voice that sounded like a box of rattle snakes. Or at least what Jack imagined a box of rattlesnakes would sound like. It crackled and hissed, barely above a whisper and with little inflection, fading beneath Ben's stronger baritone interpretation:

"When the Caieche first arrived on this land, there was already a tribe dwelling in the mountains. No one knew how long they had been there. The Caieche called them . . ." He paused and cast a quizzical glance at the old man.

"N'watu keetok taw'hey," Running Bear repeated.

Ben seemed to have difficulty translating the phrase. "The shadows . . . that . . . walk."

Running Bear shook his head, his pale eyes flaring as he said again, *"N'watu keetok taw'hey."*

"Sorry. They who walk in shadows." Ben rolled his eyes and muttered, "He's very picky about the language. We always just called them the Shadow People."

Running Bear continued with his discourse and Ben hurried to catch up.

"Anyway, they used to say the N'watu

worshiped the spirit of the mountain."

"Spirit?" Jack said, taking notes in a journal. "What kind of spirit was it?"

Running Bear went on.

"They called it Sh'ar Kouhm — the Soul Eater," Ben said. "They believed there was a gateway to the underworld deep inside the caves. Sh'ar Kouhm was the queen of the underworld and would come up at every full moon to feed on a human soul . . . or . . ." He seemed to search for the right word. "On the emotions. Fear and anger. The strongest emotions of a person's soul."

"Soul Eater?" Jack frowned. "So what happened?"

"Apparently their elders made a bargain with Sh'ar Kouhm. If the N'watu could provide her with souls from other tribes, she would leave them in peace."

Rudy raised an eyebrow. "Why didn't they just move out of the caves altogether? Y'know, find somewhere else to live?"

Running Bear peered at him in the firelight for a moment. Then he spoke in soft, broken English. "Would you give up your home so easily?"

Rudy shrugged. "Well, I wouldn't resort to human sacrifices just to hang on to it. That's for sure."

"Look," Ben interjected, "this is all just a

bunch of old stories. I mean, nobody actually *believes* this stuff anymore."

Running Bear seemed to grow agitated and responded to Ben's comment. Ben rolled his eyes again and replied in Caieche.

Jack interrupted their argument. "What's he saying?"

Ben sighed. "He claims the N'watu took his great-grandmother when his granddad was just a kid. Apparently he saw them. They were like ghosts or something."

"Wait a minute," Jack said. "He says his *great-grandmother* was actually *kidnapped* by the N'watu?"

Ben shrugged. "Like I said, that's what he says his grandfather used to tell him. But I think he may have been a little, y'know . . . few eggs short of a dozen or something. That's what I've heard, anyway."

"Were there any other witnesses? Did they try to go after her?"

"I think they just assumed she had run off with another man or gotten killed by a mountain lion or something," Ben said. "Nobody ever talked about it much."

"Still," Jack said, "it's a pretty compelling story. Does he know where the caves are?"

Running Bear spoke in a heated tone, and Ben appeared to be trying to calm him down.

"He says not to go off looking for the caves," Ben explained. "He says there's something evil in that place."

"No doubt," Rudy offered in agreement.

Jack reached into his pack and produced the papers from his father's desk. "Look, my father disappeared somewhere out here twelve years ago, and I'm trying to find out what happened to him." He pulled out the page with the image on it. "He had this drawing. I think it was some kind of artifact he was searching for. Does this look familiar at all?"

Running Bear's eyes fixed on the drawing. He seemed intrigued and yet a little sad at the same time. He spoke slowly.

Ben translated. "He says he's seen this before."

"He has?" Jack leaned forward. "Where?"

The old man rose from his chair and shuffled over to a shelf on the other side of the room. He returned with a folded piece of cloth, carrying it gingerly in his arthritic fingers, and sat down again. Unfolding the cloth, he revealed a swatch of something that looked like animal hide. He held a narrow strip of soft leather up in the firelight, where Jack could see faded red markings. Several bands of lines connected in parallel and perpendicular designs across the length of the material.

The markings looked nearly identical to the ones in the artifact. As if they were characters from the same alphabet.

Running Bear nodded and spoke.

"He says it's the language of the N'watu," Ben said. "His grandfather wrote them down long ago. He claimed to have seen this writing inside the cave where his mother was taken, then wrote it down from memory."

"His grandfather was *inside* the cave?" Jack said.

Running Bear's soft voice replied, and Ben translated.

"His grandfather once told him the story about how he had been inside the cave when he tried to save his mother."

"Did he tell him where the cave is? Does he know where to find it?"

Running Bear nodded and spoke as Ben translated. "Through the waters at the head of the Little White Eagle. In the cleft of the mountainside." Ben leaned aside. "I'm pretty sure that's White Eagle Creek. Just a couple miles north of here."

Running Bear went on.

"He wants to know where your father saw this figure," Ben said.

Jack shook his head. "I don't know. I just

found his papers a couple weeks ago. But this could prove his theories weren't so crazy after all. If I can find this cave and get pictures of the writing inside it . . . that would be *huge.*"

Running Bear spoke in a weary tone.

"He warns you not to go," Ben said, almost apologetically.

But Jack was having none of it. He wasn't going to stop for the sake of some old Indian ghost story.

"No way. I can't quit now." He turned to Rudy. "I have to find it."

Rudy held up his hands. "You didn't say anything about crawling around in caves. I'm claustrophobic."

"C'mon, Rudy," Jack said. "You know I can't do this alone."

Rudy grunted. "Dude, this trip just keeps getting better and better."

"Well, I can show you where White Eagle Creek is," Ben said. "I suppose you can try to follow it upstream and see where it leads. See if there really is a cave up there."

"I'd appreciate that," Jack said.

Then Ben went on with a grin. "Of course, you two look like a couple of city boys. Not sure it's the safest thing for you to do. Not without a guide, anyway."

"A guide, huh?" Jack raised an eyebrow.

"And I suppose you have someone in mind?"

"I sure do." Ben thumbed his chest. "US Army Rangers for ten years. I've lived in the area my whole life. Plus, I've even done a fair bit of caving in my day. If you need a guide, I'm your man. Provided the price is right."

"Price . . ." Jack rubbed his jaw and peered at the Indian. It would definitely be helpful to have someone on his expedition who was familiar with the area. As long as it fit in his budget. "How much?"

They were beginning to haggle when Running Bear stood up and shook his head. His eyes flared in the firelight.

"If you go . . . death will find you there."

CHAPTER 04

Jack and Rudy followed Ben Graywolf along the rocky bank of White Eagle Creek. The stream snaked a winding path down a rough, boulder-strewn slope through the woods. After the recent storms, water was rushing past them in a foamy torrent. The morning air was crisp, and patches of sunlight filtered down through the trees onto the forest floor of damp pine needles.

Through the branches ahead of them, Jack caught glimpses of the looming gray mountains against a magnificent blue sky. They'd gotten an early start, meeting Ben at eight o'clock at the spot where the highway crossed the creek. There was an area off the road where they could park their vehicles and head up on foot, following the creek bed westward.

Jack had to stop several times so he and Rudy could catch their breath. They weren't nearly as acclimated to the higher elevations as their older Caieche guide. For his part, Ben carried no map or compass, at least none that Jack could see, and appeared to have no pressing need to engage in conversation, either.

After another half hour of walking, Ben finally announced, "We should be getting close now. I can hear the falls."

Jack, on the other hand, couldn't hear anything over the stream and his own labored breathing.

Within ten more minutes, they emerged over a ridge onto a broad, wooded shelf at the base of a rocky cliff. A white spray of water poured out from a crevice about fifty feet up like a spigot on the side of a house. It sprayed into a large pool at the base of the cliff before flowing down the creek bed. To one side of the falls, the cliff face was sheer and smooth, but the other side was jagged and uneven, enough to afford a possible way up.

Rudy dug out his minicam to film the waterfall and surrounding area. He zoomed in on the crevice. "Don't tell me that's the cave."

Ben studied the cliff, his eyes squinting against the bright sky. "That would be my guess. It almost looks big enough to squeeze inside."

Jack drew up beside him. "Whattaya think?"

"Looks like there's some kind of ledge up there," Ben said. "But the trick will be getting to it."

They proceeded to check their gear. Ben had brought plenty of rope and climbing hardware, while Jack had brought flashlights, a couple boxes of glowsticks, and a package of flares. Their food consisted mostly of beef jerky, nuts, protein bars, and plenty of water. In addition to the supplies, Ben had also brought along a large hunting knife in a leather sheath, strapped around his waist.

"You never know what you might run into," he had said with a wink.

He took a moment to go over some safety instructions, warning Jack and Rudy of the dangers of unexplored cave systems. "Remember, when we get inside, the most important thing is to stick together. Don't go wandering off alone," he said as he adjusted his gear. "I'll climb up first and let down a safety line."

Jack could feel his heart racing as he wondered if this was the very path his father had taken during his last expedition. Running Bear had not recalled speaking with him twelve years ago, but Jack felt a sense of certainty that he was on the right trail. He was eager to find out just what kind of cave system was under this mountain.

At length Ben found a suitable area along the cliff to attempt an ascent, and he scrambled up the mountainside like a squirrel up a tree.

Jack chuckled. “Wow, he moves pretty good for an older guy.”

Rudy shook his head and grunted. “Army Ranger.”

Within ten minutes, Ben had scaled the cliff and pulled himself onto the narrow ledge. He scooted along until he came to the opening and slowly climbed inside. He disappeared from view for a minute and then reappeared, waving at them.

“It looks big enough to fit inside,” he called. “It’s maybe three or four feet wide and extends up into the cliff at about a thirty-degree angle.”

“How far up does it go?” Jack said.

Ben glanced back. “I didn’t see the end.”

They tied their packs one by one to the rope, and Ben pulled them up. Next, Rudy and then Jack attempted the fifty-foot climb while connected to the safety line. The climb was steep and laborious, but forty minutes later they had both managed to reach the ledge.

Jack gazed out as he caught his breath. The cliff dropped off right at their feet, straight down into the forest below. From this vantage point, Jack could see the foamy creek tumbling back down the slope through the woods and into a rough meadow beyond. The entire countryside below him was lit beneath the blazing sun.

Rudy stood beside him, flipped open his minicam, and panned across the vista. "Nice view, huh?"

"I'll say."

Rudy shut off the camera. "So . . . you still think your dad came this way?"

"I know I can't explain it," Jack said, "but I'm almost positive he did. I have to believe it." He turned to Ben. "So what do we do now?"

"We follow the same procedure heading up into the tunnel," Ben said. "I'll go in first and set an anchor. Then you guys follow me up."

Ben pounded an anchor into the base of the ledge to secure a safety line. Then he climbed up into the crevice over the stream of water, bracing himself against the sides. Jack peered in and watched as Ben disappeared into the darkness, trailing the rope behind him.

They waited outside for several minutes

until Ben appeared again in the mouth of the opening.

"Okay, the tunnel opens into a larger chamber about ten yards up," he explained. "There's a big pool that's feeding the waterfall, maybe twenty or thirty feet across. And it looks like there's a couple other passages leading off the main room."

Jack rubbed his hands. "Let's go."

They secured themselves to the line and pulled themselves up the incline, keeping their feet to either side of the gushing water. At one point the passage grew so narrow, Jack could barely squeeze through. He had no idea how Ben had managed to get his larger frame past it.

But the passage leveled off and opened into a large, rounded chamber just as Ben had described. Jack stood in the mud and rocks at the edge of the pool, ankle-deep in water. A narrow glint of daylight filtered up the passage and illumined part of the room, but they explored the rest of it with flashlights. The chamber was wide and low, so they had to stand slightly hunched, and a steady stream of water poured down from overhead through a number of cracks and crevices.

Rudy had unpacked his minicam again and filmed the chamber.

"Caves are very delicate ecosystems," Ben was saying, "so we need to make sure we minimize our impact. There's an old saying: 'Take nothing but pictures, leave nothing but footprints, and kill nothing but time.' "

"Yeah, well, we're having an impact just by our presence," Rudy said. "We're producing carbon dioxide and perspiration, leaving epithelial cells, and introducing new bacteria. Even our footprints could have a butterfly effect in this place."

As they talked, Jack searched the walls for evidence of the N'watu or some of the writing Running Bear's grandfather had supposedly seen. He waded around the edges, shining his flashlight along the walls, but found nothing.

Ben inspected the ceiling with his flashlight. "I'm guessing that during the spring thaw this whole chamber gets flooded."

"Is this the tunnel you were talking about?" Rudy pointed out an opening off to one side, where a trail of water trickled down and disappeared into the darkness.

"That's one of them." Ben shouldered his pack. "There's one on the other side that leads up."

He pointed his flashlight across the room to a smaller crevice. Jack could see Rudy shudder at that prospect. It did look like a tight fit. The one leading down was wide by comparison. And probably an easier climb.

"Well —" Jack swiveled his flashlight between the two options — "I vote for the lower one. It looks more promising."

"All right," Ben said. "Let me take a look around first."

He crouched to squeeze himself through the opening and crawled a few yards down the passage. "Looks like it goes on a ways."

He continued on until his light disappeared altogether. A minute later, his voice echoed back up the passage. "Okay, come on down. It looks like a pretty easy tunnel."

Jack motioned for Rudy to follow. "I'll bring up the rear," he said.

"Great," Rudy grunted as he crawled into the passage.

Jack watched him go and followed a few moments later. While he had to hunch to get through the opening, he found that he was nearly able to stand upright just a few feet into the tunnel. It led downward at a steeper angle than the waterfall shaft outside but was also rougher. The trail of water at his feet had obviously not been enough to wear the rock smooth.

Soon the passage tapered considerably and the incline grew steeper. Moreover, the ground was becoming slippery with mud as the water flow seemed to have increased, dripping down from the ceiling.

Ben signaled them to stop. "It's getting pretty steep here," he said. "And slick. I think we should keep ourselves spaced out and link up."

Jack raised an eyebrow. "Link up?"

Ben produced the rope they had used earlier and tied it to his belt harness, then to Rudy's, and finally to Jack's. "You're the anchor."

"Great."

"Keep a good ten to fifteen feet between us," Ben said. "Just in case."

They continued on, weaving between sharp outcroppings. In the meantime, the floor was growing increasingly slippery. Jack found his boots losing traction repeatedly.

Ben came to a halt. "Hold up. I want to set an anchor just to be safe."

Jack tried to stop but lost his footing and skidded into Rudy, knocking him off balance as well. They both landed on their backs but kept sliding down the passage.

"Whoa!"

It was a surreal experience as Jack felt himself gaining momentum. Kicking his feet against the sides of the tunnel, he tried to stop, but it seemed like the mud was everywhere. Limbs flailing, the two of them slammed into Ben, who was also struggling to keep himself from falling.

The chain reaction sent all three racing down a chute without a sled. Suddenly the tunnel dropped away sharply beneath them, and they plummeted nearly straight down for an endless moment through solid darkness.

Chapter 05

Jack plunged into a dark pool of frigid water. The cold tore through him like icy razors slicing his skin as he struggled to keep his thoughts from scattering into panic. He could feel gravel and rocks beneath his feet, but he was in water up to his waist and the cold was nearly overwhelming.

A light blinked on in the darkness, and Jack could make out Ben's large frame standing a few yards off clutching one of the flashlights.

Now Jack saw the pit was maybe fifteen or twenty feet across. Smooth rock walls loomed on all sides, and water cascaded from above in a steady stream. There was no place to climb up out of the cold. It looked to Jack like they had fallen into the bottom of a well.

"This is just great." Rudy's frantic voice sounded from the shadows behind Jack.

"What are we gonna do now?"

"Don't panic, for one thing," came Ben's gruff reply. "Get your ropes off."

Jack untied the rope from his waist and fumbled beneath the water for his own flashlight. He could feel his teeth chattering. "Wh-where are we?"

Ben was scanning the walls. "Looks like some kind of pit."

Jack found his light and peered up at the ledge. He spotted the tunnel they had fallen from about twenty feet up. A grim realization was beginning to set into his mind. He looked at Rudy and could tell he'd come to the same conclusion.

"W-we can't climb back up that w-way," he said.

"Check your packs," Ben said. "Make sure we have everything."

Jack swung his pack around and inspected its contents. His minicam was moist but not ruined; his canvas pack had obviously protected it during the initial fall into the water. He slipped the camera back into its nylon case and zipped it tight. It wasn't waterproof, but hopefully it would stay dry enough. Although from the look of their predicament, the fate of his video equipment hardly seemed important anymore.

He continued struggling to keep his mind

off his father, but he couldn't help wondering if he had fallen down this shaft as well and died alone here in the dark. He shuddered at the thought of stumbling across his father's bones somewhere under the water.

"W-we're gonna freeze down here." Rudy shivered.

"Shut up!" Ben's voice took on an irritated edge. "Quit talking like that. Just keep looking for a way out."

Jack pointed his light back up at the ledge. "Do you think if we boosted Rudy, he could climb back up?"

Rudy shook his head, shivering. "It's too high."

Ben shone his beam on the streamlets of water pouring down from the darkness overhead. "The shaft isn't filling with water, so it's got to be going somewhere."

Jack nodded. "Another tunnel?"

"Probably underwater somewhere." Ben began searching the perimeter of the shaft. "There's gotta be an outlet."

Then Jack got an idea. He unzipped his pack, unwrapped one of his granola bars, and set the plastic wrapper on the water like a tiny canoe. It spun in the eddies and swirls but soon began drifting toward one of the walls. As if drawn by an invisible thread.

He looked up at Ben. “What do you think?”

Ben didn’t reply. His stern, leathery countenance seemed fixated on the wrapper as it picked up speed. In moments it bounced into the smooth rock wall and bobbed against the side.

Ben looked at Jack. “Glowsticks.”

Jack dug further in his pack and produced a couple of the chemlights. He snapped them and shook them up until they gave off a pale green glow.

Ben grabbed them, sucked in a few deep breaths, and ducked under the surface. Jack was shivering at just the thought of being fully submerged again in the bone-chilling water.

A moment later Ben came back up, shaking. “L-looks like some kind of sh-shaft down there,” he said. “But I can’t see how far it goes.”

Jack was heartened by the news. “How wide is it? Can we fit through?”

“I dunno. A couple feet.” Ben set about uncoiling another length of rope and tied it onto his belt.

Rudy was shivering worse now. “Wh-what are you d-doing?”

Ben slipped off his pack and handed it to him. “I’m gonna see how far it goes.”

"Through there?" Rudy's eyes widened. "Y-you're c-c-crazy."

Ben handed the other end of the rope to Jack and took a handful of glowsticks. "Keep it tight. If I tug twice, pull me back through."

He sucked in a few more deep breaths and disappeared under the surface again. Jack felt the rope slip through his hand as he fed it into the tunnel. He soon lost track of how much length had gone in. Maybe twenty feet. Maybe thirty. Finally the rope stopped pulling, and Jack stood with his flashlight tucked under his chin, holding the coil in his numb hands above the surface.

"What happened?" Rudy asked, his face drained of all color.

Jack shrugged and pulled back gently on the rope to keep the tension. Then he gave it one short tug. A moment later he felt a single tug in reply and breathed a relieved sigh. "I think he's okay."

Nearly a full minute later, Ben emerged again, gasping for breath, his teeth chattering. "It c-comes out into an-nother chamber. The tunnel's about twenty-five feet long, and it gets a little narrow in the middle."

"How narrow?" Rudy said.

"It was t-tight for me, but you g-guys

should make it no problem."

Rudy turned to Jack, shaking his head. "Jack . . . I'm telling you, I will freak out down there."

"Well, we don't have any choice," Jack said, trying to sound firm but supportive. The last thing he needed was Rudy getting hysterical.

"I'm gonna get stuck!"

"If Ben can make it, you can too."

"But I can't —"

"Rudy." Jack grabbed the collar of his sweatshirt and jerked him close, shining the light in his face. "It's real simple. You either stay here and die for sure from hypothermia or take your chances down there. Now man up and let's do this."

Ben was already uncoiling several lengths of rope. "I'll go first. Then you send the packs through, and you two come last." He turned to Rudy. "All you gotta do is follow the rope. Hand over hand. Got it?"

Rudy was shivering too badly for Jack to tell if he was nodding or not. He slapped him on the shoulder. "You'll do fine. You'll be through before you know it."

"I'll tug three times for you to send the packs," Ben said. "Then I'll give three more tugs when you're clear to come through."

Jack and Rudy nodded.

They tied their packs to the rope, and Ben started sucking in deep breaths. Jack could see he was fighting off the effects of the cold, and Jack himself was starting to go numb. He could feel his mind shutting down as the blue beams of their flashlights began to flutter in his eyes.

Ben ducked under again, trailing the rope behind him. A minute later Jack felt three tugs and began feeding the rope through the tunnel. He could tell by the feel of the rope that one of the packs snagged a bit somewhere in the darkness, but after a sharp yank, it continued pulling through.

Rudy was rubbing his arms and hugging his slim frame. "I c-can't believe this is hap-p-pening. I knew I should've st-tayed home."

"Keep it together, Rudy," Jack said as he waited for Ben's signal. "You got to stay focused."

Suddenly the rope tugged three more times.

Jack clutched Rudy's arm. "Okay, it's our turn," he said. "You go first and I'll be right behind you."

Rudy's lips trembled. "I c-can't. . . ."

Jack shook him. "Rudy — you can do this. You're not going to get stuck."

Jack thrust the rope into his hands and

pushed him toward the tunnel, shouting positive reinforcements like some kind of desperate life coach.

Rudy sucked in several deep breaths; then Jack pressed his head under the water and guided him to the opening. A moment later Jack followed, ducking under the surface as a thousand needles of ice pricked his flesh. He fumbled blindly for the rope, following it into utter darkness.

Jack kept his eyes squeezed tight as the sharp edges of the tunnel scraped past him, closing in tighter the farther he went. It was smaller than he had expected, and at one point he felt like he would get stuck in the middle of the passage and drown. Panic began to swell inside his chest.

He could still feel Rudy's feet ahead of him, thrashing wildly, and at least took some comfort in knowing he wasn't completely alone. As the chill of the water sliced through him, memories burst in his brain like flashbulbs going off. Memories of his father. A funeral without a body. The big, empty rooms of his house.

He fought back his terror and tried to concentrate on the rope. *Move forward. Hand over hand. Keep moving forward.*

His lungs burned.

Hand over hand.

His arms throbbed from the cold.
Hand . . . over hand . . .
And then he was out.

CHAPTER 06

Jack surfaced, coughing and gasping for breath. He retrieved his flashlight from under his belt and flicked it back on, finding himself in a secondary pool within a much larger chamber. Ben was standing nearby, helping Rudy climb onto the rocky bank.

Jack waded to the side and scrambled onto the rocks. He lay there, clutching his flashlight and shuddering uncontrollably. "Wh-what do we d-do n-now?"

Ben had arranged their backpacks along the bank and was already going through them. "We need to take inventory of everything we have. I need to see what we've got to work with here."

He was moving like some kind of robot, seemingly no longer affected by the cold. Probably due to his military training, Jack thought. Meanwhile Rudy was huddled on the shore, hugging his shoulders.

"I suggest you guys get changed," Ben said. "We need to get out of our wet clothes." He stripped off his shirt and slipped on the extra clothing he'd brought along.

Jack inched his way over and felt his own extra clothes. They were still mostly dry. He pulled off his wet clothing and slipped into his shorts and sweatshirt. It wasn't much to keep him warm down in this cave, but it was better than staying in his wet clothes.

"What are we going to do?" he asked again.

Ben didn't look up. "Find another way out."

Rudy stirred at that comment. "What if there isn't one?"

Ben shone his flashlight in Rudy's face. "There's always another way out."

Rudy had brought along a pair of sweatpants and a nylon jacket in his pack. Jack tossed them over to him. "Rudy, get changed. You're not going to do us any good if you get hypothermia."

Rudy took his clothes and quietly began changing as Jack inspected the rest of the chamber. It was larger than he had first thought, more than a hundred feet across with a high, arched ceiling. Ben was already moving around the perimeter, shining the beam along the jagged black walls. The pool they had emerged from flowed out down a shallow trough along the floor of the chamber and disappeared again into a side tunnel. That tunnel seemed to be the only way out of the chamber.

Ben pointed his light down the passage. "Looks like we follow the stream."

Ten minutes later, they had repacked their gear and were headed off down the side passage. Before long, Jack began to smell something. A sharp, pungent odor.

"Ugh, what is that?"

"Sulfur," Ben said. "This whole part of the country is very geologically active. A lot of hot springs and geysers and stuff. We're pretty close to Yellowstone."

They walked down the tunnel for several minutes and emerged again in a chamber even larger than the previous one. Jack could tell it was warmer here than in the tunnel. And he was thankful for that, but the smell of sulfur was stronger as well.

The chamber was uneven, with several side passages and large boulders scattered throughout. Twisting white stalagmites rose from the floor along with various other rock formations, which gave the cavern a crowded and cluttered appearance. And the most curious thing was that everything seemed to be covered with a pale, glossy substance. It was spongy, fibrous, and slick, and it shrouded the entire room.

They'd just begun moving through the chamber when Ben stopped and pointed his light at the floor, where a large puddle of water frothed and bubbled. "It's a hot spring," he said. "Some kind of hydrothermal vent."

Jack drew up beside him and cast his light across the steaming pool, gurgling beneath a layer of thick foam. He swept his light forward and found a second pool a few yards ahead. In fact, the more he scanned the cavern, the more he found.

He noticed Rudy crouching down, video camera in hand, filming the slimy substance covering the rocks. It looked like his fear had gone — at least temporarily — and now the biologist in him seemed to be taking over. "D'you guys see this?"

Jack turned his attention to the spongy material as well. It was a light color, appearing nearly white in the glow of their lights. "What is it?"

"It looks organic," Rudy said. "Like some kind of bacterial slime."

"It's everywhere," Ben said, shining his light across the walls. He shook his head. "I've heard of bacteria growing inside caves.

But not like this."

"How does anything even survive this far underground?" Jack said.

"Bacteria are very adaptable," Rudy said. "Some strains can grow in total darkness. Even in toxic waste. Whatever this stuff is, it's obviously adapted to the dark. And it looks like it's adapted pretty well."

"That's cool," Jack said.

Rudy nodded. "It's pretty incredible, actually. We used to think all organisms needed sunlight to exist until we started exploring the bottom of the ocean and found complex ecosystems thousands of feet deep thriving around thermal vents where no sunlight ever reaches. So instead of the sun, these organisms get energy from the heat and chemicals coming up from those vents."

"Makes sense." Ben seemed to catch on. "Probably why this stuff seems to be growing more around the hot springs."

"Exactly." Rudy nodded. "The heat and water — maybe sulfur dioxide or hydrogen sulfide. I mean, I'm just guessing here. But this . . . this is incredible." He turned to Jack with a slight smile. "This could be a whole new microorganism."

Jack grinned back at him. "Aren't you glad you came along now?"

Rudy continued filming, but after a

minute he stopped. "Hey, guys, do me a favor and shut off your lights."

"What?"

"Just shut off your lights for a second. I want to see something."

They snapped their flashlights off, and darkness fell around them like a blanket. Jack could almost feel it draping over him. They stood in silence for a few moments until Rudy spoke up.

"Do you guys see what I'm seeing?"

As Jack's eyes adjusted, he saw that the entire chamber glowed with a pale light that seemed to come from all around them. It had been nearly imperceptible in the glow of their flashlights.

A sinewy network of glowing tendrils shrouded the cave floor and walls. Jack could even make out Rudy and Ben in the light.

"Whoa," Ben whispered.

"Glow-in-the-dark slime?" Jack quipped.

"Bioluminescence," Rudy said. "This stuff just keeps getting more impressive."

The light was nearly hypnotic as Jack found himself staring at the substance. For a moment he felt oddly detached, like he was far off somewhere, watching himself from the outside.

Then he shook himself out of his trance.

This discovery — as awesome as it was — didn't change the fact that they were still lost. More than that, he had yet to find evidence of the N'watu. Despite their circumstances, he needed to find some answers. He wasn't about to leave these caves empty-handed. "So which passage do we take?"

Ben stood, hands on hips, surveying their surroundings. After a minute he pointed up ahead. "That looks like a way out."

The fibrous growth clung to the floor and crawled up the walls like a network of glowing veins and arteries. Ahead of them appeared to be a small opening, as if the luminous tendrils had grown around the mouth of another tunnel.

They found a tunnel about five feet wide, though less than four feet high. The slime continued far down the passage but became less dense the farther they got from the springs.

They found they could navigate the passage by the light of the microorganisms alone. It reminded Jack of a carnival fun house he'd been to once as a kid where the trail was marked by phosphorescent paint on the floors.

"This is a little psychedelic," he said.

Ben stopped abruptly and held up a hand.

Jack and Rudy froze in their tracks.

"What is it?" Rudy whispered.

"Something's moving up ahead."

Jack drew up beside Ben, who was pointing down the passage. He saw an elongated black shape detach itself from the wall and glide across the ground maybe twenty feet away. It almost seemed like a hallucination — just a long shadow that flitted across the glowing veins on the cave floor.

In the dim light, Jack saw Ben slowly remove his flashlight and point at the switch. "Watch your eyes," Ben whispered.

Jack winced as the light flicked on, and he felt Ben move away quickly. In the commotion, Jack found himself momentarily stunned, surprised by how bright it seemed. He shielded his eyes and spotted Ben ahead of him, shining the flashlight around the passage. Then Jack felt Rudy brush past him and heard their voices elevated in excitement.

"Did you see it? Did you see that thing?" Ben was saying.

"I — I didn't get a good look."

"It was huge!"

"What was it?" Jack stumbled up to where they were standing.

Ben climbed onto a jagged rock formation along the side of the tunnel and shone his light into the cracks behind it. "I don't know. It was . . . like a centipede or something. But I mean, the thing was *huge!*"

"A centipede?"

Rudy shook his head. "I don't see anything."

"It crawled back behind this rock," Ben said.

Jack crouched beside the rock to inspect the opening. It was far too narrow to crawl through — not that he would've gone into it even if it *were* big enough.

"Shut your lamps off," he said. "Whatever it is, it's obviously trying to avoid the light. Let's wait a minute and see if it comes back."

Ben switched off the light again, and in several seconds Jack's eyes readjusted to the lower luminosity inside the tunnel. They moved away from the wall and waited.

Jack bit his cheek absently. He'd only seen a shadowy shape with no real detail. But it was far too big to be a centipede.

He felt a tap on his shoulder. Ben motioned for him to keep quiet, then pointed at something moving farther down the tunnel. Jack spotted a second shadow as it crept out from the side and paused in the middle of the passage.

Jack inched closer. It was definitely some

type of elongated creature — as Ben had described. And it was enormous — he estimated its length at roughly five feet. He also heard a gentle scraping sound, like a mouse scurrying across linoleum.

Ben pulled a bandanna out of his pocket and wrapped it over the lens of his flashlight. Pointing it away from the creature, he flipped it on. Jack could see the light was dimmed considerably but still bright enough to illuminate the area around them. Then Ben turned the light toward the animal in front of them.

Jack suppressed a gasp. "Whoa."

The creature had a solid black body five or six inches thick that looked more like a section of segmented industrial tubing than a living animal. It didn't flee but instead turned toward the light, lifting the front portion of its body. Its legs — dozens of red, fingerlike claws — wriggled in the air, and a pair of long antennae snaked forward from its bulbous head. It had no eyes that Jack could see, and only a small, horizontal opening for a mouth that munched on a glowing wad of the yellow slime.

Its antennae groped about in the air as if trying to determine where the light was coming from. Then after a moment it settled down and resumed feeding.

Jack whispered, "What is it?"

Rudy had his video camera rolling again. "It looks like some kind of . . . millipede. A very *large* millipede."

"Yeah, but how'd it get this big?" Jack said.

Rudy shook his head as if at a loss for words. "I have no idea."

"It looks like it's eating the slime. Do you think it has some kind of supernutrients or something?"

"Possibly." Rudy seemed mesmerized by the creature. "There . . . there are some pretty big insect specimens in the fossil record — centipedes and dragonflies. But there's no record of anything this big living today. This thing shouldn't be alive at all."

"Why not?"

"Well, there's not enough oxygen, for one thing," Rudy said. "The oxygen levels in the atmosphere were a lot higher in the past. But they're too low today to support the respiration of an insect this size — especially at this elevation. And on top of all that, we're underground, where the oxygen content is even lower."

"Right." Jack gestured toward the millipede. "But there it is."

Rudy rubbed his eyes. "Y'know, we might only be seeing the tip of the iceberg. There could be a whole separate ecosystem thriving down here, completely cut off from the rest of the world for ages."

Jack noticed the millipede raise its head and turn toward them, wiggling its antennae. Then it beat a hasty, zigzag retreat down the tunnel and disappeared behind another rock.

"Where's he going?" Jack said.

Ben snorted. "Maybe he got tired of listening to you guys yak."

But Jack wasn't quite so amused. He flicked on his light and swept it around the passage but saw no trace of the millipede. They stood in silence for a moment. Jack could hear the faint echo of water dripping somewhere off in the darkness. Then something caught Jack's attention. Another sound. Faint, almost imperceptible at first. But within a few seconds he could hear it clearly.

A sharp tapping sound echoed in the tunnel, like someone knocking two rocks together. Jack couldn't tell which direction it was coming from.

Only that it was getting closer.

Chapter 07

They stood in the tunnel listening to the tapping noise getting louder. Jack felt himself holding his breath.

At length Ben said, "I don't mean to be a killjoy or anything, but maybe that millipede knows something we don't."

"I agree," Jack said, gesturing to the passage ahead. "Let's keep going."

They made their way up the passage in the direction the millipede had departed. Soon the tunnel began to narrow sharply and eventually came to a dead end. Jack could tell that the bizarre sound was coming from behind them, which gave little comfort since they now appeared to be trapped.

"Okay," Rudy said, "anybody have any other ideas?"

Ben was busy inspecting the walls of the passage. "Just keep your shirt on. Let's see if there's another way out of here."

"It's still getting closer," Jack said. He could hear the *click-clack* sounds more distinctly now, but they weren't just getting louder; they had multiplied, like several people were off in the dark tapping rocks together.

Ben had apparently realized the same thing. "I think there's more than one thing making that noise." He pointed his light up at the ceiling of the tunnel. "Here! I think I found an opening."

With that, he climbed up the wall and disappeared into a small hole above them.

Meanwhile the tapping grew more intense.

Rudy aimed his camera back down the passage. "I gotta tell you, I'm starting to get a little creeped out here."

After several seconds Ben's voice came from above them. "I found another tunnel."

Jack peered up into the shaft. It was a nearly vertical passage with jagged walls, not even three feet at its widest point, but he could see Ben's flashlight shining down over a ledge about fifteen feet up.

"It's a bit of a climb." Ben's voice echoed down the shaft.

"No kidding." Jack shouldered his pack. He wondered how Rudy would manage if his claustrophobia began to kick in again. "It looks a little tight."

Rudy spun suddenly and pushed Jack up into the passage. "We don't have time to think about it."

"What's wrong? Did you see something?"

"Just get moving." Rudy's voice was tense.

Jack groped around the passage for a handhold. Sharp outcroppings on the rough surface gouged his hands, but at last he was able to pull himself higher into the tunnel. He could feel Rudy beneath him, pushing hard against his feet.

"Hurry up!"

Jack pulled himself higher up the shaft, ignoring the pain of rocks scraping his hands and arms.

Beneath him, Rudy's voice grew more urgent. "C'mon, keep going!" He gave another thrust against Jack's feet.

Jack groped around blindly, pulling himself up foot by foot. His heart pounded as he wrestled his fear both of getting stuck and of whatever was in the tunnel beneath them.

Then his hand reached up but felt only a smooth section of cold rock with no ledge or outcropping. Nothing with which to pull himself up. And Rudy was still pushing against his feet, shoving him higher into the tunnel, pinning his other arm against his side.

"Hold on," Jack said. "I'm stuck."

"Keep moving!"

Jack struggled to twist his body free, but it was no use — he couldn't pull or push himself any higher. His heart thrashed inside his rib cage like a wild beast ready to burst out. "I'm *stuck!*"

Then he felt warm flesh clamp down around his uplifted hand, and he was yanked up through the passage until at last the rock seemed to open around him, freeing his other arm.

Ben pulled Jack into the tunnel, where he rolled onto his back, gasping for breath. A moment later Ben helped Rudy scramble up out of the hole as well.

The sounds drew closer, echoing up the shaft. *Click-clack-click-click-click-clack.* Ben switched off his light, and the three of them lay in complete darkness. The noise grew louder until it sounded like the source was right at the bottom of the shaft. Jack held his breath and waited, measuring the time by counting his pulse as it throbbed in his ears. Then the sounds began to grow fainter again, and within minutes they disappeared altogether.

Jack fought to calm himself and slow his heart rate. "What was it? What did you see?"

Rudy sat up, shaking his head. "I'm not

sure. I saw something moving . . . back up the tunnel. I don't know what it was. But there was definitely more than one."

"What did they look like? Did you get anything on video?"

When there was no response, Jack flipped on his flashlight. Rudy's face was white in the glare, and his eyes seemed distant and unblinking, staring into the darkness.

"Rudy."

Rudy started as if snapping out of a trance. "I . . . I don't know what they looked like. I just . . . I didn't get a good look at them, and I didn't exactly want to stick around for one."

Rudy played back the video recording. With the night-vision setting, the amplified glow of the slime showed up as bright patches of pale-green veins running over the floor and up the sides of the passage. They were lit so brightly that the rest of the detail was fuzzy and out of focus. It looked like some kind of crazy, neon house of horrors. Suddenly a dark shape flashed into the frame. A blurred black silhouette skittered across the passage, but then the picture jerked hard as Rudy turned away and stopped filming.

"Rewind it," Jack said.

They rewound and paused the footage,

advancing it frame by frame as the shape moved into view. But it was too hazy to discern any details.

Rudy was still breathing heavily. "I think they were some sort of arthropods, but I couldn't tell how big they were."

"Look." Ben rubbed his eyes. "I hate to remind you guys that we still need to find a way out of this cave. Let's take a few minutes to eat something; then we should get moving."

It was shortly before noon when they broke out packages of beef jerky and protein bars. Jack hadn't thought about food until now and was surprised at how hungry he was. And thirsty.

"Careful with your water," Ben warned as Jack chugged his bottle. "We need to ration it until we get out of here."

They had each brought along a pair of one-liter bottles, which would last them the rest of the day, but if it took any longer to find another exit, they'd be in trouble.

There were still patches of the glowing slime nestled in various nooks and crannies of the passage, though considerably less dense than it had been in the tunnel below. They had to proceed on hands and knees through the mud and puddles. The passage wound and zigzagged through the darkness for several dozen yards until Ben stopped them again.

"You guys might want to have a look at this."

Jack inched forward and saw something that looked like a crescent-shaped melon rind wedged between some rocks. And as he looked closer, he spotted several more scattered along the passageway as though someone had just enjoyed a picnic of melons and left the garbage strewn about the tunnel.

Jack picked up one of the pieces and turned it over in the light. He held it up for Rudy to film. Its curved outer surface was smooth and black; the interior dripped with gelatinous yellow goop.

"What do you think it is?" Jack asked.

Rudy wrinkled his nose. "It smells terrible, but I'd say by the size and shape . . . it looks like it belonged to one of our millipede friends."

"Uck," Jack grunted. "What happened to it?"

"I'm not sure, but I think this guy met with a pretty unpleasant end." Rudy pointed out the other pieces. "There are segments of its body all over the tunnel. I'd say this one was, um . . . torn to pieces."

Jack just stared at him. Rudy's face was

pale. Ben didn't look well either. Jack sifted through more of the pieces and found fragments of the dark-red leg segments and a bit of an antenna.

"Okay, so —" Ben rubbed his eyes — "these millipedes feed on the slime. And now there's something else down here that's feeding on the millipedes."

"Yeah," Rudy grunted. "It's called a food chain. We just haven't come across the predator yet."

"You think it was those things that were making the clicking sounds?" Jack said.

Rudy shrugged. "I'm as much in the dark as you guys."

Ben's lips tightened. "Well, whatever it was, it managed to tear this giant millipede apart."

"That's one possibility." Jack tried to offer another, less-alarming hypothesis. "Of course, we don't know if this millipede was even alive when it got eaten. It could be that whatever did this is just a scavenger. You know, feeding off carrion."

"C'mon, Jack," Rudy said. "Scavengers don't tear a carcass apart like this. I mean, it looks like this guy put up a bit of a fight."

Jack surveyed the tunnel. Rudy was right; the segments and legs were cracked and separated, strewn about the passage.

Rudy went on. "This looks more like a predatory kill. Maybe multiple predators, operating with a pack mentality. Or like a feeding frenzy."

"A feeding frenzy," Ben repeated and shook his head. "That's great." He shifted the leather sheath around his waist and started crawling forward again. "Let's just find a way out before we run into one of them."

They crawled through the tight, damp passage, sometimes having to squeeze through sections barely eighteen inches wide. Jack was covered in mud and started feeling a chill in his arms and feet. But mostly he struggled to keep his mind off the thought of an unknown predator lurking somewhere in the tunnels.

Ben stopped and dimmed his light. Jack could see a dark shape moving between the rocks up ahead. His heart raced.

Ben whispered over his shoulder, "It's more millipedes. Two of them."

Jack and Rudy crept closer. Two of the creatures milled lazily in the passage, munching on a small patch of the slime. One appeared to be an adult, roughly four feet long, with a juvenile maybe half its size.

The two animals scurried off in the glare of Ben's flashlight, disappearing into a small side tunnel. Ben led on, and soon they emerged into a larger open area. Jack sighed in relief. His back and legs ached from crawling through the narrow passage, and he was glad now to stand straight again.

They inspected their new surroundings and found themselves at the bottom of a deep shaft. A steady trickle of water cascaded down from somewhere above them.

Rudy was filming up the length of the shaft with the night-vision setting. "This place is huge. I can't even see the top."

The other side of the shaft opened to a narrow passage that seemed to twist and turn on an angle downward like a very narrow canyon.

Ben shone his light into the mouth of the tunnel. "Looks like we go this way."

They proceeded along the passage slowly. The water trickling from above snaked along the ground in tiny rivers as if leading them on, deeper into the mountain. They'd traveled for less than five minutes when Ben stopped again.

"I see light up ahead."

"A way out?" Rudy said.

Ben looked closer and shook his head. "Don't think so. I don't feel any wind."

They moved forward, and soon Jack could see the light as well. It grew brighter with each twist in the passage until finally the tunnel opened.

Ben stood still and Rudy drew up beside him. "Wow."

Jack stood, openmouthed, staring at the sight in front of him.

"Whoa" was all he could think of to say.

Chapter 08

They stood at the mouth of an enormous cavern, easily the largest chamber they had encountered so far. Jack tried to estimate the dimensions and guessed it to be nearly three hundred feet across. Like a huge, domed amphitheater rising to a height of a hundred feet or more. Frothy springs peppered the floor and bizarre rock formations rose up across the chamber. Fat, gnarled stalagmites twisted upward from the ground; long, slender stalactites reached down from above. A few met in the middle to form statuesque pillars around the edges of the great hall.

And the glowing slime was everywhere. It grew in dense, foaming patches around the pools. Winding tendrils spread out through the cavern, creeping up the columns and walls toward the ceiling.

Jack could see several of the millipedes munching lazily on the slime like cattle out in a meadow. And there were other creatures as well. Fat, round beetles the size of overturned coffee cups marched across the cavern in a little tea-set caravan.

The light was mesmerizing. Almost dizzying.

Jack found his voice first. "It's like Las Vegas."

Rudy switched on his camera and began filming. "This is incredible."

Jack was grimy and sore, but he and Rudy spent the next several minutes traversing the chamber end to end, getting shots of rock formations, the pools, the slime, and the millipedes. And they found more of the big, plodding beetles they'd seen earlier. Rudy said he thought they looked like dung beetles. In fact, he discovered three different species and took copious shots of them all. It was odd that none of the creatures appeared to be disturbed by their presence but rather seemed content to simply graze on the slime.

They gathered around one of the larger hot springs, observing the foam being generated by the slime.

"So what's with all the foam?" Jack said.

"Well . . ." Rudy bent down to inspect the pool. "I think it's hydrogen peroxide."

Jack frowned. "How do you know that?"

"I've been working on a theory," Rudy said. "Chemiluminescent reactions require hydrogen peroxide in order to work, right?"

"Chemi-what?"

"Chemiluminescent." Rudy stood and pointed to the slime. "A chemical reaction that generates light. Glowsticks, fireflies, or our slime here. They all need hydrogen peroxide in order to glow."

"Okay . . ."

"And hydrogen peroxide is produced naturally in most organisms as a by-product of their metabolic activity."

"Of course it is."

"So this slime, whatever it is, must be generating copious amounts of hydrogen peroxide to cause it to glow like it does. It's called oxidative phosphorylation."

"It's kind of funny." Jack shook his head. "I know you're speaking English; I just have no idea what you're saying."

Rudy sighed. "If this slime is producing hydrogen peroxide and there are other microorganisms in the water that produce catalase, it would cause a chemical reaction."

"Catalase?" Jack snorted. "Y'know, I slept through biology."

"It's the enzyme used to break down hydrogen peroxide into oxygen and water.

So basically this could all be part of a symbiotic ecosystem that acts like a natural oxygen generator."

Jack was starting to understand. "Oxygen . . . So that's how the millipedes get so big?"

"It's just a theory," Rudy said. "But we got in here through that underwater tunnel. So if these caverns are sealed off from the outside and this slime is somehow giving off oxygen, it could easily raise the levels in here considerably."

"Makes sense, I guess." Jack nodded. "But my question is, why haven't they found this slime in other caves before? Why only this one?"

Rudy shrugged at that. "Maybe it's all the hot springs and geologic activity or something indigenous to this region; I don't know. But this cave has an ecosystem that's developed totally isolated from the rest of the planet. We have no idea how many other caves like this there are throughout the world. We're just now discovering new species on the ocean floor and places we've never explored. Think about it — we know more about the surface of Mars than we do about some places on Earth."

At that point Ben spoke up. "Hey, I think you guys might want to take a look at this."

They made their way over to where Ben was shining his light on an object wedged in the rocks. Jack bent down for a closer look.

It looked like some type of segmented appendage — almost like a crab leg. But bigger than any crab Jack had ever seen.

Much bigger.

Rudy gently pried it loose and held it up in the light. The smooth, hard claw portion was about twelve inches long, black with a gray underside and curved down to a point like a sword from one of those old Sinbad movies Jack used to watch. The rest of the limb was segmented by two connecting joints and snapped off just past the second joint. Shreds of white tendons and pink muscle tissue dangled out of the jagged end.

Jack straightened up. "I don't even want to know what that came from."

Ben grunted. "Looks more like something that belongs at the bottom of the ocean."

"It's definitely some kind of arthropod." Rudy turned the appendage over in his hands. "It's gotta be at least eighteen or twenty inches long. That'd give this thing — whatever it is — over a three-foot leg span."

"Probably closer to four," Ben said. He stood and looked around. Then he pointed his light toward the wall of the cavern. "I say we keep moving. Looks like there's another tunnel over there."

"Fine, but I want to take this with me," Rudy said. He got his wet shirt out of his pack, wrapped the appendage tightly, and stuffed it back inside. Then he produced a small plastic Ziploc bag of peanuts and dumped them into his pack. "I'm going to take a sample of this slime too. Just in case we actually make it out of here alive."

They made their way through the passage Ben had indicated. The tunnel narrowed quickly and soon the slime had dissipated, leaving them relying again on their flashlights for navigation. The luminescent slime had given Jack a sense of space, but now the darkness seemed to huddle around them, making the tunnel feel even more cramped.

Finally the passage opened onto a wide, oval-shaped cavern. The walls swept upward, nearly vertical, giving the chamber a basin-like shape. This room, however, had no cheerful tendrils of glowing slime. It was completely dark, and the darkness felt even heavier than inside the passage.

Jack swept his light around. Ahead of them, twenty yards or so, the chamber curved slightly and extended out of their line of sight. Jack pointed the light back toward Ben and noticed that he was staring at the wall behind them.

"Jack, you might want to get a shot of this," he said.

Jack turned to see markings scrawled on the surface of the rock with what looked like white chalk. They consisted of vertical lines with smaller lines protruding out at right angles in varying spots.

Rudy leaned in to view them. "Looks like the same kind of writing from your dad's drawing."

"We're not the first ones here," Jack said, digging out his camera to take some shots of the wall.

Ben stood with his hands on his hips. "Well, at least we know there's probably another way out of here. I'm guessing whoever drew these came in by some other entrance."

Jack zoomed in on the writing. "I wonder if these are the markings that Running Bear's grandfather saw."

They checked the wall for additional images but found none. So they spread out to inspect the rest of the chamber. Jack was searching along one wall where he'd discovered several side passages leading away from the main chamber. But they all looked too tight to crawl through. He was crouched down, shining his light into one of the tunnels, when he heard Rudy let out a sort of low groan.

Ben's voice echoed in the dark. "What's wrong?"

Rudy replied, "Just tell me this isn't what I think it is."

Jack scrambled up the rocks to where Ben and Rudy stood with their lights aimed at the ground. "What is it? What happened?"

In the dim circle of light Jack could see what looked like several long sticks lying in the mud and gravel at Rudy's feet. They had a pale, ashen color that stood in stark contrast to the black rocks. So pale, in fact, that they seemed to glow in the light. Jack tried in vain to suppress a gasp.

"Bones?"

Rudy knelt down for a closer look. "Looks like a couple femurs and maybe some ribs."

"They're human, all right." Ben's voice sounded distant and detached.

"How do you know that?" Jack said.

"Because here's the rest of him." Ben swept his light to the side, where it fell upon a skull perched amid a small pile of other bones. Wide, hollow eye sockets stared back at them, and an open jaw gaped as if frozen in the midst of a silent laugh.

Additional arm and leg bones lay strewn

within a ten- or fifteen-foot radius. Jack struggled through his revulsion to maintain a level of professional detachment, but there was something sinister he noticed in the discovery. Something familiar and darkly unsettling that he wasn't sure he wanted to share with the others.

"He's, uh . . ." Jack didn't know quite how to put it. "He's sort of . . . all over the place."

Ben flicked his light up into Jack's face, then back down at the skull. "Like the millipede in the tunnel. He's been torn limb from limb."

Jack nodded slowly. "Kind of looks that way, doesn't it?"

Ben turned away as Jack knelt beside the skull and lifted it, inspecting it for gashes or other marks of violence. He saw none. The surface was smooth, free from any bit of flesh. Like it had been picked clean.

"Jack." Rudy's voice was so soft that Jack at first didn't heed it. *"Jack."*

Jack looked up and saw Rudy standing on the edge of a rise, shining his flashlight down into the cavern on the other side.

"What?"

Rudy's voice sounded grim. "I think you should see this."

Jack drew up beside him. "What is it?"

Rudy pointed down into the cavern. "It

looks like there's more."

Jack could see more white slivers glowing in the light near the bottom of the pit. He picked his way slowly down the rocky slope as his stomach tightened and his hands grew cold. He had never been this close to death before, and he fought his rising fears. Fear of never finding a way out of this cave and of whatever might be lurking in the stifling blackness. Fear that he would end up like these corpses, lost in the dark and the mud.

And a cold, paralyzing fear that one of them might be the remains of his father.

He reached the bottom and stopped in his tracks. The shapes of white bones littered the ground amid the rocks and mud. Maybe dozens of them. Parts of an arm and a leg, at least two skulls, and what looked like collarbones and more ribs. His jaw tightened as he swept the light across the rocks.

Rudy's voice came from the top of the rise. "What do you see?"

Jack willed himself to move farther down into the chamber and saw still more pale fragments. More skulls.

"Yeah, there's more down here," he heard himself say, like he was having some kind of out-of-body experience. "I'm guessing . . . maybe a dozen or more."

Jack's legs froze and he could go no

farther. He moved the light ahead and upward and his eyes widened at what he saw. Then he turned away and retched the contents of his stomach into the mud.

Moments later he could hear Rudy and Ben shuffling down the incline.

"You okay?" Rudy said.

"Not really, no." Jack wiped a muddied sleeve across his mouth and then pointed his light up again ahead of them. As he did, he could see Rudy take a step backward.

The light chased off distorted shadows, unveiling bit by bit a tangled mass of pale bones, stacked high against the far wall of the chamber. Gaping skulls and misshapen spines and legs and arms, all twisted and contorted and heaped into a brutal white edifice. As if someone had just bulldozed them into a pile.

Rudy's breath came in throaty gasps. "There's . . . got to be . . . hundreds . . ." His voice trailed off.

Jack stared at the grotesque mound. "What is this place?"

Ben squatted down and hung his head for a moment. Then he looked up again and wiped his hair out of his face. "It's a bone pit."

Chapter 09

Jack tore his gaze away from the hideous sight and turned to Ben, who wore the vacant expression of a sleepwalker. "What do you mean, a bone pit?"

"Remember . . ." Ben hesitated a moment as if searching for a way to explain it. "The legends about how the N'watu would give Sh'ar Kouhm an offering of souls to appease her."

"So it *is* true?" Jack grimaced. "They really were making human sacrifices?"

Ben rubbed his eyes. "They were just a bunch of old ghost stories. I never took them seriously."

"Well, apparently they were based in some kind of fact," Jack said. "We're standing in front of it."

Rudy took a few hesitant steps closer to the pile. "There's so many of them." His light flitted across the mass of bones. "Look at them all."

Jack felt as if he'd stumbled across a subterranean Nazi concentration camp. Hundreds of victims killed and their bodies just dumped into this pit. His nausea was quickly turning to anger. His face flushed with emotion. "What did they do to these people? How could they do this?"

"Beats me," Ben said. "I wasn't there."

"Well, you seem to know a lot about them. You said this was all a Caieche legend."

"Look, man." Ben stood, and his tone grew sharp. "The N'watu were here way before any of us. *My* people weren't responsible for this."

"Hey, there's something here," Rudy said, pointing his light at the base of the pile. "I see something in there."

But Jack was preoccupied with Ben's comment. "I didn't say *your* tribe was responsible. I'm just struggling with the idea that someone — *anyone* — could do something like this to other human beings."

Rudy was still talking. "It looks like it's a . . ."

"Oh, really?" Ben snorted and spread his hands. "Welcome to the human race, kid. Let me tell you, this is nothing compared to what happened to thousands of Indians at the hands of —"

"Don't lecture *me* about suffering! You

know how many Africans died in the holds of slave ships?"

"Both of you, shut up!" Rudy's voice rose. "Get over here and take a look at this!"

Jack took a breath and tried to calm himself. Clearly the gruesome discovery had put them on edge, and he needed to get a handle on his emotions. He made his way over to where Rudy was inspecting the bone heap. Rudy turned and held up a small, metallic object.

Jack aimed his flashlight at it and gasped. "Is that a — ?" Before Jack could say anything further, a section of the bone pile burst outward, knocking them both off their feet. Rudy yelled and scrambled away. His light flashed back and forth, and Jack caught a glimpse of a jagged shape occupying the space where they had been standing — just a fleeting, skeletal shadow before it slipped out of view again.

Rudy scrambled backward on his heels and elbows, kicking and shrieking. Jack saw flashes of a dark shape following him. And he could hear a sort of growling hiss along with the same clicking sound they'd heard earlier.

The thing pursued Rudy with jerky movements, and only when it paused momentarily was Jack able to finally train his own light on it. In that brief second, he saw it more clearly. It was crablike in appearance and enormous — about the size of a large dog — with what looked like a bony, armored shell. And it had multiple segmented legs like a crab, with two longer ones jutting forward. Then it reared back as if up on its haunches, with its front legs coiling like cobras ready to strike.

The creature flicked forward again, out of the light. Rudy's scream jolted Jack out of his daze, and he jumped to his feet, looking around for something to use as a weapon. Just then another dark shape flashed through his beam.

It was Ben. He looked like he was carrying something. Jack thought it might've been a rock, but it was all happening too fast. Between Rudy screaming and the lights zipping back and forth across the cavern, Jack only managed to discern a flurry of movement and sounds. There was a loud, rattling hiss and three heavy thumps before his light caught up with the action again.

Jack found Rudy lying on his back, chest heaving, and Ben kneeling a few feet away with a large rock in front of him. Under the rock was a motionless, contorted mass of limbs.

Jack shone his light on Rudy. His pant leg

was torn and a trail of blood dripped down his calf.

"You okay?" Jack said, but Rudy's eyes looked as round as saucers and he gasped for breath. Jack raised his voice. *"Rudy!"*

Rudy blinked and snapped his head toward Jack. "I'm . . . I don't know."

"You're bleeding."

"I . . . I think I got cut or something."

Ben crawled over to Rudy and inspected his wound. "It doesn't look too bad." He dug in his pack for the first aid kit.

Meanwhile Jack found his attention drawn back to the creature, now lying crushed and twitching beneath the rock. He rolled the stone aside with his foot and circled the body from a safe distance. The animal lay with its legs splayed out. Jack counted eight of them. Each of the longer forelegs contained the same curved claw as the specimen Rudy had discovered.

"Is it one of those . . . things?" Rudy's voice was shaky.

"Looks like it," Jack said, kneeling to inspect the creature more closely. Its outer shell was roughly circular and about the size of a large serving platter. It was black with gray patches and had a bumpy, pebbled texture. The edges were ringed with small, hornlike protrusions. Jack made a quick mental estimate of its size. It was about three feet wide from leg tip to leg tip, and maybe four feet front to back with the longer front legs.

Jack nudged the body with his foot. "I want to try to flip it over and get a look at its underside."

Ben turned around. "Be careful with that thing. I think these cuts are puncture wounds."

Rudy seemed surprised. "What do you mean? Like bite marks? Did it bite me?"

Jack carefully lifted the outer shell and rolled the animal over. It was heavier than it looked. Its armored legs seemed to curl inward reflexively as he laid the creature on its back. From this perspective, Jack could see a distinct set of long, meaty fangs that curved out and downward. And between them protruded a pair of short, bony, fingerlike appendages, like the palps that spiders use for sensory purposes. Between them was a large slit that Jack assumed was the creature's mouth.

"Whoa," he whispered.

"What is it?" Rudy's voice rose. "Is it poisonous? Did it bite me?"

"Hold still." Ben was busy cleaning and dressing the wound.

"Well . . ." Jack couldn't tear himself from

the specimen. "It looks like some kind of giant spider with an armored shell. I've never seen anything like this before. It's *huge.*"

"But is it poisonous?"

Jack shrugged. "How would I know? You're the biologist."

"Well, we know it's predatory," Ben said without looking up. "It attacked from out of cover of the bones. Like it was waiting there to ambush prey."

"Jack." Rudy grimaced, pointing to the bone pile. "Did you see the watch?"

Jack remembered why Rudy had called him over in the first place. He swept his light across the ground and saw the scuffed and battered wristwatch lying in the mud where Rudy had dropped it. He picked it up.

"This looks pretty new," he said. "I mean, like a modern watch."

Rudy was shaking his head. "What's going on here?"

Jack peered at Ben through the lights. "Obviously we're not the only people in this cave. You said the N'watu would offer human sacrifices to the Soul Eater." He held up the watch. "I think they're still doing it. Or at least *somebody* is."

They stared at each other for a hushed moment as that thought sank in. Only the sounds of their breathing echoed in the cavern.

Ben shook his head. "This is crazy. They're just a legend."

"You saw those drawings on the wall. And all these bodies got down here somehow. They didn't just wander in on their own."

"Then we better find a way out pretty quick." Ben finished wrapping Rudy's leg with gauze. "We don't know how many of those spider things are down here, and we should probably get him to a hospital."

For a moment, Jack bristled at the thought of leaving. He knew there was real danger here and that they needed to find a way out, but still, his curiosity had been piqued. They had just discovered some actual hard evidence that the N'watu might in fact be real. And that notion was mind-boggling. Part of him wanted desperately to find out more.

He helped Rudy to his feet. "Are you okay? Can you walk?"

Rudy tested some weight on his leg. "Yeah, it just tingles a little, but I can walk." He limped over and stared down at the creature.

Jack nudged it again with his foot. "What do you suppose it is?"

Rudy shrugged. "It does look like some kind of arachnid or an entirely new species of arthropod. We'd need to do a comparative DNA analysis to modern arachnids to be sure. But these things could have been down here since prehistoric times."

He turned to Ben. "We have to bring it with us."

Ben winced. "What? You're both crazy!"

But Rudy persisted. "This is a huge scientific discovery."

Ben rolled his eyes. "Whatever. *I'm* not carrying the thing. You guys figure out what to do with it."

Rudy bent closer and inspected the carcass under his flashlight. "You realize we're going to be famous with this discovery."

"No doubt . . . but hopefully not posthumously," Jack said.

Rudy chuckled. "What should we name it?"

"What d'you mean?"

"Well, whoever discovers a new species of animal always gets to name it," Rudy said. "How about *Cavernous Arachnis Giganticus?*"

Jack just raised an eyebrow. He was thankful at least that Rudy was feeling well enough to joke, bleak as their circumstances were. "Maybe I can carry it with something or at least drag it along." He unpacked his rolled-up wet jeans and knelt down to slip them under the spider.

Suddenly the carcass jerked and erupted into a seizure. Jack leaped out of the way as the spider bumped and jittered on the ground. Rudy and Ben jumped back as well.

The creature growled and hissed, kicking in violent spasms. All of its legs thrashed about, stretching out and digging into the mud as if trying to flip itself back over.

"I thought you killed it!" Jack heard himself scream.

"I did," Ben shouted back at him.

"Apparently not all the way!"

"Shut up and kill it!" Rudy yelled, hobbling backward. "Kill it! Kill it!"

Jack was scrambling in the dark, searching for another rock, when he heard the hisses and growls turn into high-pitched squeals. He turned back to see that Ben had pounced on top of the animal and was ramming his knife deep into its center. He plunged it over and over into the soft underbelly as a viscous yellow fluid spattered his arms and face. The animal's legs thrashed and clawed in furious tremors but gradually slowed until at last the only movement was a slight twitching in one of the rear appendages.

Jack stared at the grotesque sight, not sure what to say. His heart was still pounding.

Finally Rudy spoke up from his vantage point several feet away. "Is it dead this time?"

Ben stood over the animal, wild-eyed and grimacing. He wiped his face on his sleeve. "It better be."

Jack inspected the carcass and cringed. The underbelly was a mass of shredded flesh and yellow goop. Its legs had contorted and curled inward but were finally motionless.

"You must've just stunned it before," he said after a moment.

"No way." Ben shook his head. "I hit it three or four times. And that rock weighed a good thirty pounds. No way it survived that."

"Well, that shell must be harder than it looks."

Rudy snorted. "Or maybe it was just playing possum."

Ben glared at them. "I'm telling you, I *killed* that thing."

"Great," Rudy muttered. "Giant *zombie* cave spiders."

Ben swore. "Y'know, if it weren't for me, both of you guys would be dead by —" He stopped his rant short and looked around the cavern, cocking his head.

"What?" Rudy whispered. "What's

wrong?"

"Shh!" Ben snapped his palm up and tilted his head the other way.

Then Jack heard it too. Somewhere in the darkness, an eerie clicking sound echoed off the cavern walls. It was soft and indistinct at first but growing steadily louder.

Ben turned. "We need to get out of here *now!*"

CHAPTER 10

"Wait!" Jack grabbed his camera out of his pack. He couldn't leave without recording what they'd found. "I have to at least get a shot of this place. I have to document —"

Ben clutched him by the back of his shirt and tugged him away, but Jack shrugged himself loose. Ben yelled, "You idiot, we have to get out of here!"

Rudy's breath was growing labored. "Which way?"

"Up," Ben said. "We need to get out of this pit."

"Up . . . up where?"

Jack pointed the camera around the chamber. With the night-vision setting, he could see a couple of side passages leading off the main room. One looked big enough to stand in, but the others were barely large enough for them to crawl through.

Jack got a quick shot of the giant spider and then panned over to the bone pile. In that shot, he could see Ben in the foreground shining his light up the cavern walls. Rudy was bent over and holding his side. Beyond them both, Jack could see a wide ledge just above the heap of bones. It looked maybe twenty feet high or so, but it wasn't that far from the top of the pile.

"Up there." Jack pointed. "There's some kind of ledge up there."

Ben ran to the edge of the heap and scanned his light along the ledge. He turned back and said, "We'll have to try it."

"Guys . . . ," Rudy wheezed, clutching his side. "I'm kinda . . . starting to feel a little . . . not so good." He staggered a few steps toward Jack and then fell to his hands and knees, vomiting.

"Rudy!" Jack stopped filming and ran to help, but Rudy had already collapsed into a quivering heap. Ben was there in a moment as well.

In their lights, Jack could see the ground stained dark red. Blood frothed from Rudy's mouth and nostrils, down his chin. His entire body quaked with violent tremors, and Jack could hear him struggling for breath.

"Jack," Rudy's voice rasped. His chest heaved like he'd just run a marathon, but his breath was lost in a thick gurgling sound.

He gagged and coughed. "I can't . . . I can't . . ."

"Rudy, it's okay. We'll get you out of here. Just hold on." Jack's own heart was pounding now. He felt utterly helpless. "Stay with me. Just try to slow your breathing. Take deep breaths. Stay with me!"

"I . . . can't . . ." Rudy managed two last words before his entire torso stiffened. His head arched back in a wide-eyed, silent scream. A tremor shook his body once, and then he was still.

"Rudy!" Jack shook his shoulders. *"Rudy!"*

Ben shone his flashlight into Rudy's eyes, still wide open in a look of terror. His pupils were dilated; there was no sign of any reaction to the light.

"Rudy!" Jack's voice trembled, and a strange sense of detachment flooded over him. A feeling that he was outside of his body somehow, sitting in a theater or at home watching a horror movie.

"Jack!" It seemed Ben's voice called him from the other side of the cavern. "Jack, we have to get out of here."

Jack looked up to see Ben nose to nose with him. His lips moved as if in slow motion.

"Jack . . . he's dead. There's nothing else we can do."

Ben shook him by the shoulders, and Jack blinked back to consciousness.

"He's gone," Ben kept saying. "We have to get out of here."

"No!" Jack grabbed Rudy's shoulders and tried to drag him toward the bones. "We have to get him to a hospital. Help me!"

Jack felt his head snap sideways as Ben's hand connected with his cheek. The sharp sting brought him out of his fog. The whole side of his face seemed to burn.

Ben glared at him. "He's dead! We have to leave him and get out of here."

The clicking noise was growing louder and now seemed to fill the entire cavern like an approaching chorus of castanets playing somewhere in the dark. But it was more intense now than when Jack had heard it before. And he could hear other sounds over the distinct clicking noise. Growling and hissing, like the animal that had attacked them.

Ben leaped onto the bone pile and scrambled toward the top. Bones slipped and cracked under his weight, but he kept clawing his way up.

Jack looked back at Rudy, his body limp and contorted. And still.

He grimaced, fighting back tears as he picked up Rudy's backpack and slung it over his shoulder along with his own pack. Now Jack could sense a growing shadow approaching from somewhere in the darkness behind him. He jumped onto the bone pile and clawed his way up to the ledge.

It was like climbing a snowbank; his own weight caused him to sink farther down than he was able to pull himself up. His hands clutched at thick leg bones, round skulls, and smaller ribs and hands and feet. Hard and cold to the touch, they shifted and snapped like old branches beneath his feet. The putrid scent of decay wafted up from the heap with each move he made, choking him in its stench.

He struggled to turn his brain off to the horror of Rudy's death and the corpses beneath him and focus solely on climbing, forcing his hands to keep moving and his legs to keep pumping.

As he neared the top, he saw that the ledge was higher than he'd expected. He clawed at the rock wall to find some kind of handhold. And even as he did, his feet sank deeper into the bones. It was as if the corpses were grabbing his legs to pull him down into their tomb.

But then he looked up again and saw Ben's arm extended toward him. Jack gave one final push with his legs, hoping there were enough bones beneath him to hold him stable. He jumped . . .

And felt Ben's hand close around his wrist. Jack reached his free hand up, kicked his feet against the rock, and scrambled over the ledge.

He rolled onto his back and closed his eyes, gasping for breath.

But he had left Rudy behind. Down on the cave floor. A few minutes ago, he was alive. Lungs breathing, heart beating. And now . . .

Jack peered back over the ledge into darkness. Ben switched off his light and hunkered down beside Jack, peeking over the ledge as well.

Below them, Jack could see an eerie blue cone of light shining off into the dark. It was Rudy's flashlight. Everything else around was lost in the inky black of the cavern. But the clicking sounds flooded the cave now, sounding as if they were coming from all around them.

Jack reached for the video camera and peered into the view screen. Through it, he could see the pale-green shape of Rudy's limp body lying in the mud. Then, beyond, Jack saw movement. Several shadows appeared over the rim and scurried down the incline. Sharp, bony limbs scuttling in a flurry of movement.

It was more of the spiders, some nearly as big as the one that had been hiding in the bone pile, others considerably smaller. They skittered down into the pit, converging on Rudy's corpse, tearing into it like a pack of wild dogs. Hisses turned to coarse growls and high-pitched shrieks. The flashlight shook and jittered, shooting its beam in various directions until finally it went out.

Jack closed his eyes and rolled onto his back, suppressing a sudden wave of nausea.

He thought of Rudy's parents. How would he tell them? How could he explain the kind of gruesome death their son — his best friend — had just experienced?

These creatures were everything they had feared. Ravenous and violent. Despite the presence of the enormous millipedes, the food supply in this isolated ecosystem must have been scarce.

And yet it wasn't so isolated, for they had stumbled across a subterranean killing field. Someone had been feeding these monsters human flesh, and now Jack wrestled to keep his fear from controlling him.

His nausea rose again, and this time he couldn't stop it. He rolled to his side and vomited onto the rocky ledge, convulsing in choked sobs. Rudy had been the only real friend he'd ever had. The only one he'd ever trusted. They'd been a pair of outcasts in school. A couple of geeks with only each other for company.

And now, just like that, he was gone.

Jack felt Ben's hand on his shoulder. "You okay?"

He choked back his tears and wiped his mouth. "Yeah."

"You didn't get bit too, did you?"

Jack scooted himself away from the ledge and sat up. "No . . . sorry, I just lost it there."

In the darkness, Ben's voice replied, "I'm sorry about Rudy."

"He was my best friend," Jack said. "My only friend. He didn't even want to come on this trip, but I talked him into it. I put a guilt trip on him."

"This wasn't your fault."

Jack wiped the tears from his eyes. "Yes, it was. If I wouldn't have made him come along, he'd still be alive."

Below them, he could still hear the noises of the spiders feeding. He shook his head, dazed. "He seemed fine. You bandaged his leg. . . . He was okay."

"It must've been some kind of venom. But it was so fast-acting."

"What did his wound look like? When you

were cleaning it, was there any discoloration or swelling?"

Ben paused before answering. "There were two puncture marks on his calf. Big ones. And the area was pretty red and swollen. I cleaned it as best I could with antibacterial ointment and wrapped it up. It didn't seem to bother him that much."

Jack just stared into the dark and shuddered.

"Bottom line is, we need to avoid getting bit at all costs," Ben said with a grim tone.

Jack rubbed his eyes as a rush of frustration and anger ran through him. "This whole trip was a bad idea."

"It wasn't your fault," Ben said again. "There wasn't anything you could've done."

Jack fell silent for a moment as his thoughts returned to Rudy. "How am I gonna tell his parents? What do I even say to them?"

"Let's just make sure we get out alive so we *can* tell them," Ben said. "We should get going. I don't want to take the chance those things will find us up here."

After several more minutes the frenzy below seemed to die down. Jack gathered his mental courage enough to take one more look through the camera. All was dark and quiet and the ground was still littered with bones. But Jack couldn't tell which ones had belonged to his friend.

Ben clicked on a flashlight and scanned the pit below them. He shook his head. "I can't believe this. They came out of nowhere, and now they just disappeared again."

"Probably in one of those side passages," Jack said, reeling with disgust. "Off digesting their meal."

They inspected the ledge, which turned out to be larger than they'd originally thought. They had been sitting off to one side where it was only a few feet wide, but to their right, the ledge widened further into what appeared to be a sort of natural parapet or balcony overlooking the entire pit below. And behind them a tunnel led off into darkness. It was wide and relatively level, but it twisted and turned completely out of sight.

Ben pointed down the passage. "I guess we follow this tunnel to see where it leads."

Jack felt numb and sick, and his mind was still in a fog of sorrow. "Let's go."

Ben stuck out an arm. "Hold up." He peered into the tunnel.

"Now what?" Jack said.

"Turn off your light."

Jack's arms and neck bristled as he shut

off his flashlight. Inside the tunnel he could see a dim yellow light flitting erratically across the rock walls.

Ben spoke in a tight whisper. "Someone's coming!"

Chapter 11

"Get back against the side," Ben said, herding Jack along the ledge.

Jack's throat was dry with fear as he flattened himself against the rock wall. His head was still spinning from witnessing Rudy's death. And now, when he thought things couldn't get any worse, they had. The day had begun so innocuously but had suddenly turned into a nightmare of epic proportions.

He could hear voices echoing faintly down the passage — deep and guttural sounds, but distinctly human. And there were more than one. Jack could tell some sort of conversation was taking place, though he couldn't discern anything specific. No recognizable words. And in moments he understood why.

They weren't speaking English. In fact, it didn't sound like any language he'd ever heard before.

The light coming down the tunnel was growing brighter and the voices more distinct. Jack's heart pounded, and he fought every instinct inside him that screamed for him to run. It was an unnerving experience to feel so trapped, yet so completely exposed to whoever — or whatever — was approaching through the tunnel.

Ben tapped Jack's shoulder and made some gesture, though Jack could barely see him against the glow emanating from the passage beyond. Jack shook his head, trying to indicate he didn't understand what Ben was trying to communicate.

Ben pointed over the ledge into the pit and whispered, "We have to hide."

"*What?* I'm not going back down there." Not with those spiders lurking about. Not where what little was left of Rudy's body lay torn to pieces.

The voices were growing steadily louder.

Ben moved to the rim of the ledge and pointed straight down. "We can hide in the bones."

The bones? Jack blinked. *The bones?* He wondered now whether this whole situation had caused Ben to completely lose touch with reality. But before he could say anything further, Ben crouched down and slipped over the edge, disappearing into the darkness. Jack could hear the clack and rattle of bones below him. He pressed one hand to his eyes, grimacing with frustration. Now he really *was* alone.

He leaned his head back against the rock and tried to slow his breathing. He had to control his thoughts and analyze the situation. It might be possible that the men in the tunnel weren't even dangerous, though his gut told him that was extremely unlikely. Everything he had witnessed — everything he had learned about this place — told him otherwise. Whoever was approaching most likely knew their way around these caves well enough. And the watch Rudy had discovered earlier seemed proof that whatever horrific events had led to this chamber of corpses were still going on to this day.

In any case, the spiders appeared to have departed, and the men in the tunnel would surely find him if he stayed where he was. So Jack knew with a sickening realization that Ben's plan — as crazy as it seemed — had actually been the best course all along. Jack scooped up the backpacks and paused a moment to gather his courage. Then he lowered himself over the edge.

He landed in the pile of bones, sinking to his waist in human remains. Fighting back his nausea again — which was easier now since he no longer had anything left in his stomach anyway — Jack rolled slowly to the bottom of the pile and burrowed underneath a mass of skeletal pieces. The stench was overwhelming, reminding him of a time he'd gone to the beach with his father as a boy and discovered that the tide had deposited a horde of dead fish onto the sand. He had all he could do to keep from gagging in the darkness.

He couldn't see anything but utter blackness and hoped desperately that he was buried far enough to remain hidden from whatever might be coming along. He wondered again if some of these could be his own father's bones. If his dad had met this kind of horrible death alone in these caves twelve years ago. But Jack pushed away those thoughts, determined to keep his wits about him. He had to keep still and stay quiet.

The voices continued in a stilted, halting conversation above him. Jack couldn't tell how many men there were. At least three, he guessed. Maybe four. And the words themselves were a guttural, throaty dialect.

Jack wondered if it was possible that a remnant of an ancient tribe could still be living in these caves. Had they remained concealed from all modern knowledge? Or was it merely some bizarre cult that was using a hidden entrance to come and go from the cavern, bringing terrified victims for their demonic death rituals? Whoever they were, he could only assume for now that they were responsible for the horror in this place. The cave spiders were just animals, predators doing what they needed in order to survive. It was the humans who were the real monsters.

Jack could see a faint light glimmering across the cavern from above. He peered out through a patchwork of bones and bone fragments. Minutes passed with occasional verbal exchanges from the men standing above him. Jack closed his eyes. Deep breaths would prove useless in the rotting stink around him.

After a minute or two there came another sound, a sort of soft rustling. Jack resisted the temptation to crane his neck for a better view. Meanwhile the faint light above seemed to grow brighter as well. He could hear more movement, this time clear and distinct. He wondered where Ben had gone, whether he had disappeared down one of the side passages leading from the main cavern or if he too was hidden inside the pile of bones. But all Jack could do was wonder and hope. He didn't dare risk trying to communicate.

Jack's heart began racing faster as a yellow light came into his field of view, lowering from above. He concentrated on moving only his eyes to track the light. Any turn of his head could cause the bones around him to shift, giving away his position. The light paused, lingering at the edges of his vision for several seconds, then continued its descent.

Within seconds, Jack could recognize the source of the light. A lantern of some sort was being lowered on a rope into the pit. It clanked softly against the cave wall and spun on the rope. Jack couldn't see much detail, only that there was a pale-yellow glow inside it.

It descended like a spider on a line of silk into the pit until it finally came to rest on the floor of the cave no more than thirty feet from him. It had a square metal frame with a large ring at the top and dusty glass plates on each side. He couldn't see a flame inside the glass, yet it lit up the surrounding area with a sickly yellow light.

Just behind the lantern, Jack spotted a second rope descending. Or rather, a crude ladder. A series of roughhewn wooden boards with holes in each end were suspended between twin lengths of knotted rope.

Jack concentrated on his breathing. The terror welling up inside him had tightened his chest, constricting his airflow. So he found himself unintentionally gasping for air, yet he knew he needed to keep absolutely still.

The bottom of the ladder began jiggling and wafting back and forth. Someone was obviously descending it.

Jack caught his breath as a figure came into view.

It was human as far as he could tell. From his limited vantage point Jack could see only a torso, tall and rail thin and almost entirely naked. The skin was an abnormally pallid hue — very nearly translucent — and he was clad only in a loincloth tied around his waist with a crudely beaded length of twine. Moreover, his flesh looked to be covered with a jagged network of delicate black lines. Jack at first thought it was some sort of woven netting, but as the gangly limbs moved about, he could tell it was a body etching or tattoo of some kind. The markings looked similar to the characters Jack had seen written on the wall earlier and in his father's drawing, but he couldn't make out the details in the dim light.

Nor could Jack see the man's face, merely his arms and torso up to the sinewy pectoral muscles. He was extremely thin though not sickly or malnourished. Rather, his musculature appeared to be quite well defined, enhanced perhaps by the lack of pigmentation in the skin. His hands bore long, curving fingernails also black in color. Jack guessed they'd probably been decorated by the same procedure with which the man had marked the rest of his body.

The figure stood motionless, half-crouched as if poised for action. Jack guessed he was listening for some sign of the spiders. Whatever the creatures used it for, the clicking sounds they made at least gave away their presence and warned of their approach. But other than the gentle echoes of water trickling somewhere in the big chamber, there was only silence.

Jack held his breath and waited. The man was no more than ten or twelve feet away, and Jack could hear something that sounded like sniffing. He bit his lip, hoping desperately that the man wouldn't smell him, and after several seconds he strode off, out of Jack's line of sight. Jack was amazed that with such a gangly body, the stranger moved with a fluid, almost-graceful manner, slipping barefoot across the stones without making a sound.

Terror and fascination each fought for dominance as Jack's mind bristled with questions. Could this stranger really be one remnant of a lost tribe of humans? Had the N'watu actually survived in these caverns all this time? How many more of them were there? How could they possibly have gone undetected by the modern world for so long? And were they as primitive as they appeared? Little more than a Stone Age culture? The lantern they carried seemed to indicate that they'd had at least some interaction with the outside world.

But more immediate than all of these questions was, what would they do to *him* if they discovered him hiding here? His heart pounded against his ribs as he worked to remain still.

Meanwhile the rope ladder continued swaying.

Soon another figure descended into view. The second N'watu reached the bottom and stood facing the direction in which the first one had gone off. A moment later Jack heard a voice coming from the darkness. The first man spoke in choppy, guttural syllables. But in a hushed tone. The second N'watu, standing in front of Jack, replied in a similar volume.

The first N'watu moved back into Jack's view carrying something. Jack suppressed a gasp as he saw what it was: Rudy's tattered nylon jacket. It looked like it'd been ripped to shreds. And it was covered in blood.

The two men faced each other, the one holding up the jacket in front of the other. Jack could only imagine what they were saying — no doubt discussing how someone had gotten into their cave undetected. They would probably assume the intruder had not been alone, for that's what Jack would've assumed. Living in this dark, dangerous environment, their senses — especially their senses of hearing and smell — were most likely heightened. Maybe they could even smell Jack from where he lay, under a pile of human remains.

The second man strode off into the dark and returned with the corpse of the spider Ben had killed. He held it up by its big front legs as the others dangled down, limp. Its punctured underside still dripped yellowish fluid. They talked further in what Jack thought sounded like an argument. Perhaps they were debating their next moves. Should they search for other possible intruders? Or maybe just let their spider friends take care of them?

The first N'watu kept shaking Rudy's

jacket. He seemed to be insisting on a particular point or a course of action. But his comrade did not appear convinced, nor was he quite as agitated. After another minute or two of discussion, the second man started climbing back up the rope ladder, carrying the enormous spider corpse along with him by a front leg.

The first man remained behind. He turned and faced out into the cavern again, perhaps searching for some sign of additional intruders. By now, Jack's body was aching from remaining still so long inside the reeking mound of bones.

Then Jack noticed movement in his field of view. Something dark and shaped like an overturned coffee cup with multiple legs was crawling across the bones directly in front of his face. It was one of the species of beetles he'd seen earlier.

Jack gasped and jerked backward with an involuntary spasm. The bones shuddered and immediately the N'watu's torso spun in his direction.

Jack could see the man's sinewy abdomen moving with slow, steady breaths. He held out the lantern toward the bone pile and took a hesitant step closer. Jack fought the impulse to flee. Every nerve in his body screamed at him to jump out from the cover of his hiding place and run. But his sense of reason — as if barely clinging to the edge of a cliff — kept that impulse in check.

The N'watu held the lantern out before him and crept closer. In two cautious strides he was standing directly over Jack's hiding place and crouched down to inspect the bone pile.

Then Jack got a look at his face.

Chapter 12

The face Jack saw staring in at him appeared only remotely human, marred by the same black etchings that covered the rest of his body. Jack gazed into white irises, void of any pigmentation at all and glowing eerily in the light of his lamp. His gaunt cheeks and bizarre tattoos created a face that looked more like a skull covered by a pallid layer of skin. And his head was completely hairless. Not even eyebrows.

The face moved still closer. Large, moist nostrils undulated as they sucked in the scent. Cautious, translucent eyes peered in directly at Jack. Suddenly the face reared backward. Jack cringed as the N'watu thrust one of his hands into the bone pile. He knew his life was over; this human monster was going to yank him out by his hair.

But instead of grabbing Jack, the N'watu pulled his hand back again with a softball-size beetle wriggling in his grasp.

The insect's legs clawed at the air as the N'watu held it up to the lamp, inspecting it with his ghostly, colorless eyes. Then his lips parted, revealing a mouthful of discolored, crooked teeth. He sank them into the beetle's soft underside with a sickening crunch and tore off a stringy chunk of its innards. The beetle squealed, flailed its legs, and went limp as the N'watu chewed as casually as if he'd bitten into an apple. The tip of a leg protruded from between his lips.

Jack had all he could do to fight his gag reflex.

The N'watu took a second bite, ripping out more meaty guts and a couple more legs, crunching on them with ghastly relish. He polished off the remainder of the bug in two bites, wiping out all the juicy remnants from the inside of its shell and sucking them off his fingers like a kid cleaning the last drops of ice cream out of a bowl.

He tossed aside the beetle's outer shell and wiped his mouth with the back of his arm. Then he looked around the cavern once more before climbing up the rope ladder, carrying Rudy's shredded jacket with him.

Jack could hear the N'watu arguing on the ledge above him for several minutes. He tried again to determine how many of them there were altogether, but he couldn't be sure.

The discussion continued as the rope ladder drew up out of sight, followed by the lantern, leaving Jack engulfed in darkness. In minutes, the voices faded as the N'watu moved off down the tunnel.

Jack closed his eyes, still afraid to move but too afraid to stay where he was. Then he heard Ben's voice calling softly to him from out of the darkness.

"Jack? Are you here?"

Jack breathed a sigh. A wave of relief washed across his mind.

"I'm here," he said and began digging his way out of the bone pile. "Where are you?"

A light flicked on in the darkness. Jack could see it sweeping across the chamber as he pulled himself free of the heap. He crawled out, onto the cold mud-and-gravel floor, and lay on his belly. He didn't care about the cold or the mud. He was just glad to be free of those bones — the remains of people who'd once been living, breathing souls like himself, but who had each most likely died horrible deaths, like Rudy. He could almost hear their screams and shrieks of terror in his head.

Gravel crunched underfoot, and Jack opened his eyes to see Ben standing over him, shining the flashlight in his face.

"You okay?" Ben said.

Jack nodded. He was struggling through the numbing shock of Rudy's death. But he also knew he was on the verge of confirming his father's theory.

Ben helped Jack to his feet. "Was it the N'watu? Did you see them? I was hiding on the other side of the pile. I couldn't see anything."

"Yeah, I saw them." Jack shuddered. "Almost wish I hadn't."

"What'd they look like?"

Jack forced his sorrow and shock to the back of his mind as he described the lanky bodies and the disfigured face of the N'watu. Ghostly, pale skin and demonic, colorless eyes. "They almost didn't look human," he said. "They were covered with some kind of markings. Tattoos or something — I don't know. And they looked to be pretty primitive. Although they did have a lantern with them. An old-fashioned metal one. It looked like they'd filled it with the slime we found. Like maybe they use it for their primary light source."

"All the legends say they were very clever," Ben said. "They made good use of their resources."

Jack flashed his light to the ledge. He was

quiet for a moment, trying to determine what to do next. They couldn't very well stay down in this pit. Not with the spiders still lurking about. Their best option seemed crazy on its face, but Jack decided it might be their only one.

"I think we should follow them," he said. "Try to see where they went."

"Follow them?" Ben gestured to the bone pile. "Maybe you haven't noticed, but these people don't take kindly to outsiders."

"Well, it's either them or the spiders. What do you feel more lucky with?"

Ben stared at him a moment and then grunted. "That's like asking if I prefer leukemia or pancreatic cancer." He sighed and peered up at the ledge. "I hate to admit it, but it's probably the best chance we have of finding an exit."

They climbed back up the bone heap and onto the ledge, where they took an inventory of their supplies before continuing. They still had two flashlights, both video cameras, a couple packages of flares and glowsticks, plus a fair amount of food and water. They loaded everything into their two backpacks for ease of transport. Jack also made sure he still had the spider appendage they had found and the specimen of slime Rudy had taken, glowing faintly inside the

Ziploc bag. They were too important to leave behind. He had to get them out for someone to study. For Rudy's sake.

They shouldered their packs and moved slowly into the tunnel in the direction the N'watu had gone. The passage ran thirty yards and then turned to the left. From there it narrowed sharply and wound in a zigzag path that slowed their progress considerably.

They moved in silence. Jack couldn't stop thinking about the N'watu's bizarre appearance, and after some time he spoke up. "Y'know, the tattoos they had all over them looked like writing — like the lettering from my dad's drawing."

Ben shrugged. "It doesn't look like any Indian script I've ever seen."

"That's what's so weird about it," Jack said. "That they should look so unique. Typically neighboring tribes would tend to influence each other's cultures, language, and communication. You'd think the N'watu would have at least *some* connection — some similarities to the surrounding tribes."

Ben was silent for several seconds. Finally he issued a pensive grunt. "What if they're not even human?"

"What?"

"I mean, what if they're not even from . . .

y'know . . . *here.*"

"You mean aliens?" Jack shook his head. "I don't think there's any reason to assume that."

"You said yourself they didn't look human. Maybe they're *not.* Or maybe they're some kind of hybrid. There are stories that say the N'watu were descended from a race called the Old Ones that originally came to Earth thousands of years ago from another world. Maybe they even brought those spiders with them."

Jack's chest tightened as he wondered what Rudy would have said to that. "Giant *alien* zombie cave spiders?"

Ben shrugged. "Just a thought."

They continued on, and Jack — against his better judgment — began rolling that idea around in his head. History was replete with those kinds of stories. Ancient Egyptian, Sumerian, and Indian cultures all had similar themes in their mythologies.

"What exactly do those stories say?" he asked after a moment.

Ben paused in the tunnel. "One of them says that the Old Ones came to Earth and built a huge city or fortress under the mountain. But they were dying. They . . . I don't know — they had some disease and were all going to die. And for some reason they couldn't reproduce, so they would take human women to try to preserve their line."

"So where was this underground city?" Jack said, now intrigued.

Ben shrugged. "I always thought it was here in these mountains. But I don't think anyone knows for sure."

They crept deeper into the tunnel until they came at last to a dead end. Ben's light shone against a smooth black surface. As they moved closer, Jack could see it was made of wood. Rough-hewn wooden planks covered with a sticky black substance. He couldn't see any indication of how the planks were bound together.

"It looks like some kind of doorway," Ben whispered, inspecting the perimeter. "The wood is covered with tar or something."

"Probably to preserve it from all the moisture in here," Jack said.

Jack was fascinated by the structure. He could see the framework of an imposing doorway — over eight feet tall and four feet wide. The posts, header, and threshold were also formed of timber and covered with the same sticky substance. Around the perimeter was what looked like a gravel-mortar mixture that filled all the gaps between the timbers and the rocky wall of the passage, sealing it off completely. He could only guess what lay on the other side.

Ben patted the wooden surface. "It feels pretty solid. Like they were definitely serious about trying to keep something out."

"It could be the gateway to their city," Jack said. "We have to see what's on the other side."

Ben shone his light along the edges of the wooden doorway, revealing several markings carved into the wood. Jack could see they looked nearly identical to the marks he'd seen at the entrance to the tunnel and on the N'watu themselves.

"I wish I could translate this," Jack said. "It's not pictographic at all."

"What do you mean?"

"Primitive cultures basically use pictures in their written communication. They draw images or symbols to represent objects in the world around them. But as a culture develops over time, their written language usually becomes less picture-based and uses more abstract symbols instead. And this stuff —" Jack tapped the symbols on the wood — "looks like a completely abstract alphanumeric system. That makes it harder to translate, but it's also indicative of a more advanced culture. At least more advanced than the two guys I saw wandering around here in loincloths."

Ben stared at the doorway. "So we have no idea if this says 'Exit' or 'Warning: Giant spiders behind this door.' "

"Exactly. And since we didn't see any other side passages, we can assume our N'watu friends came this way and got through somehow."

Ben pushed against the timbers, but the door didn't budge. "You think it's locked from the other side?"

Jack studied the crease between the door planks and the outer frame. "There's no handle on this side. I assume it opens inward, but I also don't see any sign of a hinge system. We can't even tell if it opens to the left or right."

"It doesn't matter if they have it locked or barred from the other side."

They spent the next several minutes pushing against alternate edges of the door but had no luck. Whoever built this door had definitely constructed it with an eye toward security.

By now, despite everything that had happened, Jack felt a pang of hunger and checked his watch. It was nearly five o'clock, and he had no desire to spend a night in this place. They decided to break for water and food. Once he'd had a chance to sit and think further, Jack hoped an idea or opportunity might somehow present itself.

As he ate, he studied the door, feeling an almost-irresistible compulsion to press on. Now more than ever — not only for his father's sake but for Rudy's as well. He'd found evidence that there was in fact a remnant of a lost civilization hidden away in these caves. A barbaric and brutal culture to be certain, but one that might hold untold secrets of the ancient world. And Jack needed to bring it into the light. It was the discovery of a lifetime. It would silence his father's detractors once and for all. And maybe, in some small way, it might bring Rudy's death some meaning.

Jack stared at the doorway. After a moment he shone his light along the bottom and crouched down to inspect it more closely. "There's a little slot cut into the wood here. I wonder if this is some kind of keyhole."

Ben peered over his shoulder. "Maybe it's like a garage door and swings up from the bottom. If it's hinged near the top, it'd be easy to push open from the inside but more difficult to pull it up from the outside."

Jack leaned back on his heels. "They'd just need to bring some kind of tool with them. Like a handle they can stick inside to pull it up." He gathered his courage and felt inside the groove. "Yeah, there's a space here. Do you have something we can wedge in here?"

They searched through their packs, and Ben pulled out one of his C-shaped metal carabiners. He worked it into the groove and twisted it to the side until it wedged into the wood. Then he pulled.

The door swung up toward them easily with only a soft creak.

"It's lighter than it looks," Ben said.

As the door swung upward, Jack could see a series of primitive ropes and wooden pulleys on the inside. "Looks like they have some kind of counterweight system rigged."

"That's not very secure."

"It doesn't have to be." Jack shrugged. "All it needs to do is keep the giant spiders out."

The doorway opened onto a narrow passage, so long and deep that their flashlight beams seemed to get swallowed by the black void.

Jack could feel his chest thumping but fought back his fear with a sober determination. He knew the answers he was seeking lay somewhere in the darkness ahead, and that compelled him forward despite his apprehension. "I guess we keep going, then."

Ben removed his carabiner and let the door close behind them.

CHAPTER 13

The air felt warmer inside the tunnel, which made sense if this was leading them to where the N'watu were living.

Ben cracked a couple of glowsticks and suggested that they proceed with their flashlights off. No need to attract unwanted attention. Besides, if the N'watus' eyesight had adapted to the darkness, the lights might prove to be a useful weapon if the situation warranted.

They followed the tunnel, keeping as quiet as possible. Jack found his palms sweaty. Since the N'watu had found Rudy's jacket, they would probably be wary of additional intruders. Then again, living for generations inside this cave system had most likely given them heightened senses of smell and hearing in order to compensate for the lack of light. For all Jack knew, the N'watu were already watching them.

The passage wound downward, and before

long Ben put a finger to his lips, then stuck his glow stick inside his pocket. Jack knew Ben must've seen or heard something, so he stashed his stick as well. In moments, Jack could see a soft glow ahead of them. It was just bright enough to outline the walls of the passage.

Ben motioned for them to proceed, and they inched their way down the passage. At the mouth, Jack found himself staring into a large chamber perhaps fifty feet across. Several clay bowls and other pieces of crudely fashioned pottery were scattered throughout the cave, each filled with a copious amount of the glowing slime. The yellowish glow provided enough light to make out some of the main features of the room, though much of it was still concealed in darkness.

But the chamber itself was empty. At least empty of any N'watu, Jack noted. Or more specifically, any N'watu that he or Ben could actually see.

Ben swiped his hand across his throat as if to signal Jack to not make a sound. A moment later he gestured for Jack to follow him. They made their way slowly around the perimeter of the room, staying in the shadows and mostly trying to keep as quiet as possible.

The chamber seemed oddly smooth, as if the N'watu had carved away the floor and walls to enlarge the room. Jack wondered how many generations of this lost tribe had dug and chiseled away at the rock to fashion their living area. What kind of tools had they used? How long had it taken? He also noticed additional markings on the walls, identical to the others he had seen.

Jack wondered if his father had made it this far — if he had discovered the N'watu — or if his body was indeed among the skeletal remains back in the bone pit. Jack's head reeled from the emotional toll of the last two hours. Who knew how long this tribe had been here? Ben had indicated the N'watu were here long before the Caieche. They could be looking at artifacts and a culture dating back thousands of years.

Ben signaled him to stop and then tapped his ear. Jack paused to listen. A low sound came from one of the openings leading off the chamber. A soft humming, deep in timbre. It was quiet at first, rising and falling in pitch and growing slowly in volume.

Jack leaned into the tunnel, trying to hear the sound more clearly. Without warning, it picked up in intensity and volume. He could tell it was the N'watu — he could hear multiple voices, though he could not discern exactly how many. It sounded like some sort of chant.

Ben gestured for him to back away from the entrance. "We need to find a way out of here," he whispered. "It sounds like some kind of ceremony or something. But as long as they're down that tunnel, we should try heading down one of these others."

"Which one?"

Ben looked around the cave and then pointed to one of the openings across the way. "That one looks like it leads up."

They crossed the chamber to the other side, and Jack paused to inspect one of the bowls of slime. They had been situated around the room like little tiki torches lighting up someone's backyard deck.

They crept into the passage and found that it did indeed angle upward. And after a few yards it also narrowed considerably. Suddenly Ben motioned for him to stop.

The droning chant they'd heard coming from the other passage now seemed to be coming from in front of them again. Ben motioned him closer. "It looks like all these side passages lead to a common chamber. We'll have to find another way."

But Jack shook his head. His curiosity was breaking through his apprehension. "Let's see what's going on."

Ben glared at him. "Are you crazy?"

But Jack dug his video camera out of his pack. "I have to see what they're doing. I have to document it. I need proof."

He crawled past Ben and within several yards he stopped, crouching low in the tunnel as Ben crept up behind him. They were looking down on a circular chamber much larger than the first and filled with bowls of the luminescent slime. There were at least a dozen N'watu figures throughout the room, crouched or kneeling in awkward positions with their heads lowered, humming a rather dissonant tune. Jack turned on the camera's night-vision setting and peered at the screen. He could see that the walls were covered with various drawings and writing. It did indeed look like some kind of ceremonial chamber.

Jack could also see another figure, smaller than the others, standing at the far end of the room. It appeared to be a woman, clothed in what looked like a shroud of black veils and adorned with beaded armlets, necklaces, and bracelets. Her face was hidden by a veil that covered her head down to her chin, but she seemed to be the focus of all the attention.

Jack leaned back and whispered to Ben, "It looks like she's the matriarch of the tribe. Like a female shaman."

Jack noticed movement at the far end as two N'watu males entered from a side passage, carrying what looked like a large papier-mâché beach ball, though it was only roughly spherical. It was a lumpy gray monstrosity, yet they bore it with great care. They sported strange headdresses, each with a set of horns that curved up and forward. And they also wore what appeared to be short leather tunics with two more pairs of the horns sewn into them somehow. The tunics draped across their backs so that the horns stuck out to the sides. Jack looked closer and could see that they were in fact the legs of the cave spiders. It was obvious their garb was intended to mimic the creatures.

The chants in the cave grew louder when these men appeared, and the woman began moaning as they approached her — a soft, rasping sound more like the yowling of an angry cat than a human voice. If there were any words, Jack could not make them out.

They brought the ball in front of the woman, and Jack could see she was holding something in her hands. A tool or knife of some sort. Jack peered closer. It was a knife — a long, crudely fashioned blade.

She muttered some further incoherent

words and plunged the knife into the ball, slicing open a small incision. Jack saw the gray mass shudder in the grasp of the two bearers. The sides quivered as if the thing were made of Jell-O. She slipped her hand into the opening and pulled out a fistful of . . .

There was something moving in her grasp, tiny, translucent, and wriggling. She held her fist up and spoke again.

Now Jack could see the thing in her hand was one of the cave spiders. A hatchling. Though only an infant, it looked to be about the size of her whole fist. Maybe three or four inches across, Jack guessed. Its transparent outer skeleton appeared to be still unformed, and its tiny limbs protruded between her clenched fingers. She lowered her hand and shoved the hapless creature into her mouth, chewing it with obvious enjoyment.

Jack recoiled, and beside him Ben's face registered similar disgust.

Jack whispered, "It looks like an egg sac. But it's huge. I've never seen anything like it before." He wished Rudy could have been there. He'd be able to offer a better analysis.

The woman reached inside the egg sac and plucked out a second spider as one of the N'watu stood and approached her. He knelt down in front of the woman as she fed the wriggling creature into his mouth. One by one, the rest of the N'watu rose and approached the woman. As they did, she would pluck hatchlings from the sac, say a few words, and shove them into their mouths like some bizarre form of Communion.

After the dozen or so N'watu had come forward, she scooped the rest of the hatchlings into a large bowl as one of the men stood beside it with a stone, mashing their bodies into a writhing slush. Jack could hear faint squeals and squeaks as the baby spiders were crushed against the inside of the bowl.

They were careful not to let any escape.

Ben pulled Jack back from the ledge. "So they *eat* the baby spiders?"

"It's like some kind of ceremony for them," Jack whispered. "If they worship these spiders, maybe they believe that eating them . . . I don't know . . . gives them a kind of communion with their spirits."

Ben stuck his thumb over his shoulder. "We need to get out of here. *Now.*"

He crept back down the tunnel, and a few moments later Jack followed quietly, his head still buzzing and his stomach churning from the horrific ceremony he'd just seen.

As he reached the first chamber, Jack heard Ben swear and stood to find himself face to face with four N'watu warriors. Their tall, gaunt, and sickly pale bodies were covered with black tattoos, and they held long wooden spears in their hands. Pointed directly at Jack and Ben.

Chapter 14

Jack stood, numb with terror, as more of the N'watu entered from the adjacent tunnel. In moments they were surrounded by at least a dozen pale-skinned warriors. Their tattooed faces held little emotion, but their fierce, colorless eyes glowed yellow in the dim light of the chamber.

Yet none of them spoke.

"What do we do?" Jack whispered to Ben. The sound of his voice sent a chorus of grunts and snarls among the warriors.

"Shh!" Ben hushed him. "Don't say anything."

Some of the N'watu leaned closer, driving the tips of their stone spearheads against Jack's throat.

Jack fought the urge to attempt to communicate with them, to make some kind of peaceful gesture. This culture, isolated as it had been from the outside world for so long, obviously held more animosity than curiosity toward outsiders. They didn't seem intrigued or fearful. They probably saw all intruders as a threat. Or more likely as a future sacrifice.

Suddenly a low, catlike voice filled the chamber. *"Yey takka hey na kaynee."*

The N'watu parted slightly to reveal the black-veil-clad woman he'd seen earlier. She stood inside the entrance of the passage, regarding Jack and Ben as if they were a pair of foxes cornered by her hunting dogs. Then she moved across the chamber between the warriors. It was clear that she commanded a high level of respect. Jack noticed that they would avert their eyes from her as she passed by. Perhaps that was why she wore the veils, Jack thought. Perhaps she was so revered by the N'watu that they were not allowed to even look upon her.

The woman approached Jack and Ben. She was shorter than he'd expected, standing only up to Jack's shoulders. In the dim light, Jack could see hints of ghostly white flesh beneath the layers of veils. She stretched a pallid hand toward Jack's face without making contact. Her bony fingers were tipped with long nails filed down to sharpened points like talons and dyed as black as ink. They hovered less than an inch from his skin. As though she could feel him without actually touching him.

Then Jack caught sight of an amulet hanging down her chest. A round medallion fashioned from some sort of metal, with markings identical to the drawing he'd seen in his father's papers. Jack froze as he recognized it. He didn't dare move or he knew they would kill him. But in the dim light he could definitely see it was the same design.

The woman muttered something else that Jack could not understand. Strident, guttural words that seemed to drip with venom. Her voice was raspy and soft — both acerbic and somehow still feminine, something wholly unnerving to Jack. He could see the glimmer of her white eyes glowing behind the veil.

Then she turned her attention to Ben and seemed more intrigued by him than by Jack, perhaps seeing he was from one of the local tribes. She reached her hand up and this time made contact, sliding her elongated, talon-like fingers gently down his cheek and jaw.

Jack tried to see beneath her veil but could make out no discernible features or expression. Just a vague white outline of her countenance and her two colorless eyes. But the medallion consumed his thoughts. If he could only get his hands on it . . .

The woman stepped back and spoke again, her tone different.

"Chenok ta-neyhee," she hissed. *"Cah-hee-chay."*

Jack glanced at Ben, whose expression seemed calm. He replied, *"Che-ahan ta-ney-hee . . . keyanok Caieche."*

Jack's eyebrows went up. Ben understood their language? Or perhaps the N'watu knew the Caieche language. Either way, if they could communicate, they might be able to talk their way out of this situation. Explain that they didn't mean any harm and weren't a threat.

"You can understand them?" he whispered.

Ben didn't take his eyes off the woman. "She speaks Caieche. The *old* tongue."

The N'watu men growled and pushed the tips of their spears closer against Jack's neck. Jack swallowed; they apparently didn't approve of them speaking to each other.

The woman spoke again — Jack couldn't tell if it was to them or to her warriors. He tried to back away, but they crowded him closer. They were outnumbered, and Jack knew he wouldn't be able to put up much of a fight before getting a spear thrust into his chest or throat.

In a kind of detached way, he saw what was left of his life play out in his mind. The N'watu would either kill them both here and feed their carcasses to the cave spiders or tie them up, drag them out to the bone pit, and let the spiders devour them alive. He hoped grimly it would be the former.

"Ben," Jack whispered, "I don't think this is going to end well. . . ."

"Close your eyes."

Jack had been hoping for something a little more encouraging. Frankly, that advice sounded a bit too defeatist for Ben.

"What?"

"Just close your eyes." Ben's tone was deliberate and tense. Maybe he hadn't given up after all.

Jack closed his eyes just as the cave erupted into chaos. He could hear unintelligible shouts and a high-pitched shriek. Someone slammed into Jack's shoulder, knocking him to the side at the same time that something sharp sliced across his upper arm.

Jack toppled over, and his eyes snapped open. A blaze of light sent bolts of pain into his skull. He was barely able to make out the image of Ben holding a bright-orange flare in one hand and with the other fighting off a barrage of flailing limbs and spears.

Above the tumult, he heard Ben's voice shouting, "Run!"

Jack scrambled to his feet and flipped on his flashlight as Ben plowed through the group of warriors toward the tunnel from which they had first entered. Jack followed close behind.

His own eyes throbbing from the brightness, Jack could only imagine how the N'watu — who'd spent their entire lives underground — were feeling. But he knew they had only a few seconds to escape before the warriors recovered from their temporary blindness.

Jack stumbled through the chaos. He could feel hands clawing at him, trying to get a grasp. He swung his arms around, hard. Clutching one of the spears, he sliced and stabbed, hoping he could inflict at least some damage. He felt the weapon making contact with several other bodies and hoped desperately that none of them were Ben.

He fought through the confused and blinded warriors, following what he thought was Ben's voice, but within moments, the howls of pain around him crowded everything else out, and he could feel hands clutching his arms and legs. They were groping for his head and neck, thrusting their spears wildly into the light.

Then Jack heard Ben calling him. "Over here!"

Jack followed in the direction of his voice but so did the N'watu warriors. Jack caught a glimpse of Ben amid flashes of light and darkness. He too had managed to commandeer one of their spears and stood by the tunnel, now with two flares and his flashlight blazing through the chamber.

Jack stumbled past him, into the tunnel, back toward the wooden door, not sure exactly why he was going that way. Maybe they could get through the door and hold off the mob.

He came to the black wood of the doorway and pushed it open, the counterweights on the inside making it easy to lift. A moment later Ben was beside him. But now they faced another dilemma. They needed to brace the door somehow, to block it so the N'watu couldn't follow them. Or at least to delay them for a few minutes.

Then Jack had an idea. "I'll hold the door, and you cut the ropes!"

Jack held up the massive wooden door while Ben crouched down and sliced his knife across the ropes holding the counter weights. The first one snapped, and the door shuddered. Jack grunted at the sudden addition of weight now transferred to him. He jammed the spear underneath to keep it propped up.

Jack could hear the N'watu approaching up the tunnel. Ben threw two flares into the passage. Maybe that would slow them down. Then Ben sliced the second rope and rolled back through the door as Jack let it slam shut.

He lay gasping for breath while Ben wedged the spear into the mud at the base of the door.

"We have to go," Ben said. "I don't think this is going to hold them for long."

Jack rolled to his feet and gathered himself. Now they were out in the cave with the spiders. He was relieved to be free from the N'watu but couldn't help feeling they had only jumped right back into the fire.

"Go where?" Jack breathed as they headed down the passage toward the bone pit. "If there was another way out, it was probably back there."

"Then we go back the way we came in," Ben said. "We just keep an eye out for those spiders."

"We can't get out that way."

But Ben seemed undeterred. "We'll figure something out. Or we'll find another way."

They reached the ledge overlooking the

inky blackness of the bone pit and paused to catch their breath.

"And what if there isn't one?" Jack said.

Ben shook his head. "There's *always* another way out."

They lowered themselves over the ledge into the bone pit, climbing down the pile of human remains as they had done before. They reached the bottom and paused to listen for any of the cave spiders' telltale clicking sounds.

The place seemed deserted. Jack swept his light across the muddy ground and spotted the still-fresh puddle of blood. He quickly averted his eyes, not wanting to see anything of Rudy's remains.

Ben seemed to sense Jack's uneasiness and tapped his shoulder. "C'mon, let's find that tunnel on the other side."

They climbed up the slope out of the pit and were starting across the cavern when Ben motioned for Jack to stop.

"Hold up," he said, tilting his head.

Jack held his breath and listened, cursing to himself. Nothing good ever happened when Ben did that.

Ben stood motionless, his flashlight shining weakly into the darkness ahead. Jack's flashlight began to tremble in his hand after several moments, and he had to remind himself to breathe again. He couldn't hear a thing except the echoes of water dripping onto the mud from somewhere above them.

"What is it?"

Ben's voice was barely a whisper. "We're not alone."

Then Jack heard it too. A scraping sound, like something being dragged across the mud and gravel of the cave floor. But he couldn't tell if it was in front of them or behind. The echoes seemed to come from all around them.

Jack spun around, shining his light behind them. Shadows skittered off the rocks and boulders strewn about the cavern floor, jerking and darting around the perimeter of his vision. Jack's heart raced as he and Ben stood back-to-back, sweeping the flashlight beams across the cave. They illuminated the immediate area but seemed to get swallowed entirely in the inky blackness beyond.

Then came another sound. Both terrifyingly familiar and yet eerily new. It was a clicking, like the spiders had made, though this sound was deeper in timbre, slower and more deliberate. Like someone tapping gently on a hollow log in a continuous though uneven rhythm. And the scraping also grew louder.

Jack swept the light around, meeting the

beam from Ben's flashlight. It fell momentarily on a large rock formation directly ahead of them. An odd-shaped boulder . . .

That moved.

Jack couldn't tell exactly what it was, nor could he determine its size or shape. Only that it was big. Very big.

Ben clutched Jack's arm and pulled him off toward the right as the cavern was filled with a shriek like knives scraping across a chalkboard. They ran at an angle away from the sound and the movement, toward the side of the cavern. Ben scrambled across the uneven cave floor, darting and weaving between rocks and holes.

Jack followed close behind, now hearing more sounds behind them — the familiar clicking of the spiders. It sounded like a whole torrent of them. Had whatever made the shriek alerted the others to the presence of fresh prey? Terror rose in Jack, gripping his chest. His breath came like a steam locomotive chugging uphill. He could see only flashes of Ben's back in front of him as his light jostled in his hand.

"Over here." Ben's voice emerged from the tumult. Jack lost sight of him and swept his light across the cave.

"Where are you?"

A light flashed in Jack's eyes. Ben was

standing several yards away to the left, waving his light. Jack hurried across the cave, stumbling over rocks. He jammed his toe against a boulder and sprawled headlong into the mud. His light tumbled from his grasp.

Out of the darkness, Jack felt something hard pounce onto his back. A shrill hissing sound growled in his ear. He cried out, rolling to the side to shake it loose. Sharp talons dug into his shoulders.

He fumbled with the clip of the backpack and shook his shoulders free of it. He scrambled to his feet, leaving the pack behind, and scooped up his light again. Without thinking, he spun back to see one of the cave spiders, a good-size one, tearing into the bag like it was dinner. It shook the sack almost like a dog shaking a rag. Suddenly it stopped and reared on its haunches, lifting its front legs up. Jack recognized that pose from the first spider they had seen. The one that had attacked Rudy. The creature's hideous, gaping maw was overshadowed by a pair of clawlike fangs that clicked together with jerky, rapid movements.

Jack knew the pose most likely indicated that the creature was ready to strike, but he was frozen where he stood. The spider's palps rapped together like castanets.

Jack blinked as another, larger shadow passed in front of him. Ben dashed into view and punted the spider off into the darkness. He turned and glared at Jack. *"Are you crazy?"*

Jack shook himself to his senses. The barrage of shrieks and clicking grew steadily louder, and he could see a wave of shadows moving across the cave floor.

Ben ran out of sight again as Jack scrambled to his feet and searched the ground around him. "My pack!"

Ben's voice came from the darkness behind him. "Forget your pack, you idiot! Just get out of there!"

But everything Jack valued was inside that pack. His camera and the appendage specimen . . . No one would ever believe he'd been here without them. He'd never be able to prove anything. He lingered a moment longer, scanning the ground until Ben's voice jolted him from his search and Jack took off after him.

In moments they came to the edge of the cavern and what looked like a dead end. Ben pointed to another opening about six or eight feet up, just large enough to squeeze through. A thin stream of water was trickling out of it.

Ben climbed the wall and scrambled into

the opening. Jack struggled up a couple feet but couldn't find any grip on the wet surface until Ben reached a hand down and pulled him up.

They wasted no time climbing the tunnel, ascending at a relatively steep angle. Water poured past them, and Jack could barely manage to keep up. The only question he had now was, could the cave spiders climb as well?

Ben and Jack continued to claw their way up until Jack's knees and elbows were scraped raw and throbbing. But he knew he couldn't slow down. Within a few moments they emerged onto a cramped, level area where Jack had to stop and catch his breath.

Ben shone his light back down the tunnel and shook his head. "What were you thinking? Why didn't you run?"

Jack closed his eyes. "I don't know. I . . . I had to get a better look at it. To see what we're up against."

"Not sure if you know this, but we're running for our lives here. It's not like we have the luxury to sit around and study them."

"Look, any details we can learn could help us survive."

"Not if you get yourself killed learning it."

Jack sat up. "Well, now I'm pretty sure they're blind. That one didn't react at all to my light. So that means they most likely make that clicking sound for echolocation. Like a bat."

"Great, they're blind," Ben grunted. "They still don't seem to have any trouble locating us."

Jack figured it was valuable information nonetheless, despite the danger he'd put himself in. Even though, had Ben not stepped in, Jack would've likely ended up like Rudy.

Jack rubbed his eyes. "But anyway . . . thanks for saving me . . . again."

"Yeah." Ben pointed up the passage. "We need to keep moving."

They crawled along on hands and knees, but the passage became increasingly narrow and soon they had to proceed on their bellies. Before long, Jack could hear the water flowing louder. And it sounded like more than just a minor trickle.

Finally the passage widened, and they found themselves in a small, mud-filled chamber. A steady stream of water poured down through an opening above their heads.

Jack's lungs burned as he sucked in gasps of air. "I . . . could use another break. . . ."

Ben paused and shone his light back down the passage. Jack rolled over to peer into the tunnel as well. Amid the shadows and rocks, he spotted a flurry of legs scurrying up the passage toward them.

"They're coming up the tunnel!"

"C'mon." Ben grabbed his arm. "I'll boost you up."

He interlocked his fingers, and Jack stepped into his grasp and scrambled through the opening overhead. Fighting to get a handhold amid the water and mud, he clawed his way into a low, wide space above them. Water streamed down through numerous fissures, some of it pouring into the opening he'd just climbed through, but the majority of the flow washed off down a secondary passage into complete darkness.

Jack heard Ben's frantic voice from the chamber below.

"Pull me up!"

Jack reached down and caught Ben's hands. He was tugging Ben up through the opening when suddenly Ben let out a terrified shriek. Jack felt him slipping back down the hole.

"My legs . . ."

Jack struggled to get a foothold, clinging to Ben's hands as the cave spiders played tug-of-war with his lower half. Ben screamed in pain and kicked his legs furiously. But the passage was too low for Jack to orient himself to gain any leverage.

"Hang on to me!"

"Pull me up." Ben grimaced. "Don't let go! Don't let —"

Something twisted Ben's lower torso, yanking his hands from Jack's grip and jerking him back down through the hole. Jack lunged forward to save him, but it had all happened too fast.

"Ben!" he screamed.

But all Jack could see in the chamber below was a light flashing erratically from inside the tunnel. Ben's screams echoed up the passage for several seconds until they finally stopped, and the only sound Jack could hear was the steady drumming of water streaming down into the tunnel.

"Ben . . ."

Jack stared down into the dark chamber. Paralyzed by fear and shock.

He rolled away from the hole and lay on his back. Water cascaded onto his face and chest. He was cold and wet and surrounded by complete darkness.

And now he was utterly alone.

CHAPTER 15

Jack lay dazed for several minutes in the darkness, water streaming across his face.

Finally he roused himself, moving purely on instinct, pulling himself down the tunnel for dear life. The passage sloped downward, and as Jack crawled forward, he could feel the angle increasing.

He had no idea where he was going, only that he couldn't turn back. He could only feel his way inch by inch through the utter darkness and hope the passage would lead somewhere safe. For all he knew, the creatures could be climbing up the hole to pursue him. He couldn't hear anything over the sound of the water rushing around him. It seemed to gain momentum the farther he crawled. Suddenly his hands slipped in the mud-slick passage, and he slid down the chute into darkness. He clawed futilely against the sides of the tunnel but couldn't slow his progress.

Then without warning, he felt the rock disappear from underneath him, and the next thing he knew, he was falling through pitch-black emptiness. He seemed to fall forever through the inky abyss until he felt impact and plunged into icy water.

He surfaced again, gulping in a lungful of air as he was swept along in the current of an underground river. His feet slammed against rocks under the surface and something sharp scraped against his shin. Bolts of pain shot up his leg and Jack winced, though he knew the pain had been deadened somewhat by the cold. He flailed his arms desperately, trying to keep his head above the surface.

After several minutes the current subsided, and Jack felt himself floating in calmer waters. But he was numb and shivering. He knew he had to get out of the water soon, before the onset of hypothermia.

Realizing he was in some sort of subterranean lake, he decided to pick a direction and swim in hopes of finding a shoreline. Or at least shallower waters.

As he paddled blindly, a profound sense of isolation swept over him. A feeling of despair as he floated in a total absence of light.

Then just as he was losing all hope, he

saw something in the cavern above him. Odd, disjointed gray shapes. He blinked and looked closer, wondering if he was hallucinating as a result of his trauma or the freezing water. But in fact he was seeing something. It was the ceiling of the cavern high above him. Vague outlines of the jagged rock formations dappled by light.

Light!

Jack looked around. Light was coming from somewhere. It was faint and diffused, but he could tell it wasn't the sickly yellow hue of the bioluminescent slime. This looked like daylight.

He floundered in the water, searching for the source. Then his feet touched bottom. It was jagged and uneven, but Jack was able to stand and survey his surroundings. In fact, he could see faint reflections of daylight everywhere around him now, wavering and jostling against the black rock walls of the cavern. It was enough for him to see the dark silhouette of the shore not far off.

Jack stumbled to the rocky ground and collapsed on a bed of smooth stones and mud. A huge weight seemed to lift from him as he lay there gasping for breath.

After several minutes he crawled to his feet and tried to assess his surroundings. The cavern seemed long and narrow, though he couldn't see to the other side. But daylight was coming up from the lake, and as Jack looked closer, he could see its source — a small, glowing patch beneath the water. He stumbled across the rocks for a better view.

The jagged outline of a narrow tunnel lay just under the water. Faint rays of daylight streamed in through the small opening, and Jack's heart raced. He maneuvered as close as he could get to the mouth of the cave. It was impossible to tell for sure, but he estimated the passage to be twenty to thirty feet in length. A long way in his weakened state, but at this point he knew he had no choice. He wasn't going to get any stronger by waiting. He took several deep breaths and submerged. It was a narrow, jagged passage, and his arms and legs ached from exhaustion as he paddled through the opening.

In the chilling darkness, Jack could make out the murky ring of daylight at the end of the watery tunnel and felt almost like he was having a near-death experience. Or perhaps it was more like being reborn.

Once through, Jack swam to the surface and emerged into a blinding glow. Daylight felt warm on his face, and he had never been so relieved to see the sun in his life. It blazed down from a cloudless sky onto the surface of a small lake. He couldn't make out many details of his surroundings in the brightness — just a blurry shoreline several yards off — but he swam madly for it.

Stumbling through the mud onto the rocky bank, he collapsed again, faceup on the shore. The sun warmed his skin and a breeze blew across his face, carrying the scent of pine trees and field grass. The sensation filled Jack with a mixture of emotions. He felt genuine relief to finally be out of those caverns and free from the creatures inside. He felt a tempered exhilaration over the discovery of the N'watu but deep sorrow as well — an almost-unbearable emptiness at the loss of Rudy and Ben. He knew the images of their agonizing deaths would be burned into his memory for the rest of his life.

But Jack also knew he wasn't finished. He had to find his way back to civilization. He had to find help. He needed to get to a phone and call the state patrol.

He rolled to his feet and tried to gain his bearings. According to his watch, it was going on seven in the evening, and the sun was starting to dip toward the horizon. He was on the shore of a small mountain lake, no more than three or four hundred feet across, with the sheer rocky face of a mountain side rising straight up on the far side and a carpet of tall pines on the other. Jack had no compass or map, but he could see the adjacent peaks running off to the right rather than the left, as he had seen when they first entered through the falls. He had obviously made it through the entire mountain and was now on the other side. It was probably a several-mile trek back to where they had parked the RV that morning. It felt like he'd been wandering through the caves for weeks, yet it had been less than twelve hours.

Jack decided his best chance was to make his way through the forest and hopefully find a highway. But he wasn't familiar with the area, and for all he knew he could be lost in one of the national forests in western Wyoming, miles from any towns. Clearly he wasn't out of danger yet.

He checked the gash in his shin. It was deep and had started throbbing. Jack guessed he would need medical attention soon. Yet another thing on his list of concerns.

Jack had never been much of an outdoorsman and now worried how he would fare out in the wild without Ben or Rudy. Logic dictated that he had better make the most of the daylight and get as far as he could while he had the light and warmth of the day.

The hot sun felt good on his wet clothes and shoes, and though the terrain was uneven through the woods, the semiarid climate made for less undergrowth. He found he was able to make good time through the forest, despite being slightly hobbled by his leg. He traveled down a rocky slope, heading on a path parallel to the mountains.

It was after seven o'clock when he finally came across a narrow, paved highway. Jack laughed and knelt down to kiss the asphalt. He knew his chances of finding help had just improved 1,000 percent. Plus, the pavement was smooth, requiring less energy to traverse.

He paused, trying to decide which direction to take. He figured that he'd already hiked a mile or two from the lake. He decided that his best bet for finding civilization was to head south. At least that would take him back in the general direction of the area where he had parked the RV.

But he had no water bottle and no food and had long ago grown thirsty. His clothes had dried and now were growing damp again with his sweat. Jack continued along the road, keeping an ear open for the sound of vehicles.

He had walked another half hour and the pain in his leg was just becoming unbearable when he finally heard a car approaching from behind. Jack turned and waved his arms as a rust-colored pickup truck appeared around the curve.

It approached, slowed, and pulled to a stop. Jack's heart felt a wave of relief as the driver rolled down his window and leaned out. He looked like a cowboy's cowboy. Lean and sinewy with short reddish hair and a large mustache sweeping out beneath his nose.

The guy nodded at Jack. "Need a lift?" His voice carried a heavy Western twang.

"Man, am I glad to see you. I got an emergency."

He looked Jack over. "You all right?"

"Do you have a cell phone I can borrow?" Jack said. "I have to get in touch with the state patrol."

The guy shook his head and waved Jack around to the other side of the truck. "You won't get any cell signals out here, but there's a little town a couple miles up with a landline."

Jack climbed in, noting how incredibly comfortable the torn-up leather seat felt after spending the day crawling around inside a cave.

The guy put the truck back in gear and continued on. "Name's Malcolm Browne."

Jack shook his hand. "Jack Kendrick. Thanks for stopping."

"So what's up? You get in an accident or something?"

"Something like that." Jack leaned his head back and closed his eyes. "We were exploring a cave up in those mountains. Two people — the two guys I was with — died in there."

"Died?" Browne gaped at Jack. "What happened to them?"

"They were . . . killed." Jack rubbed his eyes. "There's something — some kind of animals inside that cave. I just need to get the authorities up here right away."

"Well, you can get ahold of the sheriff in town. And Doc Henderson's got a phone you can use," Browne said, shaking his head. "I didn't even know there was a cave around here. What kind of animal was it? A bear or something?"

"You wouldn't believe me if I told you." Jack's voice trailed off and he shuddered.

They continued on for another mile or two before Jack spotted buildings through the trees. A wooden sign on the side of the road read: *Welcome to Beckon. You're not here by chance.*

A weathered old gas station and garage stood on the outskirts of the town, welcoming visitors with a dirt-crusted red-white-and-blue Standard sign posted out front and a small salvage yard behind it. Within the sagging wooden fence, the battered remnants of cars lay hidden by weeds and brush like an automotive graveyard. Their burned-out frames, fenders, and hoods were all smashed and rusted beyond recognition and stacked in forlorn piles, overgrown by prairie grass. Next to the service station sat a general store and, beside that, a building marked Saddleback Diner. Across the road was a row of shops and storefronts. Behind them, several houses were huddled amid the trees. And beyond the houses rose a steep, wooded bluff with an enormous log home perched on an outcropping near the top. Directly behind the great lodge, Jack could see the looming steel-gray mountain peak.

Browne pulled to a stop in front of the doctor's office, and Jack stumbled out of the truck. His leg was beginning to stiffen up, and the pain was getting worse.

Browne helped him hobble inside to a small waiting area with an empty receptionist counter and a closed-off section behind it, where Jack assumed the exam room was.

"Hey, Doc," Browne called out. "You got a patient here."

The doctor emerged from the back room. He was a bookish fellow of medium height and build, clean-shaven with light-brown hair that was sort of greased down and parted neatly to one side. To Jack he looked more like an accountant than a doctor. His eyes fixed on Jack and his forehead wrinkled. Jack assumed the guy didn't get many strangers walking into his clinic right off the street like this.

"I picked him up on the highway," Browne explained. "Just outside town. He said he had run into trouble in some caves."

"Dwight Henderson," the doctor said, shaking Jack's hand. He nodded toward Jack's leg. "Looks like you got a pretty good gash there."

"I scraped it on some rocks. But I really need to use your phone."

"Sure, just let me take a look at your leg first." Henderson motioned for Jack to have a seat in the waiting area while he retreated into the back room.

He returned a moment later with what looked like a first aid kit and pulled up a second chair. He inspected Jack's leg more closely. "We need to clean this out. You said there was some trouble in a cave?"

Jack nodded. "Yeah . . . it's kind of a long story. But I need to contact the state patrol or somebody. Two guys — my friend and a guide we had hired — were killed."

Henderson glanced at Browne and gestured toward the door. "Go on and get Carson. He's gonna want to hear this."

Browne nodded and bolted out of the office.

"Who's Carson?"

Henderson began cleaning Jack's wound. "The local law enforcement. He'll get in touch with the authorities. But your friends — how were they killed?"

Jack winced as the doctor wiped iodine into the torn skin. "I don't think anyone's gonna believe me. It was some kind of . . . I don't know, giant arthropod. Like a spider."

Henderson looked up. "Spider?"

"That's the best way I can describe them," Jack said as a shudder raked through him. "I've never seen anything like it in my life. They're huge. And they have a hard shell — like a crab — but they were more like spiders. They have venom that's extremely poisonous. And they're carnivorous. They hunted like a pack of wild dogs."

Henderson looked incredulous. "How big were these . . . spiders?"

"They were huge! The biggest ones were . . . I don't know — they had maybe four-foot leg spans. They were like big dogs."

Henderson wrapped gauze around Jack's calf, shaking his head. "Dogs? There's no way . . ."

Jack studied the guy's reaction. It seemed some part of him believed the story, and yet another part of him refused to. Like he was having some kind of internal battle. As if he didn't *want* to believe it.

Jack grunted. "Look . . . I really don't know what they are. I'm guessing they're an entirely new species."

"And you say they're poisonous?"

Jack shuddered again as his mind replayed Rudy's gruesome death. "My friend died from a bite in only a few minutes."

At that point Browne returned with a guy Jack assumed was Carson. He had a couple days' growth of black stubble on his square jaw and wore a tan shirt with a sheriff patch and a silver badge. A gun holster hugged his waist and a weathered black cowboy hat rode tight and low on his forehead.

Carson stood in the middle of the room with his hands on his hips. "Malcolm here tells me you had some kind of caving accident." His voice was gravelly and terse.

"Uh . . . yes."

"Some members of your party died?"

"Yes, two of my friends."

"And where exactly is this cave?"

Jack pointed out the front window. "Somewhere under those mountains."

Carson raised an eyebrow and produced a small notepad from his belt and a pen from his shirt pocket. "So why don't you start from the beginning."

Jack was hesitant at first but started to relate the story of his expedition. He decided to leave out the details about his father but told the rest exactly as it had happened. To hear himself tell the tale, Jack decided it all sounded too incredible to believe. Ancient Indian legends, giant millipedes and beetles, and enormous carnivorous spiders . . . like something out of a bad science fiction movie.

Then when Jack got to the part about the N'watu, he was sure they would think he was psychotic. But instead they all listened quietly, and when Jack had finished, no one said a word for a long moment.

Carson stared at Jack from under the brim of his hat. "You're saying there's a tribe of Indians living inside this cave too?"

Jack nodded. "I don't know exactly how many of them there are, or if they actually *live* inside the cave or what . . . but from what I could see, I can't think of any other explanation."

"And you came out here to study them?" Carson said.

Jack sighed. He was growing weary of all the questions. "Look, I . . . I know this all sounds crazy, but I'm telling you, I saw them — and those spider things — with my own eyes."

Carson leaned close. "Have you told anyone else about this?"

"No — I told you, I just managed to find my way out of the cave. You're the first people I've seen since I got out of there."

"All right . . ." Carson drew in a long breath as he paced around the room. "Where'd you say you parked your vehicle?"

Jack shrugged. "I . . . I don't know exactly. It was near a bridge where we picked up the trail."

"This trail to the waterfall at the head of White Eagle Creek?"

Jack was starting to get a headache. "Can we please contact the state patrol or whoever we need to contact? My best friend died in that cave, and I have to tell his family."

Carson cut him off with a wave of his hand. "I'll contact the authorities. I think right now you just need medical attention."

Jack blinked and shook his head. "I'm *fine.* We have to *do* something."

Henderson spoke up. "Listen, you've obviously been through some major psychological trauma — not to mention physical. I think it would be best for you to get some rest and —"

"I don't want to rest." Jack stood, his anger coming to a head. "I need to get out of here and find a phone!"

Carson stood by the doorway, tapping his holster and shaking his head. "Well, I'm afraid you're not going anywhere."

"What?" Jack's face flushed with anger but then quickly faded. The three men just stared at him, their expressions darker now and more menacing.

Jack backed away from them. "What's going on? Who are you people?"

A chill of fear rose inside his chest. What kind of town was this?

■ ■ ■ ■

Part II
Elina

■ ■ ■ ■

Each man must grant himself the emotions that he needs and the morality that suits him.

REMY DE GOURMONT,
SELECTED WRITINGS

Chapter 16

Western Wyoming
One Day Earlier

Deep down, Elina Gutierrez knew she was going to die. But she also knew she wasn't going down without a fight.

She dashed through the woods clutching her Browning .40-caliber pistol as the rain beat down on her in waves, drenching her short dark hair and clothes. Her feet slipped on the muddy slope and she stumbled across the uneven terrain, slamming into a tree trunk. She slumped to the ground, groaning and sucking in the thin mountain air with agonizing breaths.

Somewhere in the woods behind her, she could hear the voices.

They were getting closer.

She pushed herself to her feet and continued on, weaving between tree trunks, ducking beneath some branches and cursing as others slapped across her face, slicing off bits of flesh. She fought to keep her balance over rain-slicked rocks and gnarled tree roots. Then she spotted something through the mist and trees ahead: a smooth, flat strip of asphalt cutting laterally across the slope.

The road!

Heart pounding, head spinning, and ribs throbbing, Elina could feel herself on the verge of losing consciousness. But she couldn't now. Not here. She had to keep moving.

She had to get off this mountain.

She'd arrived in Wyoming two days earlier looking for answers but had only found more questions. For the last eight hours she'd camped out on the wooded bluff, peering through a telephoto lens into the windows of a massive, rustic lodge some 250 yards away.

The brooding mansion jutted out of the mountainside like a great diadem of log and stone. Perched in the shadow of the jagged peak, its weathered timbers appeared to have borne the brunt of many winters. The central hall extended out to the edge of a cliff, where its huge windows overlooked the little town huddled at the base of the mountain and the rough, rolling countryside beyond.

But what Elina hadn't known was that

while she had been busy watching the occupants of the lodge, *they* had been watching *her.*

It was just after noon when she heard the first echoes of voices over the rain and knew she had been found out. She jammed her gear into her backpack, abandoned her makeshift rain shelter, and scurried down the mountainside.

Now she could hear the voices echoing in the woods behind her, barking out orders to each other. They were hunting her.

But if she could reach the highway, she'd be able to get to her car.

The sound of heavy footsteps came pounding through the mud directly behind her, and a husky voice called out, "Here she is!"

Elina turned and raised her Browning as a large silhouette burst through the trees. He came into focus: a big man wearing a dark-green nylon jacket and a black cap, with a short-barrel shotgun in his grasp. Elina gritted her teeth and squeezed off two shots.

Her pursuer lurched backward with a look of surprise on his face. His shotgun fired wide, and Elina heard the pellets crack through the branches beside her head. His feet slipped into the air, and he landed on his back in the mud.

Time seemed to slow as Elina stared at the man writhing on the ground. He groaned and wheezed, pushing his feet against the mud. Then his body shuddered and went limp. Elina knew she had hit him square in the chest. Both shots. He wouldn't be getting up.

It was the second time in her life that she had killed a man.

She heard more yelling off in the woods and shook herself to her senses. The others had heard the gunshots and were converging on her location. She wasn't out of danger yet — in fact, now she was in even deeper trouble. She pushed through the pine trees until suddenly the ground fell away beneath her and she tumbled down a rocky embankment onto the shoulder of the road. Sharp gravel bit into the palms of her hands, and the Browning skittered across the wet pavement.

Elina rolled to her feet as a rust-colored pickup swerved and skidded to a halt a few yards away. The doors opened, two men emerged, and Elina found herself staring into the barrel of another shotgun.

"Don't even think about it," the guy with the gun growled at her. He was a brawny ox of a man with a dark goatee on his jaw.

The driver was smaller and leaner with

reddish hair and a thick red mustache. He snatched up her Browning from across the road and stuck it in his belt. Then he forced Elina to lie facedown on the wet asphalt while he checked her for additional weapons. After that he yanked her up to her knees, tore the pack off her shoulders, and riffled through it, pulling out her scope and digital camera.

"Well, look-a here," he said. "Whatcha doin' with all this? Some bird-watching, maybe?"

"That's right." Elina grimaced defiantly. "I'm an ornithologist."

The guy with the shotgun frowned. "A what?"

The driver chuckled. "So you got a sense of humor. We'll see how long that lasts."

At that point two more men emerged from the woods, both clad in camouflage jackets and carrying rifles. They slid down the embankment onto the road.

"She shot Carson!" one of them yelled, pointing back into the brush. "I think . . . I think he might be dead."

The driver swore and threw down the backpack. He grabbed Elina by the collar and pressed the barrel of her Browning against her forehead. The four of them surrounded her as she fought to stay focused.

Remember your training. . . . Stay calm and look for an opportunity.

The driver pulled her close, still pressing the gun to her head. "So you think you're a tough little *chica,* huh? You can shoot a gun? Maybe we'll have a little fun with you first."

The others grunted in a primal chorus of approval. Like a clan of cavemen.

"Knock it off!"

The voice came from the woods. The men backed away, and Elina could see the man she had shot — the one they called Carson — standing at the top of the embankment, clutching his chest. He looked pale and like he was in a fair amount of pain, but he was alive nonetheless. Very much alive.

Elina frowned. Kevlar. He must've been wearing Kevlar.

"We gotta bring her to town," he said. "Vale wants to talk to her."

Elina winced as they forced her hands behind her back and secured her wrists with a set of plastic zip ties. Then they hauled her into the bed of the pickup and three of the men climbed up with her while Carson and the driver got inside the cab. They turned the truck around and headed up the road.

The plastic ties dug into her wrists, but Elina knew the pain was the least of her worries now. She was completely cut off with no backup. No one even knew exactly where she was. She closed her eyes and prayed silently. And as she did, the irony struck her. Four months ago, she wouldn't have even thought about prayer. Four months ago, she was brash and hotheaded. Self-reliant and determined. Most people would have just called her angry. Four months ago, she'd had absolutely no use for God.

But that was then.

Now she sat in the back of the truck, flooded with fear and second guesses, praying desperately.

The road snaked through the pine forest. She could see patches of a jagged gray mountainside through the branches, and within half a mile they came into a clearing. The town ahead looked like little more than a clutch of ramshackle buildings hiding in the embrace of a looming mountain. A damp mist cloaked the shops and storefronts and houses, casting them in dreary silhouettes.

At the edge of town they passed a rough-hewn timber sign mounted to a pair of log posts along the side of the road. Elina shuddered as she saw the letters carved into the wood.

Welcome to Beckon. You're not here by chance.

CHAPTER 17

Midway through town, the pickup truck turned up a twisting gravel road that led to the massive stone-and-timber house. Elina tried to control her fear as they passed through a set of iron gates and pulled to a stop at the entrance, where an enormous log-beam portico loomed over a pair of ornate wooden doors.

Carson hauled her out of the truck and marched her through the front doors into a spacious, stone-tiled foyer. The decor was dark and rustic — sort of a Gothic Wild West, Elina thought — with a whole menagerie of stuffed animal heads and antlers populating nearly every wall. To one side of the foyer a wide log staircase curled up to the second-floor balcony above them.

A thin, hawk-nosed woman greeted them as they entered. Her fair complexion was surprisingly soft and unblemished — with the exception of the dark circles under her eyes, as if she hadn't slept in days. Elina guessed she was young, maybe in her twenties, but her burgundy hair was pulled back in a tight bun that made her look older. In fact, with a little mascara and lipstick — and of course a whole different hairstyle — the woman might have actually been attractive.

She looked at Elina for a long moment, and Elina could see some trace of emotion in her pale-blue eyes but couldn't quite make out what it was. Surprise? Anger? Fear? Or maybe disgust?

"This is her?" the woman asked at length.

"Yeah." Carson handed her the backpack. "He said he wanted her alive. Said he wanted to talk to her."

The woman took the pack and gestured to the hallway behind her. "He's just sitting down to lunch. Give me five minutes."

She turned and slipped down the hall while Carson yanked Elina over to a bench near the staircase.

"Sit down and keep quiet," he said.

Elina tried to get a better look at his chest. She spotted the holes in the jacket where the bullets had penetrated, but she couldn't see much of what he was wearing underneath. A black shirt of some sort. She wondered if maybe it was some kind of new ultrathin Kevlar design. After a few minutes she gathered her courage and ventured a question.

"So what happened to you? You should be dead."

"Shut up."

"Y'know, you really freaked me out."

"I said, *shut up.*"

"All right, all right . . . I'm just saying . . . I shot you nearly point blank. I thought I watched you die."

"Well, you were mistaken."

"So . . . what? You got some kind of special Kevlar vest or something?"

"Something like that." Carson snatched a fistful of her black hair and yanked her head backward. "Now *shut up.*"

Elina decided to cooperate for the time being. She wasn't going to get any more information out of Carson anyway. He was obviously pretty high up in whatever organizational structure they had in this town, but he was still subservient to this Vale character, whoever he was.

After several minutes the burgundy-haired woman peeked her head back into the foyer and waved them in. Carson nodded, pulled Elina to her feet, and shoved her along the hallway. They passed an enormous great room with a massive stone fireplace and a wide bank of windows. Next they came to the formal dining hall, which held a long, medieval-looking table. Several chairs were lined up along each side with the largest chair situated at the head of the table. The only seat that was occupied.

The man seated at the head was clearly engrossed in his meal. Elina could see it consisted of a thick red steak — very red — with a baked potato and what looked like asparagus. He had a bottle of red wine and a half-filled glass on his right; on his left was a brown folder.

Elina had gotten only fleeting glimpses of Vale through her scope, but now she saw he was a rather pale, sharp-featured man. And his complexion looked all the more pallid contrasted against his shoulder-length, jet-black hair. He was clean-shaven except for the narrow black tuft of well-groomed fuzz beneath his lower lip.

But Elina quickly noticed that his most striking feature was his eyes. When he looked at her, she could see they held a pale-green hue — nearly yellow. They were haunting eyes, like an animal's. And Elina felt almost as if a wolf were staring at her.

He chewed his steak slowly as he looked her over. Elina stood just inside the doorway with Carson right behind her; the woman had taken up a position behind Vale's right shoulder.

Vale chewed a mouthful of meat without saying a word and motioned her to come closer. She took a few hesitant steps into the room until she stood at the foot of the table.

"Did you know," Vale said through a mouthful of steak, "it was Wyoming that first gave women the right to vote?"

He sipped some wine, swirled it in his mouth, and swallowed. His voice was considerably deeper than Elina had expected. She glanced back at Carson, wondering what exactly Vale meant by the comment.

Vale sliced another piece of steak and stuck it in his mouth. "And we were the first state to elect a woman governor. Did you know *that?*"

Elina shook her head. "I'm . . . not exactly following your train of thought here."

Vale shrugged. "I'm simply saying that the people of Wyoming have always been at the forefront of societal evolution. We're very progressive, forward-thinking people."

"Okay?" Elina made no effort to hide her confusion.

"My point being —" Vale set down his utensils and dabbed his lips with a napkin — "that despite how rustic and remote our town might appear to you, don't mistake us for bucolic simpletons. Okay, Miss Gutierrez?"

"Fine."

Vale glanced at the folder beside him. "Should I call you *Officer* Gutierrez?" He flipped open the folder and browsed the top sheet. "Or . . . is it *ex*-officer? I'm not sure how this whole administrative leave thing works. You did turn in your badge, yes?"

"Wow, so you guys know how to google," Elina muttered. "I'm impressed."

Vale looked mildly amused. "You know, for what it's worth, I think you did the right thing. I really do. Even though this kid didn't have a gun . . . and wasn't technically committing a crime. I'm sure he would've gotten around to it sooner or later. It was just a matter of time. He had all the classic stats going for him, right? Single mom, no real father to speak of. The kid was just a crime waiting to happen."

Elina's jaw tightened. Obviously Vale's burgundy lady had gone through her bag and run some sort of background check while Elina was waiting out in the foyer. It wouldn't have taken much to find her recent history with the LAPD. The shooting incident four months earlier had been highly publicized and commented on by all the local news outlets — even a national program had picked up the story. Elina never imagined she'd become the center of such a media circus in only her second year on the force.

She never thought her dream of becoming a cop would turn into a nightmare so fast.

"Whatever," she grunted.

Vale leaned back and raised an eyebrow. "Though it appears you've not quite come to terms with the incident, hmm? Not made peace with yourself yet?"

"Don't worry about me."

"Well, regardless, I'm certain the people of LA are safer with one less potential criminal on the streets. I wouldn't lose any sleep over it if I were you. Some people the world is just better off without."

Elina snorted. "So is that your thing? You're some kind of therapist?"

"Hardly." Vale swirled the wine in his glass. "I just wanted to put our conversation into context for you." He took a sip. "I'm actually far more interested in what brings you from the big city to our little town. And what possessed you to trespass on my property and spy on my home."

Elina forced a tone of confidence. "Oh, I think we both know why I'm here."

Vale spread his palms. "I'm afraid you

have me at a bit of a disadvantage, Officer Gutierrez. Apparently only one of us knows."

"I'm looking for my cousin. He disappeared last month, and his family hasn't heard from him since."

"Ah, a missing persons case," Vale said.

"He had come here to find work. His sister said she saw him getting into a van with Nevada plates four weeks ago. A plain white van. She said it comes around every few weeks promising work in Las Vegas."

"So it would seem this cousin of yours is — what's the politically correct term? — an *undocumented* worker?"

"He was just looking for work. He was trying to —"

"So why aren't you looking in Las Vegas?"

"Because I followed that van the next time it came around. And you want to hear something funny? It didn't go to Las Vegas. But I'll give you one guess where it did go."

Vale shook his head. "Well, Miss Former Officer Gutierrez, Wyoming is a little out of your jurisdiction, isn't it?"

"It's a personal investigation."

"I'm sure the taxpayers of Los Angeles would be happy to know you're making productive use of your free time. But please forgive me if I don't feel compelled to cooperate with your *personal* investigation."

"I wasn't expecting you to."

Vale downed the last of his wine. "And I don't appreciate strangers who trespass on my property, invade my privacy, and accuse me of sordid activities."

"I just want to know where my cousin is."

"Then I suggest you start with the FBI. Or better yet, the INS."

"Look . . ." Elina decided to try a less confrontational approach and softened her voice. "I'm not trying to . . . to turn this into a federal investigation. I just want to find my cousin. To make sure he's safe. And let him know his family is worried about him."

"I already told you I can't help you with —"

"Javier."

Vale blinked. "Excuse me?"

"Javier Sanchez. That's his name."

"I'm sorry, Miss Gutierrez, but we really have nothing further to talk about."

"What did you do with them? There were four other men who got into that van, and I know it brought them here."

Vale's gaze grew cold. "My patience is wearing thin. I suggest you forget these ridiculous accusations and —"

"The van's plates are registered to a

dummy corporation in Nevada that pays all the fees and insurance." Elina was through playing this game. It was time to lay her cards on the table. "But guess who owns that corporation? Vale Corp International. That's *your* company, isn't it? That was *your* van. Now what did you do with those people?"

Vale stared at her for a long moment. Then he leaned back in his chair and puffed out his cheeks in a long sigh. "Very well, then. You know, when they first brought you here, there was actually a small chance that I could let you go. But only a *very* small chance."

"I'd be careful about threatening me if I were you."

Vale was silent for several seconds, but his cold, yellow-green gaze never wavered. *"Elina,"* he said at length. "Do you know what your name means?"

"What?"

"It means 'shining light.' Ironic, since that's exactly what you'll need where you're going."

"Careful, Mr. Vale," Elina said, concentrating on keeping her voice from quivering. "People know I'm here. They . . . they know what I found —"

"Yes, yes, people know where you are."

Vale drummed his fingers on the table. "And I'm sure they'll come looking for you. They'll probably search for months. And it'll be a big story for a while — they'll have your picture on all the networks. They may even find your abandoned car on a remote highway somewhere in a neighboring state. But in the end they won't find you. Not even a trace." He shook his head. "They never do."

Chapter 18

Elina felt Carson's hand clench like a vise around her upper arm. He hauled her out of the room at Vale's command, then shoved her down the hallway until they came to a security door that opened on a flight of stairs into the basement of the mansion.

Seeing the stairs, Elina tried to twist loose of his grip, but he jerked her back. Then he snapped her around to face him and she felt the jarring sting of the back of his hand across her jaw.

"Try that again and I'll break your neck!"

Elina teetered on the brink of consciousness, but she could see Carson was looking paler than he had earlier and the skin under his eyes had darkened.

She could taste blood in her mouth but grimaced at him, refusing to let her fear show. "You don't look so good. What's the matter? Not feeling very well?"

Carson only spun her around and forced

her down the wooden steps into the basement.

Elina's mind was spinning out of control. All her worst fears when she first decided to follow the mysterious van from LA to Wyoming were apparently coming true. She tried to remain rational. And she tried to reason with Carson to let her go.

At the bottom of the stairs he led her down a narrow corridor to a large supply closet at the far end. Inside were shelves of cleaning supplies and chemicals with mops hanging from a row of hooks on the far wall. He twisted one of the hooks to the side and Elina heard something click. Then he pushed against the wall and a small section of it swung out into darkness beyond.

Elina felt cool, damp air brush against her face. "Where are you taking me?"

He didn't reply but pushed her through the door and closed the panel behind them.

Elina could see they were in some sort of tunnel dug right into the mountainside. Crude lighting fixtures had been mounted into the rock overhead and cast a dim, pale-green glow. They climbed down a set of rough, uneven stairs carved into the rock, which went on for what seemed like more than a hundred yards deeper underground.

"Where are we going?" Elina whimpered again.

Still Carson didn't say anything, only forced her forward, down the steps. She could hear his breathing in the darkness, growing more labored as they walked. He didn't appear to be bleeding, but Elina guessed the gunshot had hurt him more than she had initially thought.

After several minutes they arrived at yet another door, only this one was made of solid wood. Thick, rough timbers that were fastened together with rusted iron bands and bolts. It looked like a door to some kind of dungeon.

Carson pushed the door open and ushered her into another tunnel. More dim light fixtures illuminated patches of the tunnel in the same green hue.

Now Elina could hear sounds ahead. Voices, though she couldn't make out what they were saying. She quickly discovered that they weren't speaking so much as moaning. It was as if she had descended right into hell itself.

Carson steered her into a secondary tunnel, far narrower than the first. Darkness fell around her as though someone had put a blanket over her head. After several paces he pulled her to a stop. She tried to tear away from his grasp once more, but despite his wheezing, his grip felt almost like claws digging into her flesh.

She heard a rusty metallic clank followed by the dull creaking of another door. Then came a soft snapping sound, and Elina felt the plastic ties fall away from her wrists right before she was shoved forward. She tumbled blindly onto the cold stone ground as the door creaked and slammed shut behind her, followed again by the metallic clank like some kind of lock sliding into place.

Elina flailed around in the darkness as terror welled up inside her. She felt along the floor until her palms slapped against the rough, wooden surface of the door. She balled her fists and pounded against the door, shrieking in anger at Carson. But her cries were met with silence. She screamed and raged until her voice was gone and she collapsed again on the ground, weeping softly.

Then from somewhere out in the darkness a voice called, *"Quién es usted?"*

Elina caught her breath. It was a young male voice, maybe no older than a teenager. She felt her way up the surface of the door until her fingers came across a small opening with metal bars, like the window in a prison-cell door. Outside, she could see the soft-green glow of the lights in the main corridor.

"Soy Elina. Dónde estás?"

He replied in Spanish with trembling in his voice, "I think I'm in the cell right across from you."

"What's your name?"

"Miguel," came the reply.

Elina pressed her face to the bars. As her eyes grew accustomed to the low light, she saw wooden doors across the passage from her, built right into the rock wall. Each had a small window opening with bars just like hers. There were three doors on the other side of the tunnel, and she assumed there were additional cells on either side of hers. She couldn't tell which door Miguel was behind.

He spoke again. "Where are we? What's happening to us?"

"We're in Wyoming," Elina said. "Do you remember how you got here?"

"Wyoming? They told us they had work in Las Vegas. Good-paying work. They picked us up in a van, and then . . . then I don't remember anything else. I woke up here . . . inside this dungeon."

"You don't remember anything about the trip?" Elina said.

"No . . . only that the van smelled funny when we got in it."

"How many others were with you?"

"Four others, I think. There were five of us altogether."

Elina pressed her face to the window and called out, "Javier? Javier Sanchez? Has anyone seen Javier Sanchez?"

Then another voice called out — a gravelly, hollow voice. "Elina? Elina, is that you?"

"Javier!" Elina's heart surged with emotion. Despite the darkness she suddenly felt a spark of hope.

"Elina, what . . . what are you doing here?"

"I came looking for you," Elina said. "Carmelita told me you had disappeared. She was worried sick. She said you had gotten in a van with Nevada plates."

"They said they needed five workers. They lied to us. I think they sprayed something inside the van to make us fall asleep."

"Carmelita said the van had been coming by every four weeks or so." She related how Javier's sister had called her in a panic after he had disappeared. Elina had not seen either of her cousins since they were all children. When she was a child, Elina's family would spend Christmas in Mexico every year. But after her father's death the tradition had stopped.

Then a few weeks ago she had gotten Carmelita's frantic phone call with the story of Javier's disappearance and the mysterious white van with Nevada plates. Carmelita said her family had come looking for work. Elina could guess that they had not come legally, but regardless of the circumstances, she knew she couldn't just sit by and do nothing. She had to at least find out what had happened to her cousin. And since she had been on leave from the LAPD, she had nothing but time on her hands.

Elina explained how she had been watching for the van to return for a new group of victims and how she had followed it here to Wyoming. It had arrived late the day before, and she snuck into the woods to spy on the house, trying to catch a glimpse of anyone inside. She had spent the night in the cold, watching intently, and had seen fleeting images of Vale and a couple of others. But no Hispanics. And now she had gotten captured herself.

"How long has it been? How long have I been here?" Javier asked.

"Just over four weeks, I think."

"Four weeks?" Javier groaned. "Is that all it's been? I haven't seen the sun since I've been here, and they only come down to bring us food or to take one of us away."

"Do you know where they took the others?"

"I don't know where. But everyone else I came here with is gone. Do you know?"

A frantic, high-pitched voice called out, "They are cannibals! These people eat human flesh!"

That comment got the others wailing and arguing with each other and pounding on the cell doors. The racket continued for several long minutes. Or maybe longer; Elina had no way to keep track of time anymore. She tried to calm them down but to no avail. She finally gave up, sank against the door, and put her head in her hands.

Despair turned her to memories of her father. His strong arms and gentle eyes. And his simple faith. As a girl she would always grow so nervous before a test at school, and he would pull her close to his side.

"Why are you so anxious, Little Bean? Do you think God has gotten so busy that He's forgotten about you?" he would whisper to her. "He knew you before you were even born."

Her father had immigrated to Los Angeles as a young man, newly married. He had worked hard to give his wife and children a better life, putting himself through night school to get a job repairing and maintaining commercial HVAC systems. In doing so, he had taught Elina and her younger brother, Paulo, the value of an education. He showed them the example of his genuine faith in God. He gave them the stern but loving discipline that only a father can give. He taught Elina what she should look for in a husband someday by the way he treated her mother. And in the same way he taught Paulo how he should treat his future wife. That a man should be willing to sacrifice everything for his family. And that such a man could be strong and wise and loving at the same time.

How she missed him now, and her memories only made her heart ache all the more as she longed to hear his voice again. She had been thirteen when he was killed. And in many ways his murder had been the catalyst for her joining the police department. It was a senseless, violent murder by some useless thug who killed him for the fifty dollars in his wallet. Fifty dollars. That had been the value of her father's life.

She recalled the anger that had burned inside her heart. A spark that grew out of her sorrow but soon hardened and coalesced into a steady, smoldering rage against the young black man who had pulled the trigger. A murderous punk with no job, no father, and a drug-addled mother, he'd turned to violence as a way to make himself into a man.

But her anger didn't stop there. It soon burned against all the young black men she encountered. Every one of them she saw, everywhere in the city. None of them seemed to have fathers to teach them how to be real men. How to act responsibly and do an honest day's work. They were all arrogant, misogynistic, lazy, and stupid. And violent.

So she had joined the police force to put them in jail, where they belonged.

Vale had been more accurate about her than he had probably realized. Some people the world was just better off without. Or so she'd believed.

Miguel's voice drew her out of her thoughts. He sounded weak and obviously terrified. "It makes sense, you know?"

"What?" Elina stood and looked through the opening in her door. "What does?"

"Why they choose us. Whatever's going on here, it makes sense why they choose us."

"What are you talking about?"

"Think about it. We don't have any real identification. No driver's licenses or Social

Security numbers. And most of us have no families here, at least none who would ever report us missing. We're the perfect victims. No one cares what happens to us. No one will ever come looking for us."

Chapter 19

Elina heard footsteps approaching. Multiple footsteps that echoed through the tunnels. The voices of the other prisoners began wailing, pleading for mercy in Spanish. A few seconds later the footsteps approached Elina's door and a shadow appeared at her window.

A light blinked on and flooded the tiny room.

Elina winced and shielded her eyes. She could tell it was just a flashlight, but the brightness was still painful.

"Now we can do this the easy way," came Carson's distinct voice, "or we can do it the fun way."

"What are you talking about?"

"Just do what I say," Carson said. "Turn around, face the wall, and lie down on your stomach with your hands behind you. And don't move."

While Elina's initial impulse was defiance,

she decided it would be more prudent, given her situation, to comply with the orders. They were pretty standard directions to get a suspect safely handcuffed. Besides, if they had wanted to shoot her, they could have done that through the window bars. She turned and lay down as Carson had directed.

A moment later Elina could hear them unlocking the door and a dull creak as it moaned open. Carson spoke again; this time she could tell he was inside the room.

"Keep your hands behind your back where I can see them."

Elina felt cold steel bite down around her wrists and click. Then a pair of hands hoisted her to her feet. They turned her around, and Elina could see there was another man accompanying Carson. He stood in the doorway holding the light, and all she could tell was that he was very tall and burly.

Carson pulled her roughly out of her cell and shoved her along in front of him, up the dark passage the way they had come. Elina could hear the other captives cursing and issuing warnings, but Carson ignored them for what they were. Impotent threats.

"Where are we going?" Elina said.

Carson poked her in the back. "Just walk."

At length they arrived at the supply closet entrance and marched through it back into the basement of Vale's house. They walked down the corridor and stopped at one of the doors. Here, Carson pulled out his set of keys, unlocked the door, and shoved Elina through.

The room looked like an armory, with gun racks and ammo cabinets lining three of the walls. Whoever these people were, they were well armed. In the center of the room was a wooden chair with some kind of strap system rigged up, obviously to restrain whoever happened to be sitting in the chair.

Elina knew what was coming.

Carson pushed her toward the chair as his partner, the big man, took her by her bound wrists and spun her around. He was enormous — at least six foot nine, Elina guessed — with a shaved head and a thick black goatee on his jaw. She remembered him from the road. He'd been one of the guys in the pickup truck. She struggled against his force, but the man was just too overpowering. He sat her down like a rag doll and draped her arms over the backrest while Carson proceeded to strap her feet and legs to the chair's restraints. Lastly they pulled her jacket down over her shoulders and Carson tore open her shirt halfway to her waist.

At that point two other men entered the room. Elina recognized the tall man with reddish hair and a beefy mustache as the driver of the pickup truck, the guy who'd nearly shot her with her own gun. The second man she hadn't seen before. He was small and clean-shaven with short brown hair parted to the side, and he carried a leather satchel. These two didn't say anything but stood off along the perimeter of the room with the big man while Carson paced in front of Elina. He carried something that looked like a nightstick but which Elina recognized immediately as a stun baton.

"So you're a police officer, eh?"

Elina blinked, taken aback by the question. "Um, yeah . . . I thought we had estab—"

She felt a sharp jolt and sting on her cheek as Carson backhanded her again. Elina swooned for a moment, gathering her wits. She could feel her lip swelling and her cheek throbbing.

"What?" she said. "I'm answering your question!"

Carson chortled. "I know. That was for spying on Mr. Vale." He held up the baton. "*This* is for shooting me."

He plunged the stun stick against her

chest, and Elina felt every muscle in her body seize as though a thousand needles had been jabbed into her at once. Her spine arched, and the room dissolved into darkness.

Elina heard herself groaning as she regained consciousness. Shadows swirled around her, and a sharp odor stung in her nostrils like razors. She opened her eyes to see the small man bending over her, smelling salts in his hand. He lifted her eyelids and checked her eyes with a penlight.

"She's awake," he said to Carson. Then he took Elina by the chin and whispered, "Just tell him what he wants to know."

Carson swatted him out of the way. "Okay, *chica,* let's see how smart you are. You said you followed the van. That's how you found us. Is that right? You followed it here?"

Through her pain, Elina felt a flicker of hope. She had them nervous. For all of Vale's arrogance, he *was* worried about being discovered. And he'd sent Carson down to pry information from her. That meant she had some leverage. She had something they wanted.

But she would need to proceed with caution. As soon as they got what they wanted, she would no longer be of use to them. "Yes. Actually it wasn't that hard."

"Why did you follow us?"

"Us?" Elina grinned. She could taste blood in her mouth. "So you were the one driving the van?"

Carson leaned close. "Why were you following us?"

"I told you already. I was looking for my cousin. I wanted to find out what happened to him."

"Who else knows you're here?"

"Why?" Elina almost smiled. "Does that worry you? Are you afraid other people will come looking for me? Well, you better be."

The next thing she knew, she was waking up from a second jolt. The little guy — Elina thought he must be the medic or doctor — was leaning over her again with the smelling salts.

"Stop antagonizing him," he whispered.

Carson loomed in the background, grinning. "No, we're not worried, *chica.* We'll just get a new van. And now, thanks to you, we'll make good and sure it can't be traced back to us."

Elina could barely keep her head upright. Her limbs throbbed from the jolts, but she forced a bloody smile. "It doesn't matter. They already know about the van, and they know about Vale Corp. So it's just a matter of time before they come looking."

Of course, she had not told anyone about the information she'd gathered on the vehicle. She wasn't officially part of the police department at the time and therefore not supposed to be accessing the database. Furthermore, since she didn't want Javier to get in trouble with the INS, she had truly pursued her investigation as a lone wolf. But Vale didn't know that, so at least she had some leverage, even if it was a bluff.

"Who did you tell?"

"You'll find out when they show up . . . in force."

Carson backhanded her across the other cheek. "They won't find anything. No one ever does."

The room spun and Elina's jaw throbbed. She blinked back her sweat and tears, clenching her teeth against the pain.

"That's . . . what Vale said." She struggled to get her words out. "But still, here you are . . . asking me about it. So maybe he's not as unconcerned as he pretended to be."

"He's not going to let you go. You know that, don't you?"

Elina shrugged as best she could. "Then there's not much incentive to tell you anything more . . . is there?"

Carson's grin faded, and he held the stun

stick in front of Elina's face. And that was the last thing she remembered seeing.

Chapter 20

Elina awoke in the dark, back in what she assumed was her prison cell. Her jaw and muscles ached from the beating she'd taken and from lying on the cold rock floor. She had no idea how long she had been unconscious.

She explored her cell again and found no way of escape. There was a large clay pot in the corner that reeked of human waste but otherwise nothing else inside the cell. No other bit of furnishing. Like in some squalid medieval dungeon, she half expected there to be a rotting corpse chained to the wall.

Elina found she was losing all track of time. She spent her waking hours talking either to Javier and Miguel or to God. And when she slept, it was in fitful spurts on the cold, damp ground. She struggled to keep her thoughts focused on finding a way out. She had to keep her terror at bay. Terror would lead to despair, which would cause her to give up hope.

At one point she was huddled on the floor praying for her life when she heard a voice outside her door.

"What're you doing?"

Elina looked up, startled. "Praying."

She peered through the window in her door and could see the vague features of the man with the smelling salts.

"Praying? Why?"

"Because it's all I can do at this point. And I happen to think God is listening."

"Well, it won't do any good, you know," he said. His voice held little emotion, as if he had shut himself off to it. "God abandoned this place a long time ago."

"Not *my* God. He doesn't just abandon people."

"You think so? You think He can save you? Because I've never seen Him save *anyone* from here."

"I wouldn't underestimate Him if I were you." Elina moved closer to the door. "What do you want?"

He held up a ladle to the window. "I brought you breakfast."

"Is it morning already?"

He tapped the door. "You want it or not?"

"Yes."

Elina heard something rattle and creak,

and a small slat at the bottom of the door snapped open. A bowl slid through the opening, and the slat snapped shut again. Elina picked up the bowl and sniffed it. It was half-filled with what smelled like oatmeal. He'd given her no utensil and nothing to drink.

She sat down and ate the meal, scooping it into her mouth with her fingers. She was desperately hungry, and the bland, lumpy oatmeal paste did little to satisfy her appetite. She could see the guy still looking in through the bars in her door, so she decided to venture a question.

"Who are you?"

After a moment he replied, "No one. Nobody important."

"You were part of the inquisition, right?"

"I . . . I was there to make sure you could still answer him."

"So you're a medic . . . or a doctor or something?"

Another pause. "I'm a doctor."

"A doctor." Elina stood and moved to the door. "Then can you . . . can you at least tell me what's going on here?"

"Sorry, I can't give you any information."

"Why not? Just tell me why you're keeping us prisoners here."

"No."

"At least tell me your name." Elina moved to the window and peered through.

He hesitated, shifting his weight and avoiding eye contact.

Elina persisted gently. "Mr. Vale didn't say you couldn't tell me your name, did he?"

"Dwight," he said finally.

"Dwight." Elina tried to offer a pleasant smile. "I like that. Not many parents name their kids Dwight anymore."

Dwight shrugged, still avoiding her eyes. "I guess."

Elina probed further. "What do you do here? I mean besides overseeing the torture."

"I do whatever he needs me to do."

"So Mr. Vale . . . he's the big boss man in town. Does everyone in Beckon do what he tells them to do?"

Dwight shook his head. "It's not what you think. You don't know what it's like here. We have to do what he tells us or . . . or we'll die."

"Really," Elina said. "He has that much power? He's keeping you here against your will?"

"Well . . . not exactly."

"So then you could leave if you wanted to?"

"Not exactly."

Elina sighed. "Dwight, you're not making any sense."

"It's complicated."

Just then Miguel's voice came from across the passage. *"Son todos caníbales."*

"Vamos, cómeme!" another voice yelled defiantly from down the corridor.

Dwight's face puckered in a quizzical frown. "*Cannibals?* Is that what you think we are?"

"That's what they all think," Elina said. "Can you blame them? You kidnapped them. You brought them to your little town here and locked them up in your dungeon. You tell me what happens to them."

Dwight shrugged. "Well, they get eaten, of course."

"That's what they just —"

"But not by *us*."

Elina backed away from the door. "What are you talking about?"

Dwight sighed. "Look, I wish I could help you. I really do. If it were up to me . . . you don't belong here. You don't deserve this."

"What do you mean, 'they get eaten'? What's going on here?"

Dwight stared at the ground for a moment. He looked over his shoulder and then leaned close. "There's something in the caves. Something . . . terrible."

"What are you talking about?" Elina hadn't been prepared for this. Whatever was going on in this place, she was more concerned now that this Dwight fellow was mentally unstable.

"Believe me, the less you know, the better."

"Please, just let us out."

"I can't." Dwight shook his head. "He'll kill me."

"*Please,* Dwight. Please help us. You can't just let us die down here."

"I told you, I *can't* help you. . . . I've said too much already."

Elina was losing her patience. "You're a doctor! How can you be involved in this? If you don't help us, then you're a murderer, too — you know that, don't you?"

"No," Dwight said. "I . . . I haven't killed anyone."

"Yes, you have. You know what's going on here — you're a part of it. And you could let us go, but you're choosing not to. You're just as guilty as Vale in all of this. Whatever's going on here, *you're* responsible for it."

"No!" Dwight backed away from the door. "You don't know me. You don't know anything about me."

Elina stepped forward. "I think I do. You might've been a good person once. Before you came here."

"Stop it." Dwight moved farther away.

"So what happened to you? What turned you into a murderer?"

"I told you, I'm *not* a murderer."

"It's your choice, Dwight. You don't have to do this."

"No, it's not. I can't help you. . . ."

Elina moved closer still, feeling a certain boldness despite her circumstances. "Do you really think no one will ever find out about this place? You think you'll get away with this forever?"

Dwight stammered, "I . . . I have to leave." He turned and disappeared up the tunnel.

"Dwight!" Elina called after him. "You *choose* what you are!"

Her voice echoed into the darkness, but Dwight didn't return. The other captives were shouting after him as well. Some cursing. Others wailing.

Elina slumped against her door, fighting back tears. Praying desperately. A feeling of dread wrapped around her like the darkness of the prison. She felt utterly alone. Buried so deep that no one would ever find her. All she had left inside her was a faint sliver of hope, like a thread suspending her over a vast abyss.

She'd prayed for several minutes when she

heard voices in the corridor. One of the prisoners was pleading for help. She lifted her head. Had the doctor returned?

She heard a male voice call out in English, "Where are you?"

Next she heard a woman's voice. "Here, George. Help me open it."

Elina stood and pressed her face against the bars of her door. She could hear someone rattling one of the door handles.

"They're all locked," the man said. "We have to try to find the key."

They sounded close by.

"We'll get you out. . . . Don't be afraid," came the woman again. "We'll find the key."

Elina called, "Who are you? What are you doing here?"

She could see the beam of a flashlight swinging back and forth in the corridor.

Elina reached her hand through the window. "Who are you?"

She heard footsteps as someone approached her cell. It was the woman. She stopped right outside the door and clutched Elina's fingers.

"Oh my . . . don't worry. We're going to get help."

"How did you get down here?" Elina said.

The man arrived, carrying the flashlight. "We were snooping around the lodge and found this tunnel in the basement. It's hidden. We're . . . we're just guests there."

He sounded kind . . . and Elina knew it could be a trap, but she could barely keep her hopes in check. She had to try, anyway.

"Guests? You know Thomas Vale?"

"Yes, he invited us here," the woman said.

"Then listen to me. You're in danger too. You need to get out and call the FBI. You can't trust him. You can't trust any of them. None of the people in this town."

"Who are you? Why did they lock you up down here?"

"I'm a police officer — from Los Angeles. My name is Elina Gutierrez. I was investigating a kidnapping. I followed the van here and they captured me." Elina spoke quickly. "You need to contact the FBI. They're engaged in some kind of human trafficking here. There's something horrible going on."

The man with the flashlight was searching the corridor. "We can't get these doors open. We have to go back and find the keys."

"Please help us," Elina pleaded. "You have to get help right away. Don't trust them. Don't trust any of them."

The woman squeezed Elina's fingers. "We'll get you out of here. Don't worry. We'll get you out."

Elina couldn't control her emotions any

longer, and tears flooded her eyes. "I was praying that someone would find us. I was praying He would send someone to save us."

The woman leaned in and said softly, "He heard you." She was crying too. "God heard you."

"We need to go — now." The man's voice sounded urgent.

"Listen to me," Elina said. "Be careful. There's something in the caves. They said there's something terrible down there."

"Don't worry," the man said as they started back up the tunnel. "We'll contact the FBI as soon as we can."

And just like that, they were gone.

■ ■ ■ ■

Part III
George

■ ■ ■ ■

One has to pay dearly for immortality;
one has to die several times while one is still alive.

FRIEDRICH NIETZSCHE,
ECCE HOMO

CHAPTER 21

Western Wyoming
Five Days Earlier

The old wooden sign read, *Welcome to Beckon. You're not here by chance.*

At the time George Wilcox didn't pay much attention to the sign, as he was more occupied by the rustic clapboard buildings grouped along both sides of the road. A crusty, weathered gas station stood at the edge of town like an old watchman at the city gate. Beside it were a general store and a diner among a handful of shops and houses. The whole town seemed as out of the way as it could possibly be, cradled in the embrace of a steep, wooded bluff. And high above it loomed a gray mountainside that cut a jagged edge against the sky.

George pulled their white Lexus into a parking space in front of the modest one-story office directly across from the diner. The white hand-painted lettering on the front window read, *Dwight Henderson, MD.*

"Well, I guess this is it." George shook his head and sighed. Not even the GPS had been able to locate this town, and had George not gotten directions over the phone — very specific directions — he'd never have found it at all.

Miriam sat quietly beside him, staring out the window. Her gray hair was pulled back neatly into a bun, and her gaunt face held no discernible expression. But she had come through their three-day road trip up from Texas like a trouper. Then again, she had always loved to travel. It seemed to be one of the few things about her that hadn't changed over the last four years.

George would never have driven this far with her, but the opportunity was too compelling to pass up and he was well beyond the point of desperation. Though now that he saw the town for himself, doubt was creeping back into his mind, and he couldn't shake the feeling that he'd made the worst mistake of his life.

George got out, and his aging body popped and creaked as he stretched. Being in the car for the better part of ten hours had stiffened his already-stiff joints. He was still in pretty good shape for seventy-three, but despite all the walking, swimming, and elliptical workouts, seventy-three sure didn't feel like forty. Heck, it didn't even feel like seventy.

He opened the door and helped Miriam out. It would do her good to stretch and walk around a bit.

"What beautiful mountains," she said brightly. "How long are we staying?"

George took her arm, quietly thankful that she was in a good mood. "As long as you want, sweetheart."

"Lovely. Did you see the mountains?"

"Yes, dear. They're beautiful."

George found the doctor's front door unlocked and swung it open. "Hello?"

The place was tidy and quaint, George thought, exactly what most people would've expected a small-town doctor's office to look like. But it wasn't what George had expected.

Although he wasn't sure what he'd expected.

He heard a vehicle approaching and turned as a rust-colored Ford pickup pulled up and two men got out. The driver was a tall and sinewy fellow with reddish-brown hair, wearing a red plaid shirt and blue jeans. The other man was a much shorter, mousier chap, though slightly better dressed in a white shirt and tan trousers.

The taller man smiled and waved as he approached.

"Mr. Wilcox," he said, extending his hand. "I'm Malcolm Browne, Mr. Vale's business manager. It's good to meet you."

"Thank you," George said and motioned to Miriam, who was standing nearby. "This is my wife, Miriam."

"Of course." Browne smiled and kissed her hand gently. "A very nice pleasure to meet you too, Mrs. Wilcox."

Miriam was all grins. "I've seen you on my paper towels."

Browne chuckled and turned back to George. "And I believe you already know Dr. Henderson, correct?" He motioned to his companion.

George blinked and nodded. "Oh . . . yes, we spoke on the phone a few times. Though you're a little younger than I had expected."

Henderson smiled somewhat sheepishly. "Yeah, I get that a lot."

Browne rubbed his palms together. "Well, you must be tired after your trip, and I know Mr. Vale has been very eager to meet you."

"The feeling's mutual," George said. "So where is he?"

Browne pointed up the wooded hillside to a magnificent log home perched near the top of the bluff, partially hidden by pine trees. "Just up the hill there," he said, moving back toward his truck. "You can follow us and we'll head right on up."

George shepherded Miriam into the car, and they followed the truck through town to a narrow gravel road. The road twisted up the steep, wooded incline, and as it did, George's doubts began to grow.

He knew Miriam would have counseled him to keep an open mind. She had always taken such a levelheaded approach to life. So calm and even-keeled. Mostly because of her faith, George thought, though he had only paid lip service to Miriam's religiousness before. Her devotion to her Bible and her steady reliance on prayer. He had always taken those things for granted but had come to miss their influence of late. Now that they were no longer there.

Now that she was being taken from him one memory at a time.

They had met in college fifty years earlier. George had graduated from Baylor as an aeronautical engineer and was immediately recruited by Lockheed. He worked his way quickly through the ranks of their management program while Miriam finished her degree, and they were married shortly thereafter.

George worked at Lockheed for twelve

years before striking out on his own with a pair of fellow engineers. They started Aerodigm Technologies to manufacture select components for jet engines out of a plant in Ohio, but their business quickly expanded to more complex chemical-propulsion and missile-guidance systems. In a few more short years, they had plants across the country, and George had quietly built a solid reputation with Aerodigm's largely military clientele.

Meanwhile George and Miriam purchased a four-hundred-acre ranch outside of Austin. George drove the black Jaguar to work and saved his Porsche for the weekends, while Miriam preferred the less ostentatious silver Mercedes or the Lexus. The only point of stress they might have had was that after forty-eight years of marriage, they remained childless. Miriam had often suggested that they adopt, but George refused, preferring the freedom to travel over the burden of raising children that weren't even his own. They bought a second home in Colorado and a third in Maui. Life had been good to them. Very good. And for the most part, George Wilcox had always slept well at night.

Until four years ago.

George hadn't been prepared for the reality of Alzheimer's. The pain of watching himself become a stranger bit by bit to the woman who had once known him better than anyone else had. He would have rather lost her all at once than endure this slow, steady decay of her mind.

She had been the brightest ray of sunlight in his life for nearly fifty years. But now he hardly knew her. And all he had left of their life together were a few old pictures and videos.

Ahead, the road opened to reveal a better view of the log home. Pea gravel crunched under the tires as they rolled onto the wide, circular driveway. George whistled inwardly as he got out of the car. The place was palatial — at least fifty thousand square feet, he guessed. It looked too big to be a house, more like a small inn or lodge. Thick log beams and tons of smooth river rock provided a rustic yet majestic exterior, and George found himself eager to see the inside.

"Nice place."

"It used to be a rather exclusive little hotel," Browne said, now sounding more like a tour guide. "It was originally built by the Vale family in the early 1900s. They catered mostly to wealthy city folk who wanted to get out into the country and try their hand at hunting elk and such. Mr. Vale has gone to great lengths to restore and upgrade the facilities. I think you'll find them quite comfortable."

Browne led them through the thick, wooden front doors and into an expansive flagstone foyer.

The woman who greeted them there was slender and attractive, with thick locks of burgundy hair pulled back in a tight bun.

"Welcome, Mr. Wilcox," she said. "I'm Amanda McWhorter, Mr. Vale's personal assistant. He's very eager to meet with you." She gestured to the hallway beyond the foyer. "If you'll just have a seat in the great room, I'll let him know you've arrived."

The spacious, vaulted room beyond the staircase contained a set of leather couches facing each other. Behind them, an old barrel with rusted iron bands stood off to one side of the massive stone fireplace, and an antique wagon wheel garnished the other. And above the hearth hung an impressive rack of elk antlers.

Browne motioned to the couches. "Make yourself at home. I'll have your luggage brought up to your suite."

George helped Miriam settle into one of the couches, and Dwight Henderson sat across from her. George walked over to take in the view from the wall of windows. The bank of glass overlooked a steep cliff with a dense forest of pines far below. Amid the trees, he saw sections of the gravel road that ran from the house through the wooded hillside to the town below. Beyond it lay a vast stretch of rolling bluffs that seemed to spread for miles to a row of mountains off in the distance. George breathed a sigh and shook his head. It was quite the vista.

"No matter how many times I look out there," a voice said, "I never get tired of that view."

George turned to see the man he assumed to be Thomas Vale. He looked to be perhaps in his early thirties, with an angular face and long black hair. His body appeared lean and trim beneath his black silk shirt and gray trousers.

"Welcome to Beckon, Mr. Wilcox." Vale shook George's hand. "It's good to finally meet you in person. Can I offer you a drink?"

"No, thank you," George said. He could see Vale's green eyes seemed to hold bright flecks of yellow pigment in the irises. The effect was slightly disconcerting.

Vale glanced at Henderson, who also declined the offer of a drink.

"Well, I guess I'll be drinking alone," Vale

said as he poured himself some brandy from the liquor cabinet across the room. "I imagine it must have been hard to believe when Dr. Henderson first contacted you. After all, how does one begin a conversation of this nature? I'm guessing you were pretty skeptical."

"Still am."

Vale sat down with his drink. "No doubt. But hopefully we can assuage those concerns."

"I certainly hope so." George nodded toward Henderson. "Dr. Henderson was pretty cryptic about the nature of this . . . *treatment.* Which, frankly, didn't help to inspire much confidence."

"And yet here you are," Vale said, spreading his hands. "I'm guessing you've gotten beyond a certain level of desperation. Perhaps to the point where you wondered what you had to lose."

George sat down beside Miriam and ran his fingers across her shoulders. She'd been ignoring their conversation. Lately it seemed like she'd been ignoring him more and more, slowly drifting like a boat that had lost its moorings, floating away from the dock down a dark river.

"But you said this treatment has never been tried on someone with Alzheimer's before. How do you know it'll actually help her?"

"The human body is its own best medicine," Henderson interjected. "Essentially all this treatment does is help the body heal itself."

"I'm afraid the nature of it forces us to maintain a certain level of secrecy." Vale let his gaze drift up to the ceiling and offered an odd sort of half smile. "You see, it's not exactly a *conventional* medical treatment."

"What do you mean?"

Henderson leaned forward. "It's a remedy that a local Indian tribe has been practicing for . . . well, probably for hundreds of years."

George stared at him, his mouth hanging open. "You're joking, right?"

"Now, Mr. Wilcox, we've actually —"

"You dragged me all the way up from Texas for some crazy Indian remedy? Are you *kidding* me?"

Henderson looked flustered. "As — as you recall, I explained that you would need to keep an open mind. I told you —"

"You didn't say anything about this being some hokey, superstitious nonsense. I never would have come."

"Which is precisely why we didn't tell you," Vale said in a calm tone.

"Mr. Wilcox," Henderson said, "I've

personally witnessed this treatment's effectiveness. Look, I don't believe in the supernatural either, but this is an organic compound that produces a real physiological effect. Now . . . of course the local . . . medicine woman insists on a certain ceremonial procedure, but the cure itself — I assure you — is an actual, *physical* compound."

"What kind of compound?"

"It's called perilium," Vale said.

"Yes, but what *is* it?" George said again. "You say it's some kind of organic compound, but that doesn't really tell me much."

"For the moment all we can tell you is what I explained over the phone," Henderson said. "Perilium enhances the body's natural immune system. And the body, in turn, responds to whatever disease state happens to be present. The end result is the same regardless of whether the patient suffers from cancer, MS, or indigestion. Or Alzheimer's. Perilium simply helps the body heal itself."

George glanced at Miriam, wondering what he'd gotten her into. Though it wasn't as if they had many other options. If this perilium didn't work, she would spend the next three or four years suffering with her

Alzheimer's and would eventually die. Or perhaps she'd have some sort of allergic reaction to the drug and die right away. Either way, she was no better off if he refused.

He took a breath and leaned back. "You're asking for a pretty big leap of faith. And a lot of money."

"And in exchange, you get your wife back." Vale's pleasant demeanor had evaporated a bit. "Exactly how much is that worth to you, Mr. Wilcox? How much would you pay to cure your wife's Alzheimer's? To *not* spend the next years watching her die a protracted and unpleasant death?"

George fell silent, tapping his fingers on the arm of the couch. "And if it doesn't work?"

Vale shrugged. "Then you're under no other obligation. The only condition is that you abide by the nondisclosure agreement you signed. But you and your wife will be none the worse for wear."

George shook his head. "So why do I feel like I'm being hustled?"

"Not at all," Vale said. "Say the word and I'll call the whole thing off. You can keep your money and go home." He downed the last of his drink. "The only thing you'd lose would be your wife."

George stared at the man. Vale sat on the

leather couch entirely nonchalant.

Miriam seemed equally placid and leaned into George. "I like this house," she whispered.

George looked into her eyes and could see a vague sense of recognition there, that he was still familiar enough for her to feel comfortable being with him. But he wondered how long that would last. He wondered what it would be worth for the chance to have her back. He was ready to retire and enjoy his golden years. He pictured himself living in Maui and spending his afternoons out on the ocean fishing.

But he had always pictured Miriam on the boat with him.

George took a breath. "So what exactly does this . . . *treatment* . . . entail?"

CHAPTER 22

It was just after ten o'clock when George brought Miriam up to their suite on the second level of Thomas Vale's mansion. Vale and Henderson had spent the evening making preparations for the *ceremony,* as they put it. But the whole thing was making George feel more and more uncomfortable.

Miriam hesitated in the doorway of the bedroom, her eyes darting about warily. "Where are we?"

"It's okay, sweetheart," George said, drawing her gently into the room. "This is where we're going to sleep tonight."

"Where's my bed?" Miriam said. "I want to go home now."

George had worried that all the travel would be too much for her. He tried to smile reassuringly. "But we're on vacation, remember? Up in the mountains. I made a special bed for you. Just for you."

That seemed to work as Miriam peeked

over his shoulder at the beautiful, king-size, log-post bed on a low dais. Her expression softened, and just then Henderson arrived with a small cup of hot tea. Miriam normally had a cup at bedtime back in Texas. It was the only way George could get her to take her medications.

George took the cup and cast a wary glance at the doctor.

Henderson offered what George assumed was intended to be his own reassuring smile. "Just a mild sedative. Like I said, there's nothing dangerous at all about the ritual. My only concern is that the woman wears ceremonial native garb. And we want to avoid causing Miriam any undue alarm."

Henderson had explained earlier that since the ceremony had never been performed on anyone who was "cognitively compromised," he wanted to make sure Miriam wouldn't react violently or do anything that might disrupt the ritual. It seemed that this medicine woman was hypersensitive to protocol during the rite.

But despite all of Henderson's assurances, George was still filled with misgivings and doubt. He insisted that he remain at Miriam's bedside during the entire ceremony, and Vale had agreed to allow him to stay in the room only as long as he kept out of the way.

George helped Miriam as she drank the tea and then got her ready for bed. He had brought along her favorite nightgown. Then he kissed her on the forehead and wished her a good night, just as he did every night.

Vale arrived as Miriam was settling in. He pulled George aside and spoke in urgent but hushed tones. "Nun'dahbi is on her way up. It's extremely important that you remember not to approach her or speak to her at all. And avoid any eye contact."

"Nun'dahbi?" George said, noting how strange Vale was acting. He seemed downright nervous.

"It's her title," Vale explained as he lit several candles situated around the room. "She's the spiritual head of her tribe. And this ritual is actually a process whereby they welcome a new member into their community. It's an extreme honor and should not be taken lightly."

"What tribe is this?"

"They call themselves the N'watu. They're one of the oldest tribes in North America, tracing their roots back more than two thousand years."

Henderson interrupted them and pointed to the bed. "It looks like she's asleep."

George could see the sedative had indeed taken effect and Miriam appeared to be resting comfortably. Henderson turned off the lights and stood out of the way in the sitting room. Meanwhile Vale pulled George off to the side and took up a position right beside him — George assumed it was so that Vale could prevent him from doing anything foolish during the ceremony. He stole a glance and saw a single bead of perspiration trickle down Vale's jaw.

After a moment George leaned over. "What now?"

Vale hushed him with a curt whisper. "She's here."

Just then, George heard a soft rattling sound outside the suite. The door opened slowly to reveal a shadow in the entrance. It was a figure of slight build. George assumed it to be a woman. Her face was hidden behind a black veil of some sort. In fact, she was dressed completely in layers of black garments and adorned with bracelets, beads, and necklaces of various sorts. She stood for a moment in the doorway and then seemed to glide into the room. George noticed that Vale immediately bowed his head and nudged George to follow suit.

So George lowered his head as well but kept his eyes on the shadowy figure as she approached the bed. She seemed to hiss as she walked. Though not really a hiss — more like a soft rattling sound, not unlike the sound a rattlesnake might make. In fact, George's first thought was that perhaps she'd brought a snake with her. But then he saw the source of the sound: a small gourd-like object atop the long wooden staff that the woman rattled gently. A pair of feathers and a string of claws were tied around the gourd.

She stood over the bed where Miriam lay sleeping and passed the staff over her from head to toe, rattling it softly. Back and forth across the bed, hovering just inches above Miriam's body.

Then the woman reached out a pale, thin hand and passed it over Miriam as well, making a soft humming sound that quickly grew into a low, monotone incantation, though George could not make out any words.

The woman's voice began to rise and fall, muttering and mumbling. Her tone held a gentle menace like the soft growl of a cat. It seemed at once placid and vicious. This went on for several minutes with the incantation rising and falling in both pitch and volume.

Then she stopped suddenly and turned in

George's direction. George lowered his gaze slightly but still tried to glimpse what would happen next. The medicine woman approached him, and George could feel Thomas Vale tense up.

She muttered a similar incantation to George. He raised his head instinctively and caught the briefest glimpse of vague white features behind her veil. And eyes that seemed to glow like two sparks.

Nun'dahbi hissed and snapped her staff up between them. George quickly lowered his gaze, and a moment later she continued her incantation. Her hand swept across George's face, inches away, as if trying to feel the heat radiating from his body. He could see her hand more clearly now. Her skin appeared completely void of all pigment, and long black nails had been filed into points so that they looked like claws. Or talons.

Her chanting lasted nearly a full minute, and after she finished, she took his hand in hers. George almost recoiled at her cold, bony touch as she pressed something into his palm and closed his fingers over it. Then she turned in a single fluid movement and glided out the door.

After she had gone, Vale seemed to breathe a relieved sigh, and George opened his hand to see a small glass vial with a black cap. Inside was a milky, yellowish liquid.

Chapter 23

George stared into his wife's eyes. And Miriam was looking back at him. She had finally awakened after nearly thirty-six solid hours of sleep, looking a bit groggy. But . . . she was *there. All* there, it seemed. George could see the recognition in her eyes. Her complexion had regained a rosy hue, and her eyes had brightened. In fact, she looked better than she had in years.

"How are you feeling?" George said.

Miriam stroked his cheek. "I feel fine. *You* look tired, though."

"I didn't get much sleep the last couple nights. Too busy pacing."

After the ceremony, Henderson had administered the mysterious remedy through a hypodermic. He told George that while perilium was typically ingested, due to Miriam's compromised mental state, it was wiser not to risk upsetting her by forcing her to drink the bitter substance. Besides,

Henderson said, injecting it directly into her bloodstream would provide a purer dosage than allowing the body to absorb the substance through its digestive system.

Miriam frowned. "What time is it?"

"Nine thirty. Tuesday morning."

"Tuesday . . . Where are we?"

"In Wyoming. Do you remember coming to Wyoming?"

"Wyoming?" Miriam sat up, and her gaze traced a path around the bedroom. George could see her piecing the memories together, working things out in her mind. "Did . . . did we drive here?"

George laughed. "Yes, we did. I found someone who was able to help you with your condition. Well . . . actually, *he* found *us.* They've got some kind of drug here. The local Indians originally discovered it." George struggled for the words to explain it to her. "I think it's making you better."

Miriam turned back to George and clutched his arm. "I had dreams about you. I feel like I haven't seen you in years. Only for a few seconds here and there. It was like I would catch a glimpse of you passing me on the street, and I would try to stay with you — hold on to you — but then . . . something kept dragging me away. And each time I felt like I was never going to see you again."

Her eyes moistened, and George pulled her close. "I missed you too, sweetheart," he said, fighting back his own tears. "You have no idea how much I've missed you."

George soaked in the warmth of his wife's embrace, feeling her arms around him and the flesh of her cheek against his, afraid that at any moment she might slip away from him. That she would suddenly pull away and become a stranger again. He breathed in her scent, felt her heart beating against his chest, and he wanted to freeze the moment to keep her here with him forever. Seeing her like this made the thought of losing her again that much more intense. She had been away so long.

The longer George held on to Miriam, the greater his resolve grew. He would do anything to keep from losing her again.

Anything.

George heard a knock at the door and found Thomas Vale in the hallway.

"Mind if I stop in?" he said. "Dwight said she seemed to be responding favorably. I wanted to see for myself."

George led him into the bedroom.

Miriam peered at Vale for a moment. "I remember you, I think. Have we met?"

Vale smiled. "In a manner of speaking, yes. How are you feeling?"

Miriam shrugged. "Actually, I feel great."

"Wonderful."

Henderson returned with a clipboard and took Miriam's vitals. Vale motioned for George to come out into the hallway.

"At this point, you're probably the best person to gauge her progress," Vale said in a hushed tone. "I think Dwight will be wanting to get your assessment of her recovery. Her memories and personality."

"She seems almost completely recovered." George was shaking his head. "Like her old self. I can't believe it. I've never seen anything like this before. It's incredible."

Vale nodded. "The perilium will continue to take effect throughout the day. We'll keep her under close observation for another twenty-four hours or so. But Dwight seems to think she'll be completely restored within a day or two."

George felt giddy. "You've given me my wife back. I'd forgotten how much I missed her."

"I know you're going to want to stay with her all day, but she'll need a few more hours of rest. In the meantime, there's something else we need to discuss."

Vale led him downstairs and along the

hallway to his office. A row of windows lined one of the walls behind an enormous desk. Outside, the morning sun lit up the countryside. To the right of the desk was a bookcase stacked with thick, weathered tomes and newer books on a variety of topics. Thomas Vale appeared to be an avid reader. George wasn't surprised.

Vale took a seat behind the desk and motioned for George to sit in one of the chairs opposite him. George assumed they were here to discuss the details of payment for his wife's cure. He was filled with a new hope at seeing Miriam's progress. The perilium certainly seemed to have lived up to its miraculous billing, though George wasn't ready to sign anything just yet. He needed to verify that the effects were permanent.

Vale rubbed his chin as if trying to choose his words with care. "I think we can both agree that your wife's condition this morning is better than it's been in several months, wouldn't you say?"

George nodded. "She seemed perfectly healthy to me."

"She's responding very well. However, you recall Dr. Henderson's initial discussions with you over the phone. This is not a one-time treatment."

George did recall that Henderson had

indicated the treatment would require an ongoing regimen. "He mentioned that Miriam would need to remain in Beckon for a while."

"Yes, she'll need to remain here."

George frowned. "For how long?"

Vale gazed at George for a moment, tapping his fingertips lightly together. "Indefinitely, I'm afraid."

George blinked and leaned forward. "*Indefinitely?* You mean she can't go home again?"

"Understand, we can't just call this in to your local pharmacy," Vale said. "The only person who knows exactly how perilium is made is Nun'dahbi. It can't be synthesized, and there are limits to how much she can produce and how quickly she can produce it."

"That's why you targeted me," George grunted. "You need funding to keep making more of this stuff."

"Everything has a cost. Perilium is an extremely difficult formula to produce. The organic components are indigenous to the caves here and aren't easily harvested. It's just not something we can replicate on a large scale."

"Why didn't you tell me this before?"

"Because you might not have agreed to

the procedure," Vale said.

"No, I wouldn't have agreed." George rubbed his forehead. He knew this was too good to be true. "So you *lied* to get me here."

"We didn't lie to you, George," Vale said. "We simply didn't tell you everything."

George's shock was quickly turning to anger and he stood, shaking his head. "Well, I'm not going to let you get away with this. This . . . this is —"

"What?" Vale's countenance darkened, and he stood to face George. His yellow-green eyes turned fierce. "This is *what,* George? Your wife was dying a slow and protracted death. And now we've given her back to you. We've given you the chance at a normal life together. You tell me, where is the evil in that?"

"I don't believe this." George felt his anger wavering, and he sat down again. Vale was right — what other choice did he have? "What happens if she stops taking it?"

Vale's gaze beat a trail across the room, and for the first time, George saw hesitation on his face. "The effects would . . . diminish."

"Diminish? Meaning what? Her dementia will return?"

Vale sat down. "As we explained, perilium

affects the body's immune system. But its influence is evident only as long as it remains active in her system."

George tried to process this new information, fluctuating between anger and despair. But he knew he had few options. "So how long does the effect last? How long before she'll need another dose?"

"Two or three days, perhaps." Vale shrugged. "It depends. Everyone responds differently. Dr. Henderson will continue to monitor her progress and administer another dose when her symptoms reappear."

"So . . . then what? You expect us to just move here? To Beckon?"

"You must understand that we choose our candidates with a great deal of care."

"Candidates?"

"Yes, George." Vale's eyes grew a little colder. "Your wife's condition along with your assets and skills made you an ideal candidate to join our community."

George felt himself wince. "What're you talking about?"

"I understand that over the years you've secured numerous government contracts for your company. I'm guessing you've developed your share of connections within the Beltway during that time."

George's frown grew deeper. "A few."

"I've found that one can never have too many friends in Washington. My point is that I'd like to take advantage of your political talents. You see, I occasionally find the need to deflect certain intrusive elements of the state and federal bureaucracies. And having someone here who knows which strings to pull in Washington can be invaluable in this regard."

George shook his head, still trying to get his mind around this new development. "I'm seventy-three years old. I'm not ready to start a new career anymore."

Vale's eyes seemed to sparkle at that comment. "You know, I've found that nothing keeps a man's zest for life going like his career. I've always thought that something terrible happens when a man retires. A vital part of him dies. I think a man *needs* his work in order to feel like a man. He needs something to accomplish with his life. Something he can sink his teeth into and be proud of. Something he has a passion for."

"I have a passion for warmer climates and deep-sea fishing."

"You're not a quitter, George." Vale's words became crisp. "I know you better than you think. You're driven, competitive, and demanding — not unlike myself. And you created a nice little empire during your life. However, as you and your wife are without any heirs, you must be wondering what will happen to everything you've built when you're gone. I imagine that thought must gnaw away at a man like you." He leaned forward. "I'm giving you the chance to fold your life's work — and *yourself* — into something greater. To become a part of something bigger than yourself."

The words struck a chord with George. His business *had* been his life's passion for the better part of forty years. But after Miriam's diagnosis, he had begun to gain a new perspective on the company he had created. Life was short, after all. Shorter than he had expected. One minute he was a young entrepreneur with a beautiful wife, a big house, and the world at his doorstep, and the next thing he knew, he was on the brink of retirement and his wife was slowly dying from Alzheimer's.

George had struggled with Miriam's illness from the start, hating it and raging against it like an old sea captain fighting through a squall. But he knew this storm offered no peace for him in the end. In the end, Miriam would be gone. And the worst part was that he knew those final years would be especially painful. He had denied it at first, but he knew at some point he would actually look *forward* to Miriam's death, when she would have relief. And that thought left a bitter taste in his mouth.

The truth was, he felt beaten and at the end of his rope. He had weathered her slow demise for the last four years, and now he was growing weary, like an aging boxer being pounded into submission by a younger, stronger contender. And his heart had begun to ache with brief, forbidden thoughts, fleeting wishes that perhaps something tragic might happen and she would die quickly, sparing him the torment of having to watch her die slowly. For even though Miriam was still with him in body, her mind had left him months ago.

And part of him just wanted it to all be over with.

"I understand what you're saying," George said and rubbed his eyes. "I really do. But unfortunately there comes a time in a man's life when he has to accept the inevitable. He has to learn when it's time to step aside gracefully and let the next generation have its day in the sun."

"Gracefully?" Vale scowled. "Grace has nothing to do with this. A man fights and claws for what he can get in life and then . . . what? He has to give it all up? Who made those rules?"

"It's just a fact of life," George said. "You're still young, so I don't expect you to understand. You've got plenty of years ahead of you. But I think when you get to be my age, you'll see there comes a time when you get tired of the fight. And stepping aside doesn't seem like such a bad thing anymore."

"Not likely," Vale laughed. "But the fact is, your services are nonnegotiable. I'm afraid that's just part of the deal."

"So none of this was about my wife at all? You just wanted to get my money and turn me into some kind of . . . indentured servant?"

Vale shook his head. "I think you're underestimating the value of my proposition. There are considerable fringe benefits you might find appealing. You and your wife could have your own private suite or your own home if you like. I've also managed to put together a rather extensive library and media center. Plus, you'll still have the freedom to travel. Albeit on a limited basis."

George continued to pace. Now Vale was sounding like a cheap time-share salesman. A huckster. The whole scenario was too bizarre to even be believable.

But he seemed to have them over a barrel. George had no idea what this perilium was or where to get more. And now Vale expected him to move here? To sell all of his other properties and move to this isolated town in the Wyoming mountains? George turned to the windows and stared out at the countryside. Would he be willing to do that, even for Miriam?

He couldn't help feeling like he'd been lured to this town for some ulterior reason. He felt trapped, and now each turn he took was only getting him further entangled in their web.

Chapter 24

Shortly after noon, George returned to the suite to see how Miriam was progressing. His mind was still buzzing with the events of the last few days but more specifically with the news he'd just been given by Thomas Vale.

In less than forty-eight hours, his wife's health seemed to have been completely restored, but just when he thought their lives would return to normal, Vale's additional news had turned everything upside down again. Now George and Miriam would need to make plans to move to Wyoming for good. That meant selling their homes along with most of their possessions to prepare for an entirely new life here in the mountains. Vale's home was magnificent to be sure, but it was still hard for George to get his head wrapped around the idea. More than that, he wondered, how would Miriam respond?

He opened the door to find her in the bathroom, dressed and running a brush through her hair while singing softly to herself. It had been years since he'd heard her sing. She saw him in the bedroom and came out, smiling.

"Hi, sweetheart." She wrapped her arms around his neck and gave him a long, passionate kiss.

At first, George tensed. It had been so long since she had kissed him at all, let alone kissed him like *that.* But then he relaxed and pulled her tight to himself, savoring the soft, moist touch of her lips, the scent of her hair, and the gentle press of her slender body against his. It cast his mind back to their honeymoon in Bermuda, standing on a moonlit beach with the waves sweeping up the sand to their bare feet. And he suddenly lost himself in her kiss, forgetting everything else.

Miriam finished the kiss with a soft nibble at his lower lip and pulled her head back, grinning. "Don't ever leave me again."

George cleared his throat, regaining his composure and running a hand through his thinning gray hair. "No worries there, my dear."

Miriam giggled and turned back to the mirror to finish brushing her hair. She looked positively radiant to George, more alive and effervescent than she had in years. And there was something else about her that looked different as well, something he couldn't quite place.

She made eye contact with him in the mirror. "Dr. Henderson said I should get some exercise. He said there are trails around the estate. Let's go for a nice long walk."

"That sounds like fun," George said. "Actually, it'll give us a chance to talk. We need to disc—"

Miriam turned and held a finger to his lips. "But first, I'm starving. Do they have room service here? Or do I need to fix something myself? Where do we go for something to eat?"

"The kitchen's downstairs."

Miriam grabbed his hand and tugged him out into the hallway. "Lead the way."

They made their way downstairs, past the main dining hall, and through the swinging double doors into the kitchen. The room was enormous, clearly built to accommodate numerous guests back when the place was a hotel. Miriam quickly set about foraging through the cupboards while George pulled open a metal door to what appeared to be a walk-in cooler. Three of the walls were stocked with shelving units containing stacks of meat. The shelves themselves were labeled: *Fillets, Ground Chuck, Tenderloins, Pork, Veal, Chicken, Fish.*

George stepped into the kitchen. "It looks like they've got a whole butcher shop in there. How many people are *in* this town?"

But Miriam had found bread and cold cuts in the refrigerator and had already set out making a sizable sandwich, slapping layers of beef, turkey, and ham onto a slice of bread.

George laughed. "Whoa, sweetheart. You know I'm supposed to be watching my cholesterol. Just a little turkey is fine."

Miriam looked up with a bit of embarrassment in her expression. "Oh . . . I'm sorry, dear. I was actually . . . making this for me."

George stared at her as she licked her fingers and pressed a second slice of bread onto the top. "You really *are* hungry," he said.

Miriam's eyes gleamed, and she curled up a corner of her mouth in a sensual grin. *"Famished."*

She bit into the mammoth sandwich with great relish. No formalities, no condiments, and no plate. Not even a napkin. She closed her eyes and chewed luxuriously.

She polished off the sandwich in minutes,

chasing it with a tall glass of milk. Then she began looking around the kitchen again. George was watching her with alternating fascination and concern when he heard a voice behind him.

"Oh, good, I see you found something to eat." Dr. Henderson stood in the doorway.

"Sorry," George said. "They told us to help ourselves to food. And, well . . . Miriam said she was hungry."

"No worries," Henderson said. "I was going to suggest it to you anyway. She hasn't eaten anything substantial for nearly two days."

Miriam opened the refrigerator again. "Yeah, and I'm still hungry."

George frowned at her. "You wolfed that sandwich down in two minutes; give it a few seconds to reach your stomach."

Henderson chuckled. "Actually, that's a normal response to the perilium."

"What, increased appetite?"

"It's a good sign. One of the things perilium does is increase the body's metabolic rate to aid in healing. So as the body repairs itself, it's going to naturally require a higher level of nourishment. Mostly protein."

George scratched his head. "That explains the Dagwood sandwich."

Henderson laughed again. "Yeah, you'll

notice an increased craving for meat especially. That's very normal."

Miriam wasn't paying much attention to their conversation and had set about making a second sandwich, nearly as big as the first.

George stared as she sank her teeth into the beef-laden sandwich. "You know, she used to hate red meat."

Miriam paused midchew and looked up. "What's that?"

"Nothing."

Henderson smiled and turned to leave. "I'll leave you two alone. Bon appétit."

He slipped out of the kitchen as George watched Miriam devour the rest of her second sandwich. Afterward she leaned back, belched politely, and dabbed her lips with a napkin.

"Whew, that hit the spot."

George could hardly believe this was the same woman he had married. He wondered if the perilium was having some mood-altering effects as well.

He cleared his throat. "Well, I'm guessing you could use a walk right about now."

Miriam grinned. "Let's go."

A set of glass doors off the main dining hall opened onto a wide cobblestone patio that looked out over the cliff and the town below. A narrow walkway led around to the back of the mansion and skirted a sharp ridge before coming to a set of stone stairs leading up into the woods.

George tried to keep up but found that the altitude was forcing him to pause every hundred yards or so to catch his breath. Meanwhile Miriam seemed completely unaffected by the thinner mountain air and walked as casually as if she were strolling along a beach at sea level.

At length the path emerged from the woods and came to a low, circular parapet built along the ledge of a cliff overlooking the Vale mansion and the narrow gravel drive that led to the town. Moreover, they could view the hills across the highway that stretched far off into the distance. A wooden bench had been set up on the ledge for hikers to stop and enjoy the view. George gratefully collapsed onto it.

Miriam stood, leaning out on the wide brick parapet. Her shoulders lifted as she sucked in a lungful of air and let the breeze tug at her hair. Then she turned and looked at George, who was wheezing on the bench.

"You know, I really feel wonderful."

"Good . . . that makes . . . one of us."

"I mean, I feel like God's given us another chance to be together. This medicine is a miracle. It's incredible." Then her expression clouded slightly. "Before, when I was sick, I felt like I was locked up somewhere. In some kind of prison or . . . dungeon. And I couldn't get out. I couldn't even see how awful it was. It was like having a horrible dream that I couldn't wake up from. But then it felt as if somebody just came along and opened the cell door." She closed her eyes again and let the wind flow around her.

George rose and folded her in his arms. She leaned into him, and they stood in the warm breeze for an endless minute.

"It's good to have you back again," he whispered.

Miriam kissed him. "Don't let me go back there. Please . . . just tell me I can stay here with you."

George stroked her hair and looked into her eyes. "I'm not letting you go, ever again."

She smiled. "Make love to me, George."

George blinked. "Wh— uh . . . *here?*"

Miriam pulled away and took his hands in hers. "Yeah, right out here under the sun and the sky."

George felt himself flush, and he laughed nervously. "You mean . . . right here on the gravel?"

Miriam's smile broadened. "Who knows

how long this will last. Let's make the most of every second."

"Okay." George grinned back at her. "But . . . how about we make the most of it back in our room?"

CHAPTER 25

George awoke to see the afternoon sunlight peeking in through closed drapes. For a moment he forgot where he was; then he felt Miriam curled against his bare chest, snoring softly, and it all came back to him.

She had made love to him with a passion and vigor that George had never experienced before. Perhaps yet another benefit of the perilium. And afterward they had both fallen asleep. George hadn't realized just how tired he'd been. Now he looked at the clock. It was just after three; they'd been napping for two hours.

George eased out of bed, taking care not to wake Miriam. He slipped on his shirt and trousers. He needed to get out and take a walk, clear his head. He would have to think about telling Miriam that they would be moving here. Perhaps for good.

He left the room and walked down the hall to the balcony overlooking the great room. No one was in sight. George crossed the balcony to the other wing. He'd never been on that side before and guessed this was where Vale had his own room. He needed to find out more about this man and this place.

The idea that Vale would want George to come work for him at seventy-three was bizarre enough, though George had to admit he'd made plenty of connections with congressmen and senators. He'd even had his picture taken with a president or two. He'd become an excellent negotiator in his day, making countless deals over eighteen holes and drinks, but he failed to see how his talents would be of much use to Vale — or why he would even have need of them. Besides, all that effort took a lot of time and energy, and really . . . how many good years did George even have left in him?

He came to a window at the end of the hall and saw a flash of light outside, like sunlight reflecting off something metallic. The window overlooked the main garage entrance, and George looked down to see a white passenger van backing up to one of the four bays. The windows were tinted, but George could see two men up front. The man on the passenger side got out. He was dressed in a green jacket and blue jeans with a black cap pulled low over his eyes. The driver got out as well — a giant of a man, closing in on seven feet, barrel-chested and thick-limbed. He was bald with a thick black goatee on his chin. The guy reminded George of one of those professional wrestlers.

George watched as the bay door opened and Henderson appeared. He spoke with the two men briefly and then opened the side door. From his vantage point, George could tell someone was sitting in the backseat. He only saw a glimpse of a leg, but he could swear there was more than one passenger. He just couldn't tell how many.

Henderson closed the side door quickly and motioned for the big man to back the van into the bay.

The man in the black cap followed the van inside, and then the bay door closed.

George bit the inside of his cheek. Other than Vale himself, the only people George had seen here over the last couple days were Amanda, Henderson, and Browne. And now a whole vanload of people showed up. He wondered who the two new guys were and who the passengers in the van might be. People from town? Or visitors perhaps?

He decided to head downstairs, hoping that while everyone else was occupied with the newcomers, he could get a look in Vale's office. Maybe he could learn more about the perilium.

The whole place was eerily quiet. Not a soul in sight. George continued through the lobby and down the corridor toward Vale's office.

Suddenly Vale emerged from the door at the end of the hall. George guessed it led to the garages.

George stopped in his tracks, unsure how to react. He'd been given some liberty to move about the lodge during their stay, but he hoped now that he hadn't raised any suspicions. The last thing he needed was for Vale to think he'd been snooping around.

Even though he had.

But Vale just smiled. "I hope you don't mind, but I'm planning to have the others up for dinner tonight. A little celebration in honor of Miriam's recovery. And it'll give you a chance to get to know everyone better."

George put on his best look of pleasant surprise. "Well . . . that sounds wonderful. I think Miriam will enjoy that."

"Excellent. We'll meet in the dining hall around six o'clock."

"Six o'clock. I'm looking forward to it." George beat a hasty retreat to his room, where he found Miriam up and apparently enjoying the view out the windows. She looked radiant, George thought. Better even than she had that morning.

"So Vale's throwing a party tonight," he said. "Apparently it's a celebration in honor of your recovery."

"Lovely," Miriam said. "Will there be any food? I'm starving."

"All-you-can-eat Dagwood sandwiches." George tried to sound jovial.

"In that case, I better take a shower."

They both showered and dressed and two hours later went downstairs, where they found the dining hall decked out with cocktails and appetizers while several people milled about the room. Classical music was playing in the background, and Amanda was bustling in and out of the kitchen.

Dwight Henderson was there along with Malcolm Browne and a tall brunette whom Malcolm introduced as his wife, Loraine. Loraine immediately engaged Miriam in small talk and pulled her toward the food table.

Vale waved George over and introduced him to another couple. The man was even shorter than Henderson but with a thick mop of black hair slicked back across his head. He was with a tall, dreary-looking redhead who seemed to look past George instead of at him.

"This is Sam Huxley," Vale said. "And his wife, Eleanor. Sam's the lawyer here in Beckon. In fact, we were just discussing the terms of our agreement, and he's getting all the paperwork together. I trust we can find a time in the next day or so to finalize the arrangement?"

"Yes . . . of course." George shook hands with Huxley as the enormity of this decision struck him. The *arrangement.* The multimillion-dollar arrangement that would alter the rest of his life. Not to mention Miriam's.

"Good." Vale slapped George's shoulder. "I'd also like to discuss your role in our community in more detail at some point."

George pressed a smile onto his face. "Yes . . . yes, of course."

With that, Vale steered him toward the others in the room. The first man was medium height but with a solid, muscular build, a square jaw, and a tight crew cut. George recognized him as one of the men from the van. To George he looked like a military man. Or ex-military.

"Frank Carson," Vale said. "Our local law enforcement."

George nodded.

Carson shook his hand with a tight grip and a terse "Goodameetcha."

Beside Carson stood the hulking driver with the shaved head and black goatee.

"Henry Mulch." Vale gestured to him. "He's sort of our all-around handyman."

Mulch didn't even bother with a handshake but seemed content with a nod and a grunt. And with a name like Mulch, George hadn't really expected much more.

There was another couple hovering over the appetizer table. Vale introduced them as Max and Fiona Dunham. They gave George weak, European handshakes, and from their lofty British accents he wasn't surprised.

"Delighted to meet you," they both said in highbrow, nasal tones.

"Max manages our finances," Vale explained. "He and Fiona came over from England a while back and just fell in love with Wyoming. So they decided to stay."

George noticed how Vale seemed occupied with the careers of each of his guests, as if to point out how each member fit into the community, perhaps indicating how he hoped George and Miriam would fit in someday as well.

George, however, felt increasingly uncomfortable. At first he wasn't sure why, but now it dawned on him. There was no one else his age here. Apparently no other seniors from town had been invited to Vale's little party. Not that George minded the company of younger people; he just found that age and experience often produced a certain level of camaraderie with others who'd been through the same struggles in life.

And he suddenly felt alone and out of place.

As if sensing George's discomfort, Vale gestured across the room. "Everyone here has been in the same situation you are in now, George. Each one has faced some incurable disease and found a miracle cure in perilium."

"So they all had to move here too?"

"None of them were *forced* to move here against their will," Vale said. "They were prematurely facing death and recognized this as a reasonable cost for what they were being offered."

"Better to live in Beckon than die in Texas, eh?" George grunted.

Vale spread his hands. "Is our little community such a dreary place? Is it such an unacceptable trade?"

George glanced around the room. Everyone seemed pleasant enough — perhaps with the exception of Carson and Mulch.

"And everyone here seems to have their own special job to do — their own role to fill?"

"As in any community."

"I assume they were all considered suitable *candidates,* just like us? Meaning they were wealthy enough to afford your treatment."

Vale shrugged. "Unfortunately at present there's just not enough perilium for everyone in the world. So the resulting cost makes access prohibitive for some — as is the case with any scarce resource. But you must understand: the financial resources that each one here has brought into our community have allowed our research to continue."

"Research?"

"Yes, for some time now Dr. Henderson has been working to find a way to synthesize perilium," Vale said. "Our goal is that someday we'll be able to manufacture enough for anyone who needs it."

"Very noble. I'd be curious to see his research."

"That could be arranged," Vale said.

"And what about you?" George said. "What's your role in the 'community'?"

"Balance," Vale said with a half smile. "I maintain the balance between secrecy and progress. If word of perilium got out prematurely, we would be overrun by hordes of scientists and businessmen. Well-meaning though they may be, they would ruin the delicate balance I maintain with the N'watu. I'm trying to respect their culture while attempting to —"

"Exploit their knowledge?" George raised an eyebrow.

Vale's expression darkened momentarily, but then a thin smile curled on his lips. "Think about it, George. A day is coming when we can potentially wipe out all disease. When cancer and diabetes and even Alzheimer's become things of the past." He leaned close, and his tone grew serious. "Imagine what kind of world that would be."

George looked across the room, his thoughts coiling around Vale's words. What kind of world indeed. Free from sickness and disease and the stigma that accompanied them. He'd always thought such dreams were the realm of wishful thinkers or religious hopefuls.

He felt Vale's hand on his shoulder. "I'm offering you the chance to be a part of it, George."

George watched Miriam laughing as she chatted with Loraine and Malcolm Browne and the Huxleys. Just a few days earlier she'd been all but a stranger to him. But now it was as if he'd gotten her back from the dead. This perilium was perhaps the most significant discovery in the history of the world. Its impact would be enormous. How could he not be involved?

Amanda came up to Vale and said softly, "We're ready to eat."

Vale called for attention. The lights dimmed, and everyone took their places around the main candlelit table with Vale at the head and George and Miriam sitting to his right. Numerous covered platters had been set out along with several bottles of wine. But before anyone began eating, Vale stood and raised his glass.

"My friends, it gives me great pleasure to welcome George and Miriam Wilcox into our circle of fellowship. As most of you know, Miriam was suffering from advanced Alzheimer's when she arrived the day before yesterday. Just two short days ago she could barely recognize her husband of fifty years, and yet now she sits among us completely restored. Their marriage has been made whole again, and she becomes a privileged recipient of nature's greatest miracle." He turned to George and Miriam. "May you be blessed to enjoy a long and healthy life together."

"Hear, hear," Max Dunham said to a chorus of clinking glass.

Amanda circled the table, lifting the covers off the platters to reveal steaming vegetables, fresh-baked dinner rolls, and a large salver of meat. Fillets and tenderloins were stacked high on the plate.

All of them quite raw.

George suppressed a gasp. Was something wrong? Was this some kind of sick joke? Miriam seemed repulsed as well and clutched his arm. George looked around the table, but no one else appeared to be disturbed by the sight. Everyone was serving themselves and shoving forkfuls of the red, bloody meat into their mouths. Vale was enjoying a particularly thick fillet, mopping the blood up with a dinner roll. He seemed to notice George's look of disgust and smiled. "I see our custom doesn't sit well with you."

George grabbed a roll. "I guess I just prefer my steak grilled."

Vale clucked his tongue and slipped another forkful of meat into his mouth. "Did you know that the Inuit in the Far North eat raw meat almost exclusively? So do the Masai of Africa. Both of these cultures are known for their extraordinary health and freedom from disease."

"Still . . . if it's all the same to you, I'll stick with cooked meat."

"Suit yourself. I can have Amanda put something on the grill."

"Actually," George said, "it's all right. I'll be content with vegetables and some rolls."

Malcolm Browne was seated across from George. He wiped a few drops of blood from his chin. "You know, I was the same way when I first arrived. But I discovered it's an acquired taste."

"So I've heard."

George was no longer hungry. The Inuit notwithstanding, this was one custom he was definitely not going to adopt. Miriam, however, was staring at the platter. George watched her expression slowly turn from horror to curiosity as she studied the others dining on the raw flesh.

He leaned over and whispered, "Tell me you're not thinking about trying that."

Miriam's lips tightened. "I'm starving."

"So have some vegetables."

"Haven't you ever felt a craving for something? A certain kind of food? And no matter what you try, nothing else seems to satisfy it?"

George was mortified. "You're not serious. It's *raw.*"

Miriam looked away. "Just a little taste."

She reached out and plucked a small fillet off the platter with her fork, then sliced off a thin piece while George looked on, dumbfounded. She doused it with table salt, raised it to her lips, paused a moment . . . then put it in her mouth. George watched her chew on the morsel. Her eyes closed and George's widened. She looked like she was actually *enjoying* it! She carved off a second slice. Her expression looked like a person dying of thirst getting her first sips of cold water.

Vale took a drink of his wine. "The human body craves protein, George. It needs it to survive. We're built from it, after all. There may be other sources — nuts and legumes and such." He grinned. "But nothing provides the raw material our bodies need like real, fresh meat."

George was feeling slightly faint. "Fine, so why not cook it? At least sear it a little."

"The body assimilates the protein more readily when it's ingested raw," Vale said. "Understand that as perilium accelerates the rate at which the body repairs itself, it naturally requires a ready store of raw material with which to work. The best source of this is through the regular consumption of protein. Copious amounts of protein."

George wrinkled his forehead. "Copious

amounts . . ."

Miriam had polished off her fillet and reached for another. As George watched her eat, he couldn't help feeling as if she was somehow drifting away from him again.

George barely made it through the meal. The conversation around him ranged from art to politics to philosophy, with Vale behaving as though he were holding court in the dining hall, encouraging debate and discussion among the other attendees.

Dwight Henderson and Malcolm Browne diverged on the specific points of obscure economic philosophies, while Max Dunham and Frank Carson got into a rather heated tangential debate over whether or not the reparations in the Treaty of Versailles had led to hyperinflation in Germany and ultimately to the Second World War.

George alternated between fascination and disgust. The level of intellectualism in the room was staggering, yet all the while they were chewing on raw meat like cavemen.

Afterward, Loraine continued to monopolize Miriam's attention, so George, wearied as he was by Vale's cohorts, went out to the patio for some fresh air.

He leaned on the railing of the narrow parapet and gazed down the sheer side of the cliff into the jagged rocks and twisted pine trees more than a hundred feet below. Above him, the sky looked like a diamond-studded, black velvet blanket. It seemed like he could see into eternity. He was lost in thought when the door opened behind him and Amanda stepped outside.

She didn't seem to notice George standing in the shadows as she walked to the rail, placed her hands on it, and leaned over as far as she could. The woman, George noted, did not seem happy. He had not seen her smile at all during the meal nor talk much to anyone. And yet she was actually quite beautiful, though she wore no makeup, pulled her hair back in a simple fashion, and was dressed far more plainly than George would have expected a woman of her looks to be.

He was intrigued. "It's not that bad here, is it?"

She straightened up quickly and spotted him. "What?"

"Sorry, I didn't mean to startle you." George smiled and nodded over the edge of the rail. "For a second there it looked like you were going to jump."

Amanda wiped the errant strands of hair from her face. "It's just been a long day." She didn't smile, though George noted that she didn't appear rude. Simply tired.

"Do you cater all of Vale's parties?"

Amanda offered a mild shrug of her shoulders. "Everyone in town has a job." Her eyes flicked back toward the mansion. "Mine is managing the food services . . . among other duties. I make sure there's enough for everybody to eat."

"And how long have you been here?"

Amanda let out a sad sort of chuckle and gazed over the cliff as a breeze brushed her hair back. "Too long. Most of my life."

George moved closer. "So . . . are you happy here?"

"Happy?" She frowned. "I don't remember actually being happy in a long time."

"Why not?"

"Because sometimes this place feels like a prison," she said.

"How did you end up here?"

"When I was young, I had cancer. I was dying. My father was an investment banker in Philadelphia and was very wealthy. My parents tried everything, but all their money couldn't save my life. The doctors couldn't do anything for me. Then one day Mr. Vale contacted them and told them about this miracle drug. He said it would cure me. He guaranteed it."

George nodded. He'd been right — Vale

had built his little empire by offering his perilium only to the very wealthy. "He *is* a shrewd businessman."

"It cost my father his entire fortune," Amanda said. "Vale had asked him what he would pay to save his only daughter's life. What it was worth to him."

The question hung in the air for a moment, and then George sighed. "Everything."

"The only condition was that I had to come live here in Beckon. Become a part of his community, as he called it."

"And what about your parents?"

"They stayed in Philadelphia at first so my father could keep working. They came to visit as much as they could. But they were struggling financially. My father died a few years after I came out here. And my mother died not long after."

"So now you're . . . what? You're stuck here? Working for Vale?"

Amanda sighed. "Don't get me wrong. I'm grateful to be alive, I guess. And Beckon's a beautiful place; I . . . I love the mountains . . ."

She looked out into the night.

"But I can never leave."

Chapter 26

George awoke the next morning to find that Miriam was up already. The light in the bathroom was on, but the door was closed and he could hear water running inside. George got up and opened the curtains. The morning sun wrapped the rolling countryside below in a warm amber hue.

It had been nearly midnight by the time they got back to their room last night. George had been contemplating how to explain their circumstances to Miriam, but he wasn't ready to do that just yet. Perilium was truly a miraculous substance, even if the effect was only temporary. But still, there were a thousand unanswered questions. George's background was engineering, not biomedical research, but he knew enough to know that you couldn't just bypass the system like Vale was attempting to do. Maybe what Vale wanted was for George to help facilitate the process of herding this project through the proper government channels.

Or maybe he had other ideas.

Over the sound of the water in the bathroom George heard a gentle sobbing.

He knocked on the door. "Sweetheart? Are you okay?"

"I . . . I don't know. . . ."

Miriam opened the door, and George gasped. "Miriam?"

He grabbed her shoulders and moved her into the light. She looked like a different woman altogether. Her skin was smooth and the crow's-feet at the corners of her eyes had practically disappeared. The creases around her mouth were nearly gone as well. And her hair . . .

Most of her glistening black hair color had returned, leaving only vague traces of gray. She looked twenty years younger — or more. George turned her toward the mirror and stared at the two of them side by side.

"You . . . you look like you could be my daughter."

Miriam touched her cheeks and laughed as tears continued to stream down. "I don't believe this is happening." She looked up at George. "How do I know I'm not still senile and just imagining all of this?"

George shook his head in disbelief. "Then

I must be too." He held up her hand in his and inspected them both. All the telltale signs of her arthritis had vanished, most of her liver spots had faded, and the skin around her knuckles and wrists was smooth. His hands were gnarled and leathery, creased and mottled with years of work and stress.

"How can this be happening?" Miriam said.

George was almost too stunned to think. "I'm guessing there's more to this perilium than they told us about."

They dressed and went downstairs, where they found Thomas Vale sitting alone at the table in the dining room, eating breakfast. He stood when he saw them come in and smiled at Miriam as they sat down.

"I see the full effects of the perilium have begun to manifest themselves."

"The *full* effects?" George frowned. "So it's true, then . . . this stuff reverses aging, too?"

Vale shrugged. "Of course. Aging is merely caused by the body's inability to keep up with overall cellular deterioration. Perilium increases this ability."

"So why didn't you mention this before?"

Vale chuckled and sipped his juice. "There are some things people need to see for themselves. We felt that claiming a cure for Alzheimer's had already stretched your credulity far enough. You never would have agreed to participate in the treatment if we explained all the benefits."

George leaned back in his chair. "You're right. I would've thought you were crazy."

"What exactly is this perilium doing to me?" Miriam said. "I look . . . I *feel* like I'm twenty years younger."

Vale lifted the corner of his mouth in a smile. "You've met Sam and Eleanor Huxley?"

"Yes."

"Eleanor was dying of cancer when they first arrived. She was seventy-nine and Sam had just turned eighty."

"What?" George and Miriam gasped in unison.

George's head was spinning. "But . . . they don't look a day over thirty. Neither one of them."

"No, they don't. Not since they began taking perilium."

"How long ago was that?"

"Oh . . . I think it was 1972. Thereabouts."

Miriam gasped. "That would make them around 120 years old."

George couldn't believe what he was hearing. The whole thing was just too bizarre to be true. These people had stumbled on an actual fountain of youth? No wonder Vale went to such lengths to keep it a secret.

He found himself stammering, "Well . . . I mean, that . . . that's amazing. You've actually discovered a legitimate anti-aging compound. I wouldn't have believed it if I hadn't seen it with my own eyes."

"Now do you understand the impact of what I'm offering you?" Vale said, looking at George. "*Both* of you?"

George blinked. "Both of us?"

"You didn't think we would give your wife this gift and not make it available to you as well."

George was momentarily stunned as he considered the opportunity Vale offered him. This perilium not only gave people a second chance at life, but a whole *new* life altogether. It was almost too incredible to wrap his mind around. He was seventy-three years old, and by drinking this substance once every few days he could turn the clock back . . . forty years? Fifty?

Miriam leaned forward. "So then . . . excuse me for asking, but how old are *you?*"

"I was born in Richmond, Virginia, on October 16 . . . 1847."

"Eighteen . . . ," Miriam breathed. "But . . . that's impossible."

"Impossible?" Vale raised his eyebrows. "You've looked in the mirror. Is *that* impossible? Is *that* too good to be true?"

George was shaking his head. "So you're more than 160 years old?"

Vale's smile faded slightly and his yellow-green eyes were solemn. "Now you understand why I must keep perilium a secret. And why I have to go to such lengths to protect this place."

George could barely think clearly enough to consider the ramifications of what Vale was saying. This was the most significant medical discovery in history. It screamed to be shared with all of humanity, yet George understood what chaos would ensue if this ever became known. Vale's little retreat would be overrun by the masses. Everyone in the world would come to Wyoming seeking a slice of immortality.

But now — to make the matter more intriguing — Vale was offering this miracle to *him.* George looked again at his own aging hands. What would he give for the chance to reverse the effect that time had had on him? The chance to be young again with Miriam? The chance to live . . . forever?

Then Miriam's voice drew him from his thoughts.

"This isn't natural." She put her hand on

George's arm. "You can't just cheat death like this. Not without suffering some consequences."

"Consequences?" Vale said. "Do you mean consequences like having three lifetimes' worth of acquired knowledge and experience? Perfect health? Resistance to illness and injury?"

"Injury?" George repeated.

Vale nodded. "The body's natural healing processes are hyperstimulated. We're not certain precisely how it works, but we're getting close."

George looked from Vale to Miriam. "So someone taking perilium can't be killed?"

Vale chuckled. "I wish that were the case. No, our bodies can sustain physical trauma to such a degree that not even perilium can help. It won't grow back a limb, for example. Nor does it prevent someone from, say . . . drowning or suffocating. But I can tell you that most injuries — even gunshots, if not immediately fatal — can heal within minutes. Broken bones, depending on the severity of the break, will heal within a few hours."

Miriam was shaking her head. "So . . . forgive my cynicism here, but what's the catch? I can't believe this perilium has no negative side effects."

Vale narrowed his eyes at George. "You haven't related our conversation to her?"

Miriam frowned and turned to George as well. "What conversation?"

"Uh . . . well . . ." George had hoped to explain the situation to her in his own time. On his own terms. But truthfully, he hadn't even figured out exactly how he was going to broach the topic. Now he stammered, trying to find the words to explain it all to her.

Finally Vale interjected, "The beneficial effects of perilium require a regular regimen to maintain. But as long as you continue your treatment schedule, you should retain your health — and youth — indefinitely."

"Regular regimen?" Miriam fell silent a moment. "What exactly does that mean? Just how often do I have to take this stuff?"

"That all depends on your body's specific response to the treatment," Vale said. "But in your case, most likely once every few days."

"And how often do *you* have to take it?"

George stared at his wife. A few days ago she didn't even know her own name. Now she was back to her old self again, going after Vale like an attorney questioning a beleaguered defendant on the witness stand. George watched Vale draw a breath and could see a slight tightening of his lips.

"Those of us who have been here longer take a daily dose."

"Daily," Miriam said. "So then, the older you get, the more you need."

"A minor consequence." Vale tried to shrug off her comment. "It was to be expected."

"And if you *stop* taking it?"

Vale's eyes narrowed. It was as if that thought had never even crossed his mind. "Then of course the beneficial effects would wear off as well."

"And I assume everyone in town . . . they all have to get their daily allotments from you?"

"Yes."

"And where do *you* get it?"

Vale glanced at George as if expecting him to intervene, but George could only shake his head. Vale's eyes flicked back to Miriam. "From a local tribe called the N'watu," he said. "They discovered the secret of perilium a long time ago."

"But you don't know what it is."

"We're . . . addressing that issue."

"Addressing it? So this tribe — the N'watu? — right now they're the only ones who know how to make this perilium?"

"From what we've been able to determine,

the primary element is an organic component that we believe exists only in the caves in this area."

"But still," Miriam pressed, "you don't know how to make it yourself."

Vale sighed and seemed to concede the point. "It's an ancient secret, yes. They're very guarded about it."

Miriam laughed. "So you're just as much a prisoner here as everyone else."

Vale shook his head. His tone grew terse. "To be completely free from disease, from aging — you call this a prison?"

"It's not just disease and aging we suffer from, Mr. Vale," Miriam countered. "You can never leave this place, can you? You're like a drug addict. And you have to do whatever they tell you to; am I right? The one who supplies the drugs always has power over the ones who take them."

Vale stood. George could see his pale complexion turning pink. "You're making judgments about things you know nothing about, Mrs. Wilcox. I suggest you discuss this decision in depth with your husband. If I can't persuade you of the benefits of this arrangement, perhaps he can."

As soon as Vale had left the room, Miriam turned to George. "How could you have gone along with this?"

George hung his head. Now he was on the stand. "You don't know what it was like to watch you drift away from me over the last four years. To have you looking at me like I was a stranger. To watch you . . . fall out of love with me."

"*I* was the one with the disease, George."

"And you said yourself you didn't want to go back there again. You know how terrible that was. What would you have done for me?"

Miriam paused, her lips tightened a moment, and she looked down. "Do you really think you can live forever?"

"I don't know what to think," George said. "They told me it would cure your Alzheimer's. They didn't say anything about longevity. Or that we'd have to move here. I just knew we'd be together again."

Miriam touched his cheek. "Sweetheart . . ."

"But we could live another eighty or ninety years at least. Maybe twice that. What could we do with that kind of time? Think of all the things we could accomplish."

"But is it worth it?" Miriam said. "What good is living so long if we have to spend it cooped up in this town? Doing whatever Vale tells us to do? That's not life — not *real* life."

"We'll be together. That's enough for me."

"George —" Miriam's voice grew gentle — "I know what you intended, but this feels like we're trying to cheat the natural order of things."

"Natural order?" George grunted. "If your Alzheimer's was part of the natural order of things, then I'm fine with cheating it. I refuse to let you go back to that condition. I don't care what it costs me."

"I'm not saying this isn't a wonderful opportunity. It's incredible and I'd love for it to last forever. But something about it just *feels* wrong. Everything has a cost to it — more than just money."

Miriam's comment was hauntingly perceptive. George knew if he were Vale's employee, he would end up having to do as he was told. And he would be helping keep this place a secret. George had never been above bending the law a bit in order to get a business deal done or to gain leverage over a competitor. Still, he'd never gone so far as to do anything overtly illegal. But then, he'd never had quite so much to gain before.

Or so much to lose.

He felt Miriam's hand on his arm. "You know what I believe, George. I've lived a good, long life — a full life. And I know there's something better waiting for me after it. So much better than this. I'm not afraid to die."

"I am."

She rubbed his arm. "You don't have to be. We were meant for something better than this world. For eternity. This body is wasting away no matter what we do — even their perilium can't stop it completely. They might live for hundreds of years, but eventually death will catch up with them."

"But what's wrong with trying to put it off for a while?"

"I think we would be miserable here."

"Well, the others all seem happy enough with their arrangement. You talked to them, right? Did they seem miserable?"

Miriam sighed. "I suppose not. The Brownes and the Huxleys seemed to love it here. I couldn't get them to shut up about it."

"Did they feel like they'd been cheated? Did they have any regrets?"

"No." Miriam rested her chin in her palm and drummed her fingers lightly on the table. "No, they seemed perfectly happy."

"Well, there you go," George said. Though he'd gotten a very different impression from Amanda McWhorter out on the patio last night. She was anything *but* happy. Now he wondered how long she had actually been out here and how old she really was.

Miriam continued, "But we'd have to move away from all our friends. And church. What are we going to tell everyone?"

George shrugged. "Maybe you've forgotten, but you haven't been very close with anyone for a couple years now. I stopped bringing you to church when you stopped recognizing anyone. I think in their minds, you're already gone. You were gone a long time ago."

"I just get a bad feeling about this place, George. Why does he have to go to so much trouble to keep it a secret?"

"Can you imagine what would happen if word of this ever got out? I mean, if the public found out there was a cure for cancer or Alzheimer's or *any* disease out here — let alone a fountain of youth — this place would be overrun with crazies. And if that happened, no one would benefit from it."

"So instead they keep it a secret only for a select few? The very wealthy? That's not right either."

"There's just not enough of it for everyone. Besides, even if it could be mass-produced, can you imagine the nightmare this planet would become if everyone lived two hundred years? Or three hundred? We're stretching our resources thin the way it is. Talk about hell on earth. . . ."

Miriam turned away, frowning. "It just smacks of elitism, George."

"Then so be it." George felt a certain resolve growing inside him. He could see the logic to Vale's methods. Elitism or not, he was starting to see the rightness of it.

Besides, it wasn't like they had much of a choice anymore.

CHAPTER 27

They spent the rest of the day indoors. Miriam had said she was feeling a bit restless, so she offered to help Amanda in the kitchen. The two of them spent most of the day together talking while George lingered on the periphery. It looked like they had struck up a bit of a friendship, and he was thankful for that. Amanda seemed to be a rather lonely person, and George knew it would be good for Miriam to have a friend as well.

Amanda shared some of her life story with them. She had apparently arrived in Beckon in 1923 at the age of seventeen. It was incredible to think that she was over a hundred years old. She looked barely twenty-five. Miriam peppered her with questions about the perilium, the town, and mostly about Thomas Vale. Amanda provided only vague answers to most.

George frowned inwardly; a hundred years

was a long time to be so miserable.

He also heard them talking about God at one point and wasn't a bit surprised. Miriam had always been able to worm her beliefs into almost any conversation. There was a time in his life when it had annoyed George. Now? Not so much.

And rather than seeming put off herself, Amanda looked genuinely interested in what Miriam had to say. Something about what Miriam was sharing appeared to have struck a chord.

That evening Miriam complained of feeling tired, so they went to bed early. George slept fitfully. He kept thinking about the van he'd seen the day before and wondered what the story was behind it. Who was inside, and why were they here? He was hesitant to ask about it since the only way he'd been able to see it was through the window in the other wing, and he didn't want Vale to know he'd been poking around.

He woke up the next morning to gray clouds and a heavy rain pounding the glass and drumming on the roof. And for the second morning in a row, he found Miriam in the bathroom weeping softly. Though this time it sounded different.

George knocked on the door. "What's wrong now?"

A moment later Miriam opened the door. "I don't feel very well."

Her complexion was pallid with dark circles lining her eyes. Her forehead was cold and clammy to the touch.

"I just feel . . . a little dizzy."

George helped her back to the bed. "Lie down and I'll get Dr. Henderson."

He went downstairs. It was still before eight o'clock, but he hoped Amanda would be up early. He went to the kitchen to find her preparing a tray of food.

"Where's Dr. Henderson?" George said. "Miriam's not feeling very well; I think she might need more medicine."

Amanda frowned, then pushed past him and hurried down the corridor with George on her heels. "Where is the doctor?" he was saying. "Can you call him?"

But Amanda just said, "Wait here," and disappeared inside Vale's office.

George called after her, "Can you please just call the doctor?"

Amanda emerged from the office a few moments later with a glass vial in her grasp. George followed her back to their suite and the bed where Miriam was lying, now drenched in sweat and struggling, it seemed, just to breathe.

"Do you know how to administer this

stuff?" he asked.

Amanda helped Miriam sit up in the bed, then uncapped the vial and held it to her lips. "Drink this down. Swallow it all and don't spill any of it."

Miriam gagged slightly but swallowed the perilium from the vial. Amanda made certain she drank every drop. Miriam seemed to relax; her breathing slowed and she settled back against the pillows.

Amanda felt her forehead, then got up from the bed. "She should be all right in an hour or so. Let her rest for now. I'll call Dwight and he'll come up and check on her."

Amanda left the room, and George sat in silence for several minutes watching his wife. Vale had said that the effects of the perilium would wear off, but George hadn't expected it to happen so quickly.

When he was satisfied Miriam was sleeping again, George dressed and slipped downstairs. He found Amanda in the kitchen, leaning against the big aluminum sink, her head down, the water running.

"What was wrong with her?"

Amanda didn't look up. "Did they tell you what would happen if she ever stopped taking it?"

George shrugged. "They said that the effects would wear off. And that her Alzheimer's could eventually come back."

She shook her head, and her eyes glistened. "Well, let's just say if she stops taking the perilium, Alzheimer's will be the least of her worries."

"What? What are you talking about?"

She turned back to the sink. "Never mind. I already said too much."

George grabbed her arm and spun her around. "What will happen to her?"

She pulled free from his grasp, her eyes flaring. "Why did you bring her here?"

"To save her. I had to try to save her."

"Really? Did you do it for her or for yourself?"

George stepped back and blinked. "What?"

"I mean, was it *her* suffering you were trying to ease or your own?" Amanda wiped her eyes, and her tone suddenly grew cold. "Who were you really trying to save?"

She pushed past him and left George standing in the kitchen struggling with his thoughts. Her question hung in the silence, pricking his conscience. Had he brought Miriam all this way for her sake or his own? He recalled hearing Alzheimer's described just that way: a disease where the patient's family suffers more than the patient. He hadn't thought about it quite like that before. But now part of him had to concede it was true. He'd been more occupied with how her disease had affected him. *His* life. *His* plans.

George returned to his room and sat at the bedside as Miriam slept. An ominous thought overshadowed him as he considered the miracle drug and its side effects. Vale had purposely withheld the information about its rejuvenating abilities until it suited him. George wondered now what else Vale hadn't told him. What other side effects were there? He couldn't trust Vale for information. He would need to find out for himself.

After a time he dozed off and woke up again shortly after noon. He glanced out the window and saw that the rain had let up some. Miriam was still asleep but George was starving, so he decided to head back to the kitchen and find something to eat.

In the hallway he heard voices coming from the dining room. It sounded like Thomas Vale. And George thought he heard another woman's voice as well. It wasn't Amanda, and it didn't sound like any of the other women he'd met at the dinner party two nights ago.

George heard Vale's voice drifting up

through the foyer. "She wanted to find her cousin. Go take her to him."

George snuck along the hall until he came to the balcony over the foyer, where he saw Carson escorting someone down the corridor below him. It was a woman, her shoulder-length black hair hanging in wet clumps. She was drenched. George couldn't see her face, and it almost looked like she had been handcuffed.

"Idiots!" Vale was saying now. "How could they *not* have known they were being followed? Is he completely incompetent?"

"What are you going to do with her?" Amanda's voice responded.

"We don't have any choice," Vale said. "She didn't leave us any."

George watched as Vale and Amanda emerged from the dining room and walked down the hallway.

"See what else you can find out about her," Vale said. "I need to know if she was telling the truth or not."

"Yes, sir."

They headed down the same corridor where Carson had taken the prisoner. Vale exited through the door at the far end of the hallway, and Amanda turned into one of the other doors.

George stole down the stairs quietly and

listened. Maybe now was his chance to check in Vale's office. It was obviously the place where he stored the supply of perilium, or at least some of it, and George needed to find out what else was in there. It was also where George recalled spotting the only phone he'd seen in the entire complex — on Vale's desk. And since his cell phone had no reception in these mountains, it was the only connection George had to the outside world.

The door was closed, but George pushed it open silently. The office was empty, as he suspected. The big oak desk stood at the far end of the room, and George's heart pounded as he sucked in a deep breath and stole inside.

He moved past the bookshelves and picked up the phone but heard no dial tone. The LCD screen indicated that a pass code was required in order to dial out. George wasn't surprised. Vale's mission was to keep this place a secret. And that meant no unauthorized communications.

To the right of the desk was a second door. George tried the knob, and it opened to a room filled with what looked like storage equipment and monitors. It was small and dimly lit, containing two large refrigeration units built into the walls, with temperature monitors and a security system connected to a large console in the middle of the room. Across from the refrigeration units was another door that led to some sort of supply closet.

At that moment George heard voices in the hallway. Vale was coming back. George slipped inside the closet, leaving the door cracked open. The room was dark and smelled of paper.

In a few seconds Vale entered the refrigerator room and flipped on the lights. He was followed by Frank Carson. George nearly gasped at the sight of the man. He looked pale — almost ashen in appearance — with beads of sweat dripping down his forehead. He was clutching his chest and panting like he'd just run a marathon.

Vale went to one of the refrigeration units and punched in a code on the security keypad. The door beeped once, then clicked and opened with a soft hiss. George could see several glass vials of the perilium in a rack on the shelf.

Vale took one of the vials and held it out to Carson. But as Carson reached for it, Vale drew it back again just out of his grasp. "You know, I'm seriously debating whether or not to dock your pay by one dose. Just for sheer incompetence."

Carson's hand hung in midair. His eyes went wide and he stammered between gasps of air, "I'm telling you . . . I didn't . . . didn't see her."

Vale scowled at him and then finally relented. Carson grabbed the vial and unscrewed the cap with trembling fingers. He swallowed its contents in one gulp and collapsed into the chair at the computer console.

"You didn't see her?" Vale stood over him, shaking his head. "She followed you all the way from California, you idiot. You didn't *see* her?"

But Carson seemed too weak to respond.

Regardless, Vale was not done ranting. He paced the room. "And then you couldn't even apprehend her without getting shot!"

After a minute Carson sat up again. His breathing had slowed slightly and he wiped the perspiration from his forehead. "I'm telling you . . . she won't be a problem. You don't have to worry about her."

"And what if she *did* tell someone else?" Vale said. "We'll have even more guests."

"She was . . . ," Carson wheezed. "She was just bluffing."

"Well, I'm not sure I trust your judgment anymore, Frank. I don't need this distraction. Especially now." He leaned into Carson's face. "You find out what she knows and who she talked to. Do whatever you need to — just *get her to talk!*"

Vale stormed out of the room and Carson followed a few seconds later, muttering curses under his breath. From the closet George could see out into the main office, where Vale was moving around. After a short time it appeared he had left the room. George waited several more minutes before gathering enough courage to emerge from the closet. He peeked through the door into the office, saw it was in fact empty, and breathed a sigh.

He returned to his suite, where he found Miriam still asleep, and sat down in the other room to collect his thoughts. And formulate a plan.

Everything had just taken a serious turn for the worse. What he'd seen in Vale's office convinced him he could no longer trust the man. He could no longer trust anyone in this town.

They were holding a woman prisoner either in the lodge or somewhere in town. And it obviously had something to do with the van he'd seen the other day. This woman had followed Carson from California. But what had Carson been doing in California?

And Carson's appearance had been more

than a little disconcerting. His symptoms were similar to Miriam's, only more severe. An unsettling thought grew in the pit of his stomach as he wondered again what the other side effects of this substance were.

Right now everyone he had met in Beckon seemed to be in the same predicament as Miriam. Frank Carson and Amanda, the Brownes, the Huxleys, and the Dunhams. Probably even Henderson.

George felt sick inside as he wondered what he'd gotten Miriam into. She had been right about Vale. Judging by the way he had just treated Carson, he seemed to have no trouble exercising his complete authority over everyone in town. They all needed the perilium, and he controlled the supply, which meant he made the rules. Quite the monopoly he had going.

But George was at a point of no return. All moral squeamishness aside, right now his top priority was to make sure Miriam had unfettered access to the perilium. At all costs. Unfortunately that meant he would need to cooperate until he could find a way to change the rules of the game in his favor.

Fortunately Vale was a prisoner too. Miriam had determined that much herself. He was beholden to Nun'dahbi — whoever she was — to keep him supplied. Vale had indicated that she was the only one who actually knew how to make perilium, which meant she was the one with the real power.

Which also meant Vale had a point of vulnerability.

Chapter 28

Later that afternoon, George found Thomas Vale in the great room standing at the windows, gazing out across the mist-covered landscape. Vale turned from the window, and George could see he was holding a drink.

"I trust Miriam is resting comfortably," Vale said. "Amanda told me what happened this morning."

"It gave me a pretty good scare. You didn't tell me perilium would have that kind of side effect."

"A minor consequence," Vale said and sipped his drink. "But they can be avoided easily enough. Fatigue is one of the early warning signs that she's ready for another dose. I suppose we should have given her one last night before going to bed. But I wouldn't worry about it. It won't happen again."

George was taken aback at how casually

Vale seemed to dismiss the incident. But he knew he needed to refrain from being overly confrontational at the moment. "How can you be sure?"

"Trust me, George, I don't like it any more than you do. But we must deal with it and move on. I've survived for more than a hundred and thirty years without serious incident. I'm living proof it can be done."

George shook his head. It was odd to think he was talking to a man who had lived through the Civil War, not to mention the entire twentieth century and now well into the twenty-first. Vale had seen so much history and yet he'd seen it only from this small corner of the world. No wonder the man could be so callous. He'd been the center of his own universe for too long.

"I'm curious . . ." George went to the liquor cabinet and poured himself a drink. It had been a while since he'd had a formal business meeting, but now he found himself slipping easily into negotiation mode. It was just like riding a bike. "Everyone in Beckon seems to have a very specific function. You've given me some idea of what my role here would entail, but what exactly will you need me to do?"

They sat down on the leather couches, and Vale drummed his fingers on the wide armrest. "Our lives here are about balance. We have to maintain a very delicate balance in order to succeed — for *all* of us to succeed. And what I need is your help to maintain the status quo."

"What status quo?"

"With the N'watu," Vale said. "We have a very old treaty with them. We give them what they want, and in turn they give us what we need."

George smiled inwardly. This was an interesting bit of information. Vale had obligations himself. Some sort of symbiotic relationship with the N'watu.

"So obviously you need a steady supply of perilium from them, but what exactly do they want in return?"

Vale took another sip of his drink. "Isolation."

"I don't understand."

"The N'watu are a very ancient culture and fiercely xenophobic," Vale said. "I first arrived in Wyoming back in 1878 looking for gold. And when I stumbled across the cave entrance, they captured me. I had to think pretty quick in order to save my life."

George's eyebrows went up. "They were going to kill you?"

Vale nodded. "If I hadn't had one of the local Indians as a guide, I'd be dead. But fortunately he spoke their language, and I was able to negotiate with them."

"But what did you have to bargain with?"

"The most powerful commodity on the market."

George furrowed his brow. This should be good. "What's that?"

Vale's icy yellow-green eyes narrowed. "Fear."

"Fear? Of what?"

"Well, that's the real trick, isn't it?" Vale said. "The key to any negotiation — as I'm sure you well know — is finding out what the other party is most afraid of and exploiting that to your advantage. Fear of losing their business or losing market share. Or losing their life."

"So what do the N'watu fear?"

"Losing their home," Vale said. "They have a deep spiritual connection with this mountain. I think they see themselves as guardians in a way. Priests. I got the sense that they were protecting something. Something deep inside the cave. So I explained to them how the white man was moving ever westward and even if they killed me, it would only be a matter of time before others would come. And come with more guns. I convinced them that soon their way of life, their whole existence, would be threatened."

"Very clever," George said. He hadn't realized it before, but to one degree or another he'd been employing those tactics in the business world his whole life. A thought that, after meeting Thomas Vale, was a little unsettling. "What did you offer to alleviate those fears?"

"I assured them that I could keep them safe. I could conceal the entrance to their cave and keep their home hidden away from prying eyes, as it were. I staked claim to the surrounding land and built this lodge to conceal the entrance, and eventually the town to conceal the lodge."

"Hidden in plain sight," George said. "Brilliant."

Vale chuckled and sipped his drink. "You know, I used to think I stumbled across that cave by accident. Pure dumb luck. But now I know it was fate. It was my destiny to discover the N'watu. We found each other, really. We each supplied what the other was looking for."

"Kismet." George nodded. "And now your whole life is focused on keeping this place a secret."

Vale gestured out the window. "I'm still trying to keep the white man away and keep the N'watu hidden from the modern world. But as I said, it's a balancing act. And that's why I chose you. Politicians are tireless busybodies, and I need you to help keep them out of my business."

"So this cave . . ." George rubbed his jaw. "Where exactly is it?"

Vale gestured to the floor. "Right beneath us. As I said, I built this lodge over the entrance. I've provided the N'watu with complete privacy for the last 130 years in exchange for their sacred elixir of youth. Not such a bad trade-off, I'd say."

"They're still living inside the caves?" George could hardly believe an entire tribe of human beings could be living under such horrid conditions. Why would they want to? He couldn't conceive of any benefit or reason for it. "But how can they possibly survive? It's inhumane."

"Ah yes, they'd be much better off with cell phones and mortgages." Vale snorted.

"No, I mean, how do they live? What do they eat?"

"I've only been down there once in my life. But from what I saw, a part of that cave system has been isolated from the outside world since the dawn of time. There's a whole self-contained ecosystem thriving down there, and the N'watu are an integral part of it. They adapted to it long ago. It's all the world that most of them have ever known. For them, coming up to the surface, into the sun, would be as alien and unsettling as it would be for you to live underground. And they are keenly single-minded in their religion. They have no real material needs, and all they want is to be left alone."

It all seemed so bizarre to George. The N'watu should have died out from a lack of vitamin D, for one thing. Sunlight was such a necessity for human life in numerous ways. Unless they were able to compensate for it in some way. And that was probably where the perilium came in. George wondered how old they were. And how many were left. He'd only ever seen the one woman. Nun'dahbi. And she had been so covered in black veils that he wasn't even sure what she looked like.

But George also recalled the power Nun'dahbi seemed to have over Vale when she came into the room that first night. Vale had acted like a frightened child in the presence of his domineering mother.

"I assume the N'watu need perilium to survive as well," George said.

"Correct."

"And by moving here — by joining your community — I can basically get my youth back?"

"And then some," Vale said. "It's quite

literally the chance of a lifetime."

George shrugged. "Where do I sign?"

A smile curled onto Vale's lips. "You're on board, then?"

George spread his hands and smiled. "At this point, I already have a vested interest in your community."

George knew he was most definitely *not* "on board" with Vale. Not the way he ran things in Beckon. The fact was, George was going to make it his sole mission to undermine Thomas Vale's little empire and usurp his position of authority altogether. If George was going to live here, he wasn't about to put himself in submission to Vale. If he and Miriam were going to have a second chance at life, then *he* was going to be the one in charge. Then he could get perilium into the hands of real scientists and find a way to replicate it or even improve it and eliminate the side effects.

He would drag this whole town into the twenty-first century. And hopefully live to see the twenty-second.

"Glad to hear it." Vale slapped George on the shoulder. "*Very* glad to hear it."

Satisfied that he'd waylaid any doubts Vale might've had about his commitment, George went back to the room to check on Miriam once more. It was getting late in the afternoon and she'd been in bed since her episode that morning.

But the bed was empty, and there was no sign of his wife in the suite. George recalled Miriam's voracious appetite after her last dose of perilium and returned downstairs to see if she was in the kitchen.

He found her there, wearing her robe, sitting at the table across from Amanda with her back toward him. Amanda looked up at George and winced. An odd expression, George thought.

"I figured you'd be down here," he said to Miriam. "How are you feel— ?"

He choked his words off as Miriam turned to face him. He blinked and took a step backward. "Miriam?"

Her complexion held no trace of line or wrinkle whatsoever. Her skin was like unblemished alabaster. Her hair fell in pure dark waves to her shoulders. A glossy black sheen, just like when they had first met.

She stood, her expression somewhere between joy and terror, traces of blood around her lips. On the plate in front of her was a half-eaten slab of raw meat. "George . . ."

George was stunned. His mouth hung open and he shook his head. "You . . . you look . . ."

Miriam ran to his arms and George held her close, wondering why he was shocked when he should have expected this. She looked as young and vibrant as a woman in her twenties.

Chapter 29

"George . . . I don't want to stay here anymore," Miriam whispered.

"Look at you! You look like you're eighteen again."

"But what this stuff is doing to me — it's not natural. None of this is. Please, can't we just go home?"

"No. You're going to need another dose in a day or two."

"I don't care," Miriam said. "I can't live here. I don't care what this drug does to me. I don't care how young it makes me. I just don't want to stay here anymore."

"Listen to me." George clutched her shoulders. "Just give me some time to figure a way out of this."

"I don't trust him." Miriam's eyes glistened. "I don't want to be a prisoner in this place, and I don't trust Vale."

George held her close in a long embrace. Clearly the stress of regaining her sanity and her youth had become too intense a strain on her mind. She needed time to adjust, he told himself. She just needed to get used to the idea that she was young again.

"You need to get some rest," he whispered. "Clear your mind. Why don't you go back to the room and lie down?"

"I don't want to lie down!" She pulled away and her tone grew sharp. "I've been doing nothing but *resting* all week. Stop treating me like I'm still an invalid."

"Fine," George said. His voice softened. "You're right; let's find something else to do." He looked at Amanda. "What do you do for entertainment around this place?"

Amanda showed them the fitness room in the south wing and the entertainment center stocked with all manner of games, movies, and other crafts and activities to pass the time. Miriam found an old game she used to play as a child, and her spirits seemed to lift slightly. And with a little effort, George persuaded her to go back to the room and get dressed. The two of them would get in a light workout together and perhaps sit in the hot tub for a bit. Her mood brightened further at that suggestion.

Miriam left, and once George had Amanda alone, he cornered her in the game room. "Okay, tell me what's going on here.

Who was the woman they brought in?"

"Woman?" Amanda stammered. "What . . . woman?"

"Stop with the act. I *saw* her. I saw Carson leading her away in handcuffs a couple hours ago. Who was she? And who did they bring up in the white van?"

"No." Amanda shook her head. "I can't say anything. He'll find out. And it's not your concern."

"Where are they?" George persisted. "Are they down in the caves? Does it have something to do with the N'watu?"

"Stop it." Amanda's eyes darted away. "I have to go. I have work to do."

George grabbed her arm. "Answer me! Whatever you people are doing up here, you won't get away with it."

"You have no idea what we're doing." She yanked her arm from his grasp. "And if I were you, I wouldn't even think about crossing him. Not if you want her to live."

George glared at her but he could see only fear in her eyes. She wasn't his enemy. She was just a fellow prisoner living in fear. She had been shipped out here by her desperate parents, however well-intentioned they might have been. They were trying to save her life but had unwittingly relegated her to a living nightmare. An unending one. What would it be like, George wondered, to work for a man like Vale for ninety years? He could only imagine what other sorts of jobs Vale would have found for her, and he wondered if such longevity as perilium offered could become more of a curse than a blessing.

Miriam returned and they spent the rest of the afternoon together. Her strength and stamina were clearly heightened by the perilium's effect as she long outlasted George on the treadmill. Then they sat in the outdoor hot tub and played a game of cribbage before dinner.

Vale had invited the other residents again for dinner — raw meat and all. This time Amanda provided George with a cut of meat that was cooked. George did his best to appear amiable, though deep down he had just wanted to spend the evening alone with his wife. His young, vivacious wife.

It seemed the group all came together a few evenings each week. They gathered around the big dining table as though they were at a medieval feast. And Vale sat at the head, directing conversations and moderating debates, always having the final word.

George wondered what it would be like to live within such a small community. Seeing the same few faces year in and year out.

Some for more than a century. From the conversations, George gathered more details on how each one had arrived in Beckon. In most cases, their stories were not so different from his own: wealthy souls, stricken with some disease and willing to pay a fortune for the chance to cheat death.

Vale had practically built the town himself after discovering the cave in 1878. At first George wondered why he would build a town in the first place. Why draw people to the very place you're trying to keep hidden from the public?

But then it struck him: it was obvious that Vale needed some type of human community just for his own survival and sanity. Or ego. Though still, it seemed an odd way to keep a secret.

George surmised that eventually Vale's fortune would have begun to wane and he would've needed additional funds to maintain his way of life. He was a businessman at heart. So he had found a way to use the perilium to his advantage and began his search for others whose circumstances he could exploit, then convinced them to join him. Or perhaps *lured them here* would be the better description.

George learned that Malcolm and Loraine Browne had arrived in 1893, followed shortly afterward by Frank Carson, who'd once been a colonel in the Union army. And then in 1897 came Dwight Henderson, who had been a physician at the time. Henderson was tight-lipped about the precise circumstances that had brought him to Beckon, but George got the feeling he might have been trying to save someone. Someone close to him.

He also discovered that Max and Fiona Dunham were low-level British royalty who had arrived from England in 1914 just as the First World War was breaking out in Europe. Fiona had suffered from some sort of aggressive cancer.

George already knew that Amanda had arrived in 1923 and the Huxleys in 1972, but there seemed to be a big stretch of time between them, and he wondered if there had been others that he didn't know about. Others who perhaps didn't wish to remain under the rule of Thomas Vale. Not for all the perilium in the world.

George noticed that Henry Mulch was not present. When he asked, Vale simply said that Mulch was busy with a job he'd asked him to do.

He made it a special point to look for any hint of dissatisfaction among the group, but the general mood was light and jovial.

The gathering began to disperse shortly after ten o'clock, so George and Miriam excused themselves and retired for the evening. George wanted to get to bed early. He had plans for a morning excursion to locate the cave under the lodge. It was a risky maneuver, but he needed to find some answers.

So he arose early the next morning and slipped downstairs to look around. The place was quiet. He followed the corridor past Vale's office and discovered a door hidden in a narrow side passage off the main corridor. It opened onto a stairway leading down into darkness. George caught his breath as a sudden wave of apprehension seized him.

"Where are you going?" Miriam's hushed but urgent voice came from behind him.

George nearly jumped out of his trousers and cursed. "What are you doing? I thought you were asleep."

"I woke up when you left," she said. "And I've been following you, snooping around."

George shushed her. "I'm not snooping. I'm . . ."

"Nosing? Sneaking? Spying?"

"Exploring."

"Ah," Miriam said with a stern tone. "Then I'm coming along."

George stuck out his hand and stopped her short. "No, you're not. You need some rest, so go back up to the room and —"

Miriam brushed his hand aside. "I am not going back to bed while you go exploring. I'm coming with you."

George sighed. The last thing he needed was for Miriam to see more of this place than he wanted her to. But he also knew she wasn't going to listen to him. Besides, she was now probably stronger and nimbler than he was, so even if he wanted to stop her, he doubted he'd be able to.

"It might be dangerous," he said, lowering his voice.

Miriam peeked past him down the darkened stairway. "It's a basement. I've seen basements before, George."

"Yeah, well . . . somehow I don't think this is going to be a normal basement. And I don't want —"

"I appreciate your chivalry," she said, placing her fingers against his lips. "But if you're going down there, I'm coming with you. It's as simple as that."

George clenched his jaw and muttered to himself. "Fine," he said at last. "But keep quiet."

They proceeded down the stairs until they came to a narrow corridor with a door on either side and one at the end of the hall. Cold, flickering fluorescent lighting gave the area a pale glow. George tried both side doors only to find them locked. The door at the end was another supply closet containing mops and brooms and a couple of shelving units packed with cleaning supplies.

George closed the door with a frustrated sigh. Miriam frowned. "This basement looks like it should be a lot bigger."

George tried the two locked doors again. "Yeah, I'm guessing there are more rooms behind these door —"

Suddenly they heard the door at the top of the stairs open and footfalls start down the steps.

Miriam's eyes went round and she stifled a gasp. George pushed her back into the space under the stairwell. They watched a pair of legs descending with a five-gallon pail. It was Dwight Henderson. He continued down the hall to the closet at the end and disappeared inside.

"Let's go back up," George whispered.

Miriam pulled him back into the shadows. "No, he'll come out and see us. Let's just wait for him to leave." They waited beneath the stairs. And waited.

And waited.

Three full minutes passed.

"What's he doing in there?" Miriam whispered.

Another minute passed and George whispered again, "Let's just go."

Miriam hushed him and slipped out of their hiding place.

George grabbed her arm. "What are you doing?"

She pulled herself loose, slipped down the hall, and put her ear to the closet door. "I don't hear anything."

George stood at the foot of the stairs and waved her back. "Good. Now let's *go.*"

But he could see Miriam was having nothing of it. She pointed to the bottom of the door. "There's no light on." She tapped on the door.

Nothing.

Then she opened the door and stepped back. George held his breath and drew closer for a better view.

But aside from the mops and supplies, the room was empty.

CHAPTER 30

George snuck down the hall as Miriam flipped on the light. "We did see him come in here, right?"

Miriam shrugged. "There must be another way out. Some kind of hidden door?"

The room was small, with shelving units on both sides and a large pegboard with hanging hooks along the back. They inspected each of the walls and the floor, looking for anything that might be an entrance.

Miriam was shaking her head. "I don't like this. Why would they have a secret passage? What are they hiding?"

"I don't think I want to kn—"

Suddenly they heard muffled footsteps approaching and one of the hooks along the pegboard wall began to move, twisting to the left. George switched off the light and pulled Miriam into the corner just as a section of the back wall swung outward and a pale-green light shone in through the opening. They moved farther into the corner, behind the shelving unit, as a figure emerged.

In the shadows of the closet they could see it was Henderson again. He was still carrying the bucket, but his face looked somewhat distraught in the pale light. George held his breath as Henderson pulled the secret door closed again behind him. They heard a metallic click, and then Henderson exited the supply room through the main door. They listened to his footsteps retreat down the hall and climb back up the stairs.

Then they both breathed a long sigh.

"I'm too old to go sneaking around like this," George whispered into Miriam's ear.

"We need to find out what's back there."

"It's too dangerous." George flipped the light on. "If they catch us . . ."

But Miriam was busy feeling around the wall where Henderson had emerged. "We've got to find out what's going on out here."

George knew it was better not to argue with her. He pointed to the hook he'd seen move earlier. "I think this might be some kind of latch."

He tried twisting it to the left and could feel it swivel on its mounting bracket. He continued turning until he felt it snap into place like a dead bolt. The doorway was disguised as a section of pegboard mounted to the cinder-block wall, hooks and all. The board had numerous mop heads and brooms hanging from it along with other supplies. It was ingenious, really. George never would have suspected it was a doorway had he not seen it in use.

The board loosened on its hinges, and George was able to push it outward. It opened into a rough-hewn tunnel carved into solid rock with a series of stone steps leading down and out of sight. A line of light fixtures was mounted to the rock ceiling, each with a pale bulb, casting a sickly glow into the tunnel.

George glanced at his wife, still not quite used to her youthful appearance. "What do you think?"

Miriam grabbed a flashlight from one of the shelves and handed it to George. Then she gestured into the tunnel. "Let's go."

George nodded, his jaw clenching. "That's what I was afraid you were going to say."

They stepped through into the tunnel beyond and George pushed the door closed behind them, turning the locking mechanism back into place. Then they crept down the stairway, ever listening for any sounds. George wondered how many of the other residents knew about this passage. He was certain that Vale did. And obviously Henderson was using it too. He also assumed Frank Carson knew about it, since he was the one who'd brought the woman down here in the first place. In fact, it wouldn't have surprised him if all the residents of Beckon were aware of the passage. And if that was the case, why bother keeping it a secret?

The lights were spaced every forty feet or so, creating brief, dimly lit patches amid lengthy sections of darkness. They descended the stairway as it curved away out of sight, making it difficult to see too far ahead at any given time. After several minutes of cautious descent, they arrived at a large wooden door. It looked to him like something out of a horror movie. Thick wooden beams held together with iron bands and bolts.

George put his ear to the wood but couldn't hear anything. He pushed against the handle and felt it swing open with a dull creak. On the other side the tunnel continued straight.

They had come this far; they might as well keep going. But once through the door, they paused to listen again, and what they heard sent chills down George's spine. Voices echoed up through the dark passage. Wailing and moaning as if in torment. George's heart pounded and his throat went dry. It was as if they had in fact descended into some subterranean dungeon of horrors. They had left the modern world behind them and gone back into the Dark Ages, into a torture chamber.

Miriam gripped his arm. "Those are people, George. . . . What is this place?"

George felt sick inside. The voices grew louder as they made their way down the passage, and soon they came across side tunnels off the main corridor. At this point, George was glad Miriam had found the flashlight in the supply room.

He shone the beam down one of the tunnels. There were in fact more doors built into the rock walls. It was a prison of some sort. They could hear a weak male voice pleading to them in Spanish, but George couldn't make out what he was saying.

He called out, "Where are you?"

The voice grew more earnest, and in the beam of the flashlight George could see fingers reaching out from a slat in one of the doors.

Miriam rushed down the corridor to the door. "Here, George." She pulled on the iron latch, but it wouldn't budge. "Help me open it."

George followed her and inspected the handle. "They're all locked," he said. "We have to try to find the key."

Miriam peered in through the opening. "We'll get you out. . . . Don't be afraid. We'll find the key."

Then George heard a voice from one of the other doors. A woman's voice, speaking English. "Who are you? What are you doing here?"

George panned the light toward the new voice and saw a hand reaching out through the bars.

"Who are you?" the woman said again.

Miriam turned and clutched the woman's fingers. "Oh, my . . . don't worry. We're going to get help."

"How did you get down here?"

George leaned in. "We were snooping around the lodge and found this tunnel in the basement. It's hidden. We're . . . we're just guests there."

"Guests? You know Thomas Vale?"

"Yes, he invited us here," Miriam said.

"Then listen to me. You're in danger too. You need to get out and call the FBI. You can't trust him. You can't trust any of them. None of the people in this town."

"Who are you? Why did they lock you up

down here?"

"I'm a police officer — from Los Angeles," the woman said, her voice cracking with emotion. "My name is Elina Gutierrez. I was investigating a kidnapping. I followed the van here and they captured me." Her tone became insistent. "You need to contact the FBI. They're engaged in some kind of human trafficking here. There's something horrible going on."

George's head spun as he searched the corridor. These had to be the people they'd brought in the van and the woman he'd seen the day before. "We can't get these doors open. We have to go back and find the keys."

"Please help us," Elina pleaded. "You have to get help right away. Don't trust them. Don't trust any of them."

Miriam was squeezing Elina's fingers through the bars. "We'll get you out of here. Don't worry. We'll get you out."

Elina began weeping. "I was praying that someone would find us. I was praying He would send someone to save us."

Miriam leaned close and said softly, through her own tears, "He heard you. God heard you."

George suddenly felt as if the darkness were closing in on him. As if something were pursuing them. He grabbed Miriam's arm. "We need to go — now."

He led her back up the tunnel as Elina's voice came from behind him.

"Listen to me," she said. "Be careful. There's something in the caves. They said there's something terrible down there."

George steered Miriam away. "Don't worry. We'll contact the FBI as soon as we can."

They hurried back the way they had come. Through the wooden door and up the stairs. George was puffing hard as they climbed the stairs, but now Miriam pulled him onward, her new youthful stamina driving her.

"What is this place?" she was saying between breaths. "Why would they have these people locked up?"

"I don't know," George wheezed. "I saw her . . . yesterday. . . . Carson took her away like a . . . prisoner."

"What?" Miriam turned on the stairs and glared at him. "You *saw* her? You *knew* about this place and you didn't tell me?"

"I didn't know about this place," George said. "And I didn't know . . . who she was. I just . . . didn't want to upset you until I found out what was . . . going on."

Miriam started back up the stairs. "We

have to call the state patrol or something."

"I tried, but the only landline is in Vale's office, and you need a pass code to dial out." George pulled Miriam's arm and she turned around. "Look, if Vale thinks we're going to cause trouble, he'll have us both killed."

"How could you get mixed up with these people?"

"I was desperate!" George hissed in a hushed tone. "I would've done anything to save you. You have no idea what it was like living with you like that. All our money, and I couldn't even . . ." He could feel his emotions swelling up and choked off his words. In fifty years of marriage, he'd never cried in front of Miriam; he wasn't about to start now.

She hugged him. "I'm sorry, sweetheart. I don't blame you. But we have to get out of here. We can't stay here any longer."

"We *can't* leave."

"George." Miriam looked him in the eyes. "I don't care what happens to me. I am not going to let you become Vale's slave for me. I won't let you live in that kind of fear."

"I can figure out a way to get rid of him. I'm not afraid of him."

"And *I'm* not afraid of death."

They continued on to the top of the stairs.

George pulled open the hidden door to the storage room. They both clambered through into the room and stopped in their tracks.

Thomas Vale stood in the open doorway. Frank Carson and Henry Mulch stood behind him in the basement corridor, arms folded.

Vale sighed and shook his head, a look of disappointment on his face. "I suppose it's too much to hope that you were just out for a morning stroll."

■ ■ ■ ■

PART IV
THE SOUL EATER

■ ■ ■ ■

You don't *have* a soul. You *are* a soul. . . . You *have* a body.

WALTER M. MILLER JR.,
A CANTICLE FOR LIEBOWITZ

Chapter 31

Twelve Hours Later

It was going on eight o'clock in the evening and Jack was huddled in the back of the rust-colored pickup as it wound its way up a gravel road through looming pines to the top of a craggy bluff.

His clothes were torn and muddy from his ordeal in the caves. The gash in his leg was bandaged and his hands were cuffed behind his back. And the sheriff they had called Carson — who Jack now knew was no real sheriff at all — sat beside him with a gun in his hand pointed at Jack's chest. Malcolm Browne, the guy who had first picked Jack up on the highway, was driving. And the doctor named Henderson, who had bandaged Jack's leg, was sitting beside Browne in the cab.

They continued up the wooded hillside until the road leveled off and the trees parted to reveal the enormous log-beam mansion perched near the top of the bluff. It was quite impressive — a place that normally he'd like to spend a week in. Though considering his current circumstances, Jack could only feel a sense of great peril waiting for him inside.

Carson yanked him out of the truck and ushered him up the gravel drive through the main entrance. He escorted Jack across the foyer into an expansive central hall.

A man stood with his back to a wide bank of windows. He was lean and quite pale with a thick mass of black hair and very light-green — nearly yellow — eyes that gave his appearance a disturbing, vampirish feel.

He strode across the room somewhat casually, as if to give Jack a closer look. "Welcome to Beckon. My name is Thomas Vale. They tell me your name is Kendrick. Is that right? Jack Kendrick?"

Jack looked around at the others. "Do I know you?"

"No," Vale said simply. "They also say you've been inside the caves."

Jack could see where this was going. He suddenly realized that the less he knew, the safer he might be. "Uh . . . no. I haven't been in any cave. I've just been out hiking —"

Vale waved off his attempt at a lie. "Because you may just be the only person to have ever made it out of there alive." He circled Jack as if inspecting him. "I can't tell you how fascinating that is. I have a million questions."

"So do I."

"They tell me you're some sort of anthropologist, yes?"

Jack shook his head. "I'm not answering any questions until I get a phone. I want to call —"

"Call who? The authorities?" Vale gave an icy chuckle. "Jack, in this town I *am* the authority."

"What's going on here? Who are you people?"

Vale ignored him. "It's pretty impressive, really. I mean . . . finding a way *into* those caves was unlikely enough. But actually finding your way *out* again . . . well, that was just extraordinary. You have no idea how lucky you are."

"Funny, I don't feel very lucky at the moment."

"Oh, but you are," Vale said. "You see, the N'watu hate outsiders with a passion. And for you to have survived your encounter is nothing short of amazing."

Jack leaned forward. "What do you know about them?"

Vale scratched the back of his neck. "Not nearly enough, I'm afraid. Though probably more than anyone else."

"Who are they?"

"The last remnant of a pre-Columbian civilization that predates the Mayans. Probably even the Olmec."

Jack frowned. His father's theories continued to be validated — a fact that both thrilled and frightened him as he feared he would never escape to share the discovery with anyone else. There was something obviously sinister going on in this town, and Jack wondered if his father had stumbled across this place and perhaps been kidnapped as well. In either case, he needed more information. He needed to find out what this guy knew about the N'watu.

"And they still exist today, living entirely underground?"

"Yes . . ." Vale looked almost giddy, like a parent talking about his child. "The truly incredible thing is that their culture has survived essentially intact for thousands of years, completely undetected by the modern world." He paused, and his expression grew somber. "Of course, my intention is to keep it that way."

"Why?"

"Why?" Vale looked incredulous. "You're

an anthropologist, aren't you? To preserve their culture. To protect them from the invasive scrutiny of modern society."

Jack scowled. "But science is all about scrutiny. It's about exploration and discovery."

Vale clucked his tongue and shook his head. "Perhaps some things weren't meant to be discovered. I'd have thought you would understand the consequences to their way of life if news of their existence ever got out."

"Way of life? What kind of a life do these people have? They're living inside a cave at a Stone Age level of existence."

"This culture has evolved in a completely isolated subterranean environment. The N'watu live their entire lives underground. And yet somehow they've managed to survive. Think about how remarkable that is."

"I guess I just don't share your enthusiasm," Jack said. "Besides, I think they've had more contact with the outside world than you're leading me to believe."

Vale's eyes flicked to the three other men in the room, then back to Jack. "Do you have any clue what kind of secrets such an ancient culture might hold? And what we can learn from them?"

"Oh? Like offering human sacrifices?"

Vale leveled his gaze at Jack. "You say that with such vitriol and judgment. But is our modern, *civilized* society any better? How many innocent lives have we surface dwellers taken in the name of progress or security? Or just plain convenience?"

"So I assume you know about their bone pit."

"I've never actually been that deep into the cave," Vale said. "But I don't presume to judge their religious practices."

"*Religious?* They've been practicing ritual human sacrifices for years. And I'm guessing you've either known about it or have been directly complicit in the act."

Vale laughed and shook his head. "I don't think you have a clue what's going on here."

"I think I've seen enough."

Vale nodded to his men. "Excellent; then let's see how much you know."

Carson yanked Jack backward, and they followed Vale down a corridor off the main room. Browne and Henderson brought up the rear. They turned down a narrow side hall, where Vale led them through another door and descended a flight of stairs.

They arrived in a dimly lit basement, where Jack found himself in a narrow concrete-block corridor with three metal doors: one on each side of the hall and a third at the far end. Vale opened the door on the right and ushered Jack into a large room lined with cabinets and shelving units and lit by two rows of cold fluorescent lights. Situated throughout the room were several long tables, each one cluttered with a variety of laboratory equipment.

At the far end of the room was a pair of enormous glass terraria, five or six feet in length. Vale strode to the first terrarium and tapped on the glass. "Have you fed them yet today?"

Henderson cleared his throat. "Uh . . . no. I figured you might want to do that yourself."

Vale waved Jack over for a better look, and after a sharp nudge from Carson, Jack complied. He could see that the bottoms of both tanks were covered with a layer of mud, pebbles, and small rocks. On one side of each tank was a large pile of leaves and sticks. Jack could see the leaves jittering as Vale tapped the glass.

"Bring me a rat, please."

Henderson went over to one of the shelving units along the wall. It was packed with rows of wire cages. And each cage contained one or more of a variety of rodents: rats, mice, guinea pigs, and even a few rabbits.

He retrieved a white rat by the scruff of its neck and handed it to Vale. Vale flipped open a small plastic hatch in the cover and dropped the rat into the terrarium.

The rodent sat there for a moment, its whiskers twittering as it inspected its new surroundings.

Suddenly the leaves shook as something emerged from under the pile. Jack let out a yelp and jumped backward.

Vale grinned. "You've seen this before, yes?"

Jack's throat was dry. "Yes."

The armored arachnid was a miniature version of the monsters Jack had seen inside the caves. It was only six or eight inches across but had the same dark coloration on its top and a pale-gray underside. It reared back, raising its saber-like forelegs in the same menacing pose that Jack had seen before. Its two palps slapped together in rapid bursts, creating a soft but all-too-familiar clicking sound that sent chills down Jack's spine. And while this spider was much smaller, it looked no less fierce under the brighter lights. A moment later three more had appeared from under the leaves.

Vale leaned close to the glass as the creatures pounced on the hapless rat, overwhelming it. Fangs punctured fur and skin.

Claws dug deep into its flesh, twisting and yanking the limbs in various directions, and their tiny jaws tore off bits of tissue while the rat squealed and writhed. Jack grimaced as he watched the horrid spectacle.

Thankfully, the rat was dead within seconds, and the spiders began systematically dismembering its corpse.

No, Jack thought, it was hardly systematic. It was a frenzied, monstrous attack like he had seen in the caves. Vicious and chaotic. One of the spiders clutched a hind leg with its fangs and forelegs and spun its body to twist off the limb much like a crocodile would do to an antelope. The others tore into the carcass with their claws, gnawing flesh off bone. A flurry of blood and fur spattered the glass. Jack had never witnessed anything so brutal in his life.

He noticed Browne and even Carson kept their distance from the terraria.

But Vale seemed positively giddy and grinned at Jack. "The N'watu call them kiracs. It's derived from their word for *terror.* Aptly named, wouldn't you say?"

Henderson sounded less enthusiastic. "We believe they live in a colony structure with dozens or even hundreds of male hunters serving a single queen."

Vale leaned close to the glass, pointing at

the carnage. “See . . . the males — the warriors — they’ll eat anything. Bugs, birds, reptiles, mammals . . . even each other.”

Then he straightened up and moved to the second terrarium. “But the female, the queen . . . now, she’s more discriminating in her tastes. She’s far more . . . *refined.*” He tapped the glass.

Jack’s eyes widened at what he saw.

The queen kirac crept out from under the sticks and leaves, revealing her gnarled, armored bulk inch by inch. She was at least three times the size of the males and completely black with yellow spots dotting the top of her jagged shell. She moved slowly and deliberately . . . menacingly . . . clicking her palps in search of prey.

Vale motioned for Henderson to bring him another rodent. A guinea pig this time. Vale held it by the scruff of its neck outside the glass. The queen seemed to ignore it completely, though the guinea pig wriggled and twitched at the sight of the kirac, struggling to free itself from Vale’s grasp.

“See, the queen doesn’t eat flesh,” Vale said. “She only drinks the blood. But here’s the thing: it has to be a living victim.”

He lifted the lid and dropped the guinea pig into the cage. The queen turned, clicking her palps in short flurries. She seemed to locate her target quickly. The rodent scrambled away, instinctively backing up to the glass. Its nose and whiskers twitched furiously as it rose up against the glass in search of an exit.

The queen crept closer with slow, menacing strides. She first backed the guinea pig into the corner and then quickly moved in for the kill. The rodent jerked and struggled in a futile attempt to flee, but the queen clutched it with her massive forelegs. Jack could see the agitated animal growing increasingly desperate as the queen closed her legs around it, pulling it tightly into her embrace. It kicked against the rocks but couldn't free itself from her bony grasp.

Vale had a look of pride as if watching his prize hunting dog corner a fox. "And she doesn't poison it, either. She overpowers it, holds it tightly, and sucks out all of its blood."

Jack saw the queen sink her long fangs into the throat of the guinea pig. The animal's sides pulsed with each frantic breath but gradually slowed and within a minute had stopped altogether.

After another minute, the queen slowly loosened her grasp and moved off toward her lair, leaving the rodent's corpse lying in the mud.

Henderson lifted the lid and picked up the limp guinea pig with a pair of tongs. Then he dropped it into the first terrarium, where the ravenous males dispatched the carcass with the same speed and ferocity as they had the rat.

Jack swallowed back his nausea. "So she lives off the blood?"

"It's more than just blood. We think there's something else." Vale glanced at Henderson, who seemed to take his cue.

"We know she won't touch a corpse," he said. "She has to have live prey. But when we give her a choice between two identical rats, one of them sedated and the other fully conscious, she'll ignore the sedated one even though it's an easier kill."

Jack frowned. "She only picks the conscious one?"

"Every time. She won't feed on a sedated animal even if that's her only option."

"So . . . her instincts are based on movement?"

Henderson shook his head. "That's what we thought at first, but when we suspended a sedated rat from a string to keep it moving, she still wouldn't go for it."

Jack nodded. "She must be keying in on something else. Maybe respiration or heart rate . . ." Jack recalled something Running

Bear had said. The N'watu believed that Sh'ar Kouhm — the Soul Eater — fed on emotions.

On fear.

"The Caieche said the Soul Eater feeds on fear and anger." Jack scratched his head. "So what if she can sense fear in her prey? Fear has a physiological effect on the body. Elevated heart rate, respiration . . ." He shrugged. "Maybe she has a taste for adrenaline."

Vale offered a thin smile. "Very good, Jack. I'm impressed with your powers of deduction. I want to know everything that happened in those caves. I want to know everything you know about these things."

"What?" Jack scowled. "Why should I tell you anything?"

Vale shrugged. "Because the only thing keeping you alive at the moment is that I believe you have information that could be useful. So as long as you stay cooperative, you'll stay alive."

Jack felt his jaw tighten. He had no doubt these people would make good on that threat. He had no interest in helping them, but he also needed to learn more about what was going on in this town.

He sighed. "Fine . . . what do you want to know?"

Henderson gestured to the glass. "I've been studying these things for a while now, but there's still so much I don't know. What can you tell me about what you experienced in the caves?"

Jack just stared at the kiracs, wishing Rudy were still alive. *He* was the biology major with all the theories. Jack shuddered again at the memory of his friend succumbing to the spider's poison.

"Well . . . we found out their venom is extremely toxic. And fast. It causes massive internal bleeding and . . . a very painful death."

"We know," Henderson said. "But only the males are venomous."

Jack pointed to the terrarium. "The ones I saw in the cave were enormous. Five to ten times the size of these. Are they all juveniles?"

"No, they're fully mature at twelve months," Henderson said. "But some arthropods never stop growing."

"My friend had a theory," Jack said. "We saw enormous millipedes and beetles feeding on some kind of bioluminescent microorganism — bacteria or something. And he thought it might be producing oxygen. Through some kind of reaction."

Henderson was nodding. "So an increase

in the overall oxygen levels would support the increased mass . . . provided they had a sufficient food supply."

Vale interrupted them. "Well, it sounds like you two have a lot to discuss." He seemed satisfied with Jack's cooperation. "I have some matters to attend to upstairs. Let me know if you come up with anything useful."

Vale left the lab, followed by Malcolm Browne.

Carson checked to make sure Jack's handcuffs were still secure. "Don't try anything stupid, kid. I'm right outside."

Carson left and locked the door behind him, leaving Jack and Henderson alone in the lab.

Jack sat down on a stool, suddenly overwhelmed by fatigue and hunger. "Look, you seem to be the only one in this town who's not psychotic. Can you please just tell me what's going on?"

Henderson looked away. "It's complicated."

Jack shook his head and laughed a hopeless, empty laugh. He truly felt at the end of his rope. "Of course it's complicated. There's a pile of human bones down in those caves. There are legends of human sacrifices. And now you people are holding me captive, I assume because I've seen too much and you can't let me go."

"You're here because you serve a purpose for Thomas Vale," Henderson said. "All of us serve some kind of purpose for him."

"So . . . are you saying you're being held here against your will too?"

Henderson bit the inside of his cheek. "I suppose I could leave if I really wanted to."

Jack wrinkled his forehead. "I don't get it. Don't you want to leave?"

"More than anything."

"Then what's the problem?"

Henderson's gaze fell and he shook his head. "The problem is, I'll die if I leave. And I'd die a pretty painful death."

CHAPTER 32

George peered out his window yet again. It had been hours since Vale brought them back to their suite and posted Henry Mulch outside their door. George paced through the suite, checking every window numerous times for an avenue of escape. But none of them were very promising. All the windows, George had discovered, were of an odd configuration that opened enough to let in a breeze but not enough to let someone escape. Not without breaking the glass and bringing Mulch in to investigate.

And more than that, it was at least a fifteen-foot drop to the ground from any of their windows or balconies, and there was no way to sneak from one balcony to another. It was as if Vale had designed his guest quarters with an eye for security as well.

This prison cell was a bit more comfortable than the ones George and Miriam had seen in the dungeons far below the lodge. But it was a prison nonetheless.

George checked in on Miriam again. She had complained of a headache and gone to the bedroom to lie down a couple hours ago. She'd been somewhat sullen since their trip into the tunnels beneath the lodge, which surprised George. He had expected her to respond with more emotion to the situation she had witnessed in Vale's dungeon. More indignation, more anger. Something. But she looked like she was preoccupied. Or perhaps slightly disoriented.

Vale had essentially sent them to their room without any supper. He'd had a small tray of food brought up for lunch, but it'd hardly been filling. It was well past the dinner hour and George was starving. He could only imagine how Miriam must have been feeling.

At length George grew tired of pacing and sat, brooding, in one of the chairs out in the sitting room of the suite. He had given up hope of escaping. Or leaving. Vale had muttered something about instilling a sense of priority in them — whatever that meant.

After seeing the prisons down in the tunnels, George knew Vale would be capable of anything. Neither he nor Miriam was safe at this point.

It was getting dark by the time Mulch came in. "Mr. Vale would like to see you now. Just you."

George made his way down to the great room, where Thomas Vale, Malcolm Browne, and Sam Huxley were already waiting. A fire was blazing in the fireplace. And Huxley was holding a folder with a sheaf of papers inside.

Vale still wore his pained expression as if George had deeply offended him. George stood in front of him like an errant son waiting for punishment to be handed down by his father. Not so far off, George thought, as Vale was more than twice his age.

"I want you to know that I'm willing to overlook your indiscretion earlier today and am still prepared to move forward with our arrangement." He gestured to the folder in Huxley's hand. "I have the papers here ready for your signature, George."

George blinked. "Signature? You really expect me to go through with this deal after seeing your dungeon down there?"

Vale shrugged and went to pour himself a drink. "Yes, I expect that once you understand what's at stake, you'll sign this contract. Gladly."

"Well, you can toss that contract in the fire, because after what I've seen, I don't want anything to do with you or your little *community.*"

"You know, I don't make these types of decisions lightly. So when I offer someone such an opportunity, I don't expect him to start nosing around my home. It's an odd display of gratitude."

"When we're dealing with the kind of money you're asking for," George said, "you can't expect me to make *that* decision without trying to find out what kind of man you are."

"Such relationships must be based on trust, George. You trusted me to help your wife, and I trusted you to respect my property and privacy."

"Privacy? You kidnap people and lock them up in your own personal dungeon. That's not a matter of privacy. It's criminal!"

Vale sipped his drink and paced the room as if contemplating his next words. "I don't think you fully grasp the scope of the gift I'm offering you. Perilium is not just some remedy for cancer or senility. It brings the human body back to its original design. Immortality, the way God intended it. Just as it was in the Garden."

George shook his head. "We won't be a part of what you're doing here."

"Oh, but I'm afraid refusal is no longer an option," Vale said. "You see, perilium is an exacting master, not something to be taken casually. She requires your full commitment. And once you've tasted the elixir of life, you become one with it. There's no turning back."

George felt his neck bristle with a chill. "What do you mean?"

Vale drew another sip from his glass and looked at his watch. "It would actually be more dramatic for me to show you."

He motioned to Browne, who left immediately.

Vale went on. "The survival of our community depends on two basic elements. One is a fair amount of seclusion from the rest of society. As you can imagine, we don't wish to attract too much scrutiny here.

"And the other is balance. Every member of our little family has a specific function. We're all dependent on one another to ensure the continuation of our way of life. So when one of us is no longer willing or able to function, they must be . . . *reevaluated.*"

Browne returned, leading Amanda into the room, her hands cuffed in front of her. She was sobbing. And George could tell immediately that something was wrong with her. Her complexion was pallid and her hair and clothes were nearly drenched in sweat.

Vale gestured toward her. "You see, Amanda here requires a daily measure of perilium just like the rest of us. Typically right after breakfast. But today I had to withhold her allotment as there were certain issues I felt we needed to discuss."

Amanda sank to her knees, sobbing. "P-please . . . why are you . . . doing this?"

George frowned. "What's wrong with her?"

Vale tapped his watch. "She's nearly twelve hours overdue."

He reached into his trouser pocket and held up a glass vial of the yellow liquid.

Amanda saw it and struggled to her feet. "Please . . ." She tried to reach for it, but Vale held it just out of her grasp and she collapsed again to the floor.

George looked on in horror. "What's happening to her?"

"As I said, perilium is an exacting master." Vale stared at the vial in the firelight. "And she demands a heavy price for disobedience. The body goes into a sort of toxic shock if not supplied with a regular dose. It's a rather unpleasant sight to witness."

"What did she do? Why are you doing this to her?"

"To make an example," Vale said. "See, I've been observing her over the last few days, and lately I'm just not so certain of her commitment to our community. She seems to have developed something that could be an impediment to our existence."

George couldn't bear to look at her any longer. "What is it?"

"A conscience." Vale knelt beside Amanda's quivering form, dangling the vial over her head. "Apparently she's been having doubts about our way of life. And I'm afraid we can't tolerate such a lack of moral clarity. We have far too much to lose — all of us. We all depend on maintaining that precious balance, and she has become the weak link. A dry branch that needs to be pruned."

Amanda reached again for the vial. George could see genuine terror in her eyes. "I . . . I've always been faithful. . . . I've done everything you asked. . . ."

But Vale withdrew the vial once more and stood.

George stepped forward. "Stop it! Just give it to her!"

Vale wagged his head. "Here's the thing, George. I have to make room for Miriam, and if I were to keep Amanda on, I wouldn't have enough perilium left for your wife. I'm afraid there's just not enough for both of them."

George blinked. "Not enough? But you said —"

"What I said is that we must maintain a delicate balance. So if Miriam is to join us here, then unfortunately there will be no room left for dear Amanda."

George cursed at him. "You're a monster."

"Monster? Me?" A cold smile spread on Vale's face. "But this is *your* choice, George." He held up the vial. "Amanda or Miriam — which one will it be?"

Amanda writhed on the floor, gasping for breath. "George . . . p-please . . . help me."

George could feel his rage growing, but his old body would be no match for Vale in a physical altercation. He just shook his head in frustration and swore.

"Her life is in your hands, George," Vale said again. "Just say the word."

Seconds ticked by. George couldn't bring himself to speak. Part of him didn't believe Vale would help Amanda regardless of his choice. But it was a moot point. He couldn't risk it. He couldn't let Miriam die.

"Or . . ." Vale narrowed his yellow eyes. "Have you already made your choice?"

Amanda's tremors quickly became more violent. Her spine arched with a sharp spasm and her eyes rolled back in their sockets. Her quivering body bumped and jittered on the floor as the rest of them looked on. George watched, horrified but unable to turn away.

The seizure lasted for more than a minute before it finally ended in a long, painful groan. Amanda's body lay in a contorted, twisted mass on the floor.

Vale sighed and clucked his tongue as though he'd just lost a pet fish. Nothing more. "Now we're both monsters, George. But more to the point, I think you needed to see precisely what awaits your beloved wife if you cross me again. Or in case you were thinking about leaving our community."

George growled, "I'll kill you."

Vale laughed, replacing the vial inside his jacket. "Well, it wouldn't be the first time. But you may want to reconsider your refusal of my offer. I'll give you another twelve hours to think it over."

CHAPTER 33

Henderson opened a small refrigerator and produced a glass vial. He held it up for Jack. It was sealed with a black cap and inside Jack could see a yellow viscous substance.

He wrinkled his forehead. "Okay . . . what is it?"

Henderson gazed at it and shook his head. "It's called perilium. And it's probably the most valuable substance on the planet. *And* the most dangerous."

"Why?"

"It's an organic compound that the N'watu have been producing for centuries now. They ingest it for medicinal purposes."

"Medicinal?" Jack didn't know if he was joking or what. "What do you mean?"

"Perilium appears to hyperstimulate the body's immune system, making it far more aggressive at repairing damaged cells or destroying diseased ones."

"So basically it helps the body heal itself faster?"

"Exactly."

Jack folded his arms. "How fast?"

Henderson just stared at him a moment and then rummaged through one of the drawers until he found a box cutter. He rolled up his sleeve and held his arm out for Jack to see.

Jack frowned. "What are you doing?"

Henderson winced as he ran the razor down the length of his forearm, slicing open his skin along an eight- or nine-inch track. A dark trail of blood rolled off his arm onto the cement floor.

Jack backed away. "Are you crazy?"

"Just watch." Henderson held his arm still under the lights.

Jack watched as the wound stopped bleeding all on its own. The skin seemed to close up right before his eyes, as if someone were zipping it shut from the ends toward the middle. In seconds, a bright-red scar formed and faded back to the color of the original flesh.

Within two minutes' time the scar completely disappeared and Jack could see no trace of the wound whatsoever. He blinked and shook his head. Was his extreme fatigue playing tricks with his mind? Had Henderson performed some kind of sleight of hand?

"I don't believe it," he said. "How does it work?"

"I told you. It enhances and accelerates the body's natural ability to heal itself."

Jack's hands were still cuffed behind his back, but he leaned forward to examine the vial. "So . . . what? You just drink this when you're sick or injured?"

Henderson rolled his sleeve back down. "Something like that."

"And . . . a person who drinks this . . . can't be killed?"

"Not exactly. If the physical trauma is too severe, the body may not have time to heal itself before succumbing to death."

Jack nodded at the terraria. "And you think the spiders — the kiracs — are the key to how they make the perilium?"

"That's our theory," Henderson said. "They exhibit an uncanny resistance to disease and extremely fast recuperative abilities when injured."

Jack recalled the spider Ben had tried to kill. It wasn't until he had caused enough physical tissue damage with his knife that the animal finally died.

"But you don't know how it's made."

Henderson shook his head. "The N'watu guard this secret closely."

"No doubt." Jack sat on the stool. For now all of his weariness had left him. His mind was active with the possibilities this substance presented. It needed to be shared with the world. So why was it being kept a secret?

"There's some catch to it, isn't there?"

Henderson sat down at the table across from Jack. His expression turned grim. "The impact on the body is enormous . . . but only temporary. Once perilium enters the system, the body requires regular doses to survive. Otherwise, it goes into shock. Convulsions, seizures . . . and death."

Jack's mind was racing. It was making sense now. These people needed a constant supply of this perilium, and the N'watu were the only ones who knew how to make it. So they had some kind of contract. He recalled Running Bear saying the N'watu had made a similar bargain with the Soul Eater. To offer it human souls in exchange for their own lives.

"So this is where the legend of the Soul Eater comes from?" Jack said. "The N'watu worship these kiracs. They offer up human sacrifices and get this perilium in return."

"We figured you knew about the legend." Henderson drew a long breath. "The N'watu will only accept a human soul. The legend goes that the Soul Eater consumes the life force of the soul, and by drinking her nectar, a person can gain the power of the other's life force. One life for another."

"One life . . ." Jack couldn't believe what he was hearing. He could still see the tribe inside the cave, gathering round to eat the baby kiracs right out of the egg sac. And how the others were thrown into a bowl to be mashed up. This must have been the way they produced the perilium. He looked again at the vial on the table. It was something inside the spiders' physiology that the N'watu — and the people here — were ingesting. He shook his head. "Is that where you all come in? You supply them with fresh souls to be offered?"

Henderson's jaw clenched. "We do what we have to do to survive."

"Do what you *have* to do?" Jack cringed. "You're *killing* people!"

"Don't you get it? We'll die without the perilium."

"Then die! What gives you the right to take someone else's life like this?"

"That's why I've been studying it," Henderson said, raising his voice. "If I can synthesize it or find a way to replicate it, we can make it ourselves and I can end this nightmare!"

"And in the meantime . . . what?" Jack said.

"In the meantime we have to maintain the status quo."

Jack eyed him with disgust. "Status quo? Meaning you keep herding innocent people to the slaughter?" He nodded again to the terraria. "To be fed to those things in the cave?"

"No." Henderson shook his head. His eyes seemed to glaze over. "To be fed to *her.*"

"Her?"

"Sh'ar Kouhm. They feed them to the queen. The others — the males — just get the leftovers."

Jack sat dumbfounded, staring at the second terrarium and recalling the larger specimen and how it fed. His heart raced at the thought of one of the queens lurking in the caves. Something even more terrifying than the males he had encountered. He remembered the massive shape he had glimpsed in the cave as he and Ben were making their escape. Could that have been the queen? Jack shuddered. "And she drinks their blood?"

"Drinks their souls, yes."

"And since she feeds on fear," Jack went on, "these victims are alive and kicking. They're filled with terror when they get thrown to the Soul Eater?"

"I don't know how the ritual is performed."

Ritual? Jack squeezed his eyes shut and took a deep breath. "Look . . . Dwight. This . . . this has to stop. You can't let this continue. These are *people* you're killing. Human beings!"

Henderson stood. "I haven't *killed* anyone. I'm trying to end this."

"But you're helping them do it."

"And I'm telling *you,* your only chance of staying alive is if Vale thinks you still have some value to him. So you decide. Help me find a solution and live. Or stand there moralizing and get thrown into the pit."

Jack took a long breath. "Is everyone in Beckon trapped here like you? They're all involved in this?"

"Everybody in this town was lured here by Thomas Vale at some point; they were chosen for a reason. They each had something Vale wanted to exploit. Money, expertise . . . Malcolm Browne was a businessman worth millions. Sam Huxley was a lawyer. Frank Carson is ex-military and Vale wanted him for security purposes. And the others . . . we were all facing death in some way and gave up everything for the promise of a miracle. A second chance at life."

"A second chance?" Jack frowned at him. "So wait a minute. If this stuff can eliminate disease, then how . . . ?" Jack was trying to piece together the information Henderson was giving him, but he couldn't think of how to frame his next question. It sounded too crazy. "Exactly how long have you been here?"

Henderson just looked at him for a moment. "You're starting to understand the true secret of perilium."

"So you're saying this stuff . . . enhances longevity?"

"Significantly."

Jack blinked away his shock. "Seriously . . . how old *are* you?"

"Let's just say I'm older than I look."

Jack's mouth hung open. This guy looked like he was in his twenties. Thick, chestnut-brown hair without a hint of gray. And perfect complexion. Not a trace of age lines by his mouth or crow's-feet around his eyes. No moles or liver spots. But how old was he in reality? Forty? Fifty? Jack pressed him for an answer, but Henderson refused to provide further details. Finally Jack shook his head in frustration. "But you're telling me that if you leave here or stop taking the perilium, you'll die."

Henderson nodded and his lips grew tight.

"I've seen it before. There have been others. The day you fail him or the day he decides you're no longer useful to him, he cuts you off."

Jack fell silent for a moment, taking this all in. Then he snorted. "So basically your whole job here is to find new victims for the N'watu to sacrifice."

"Because if we don't, the flow of perilium stops. And we all die."

Jack stared at the first terrarium. The kiracs had picked clean both the carcasses of the rat and the guinea pig. All that was left were bloodstains and bones scattered around the cage.

"What happened to you?" Jack asked. "You're a doctor. You used to value human life, didn't you? You should know better."

Henderson issued a long sigh. "You need to see things with a little more objectivity."

"Objectivity?" Jack said. "You kidnap innocent human beings and bring them here to die."

At that point the door opened and Vale entered, shaking his head as if he'd been listening in on their conversation the whole time. "You know, Jack, I was really hoping you would work out here. That you'd be able to see the bigger picture."

"I've seen enough," Jack said, his teeth

clenched. "I'd tell you how wrong all this is. How evil. But I'm guessing you're beyond even grasping those concepts."

Vale chuckled. "It's funny how quick people are to judge evil, while so blind to seeing it in themselves."

"Don't you drag me down to your level."

"Oh, I think you would be capable of greater things if properly motivated. We're all willing to sacrifice others for our own purposes."

"Not like this," Jack said. "Not like you."

"No? Tell me, Jack Kendrick, what moved you to come here in the first place? What drove you to search those caves? Something did. Some ambition. What was it, Jack?"

Jack's jaw clenched. Did he dare bring up his father? Would these people know what had happened? Or had his father just been one of a multitude of victims? Despite how painful the truth might be, Jack needed to know.

"I came here to find out what happened to my father."

Vale narrowed his eyes and the corner of his mouth curled up slightly. "Your father?"

"His name was David Kendrick, and he disappeared somewhere out here twelve years ago." Jack found his voice quaking slightly. "He was an anthropologist doing some research. I'm guessing you probably remember him. You know what happened to him."

Vale merely shrugged. "But unfortunately I don't."

"I don't believe you."

"Sorry to disappoint you," Vale said. "It's sad, really. You coming all this way, looking for answers and not finding them. And it sounds to me like your friends paid the ultimate price for it."

Jack opened his mouth but could find no answer. His anger drained away as he pictured Rudy's terrified convulsions and death. And he could still hear Ben screaming as he was pulled back down the tunnel by the same creatures.

"So was it worth it, Jack? Was it worth their lives?"

Jack stared at the floor. "I . . . I didn't kill them."

"No? It was *your* obsession . . . *your* desire to find answers that killed them."

Vale gestured to Frank Carson, who entered the room with a dark grin. Fear and anger gripped Jack as he snapped out of his guilt and looked for some way of escape. But there was only the one door, and his hands were still bound behind his back. Still, he made a dash for the doorway, trying to plow through Carson. But Carson grabbed him and wrestled him to the floor, knocking a table over in the process and scattering papers everywhere.

He yanked Jack to his feet and slapped the back of his knuckles across Jack's face. Jack swooned momentarily and his legs buckled as he struggled to stay standing. He blinked the stars from his eyes and looked up at Vale.

"What . . . what are you going to do with me?"

Vale's yellowish eyes stared at Jack, seemingly void of any emotion. "Unfortunately you pose too great a risk for us. So you might say we're donating your body to science."

Chapter 34

Jack felt himself being half carried, half dragged through darkness as the world spun around him. His head and jaw throbbed from where Carson had belted him, and Jack dimly added a concussion to his mental list of injuries. Only vaguely aware of his surroundings, he could tell he was descending deeper into darkness as shadow and cold folded around him and a sickly familiar scent of damp earth and stone filled his head.

Fear swirled inside his chest, though he was too groggy and disoriented to realize just how afraid he should be. Far down in his consciousness, he knew they were taking him back into the caves. Back into the horror from which he had barely escaped.

He heard metallic sounds: the jingle of keys and some kind of latch and then the dull wooden creak of a door. And then he fell flat onto a cold, hard stone floor. Human voices wailed and moaned in the darkness.

Above them all, Carson's harsh voice muttered something, but Jack couldn't respond; then the sound of their footsteps quickly receded into the darkness. And as Jack lay on the floor, he felt an insurmountable sense that he was completely alone.

"Hello?"

A woman's voice echoed somewhere nearby. Jack wondered if he was dreaming. Then a male voice — also nearby — responded. Jack thought he was speaking Spanish.

Jack opened his eyes. He lifted himself off the ground and surveyed his surroundings. He could see the vague rocky surface of walls. Along one side, a pale beam of green light streamed in through an opening. Like a small window in a door. Jack squinted. A prison door.

He rubbed his head and jaw, which still throbbed, though less intensely now. Carson's punch had packed considerable wallop. He almost thought he had heard voices calling to him.

"Hey in there . . . can you hear me?" The woman's voice came again.

Jack felt his way to the door and peered out into what looked like some kind of tunnel. Across from him, he could see another wooden door with a small window cut into it. Iron bars were embedded in the wood. A sick feeling grew in the pit of his stomach.

"I . . . I can hear you," he said.

There was a pause. Jack was both relieved and disconcerted to hear others down in the darkness. Obviously this was where Vale was stockpiling new victims for his monsters. Then the voice came back.

"My name is Elina Gutierrez. I'm . . . I used to be a police officer from Los Angeles."

"Los Angeles?" Jack said. "How did you get here?"

"I was looking for my cousin, Javier. He'd been kidnapped and brought here. I followed their van from California but they caught me, too."

At that point Jack heard another male voice off in the darkness, speaking Spanish. Elina responded in Spanish as well.

"Who are they?" Jack said.

"That's Javier. They brought a whole vanload of workers — they said they had jobs in Las Vegas but then brought them here four weeks ago and locked them in this place. I think they've been doing this for a while."

Jack grunted. "Huh . . . I guess that makes sense."

"Why? What are they doing to them?"

Jack leaned his forehead against the bars. "You don't want to know."

"They said there's something down in the caves. Do you know what they're talking about?"

Jack couldn't bring himself to tell them what he knew. He could barely stand to think of it himself.

After a moment Elina's voice came again. "What's your name?"

"Jack."

"Jack . . . how did *you* get here?"

Jack closed his eyes for a second. He had lost track of time. It had been only a matter of days, yet it seemed like forever. "I was in the caves, trying to find some evidence of an old Indian legend. . . ."

He gave her all the details of his expedition. How he had discovered his father's papers and the article on the Caieche. He told her about the legends of the N'watu and the Soul Eater. He described how they had found the cave and the kiracs in the bone pit. His voice grew a little shaky as he described Rudy and Ben and how they died. He told her about his encounter with the N'watu remnant still living in the caves and his escape. And finally how he had been captured by the people in Beckon and everything he had learned about perilium and their dark history of human sacrifices to the Soul Eater.

Elina seemed particularly interested in that part. "Perilium? Well, that explains how Carson recovered from his gunshot wound."

"Gunshot?" Jack said. "When did that happen?"

Then Jack listened as Elina told him about her own encounter — how she had followed the white van with the Nevada plates to Wyoming and how she had shot Carson nearly point-blank and he had appeared to recover.

"But the trouble is, they all have some kind of addiction to it," Jack said. "If they ever stopped taking it, they would all die."

"So they've been smuggling illegal immigrants for years," Elina said. "Now I know why."

"But they don't know how to actually *make* this stuff themselves," Jack said. "So they've been forced to keep this bargain with the N'watu."

"Well, you said they thought it was somehow connected to these creatures."

"Yes, but they don't know how exactly," Jack said, lowering his voice. "When we were inside the cave, we saw the N'watu performing some kind of ceremony where they pulled the hatchlings out of an egg sac and ate them. Then they poured the rest into a bowl and started mashing them up."

"So you think they make perilium out of the . . . baby kiracs?"

"And that's what the Soul Eater legend says," Jack said. "The queen kirac supposedly devours a human soul and then imparts its energy back through her nectar."

"That's disgusting," Elina grunted.

"Yeah, but it makes sense," Jack said. "There must be something in the kiracs' physiology — some type of enzyme or something, maybe active just during that stage of their development — that causes the effect on the body."

"There's one thing I don't get," Elina said. "How has this tribe been able to survive for so long? You said you only saw the one female in the cave. That's not much of a gene pool."

Jack shrugged. "I don't know. There must be more of them that we didn't see."

"Or maybe they're just like those creatures," Elina said. "Like you said, a group of hunters around a single queen."

"Maybe." Jack rubbed his eyes. "I don't care anymore. I just want to find a way out."

Elina seemed to brighten. "There were two people who came down here earlier. I don't know who they are, but I don't think they're part of all this. They said they were guests or something. They were going to try to get help."

"If they're guests *here,* I'm not so sure we can trust them," Jack said. "I wouldn't trust anyone connected to Thomas Vale."

"I don't think they knew what was going on here. They said they were going to try to contact the FBI."

"I hope you're right."

Although *hope* was not something he sensed much at the moment.

CHAPTER 35

George had watched Miriam sleep fitfully throughout the night. He had tossed and turned himself, as he found he couldn't get the vision of Amanda's agonizing death out of his mind. And Vale leering over her, playing mind games with him. The man was clearly used to manipulating his subordinates and circumstances, all to his own advantage.

George woke every time Miriam coughed or rolled over, afraid she would start having seizures during the night. And by the time morning came, he'd not slept more than a few minutes at a time and was still bleary-eyed when he heard voices outside the door.

George slipped out of bed to see what was going on just as Dwight Henderson entered with a tray of food. Through the doorway, George spotted Mulch still standing guard outside.

Henderson set the tray on the table and

glanced into the bedroom. "How is she doing this morning?"

George glared at him. "As well as could be expected."

Henderson was silent for a moment and then shook his head. "Why did you go nosing around? Why did you have to go down into the tunnels?"

"Why were *you* down there?" George said. "What does Vale have you doing? Checking on all his prisoners?"

"You don't know the whole story."

George could see some kind of conflict in Henderson's eyes. Whatever was going on in this town, it looked like Henderson was more of an unwilling participant. Much like Amanda had been.

"Then why don't you tell me? You can start with how you got here."

"It's not important." Henderson looked away. "It was a long time ago."

George sighed. "Vale lured you here the same way he did us, didn't he? To save someone you loved?"

Henderson didn't answer.

"Who was she?"

Henderson's gaze fell, and after a moment he took a long breath. "Her name was Julia. She was my wife. But she's been gone more than eighty years now."

"From the perilium?"

"No . . ." Henderson sat down. "No, she hanged herself."

"Suicide? What happened?"

Henderson's gaze shifted around the room. "I was a doctor in San Francisco when Julia became ill with leukemia. It was 1897 and we tried every treatment available to us, but she only got worse. And that's when Vale contacted me. I . . . I don't know how he found me, but Julia was quite literally on her deathbed and Vale said he had this medicine — an old Indian treatment that would heal her. But he said it would come at a cost. My family was quite wealthy, but he said he didn't only want our money. He just said the cure would require us to move to Beckon."

"Sounds familiar," George grunted.

Henderson shrugged. "We were desperate, and I would have done anything to save her. So, of course, I agreed. We were both in our fifties at the time and soon I found what you did. That perilium reverses the aging process and makes a person young again. Within days, Julia looked like she was thirty years younger."

George nodded. "You thought it was a miracle."

"Yes," Henderson said. "He offered it to

me as well, but he said he needed me to return to San Francisco for a few years. He said he had work for me to do."

George frowned. "What kind of work?"

"Horrible work." Henderson looked down and shuddered. "The devil's work."

"What was it?"

"He said he needed . . . *specimens,* he called them — five or six every month. He gave me very detailed instructions on what to do and how to have them sent. He said I would find plenty of suitable subjects in San Francisco. People no one would miss. Vagrants, prostitutes, criminals. He said I would be doing the city a favor. All I had to do was sedate them and have them transported to Wyoming. Henry Mulch would arrive with a coach every month like clockwork. And Vale said if I missed a single deadline, the perilium would stop and Julia would die. If I told anyone or tried to send help, Julia would die."

George recalled Vale's boasting about his negotiation skills. "So he found out what you needed most and exploited that to get what he wanted. He used your fear against you."

"It's what he does best. It's how he has survived here for so long."

"So what did he do with them? The . . .

specimens?"

Henderson grew pale at George's question. "There's something down in the caves. The N'watu call it the Soul Eater — they worship it like some kind of god. And it's the source of the perilium." He turned away. "The N'watu must supply it with a new offering — they . . . *feed* it a human soul in exchange for the perilium."

"*Feed* it?" George couldn't believe what he was hearing. "What do you mean? What is this thing?"

"It's . . . some kind of animal." Henderson seemed to struggle for words. "A creature that drinks the blood of its prey. The N'watu say it feeds on a human soul and in exchange provides that soul's energy back to them."

"This is crazy!" George found his mind reeling again. He got up and paced the room. The more information he gained about this town, the more hideous and terrifying it became. "So then everyone's role here is somehow involved with finding new victims."

"One way or another," Henderson said. "If we don't provide the N'watu with a new sacrifice, the perilium will stop. And if the perilium stops, we'll all die. Just the way you saw Amanda die."

"How many *specimens* did you send him?"

"I don't know." Henderson rubbed his eyes. "I wouldn't keep count. You have to understand, I had to become another man altogether to do this work. Like Jekyll and Hyde. Sometimes I would find two or three at a time to send. I swear I didn't know what he was doing with them."

George grew indignant. This man truly believed he had done nothing wrong. He had justified his role in the deaths of possibly hundreds of innocent human beings. "What did you think he was doing? You're a doctor. You're supposed to *save* lives!"

"I saved *Julia's* life. As long as Vale kept getting his specimens, she had enough perilium. Don't tell me you wouldn't sacrifice a stranger — or a thousand strangers — to save Miriam."

George's indignation suddenly abated. He'd made just such a choice last night. Amanda's life had been in his hands and he'd sacrificed it for his wife's. He no longer had the moral high ground from which to judge Henderson.

He wondered how long Henderson had kept this secret bottled up inside him. His voice softened. "Then what happened? How did you end up here?"

Henderson sighed and sank onto the couch. "It got to be too dangerous for me to stay in San Francisco. I was getting old by then and in danger of getting caught. Vale said it was time and I could come to Beckon to stay. He said he would give me the perilium and he had additional work for me to do."

George frowned. "You wanted the perilium too? Even after everything you knew about it?"

"For a chance to regain my youth? To live with my Julia forever? Yes, more than anything. I drank it too."

"Despite all the people that had been killed."

"These were vagrants, criminals. After a time I came to accept what had once been unacceptable." His gaze turned cold. "Don't judge me too harshly. It's not as hard as you might think."

"And what happened to Julia?"

Henderson turned away. He went to the window and hung his head. "She never knew the truth about her cure or the things I had done on her behalf. She only knew that perilium was a fountain of youth, and she was perfectly happy in her ignorance. Then one day she found my journals. She confronted me and I had to tell her everything. She hanged herself not long afterward."

George didn't know whether to hate the man or pity him. Despite his complicit role in all this evil, George couldn't help but feel sorry for him. Because now he found himself in the same predicament.

Henderson left, and George woke Miriam to give her some breakfast. She ate quietly, not speaking much. George knew she must be preoccupied with thoughts of her own mortality. He tried to engage her in conversation but with little luck.

Vale kept them consigned to their room, and as the hours passed, George could see Miriam was growing more and more withdrawn. By noon she complained of a slight fever and a headache that grew worse as the day wore on.

George sat at the bedside, wiping the sweat from her forehead with a cool, damp washcloth. He still couldn't get the vision of Amanda's death out of his head. And now as he watched Miriam's condition worsen by the hour, he found his own resolve weakening.

He stood over her bed as she opened her eyes, shadowed by dark circles, and offered him a weak smile.

"I can't do this," he said at last, his voice

shaky. "I can't just stand around and watch you suffer."

"George . . ." Her voice was soft and her breathing grew labored. "This place — this man — is evil. You need to be strong. You can't . . . give him what he wants."

"I'm not going to let you die."

"I'm . . . not afraid. You need to let me go. You'll never be free of him if you don't."

George shook his head. He'd just gotten her back after four years, and he wasn't about to let her go again. He went to the door, where Mulch was standing guard.

"I need to see Vale — *now.*"

Mulch led him to the dining hall, where everyone was gathered eating. The Brownes, the Huxleys, the Dunhams, along with Carson and Henderson. George noticed that this evening there was little conversation and the general mood seemed more subdued. And no wonder, George thought. Vale had just killed off one of their own with about as much detachment as if he had traded in a used car for a newer model. He sat in his normal place at the head of the table and raised an eyebrow as George entered.

"Hello, George," he said, glancing at his watch. "I've been expecting you. I assume you've had a change of heart?"

"Yes." George tried to mask his contempt. "You win. I'll do whatever you want me to do. Just give her the perilium."

"A wise choice," Vale said. "I'm looking forward to integrating you into our group. And now that Amanda has left us, I think Miriam would fit this role perfectly."

"I wouldn't be too sure of that." Miriam's voice came from the doorway.

George turned. "What are you doing?"

Miriam's face was deathly pale and glistening with sweat. "I'm coming here to s-stop you from making . . . a mistake."

"It's okay," George said. "The money doesn't matter to me."

"It's not about the *money,*" Miriam said, stepping gingerly into the room. "It's about your soul. I can't let you . . . get involved in what they're doing here. I won't do this."

"Come now, Mrs. Wilcox, get off your high horse." Vale gestured to the others at the table. "In Beckon, we have found an end to disease and suffering. And even time has no power to ravage your body. I've made you young and beautiful again."

"On the lives of those people down there?" Miriam looked at the others. "Do they have to . . . die so you can live?"

"All species live at the expense of others," Vale said. "That's the way it is in nature."

"Perhaps that's the way of animals. Not us."

"Criminals, indigents, and the dregs of modern society. Those are the types of people down there. We have made the world a better place by eliminating them."

"Those are human beings. Created in God's image. You have no right —"

"God's image?" Vale laughed. "In a great house, there are vessels designed for noble purposes and others for ignoble, remember? God Himself creates the distinction. God Himself destined them for this purpose. To be given for us. We're simply ridding His house of the ignoble vessels. In our own way, we're doing His divine will."

"You are not God . . . and this is not His will." She looked at the others gathered around the table and sucked in a long breath. "He's played on your fears . . . and used them against you. You were all so d-desperate to save yourselves or your loved ones that you were willing to do anything. *Anything.* And now look at you. You're like slaves. You do whatever he tells you to, no matter how terrible. You think . . . you're immortal . . . but you've lost your souls long ago."

"I don't care." George grabbed her shoulders. "I can't lose you again."

"Lose me?" Miriam touched his cheek and smiled. "After all these years you still don't . . . understand? Death isn't the end, George — not for me. I'm . . . just going home."

"Are you so sure of that?" Vale pointed to the windows. "Death and disease rule out there. But I saved you from it. Here in this town, *I've* given you immortality."

"You've made them prisoners," Miriam countered. "They live in fear of you. Afraid that one day you'll take it all away from them."

Vale's eyebrows went up. "And you would have them believe you're *not* afraid of dying?"

Miriam shook her head. "I may be . . . afraid of dying . . . but I don't fear death."

Vale grunted. "And why is that?"

Miriam grimaced and doubled over, leaning on George for support. And then with all her strength, she straightened again, leveling her gaze at Vale and the others. But George saw in her eyes neither hate nor anger nor even defiance, but rather . . .

Compassion.

"Because . . . I know the Author of life."

Vale scowled and looked away from her. "It's not too late, George." His voice was even and confident. He got up from the table and slipped a glass vial from his pocket. "I can stop her suffering. I have it in my power."

"Yes!" George reached out his hand. "Give it to me."

But Miriam clutched his arms, refusing to let go. "No! I won't live like that."

"George?" Vale held out the vial and moved closer. "Do we have an agreement?"

"Yes, yes. Give it to me."

Miriam lunged forward, snatching the perilium from Vale's grasp. She fell in a heap, smashing the vial onto the floor. Glass shattered and the yellow liquid splashed across the tiles. The others gasped and scrambled to their feet.

"No!" George slumped to his knees and wrapped his arms around Miriam, lifting her to his chest. "What are you doing?"

Miriam's breaths came in choppy bursts. "Setting . . . you . . . free. . . ."

Tears poured from George's eyes as she began to shake, her arms and legs quivering with increasing violence. He wept with bitter moans, desperately trying to hold her body still. But she arched back in his arms. Her head twisted and she groaned through her clenched teeth.

"No, no . . . dear God." George sobbed like a child. "Please don't leave me."

Miriam's body shook in violent surges, and he tried to hold her tightly but couldn't prevent the ravaging onslaught of her spasms. He couldn't ease her suffering or fend off death. He couldn't . . .

He couldn't save her.

George felt the whole world shift as his brain shut down to the trauma. This wasn't happening. Miriam wasn't dying. They never came to Wyoming. He never heard of perilium.

Seconds crawled past like hours. Eventually her tremors weakened, her body relaxed, and her eyes rolled back down. They seemed to fix on him for a brief moment as a sigh escaped her lips.

"No . . . sting . . ."

Then her eyes lost focus and she fell limp in his arms.

CHAPTER 36

Elina still had more questions than answers. This newcomer, Jack, fascinated her, but his story was chilling. And while there were still some missing pieces, he had certainly shed light on the N'watu and why the people of Beckon were doing what they did.

But she didn't know how many others there were. Was the whole town infected by this substance? This perilium?

And she wondered further about the couple she had encountered the day before. They seemed genuinely unaware of what was going on in this place and completely appalled by their discovery of the dungeons below Vale's palatial lodge.

But it had been too long since their encounter. Clearly, if these people had been able to call for help, they would have heard something by now. Either they had been caught or killed — or worse, perhaps they were both part of the town's conspiracy and had just been toying with them by pretending to help.

Elina felt like screaming. She hated not knowing what was going on. Hours had passed since they had brought Jack, but she couldn't tell what time it was or even what day it was. She was filthy and hungry and now more angered than scared. But at least with Jack she had someone who knew more about what was going on.

They discussed various theories about the N'watu and the creatures that were apparently lurking farther down in the cave. They talked for hours, but Elina was getting more and more frustrated. All this talk was just fine, but it wasn't getting them any closer to escaping — even to formulating a plan for escape. And in the back of her head, Elina knew it was only a matter of time before Vale came for another sacrificial offering. Before it was time for the Soul Eater's next meal.

She peeked out the window in her door. "Jack, I can't just sit here and wait around for them to come and get one of us. We have to try to escape."

She heard Jack's voice reply, "What exactly did you have in mind?"

"I don't know, but I'm tired of waiting."

"How many others are down here?"

"The best I can tell is maybe five or six," Elina said.

Elina could hear Jack testing his cell door, inspecting the lock, the hinges, and the window bars. After a few minutes he issued an exasperated sigh. He sounded like he was giving up hope. And she couldn't let that happen. Down here, hope might be all they had.

"Jack . . . do you believe in God?"

There was silence for a few seconds. "I guess so. I mean, my father would take me to church when I was a kid, but it always seemed so . . . I don't know. Lifeless. And when I see places like this, I wonder if He's even real at all. And how He could allow stuff like this to happen."

"I don't have a very good answer for you there," Elina said. "I've only been going to church for a couple months."

"A recent convert?"

"Well, more like a revert."

"What do you mean?"

Elina sighed. She'd never shared this part of herself with anyone before. She had never seen the need to. She had always been too arrogant and independent. But her current circumstances seemed to provide an opportunity.

"My father was such a good Christian

man. I was only thirteen when he was murdered . . . and something happened to me. I guess I just stopped caring about God. I couldn't forgive Him for letting my father die."

She heard Jack grunt softly. "I think I can relate to that."

"So I was angry most of my teenage years and even through college. And when I joined the LAPD, I was an angry cop. A good cop, but an angry one."

"You said you *used* to be on the police force. What happened?"

Elina's chest began to ache. "I was on a call, a robbery. And I ended up pursuing a suspect. I followed him down an alley and lost sight of him for a moment. When I found him again, he had turned and was walking toward me."

"Was he armed?"

"I thought he was, so I fired my weapon. But I didn't warn him. I didn't identify myself. I just fired. Three or four shots. One to the head. And I didn't care. I didn't know who he was, but I hated him and I wanted him to die because he was just a thug like the one who killed my dad."

"But it wasn't the right guy, was it?"

"No. . . ." Elina could feel the tears in her eyes. They dripped down, cutting a salty path through the grime and dirt on her cheeks. "He was just some kid. Some innocent kid the guy had passed in the alley. Some kid just walking home from a party."

"Let me guess — an internal investigation, a reprimand. Mandatory leave?"

"The suspect was black. The kid was black, and the guy who killed my father was black. . . ."

"So . . . they tried to make it a racial incident?"

"Somebody had heard me make derogatory comments in my rookie year, and all that came back to haunt me too."

"So *was* it about race?"

"That's the thing," Elina said. "I've been hating black men since my father was killed. And I didn't care what people thought."

"I guess there wasn't much tolerance on the LAPD for that mentality."

Elina wiped her eyes. "I kind of hit rock bottom. I had lost my job and stirred up all kinds of racial tension in my neighborhood. Then a few months ago I started to rethink some of my values. Started going back to church. Praying more. You know, trying to humble myself before God."

"Do you still hate black men?"

"Not since I've come back to God." Elina

chuckled softly. "Now I only hate some of them."

Jack laughed. "So why are you telling me all this?"

Elina sighed. "I don't know. I guess it's a little cathartic to talk about it. But mostly to pass some time."

She could hear Jack moving around in his cell again. His voice held a tone of frustration. "There's got to be a way to break out of here."

"I haven't seen any way out," Elina said. "They feed us twice a day, I think. A bowl of oatmeal slop and a cup of water in the morning and evening. No utensils."

"Have they taken anyone away during that time?"

Elina paused. "Mmmm, no. Not that I heard, anyway."

"So as far as we know, it's been at least a few days since this thing was fed. I wonder how long it goes between meals."

Then Elina heard voices echoing up the tunnel, getting closer. Her heart began pounding. "I'm guessing a few days."

The chorus of wails and curses from the other prisoners started up again, and Elina pressed her face against the bars, straining to see into the main passage. She glimpsed the erratic beam from a flashlight glancing off the sides and floor of the tunnel.

In moments a group of figures appeared around the corner. In the painful glare of the flashlight, Elina thought she saw four men. One in the lead with two others behind him, carrying a fourth man between them.

One of the men chuckled and Elina recognized his voice: Carson.

"It's like Grand Central Station down here."

The man in the lead stopped at the head of the passage and pointed to the door next to Elina's. "Put him in that one." She could tell it was Vale.

The other two dragged the man past Elina's cell. She caught a glimpse of his face and gasped.

It was the man who had discovered them yesterday. The man she had hoped was going to call for help.

They deposited him in the cell with a sick-sounding thump and closed the door. Vale shone his flashlight in the window. "I'm sorry your wife lacked the vision to join us, George," he said. "But I'm a forgiving man. You know that you're more than welcome to come back, should you have a change of heart. You could still have a long and happy life here with us."

Elina heard muffled curses from behind the door, but Vale only laughed and then turned his attention to the other cells, peering in through the bars.

"Good evening, Jack," he said. "You must be feeling a bit of déjà vu, I bet."

Then he crossed over to Elina's door, and she backed away from the window.

"Ahh, Former Officer Gutierrez." Vale peered in at her. She could see his yellow-green eyes inspecting her for what felt like an endless moment. "Yes . . . it's been quite some time since she has enjoyed the taste of a woman."

Elina retreated farther into the cell. "What are you talking about?"

Vale chuckled. "You mean you haven't told them what's waiting for them, Jack? Down in the caverns? You haven't told them about Sh'ar Kouhm?"

"Of course I told them," Jack shot back.

"She's hungry tonight." Vale's eyes again appeared in Elina's window. "She feeds on fear, you know. She can smell it in your blood. It's like a drug to her. And women are capable of generating such . . . pure, unbridled fear."

Elina's pulse raced and she pressed against the wall as Carson unlocked her cell door. She could hear Jack and the others yelling and pounding their doors. Her senses heightened as adrenaline surged through her veins. Elina coiled down, ready to attack. She was outnumbered by bigger, stronger men, but she refused to go with them quietly. The door opened and Carson entered, carrying the black stun baton. Elina gritted her teeth against the pain she knew was coming. She would make them kill her rather than take her to this creature. She sprang forward, aiming her foot at Carson's groin.

She was still in the air when Carson swung the stick toward her. She saw a blue spark of light and felt her limbs involuntarily stiffen. She hit the ground like a sack of rocks, her throat tightening so violently that she couldn't breathe.

Then Carson pulled the stick away, electricity still sparking from the tip. Elina lay completely stunned and gasping for breath as the other man entered with a rope.

Chapter 37

Jack screamed until his throat was raw, his throbbing fists pounding against the door. He alternated between threatening and reasoning with Vale as Carson and another man entered Elina's cell.

But Vale ignored Jack, and a few minutes later his men emerged again, carrying Elina between them. She was bound and gagged, her hands and feet wrapped tightly with rope.

They hauled her back up the tunnel, around the corner, and out of sight. Jack leaned his head against the bars, listening to the other voices echo curses through the tunnels.

Jack closed his eyes and struggled to keep his thoughts focused. He tried to talk to the man in the cell across from him. The newcomer they had just brought down. Vale had called him George.

"Hey . . . hey, George."

Jack could see a vague shadow moving behind the bars in the window.

"George," Jack called again. "Did you ever find a way to contact the FBI?"

A voice replied from behind the door. It was husky and hollow, empty of emotion. "No. They were waiting for us as soon as we got out of the tunnel. Vale's had us locked up in our room ever since."

"Elina said you were with someone else. . . . Was that your wife?"

"Yes."

"What happened to her?"

Jack could see the vague shape of George's face through the bars of his door. "She's dead. They said they had a cure for her Alzheimer's, but . . . they lied to us. It killed her instead."

Jack heard him begin to sob in the darkness. He stepped back to process this information in silence. It was just like Henderson had described. Vale lured people to town with the promise of curing some disease. George was probably wealthy or had something else Vale needed to continue his smuggling of human beings into town. That must have been why they were chosen.

"I'm sorry for your loss" was all he could think of to say.

The soft echo of footsteps brought Jack

up from his thoughts. He strained to listen. Someone else was approaching.

A minute later another figure appeared in the tunnel, carrying a flashlight. He moved slowly down the passage, peering into the cells. The light glared in Jack's eyes for a moment, then flicked away.

"He's going to kill her," a voice said.

Jack's hope lifted. "Dwight?"

Dwight Henderson's eyes darted around the tunnel. "We . . . we have to save her."

"Save Elina?" Jack said. "Yes, we do. But you need to let us out so we can help you."

Dwight shook his head. Jack thought he looked disoriented. "I — I begged him not to take her, but . . . he said she was too dangerous to keep."

"Dwight, let us out of here. We're running out of time."

Dwight shone the light into George's cell. "I'm sorry about Miriam. I'm sorry that you lost her."

George's voice took on a biting tone. "Oh, I'm sure you are."

"Why didn't she want to live here? Why would she do that?"

"Because she wasn't afraid to die," George said. "She would rather die than be a part of what you people are doing here, and she wanted to set me free. She . . ." His voice cracked. "She believed something better was waiting for her when she died."

Dwight leaned closer to George's window. "Do you?"

George was silent for a moment, then said, "I don't know."

"Dwight," Jack said, "do you have the keys?"

Dwight held up a ring of keys. "He'll kill me for this."

"We'll help you," Jack said. "Just let us out of here."

"He'll kill me." Dwight stared at the keys, though his gaze seemed unfocused. "He'll get rid of me like he did with Amanda. He's going to kill all of us sooner or later. Eventually we'll all stop being useful to him."

"Listen to me," Jack persisted. "We can help you."

"No, you can't, Jack. No one can." He turned back to George. "Do you think Miriam was right? Do you think there's anything waiting for you when you die?"

"If there is a hell, I know you'll be there. You and all the rest of the people in this town."

Jack could see Dwight wavering in the darkness. Teetering on the brink between hope and despair. Struggling perhaps with a newfound conscience. A sense of moral doubt that had been buried too deeply and for too long but that now seemed to be reemerging. Jack tried to tip the balance further, even if he wasn't quite sure of it himself.

"That's not true, Dwight. There's still hope."

"No, there's not. I've done terrible things."

"I know it," Jack said. "Horrible things. I don't have all the answers, but I have to believe that God's bigger than all that. I have to believe He can forgive you. That He *wants* to forgive you."

"That's what she thought too." Dwight furrowed his brow and snorted. "But God left this town a long time ago."

"No, He didn't." Jack felt his heart swelling now with courage. He could sense the tiniest spark of hope in this dungeon. Elina had ignited it in his heart almost without his knowing it. And now it was struggling to shine again right on the other side of his prison door. He just needed to coax it a little. To fan it into flame. "I used to think that way too, but maybe God's here now. Right here in the darkness. Maybe it's why He brought Elina here. To help you find Him. Now please, let us out so we can save her."

Dwight blinked and looked down at the

ring in his hands. His jaw clenched, and he slipped the key into the lock.

Jack pushed the door open with a rush of emotion flooding over him. He grabbed Dwight by the shoulders, wanting to hug the man there in the tunnel. "We have to free the others."

They unlocked George's cell and the one on the other side of Jack.

The young man who emerged from that cell was emaciated and filthy. He looked barely eighteen or nineteen and rail thin. His tattered clothes reeked. He was talking rapidly in Spanish. Jack handed him the keys and motioned for him to open the other cells.

George emerged from his cell as if in a daze. Jack could see he was an older man, maybe in his seventies. He was tall and perhaps at one time rather distinguished-looking, but now his face looked gaunt and gray as if worn out by sorrow. A large purple bruise puffed out on his upper cheek.

"We have to go after them," Jack said to Dwight and George. He could hear the other cell doors opening, accompanied by yelps and hoots of relief.

Dwight was shaking his head. "You need weapons first. Frank has a gun."

By now, the other kid had returned, out

of breath and followed by six exhausted-looking Hispanic men. They were all speaking Spanish, and Jack couldn't understand what they were saying.

He turned back to Dwight. "Where are the weapons?"

Dwight pointed up the tunnel. "Frank's ex-military. He's got an armory in the basement, right across from my lab."

Jack looked at the group of Hispanic men. "Which one of you is Javier? Who's Elina's cousin?"

One of them stepped forward, the tallest of the group. His long black hair was matted and tangled.

"We have to save Elina," Jack said.

Javier started to reply in Spanish, but Jack shook his head.

"Wait . . . uh, *no . . . no habla es—*"

Dwight cut him off. *"Han llevado a Elina a la cueva. Tenemos que ir por ella."*

Javier nodded excitedly. *"Sí, vamos a prisa!"*

They rushed through the tunnel and up the stairs into the basement of the lodge. All of them shielded their eyes from the fluorescent lights and moved out into the corridor.

"Here," Dwight said. He stopped at the door across from his lab and fumbled with the keys. "It's this one."

All of the prisoners with the exception of Javier scurried past them toward the stairs.

"Hey, wait! Hold up," Dwight called after them. *"Espera, espera!"*

But they ignored him, obviously too relieved to be free.

Dwight looked at Jack and George. "We have to stop them. The others are still upstairs. If they find out what's going on . . ."

George's eyes took on an icy glare. "I'll take care of them; you guys go after the girl."

Dwight unlocked the door and opened it into a small room with gun racks on the walls and a shelving unit crammed with boxes of ammunition. They snatched weapons and ammo in a mad flurry. Jack found a rack of shotguns.

He tossed one to George along with a box of shells. "Guard the entrance. Make sure none of them come after us."

George nodded and headed up the hall, loading the shells as he went.

Dwight was busy loading the other shotguns. He slung one over his shoulder and handed another to Jack. Jack looked it over, familiarizing himself with the weapon. He had fired a gun a few times on a target range, but he'd never used one in any kind of violent action.

"Point and pull." Dwight tapped the barrel. "Just don't point it at me." He gave one to Javier as well and rattled off some instructions in Spanish.

Jack spotted a box of flares on one of the lower shelves. He grabbed a handful and shoved them into a canvas bag.

Meanwhile Dwight had loaded a pair of .45 revolvers; he shoved one in his belt and held the other ready. Inside of three minutes they were loaded and ready for war.

Dwight stopped on his way out the door. "Hold on."

He grabbed a couple items off one of the shelves and showed them to Jack — small, black metallic spheres with handles on one side.

Jack's eyebrows went up. "Grenades? He's got hand grenades too?"

Dwight shrugged. "Like I said, Frank's ex-military."

Jack glanced back along the corridor where George had disappeared up the stairs. Then he turned and followed Dwight and Javier through the storage closet and down into the tunnel.

Chapter 38

Elina struggled against the ropes, but they were far too tight. Obviously these guys had done this before and knew the best ways to subdue and transport their prisoners. They had gagged her as well.

They carried her out of the cell and down into the darkness of the tunnel. There was no more lighting and no stairs carved beyond this point, so the two men moved slowly through the rough passage, lugging her between them. Vale stayed in the lead with the flashlight.

They carried her for nearly ten minutes, descending deeper into the cave until they came at last into a larger chamber. They set her down on the ground, a cold mixture of pebbles and mud. Elina watched her two bearers step back while Vale moved forward to a section of the wall where Elina could see what looked like wooden timbers. Another doorway built into the rock.

Vale picked up a large stone and pounded it against the wood. A dull, hollow thump rang out in the cavern. Then he stepped away. The other two men retreated even farther, taking cover behind a large rock.

At first nothing happened. And then came a long, low creak as the door swung open. Vale shut off his flashlight, plunging the entire chamber into blackness.

In the middle of the darkness, Elina saw two lights glowing. She peered more closely, her heart racing now. These weren't flashlights or torches she saw, but rather they emitted a soft, steady glow. Two orbs of pale-yellow light suspended in the darkness.

And yet Elina saw the lights were moving, floating closer until she could see they were in fact two lanterns of some sort, being carried by a pair of human figures walking toward them. It wasn't until they were much closer that Elina was able to determine what they looked like.

And then she wished she'd never seen them.

They were tall and gaunt and ghostly pale, their skin reflecting the light of their lanterns with an eerie luminescence. They moved with smooth, sure-footed strides through the dark cavern, naked except for the loincloths tied low around their hips. Their translucent white skin was covered with strange black markings, just as Jack had described. But in fact the N'watu were more terrifying by far than Elina had imagined from Jack's account.

Now she could see four of them, each one carrying a thick spear topped with a long, serrated tip that looked like it had been carved from some sort of bone or shell. And behind them, Elina spotted a diminutive shadow moving. Black against the darkness beyond.

The N'watu approached Elina and loomed over her with eerie, colorless eyes gazing down. Their skeletal faces were hideous — fierce and misshapen. If Carson hadn't stuffed the rag in her mouth and tied it there, Elina would have been screaming.

Then the fifth figure drew up behind them. The woman Jack had described, dressed in veils and dwarfed by her accompanying warriors, approached Elina. She bent down as if to inspect her, like a woman examining a cut of meat at a butcher shop. She hissed some muttered incantation over her, then straightened and faced Vale.

Vale bowed low in her presence. "Nun'dahbi."

"Another outsider," the woman's voice hissed. The sound was somewhat unnerving to Elina, at once beautiful and yet filled with venom.

"Yes," Vale said. "She . . . she wandered into town — and she knew too much for us to let her go."

"She will be missed. More will come searching."

"No, Great Mother, they won't find anything," Vale said. Elina could tell he was trying to exude confidence, but he looked nervous. "I'll make sure of it."

"There were other intruders. You could not keep them away."

Vale nodded in earnest. "We captured one of them, and the others are dead. They had discovered another entrance into the caves. A hidden entrance. But we will block that also so no one else will find it. Your home is still safe."

Nun'dahbi paused. Elina could not see her face and so could not tell if she was satisfied with his assurances. "They are growing too numerous," she said at last. "More and more they come."

"Your home is safe, Nun'dahbi."

"But for how long?"

Vale looked surprised. "I . . . I assure you," he stammered, "we . . . we have everything under control."

Nun'dahbi paused a moment — perhaps

to let Vale stew in a bit of uncertainty, Elina thought. He might have been in charge up on the surface, but clearly he was the subordinate down here.

Then Nun'dahbi produced a vessel of some sort from the folds of her cloak and held it out in white, bony hands. It was a tall, dark-colored decanter that Elina could see held some sort of liquid. Vale bowed his head and reached forward to take the jar from her hands, but she clung to it a moment.

"Do not fail me." Her tone was soft but strident.

Vale looked up sharply. "I . . . I have never failed you, Great Mother."

The faceless veil issued a soft hiss, a sigh perhaps. Or perhaps it was a laugh. Elina couldn't be sure. But after a moment Nun'dahbi released the jar into his grasp.

"See that you don't."

Then she turned away and with a brief gesture of her clawed fingers waved him off.

Vale skulked away, clutching the jar in both hands as two of the N'watu lifted Elina by the ropes and carried her through the doorway into the tunnel beyond. She could hear a heavy, wooden groan as the door swung shut behind her. Elina found her pulse racing as she struggled against the ropes.

They carried her through the passage. Elina could see one lantern ahead of her and one behind, both casting a pale glow against the jagged walls and ceiling.

Before long they came into an open space, a larger cavern. Situated about the chamber were dozens of lanterns like the ones the two warriors carried. Their glow lit the cave in a mesmerizing yellow light. Elina struggled to stay focused and aware of her surroundings. The room was about a hundred feet across and the floor was smooth and flat, almost artificially so. Not like a natural cavern. The walls as well were too straight to be natural formations, with openings cut into them leading perhaps into other rooms.

They came to the edge of a precipice that plunged into darkness. She glanced, wide-eyed, down at the abyss.

They moved along the edge of the pit until they came to a wide, stone slab and laid her on it. Elina noticed now that several other warriors had joined them, and she fought through her fear to try to count them. Nearly a dozen of them but still the woman, Nun'dahbi, was the only female Elina had seen.

She was lying on some sort of table in a large oval-shaped chamber. Recalling her training, Elina tried to get her bearings. In the middle of the chamber was the large, round pit. Elina guessed it was twenty or thirty feet across. And on the ledge she could see the outline of a large structure — a stone base supporting a thick log that extended out over the mouth of the pit.

Nun'dahbi strode into Elina's view, carrying a staff with beads and feathers dangling from the top. She swept it over Elina's body from head to foot and back again, muttering a gargled series of incantations. She motioned to some of the men standing around her, and they brought a few lanterns closer, setting them on the edges of the table. Another man brought a small wooden bowl, the size of a coffee cup, and set it beside Elina's head. She squirmed and rolled on the table, determined to make whatever procedure they might have planned as difficult for them as possible.

But apparently Nun'dahbi would have none of it. She hissed something at her men, and four of them stepped up to place their long hands firmly on Elina's body and hold her still. For all their lean and bony appearance, these men seemed to possess great strength. Elina felt like she was being held by iron restraints.

Nun'dahbi leaned close over Elina's face. Behind the veil, Elina could see vague, pale features and colorless eyes gazing down at her. The woman reeked of human stench. Elina's breath came in sharp, rapid bursts, and she could feel herself choking on the rag.

Nun'dahbi whispered another unintelligible phrase and then slowly lifted her veil.

Elina's heart pounded hard inside her ribs.

The woman's face was as hideous as it might have once been beautiful. Her skin held no pigmentation whatsoever, though it was perfectly smooth and without blemish, like a layer of white latex stretched over a human skull. Only her thin lips and eyelids held any color, painted as black as her fingernails. And she was completely hairless. No eyebrows or even eyelashes that Elina could see.

She picked up a stick out of the bowl. It was long and slender like a quill of some kind, and Elina could see the tip dripping with a viscous black liquid.

Nun'dahbi issued a sharp, guttural command, and two more of the men grabbed Elina's face. Cold, hard fingers clamped onto her jaw and skull, holding her immobile as the woman leaned close.

Elina screamed through the mouthful of rag, choking and sobbing as the woman etched marks across her face, whispering unknown words that only Elina could hear.

CHAPTER 39

Jack, Dwight, and Javier followed the tunnel deep into the mountain. Dwight had taken the lead, carrying his flashlight in one hand and a revolver in the other. As they descended, the tunnel became rough and harder to navigate.

Jack found himself praying desperately as he plunged further into danger. It was a strange sensation. Before meeting Elina, he hadn't even thought to pray. Not earlier in the caverns. Not even when he was being chased by the N'watu. But now . . . now he was heading back into the pit. Back into the danger he'd escaped from just one day before to try to save a woman he hardly even knew. And he wondered if there really was a God who would help him. Or at least give him some answers. Was this the right course? Or would they have been better off staying on the surface and contacting help?

But he knew Elina didn't have the luxury

of waiting for the authorities to arrive. He also knew every step was leading him back into the horrors to which he had sworn he would never return.

Dwight held up his hand and shut off his light.

"What's the matter?" Jack said between breaths.

Dwight whispered, "They're coming. I hear voices."

Jack squinted into the darkness. He could see a faint shaft of light drifting across the tunnel up ahead. "What's the plan?"

Dwight flicked his light back on and inspected their surroundings. The cavern passage was low and wide and marred by numerous rock formations that had slowed their progress.

"Take cover off to the side," he said. "We can ambush them when they come by."

Jack's pulse was racing as Dwight explained the plan in Spanish to Javier. Jack had never fired a weapon on another human being before. Now he wasn't sure he'd be able to. But he heard himself saying, "Fine."

They found a couple of rough boulders against one of the cavern's sides and took cover behind them. Jack crouched in the darkness, watching the light approach and now hearing voices as well. It was Vale all right, and Carson, but Jack couldn't make out what they were saying.

Minutes crept by, and finally the men came into view. Jack couldn't see well enough to shoot at any of them. And on top of that, he was having doubts about killing anyone in cold blood. No matter how much he felt they deserved it.

"Aim for the head," Dwight whispered. "Perilium begins the clotting cascade almost immediately, so hitting them anywhere else may not do the trick."

Vale and Carson were discussing something about the prisoners. Jack thought they were trying to decide whom to sacrifice next. The big man was following close behind.

Suddenly Javier leaped from cover and started firing his shotgun toward the flashlight. Which immediately blinked out, plunging them all into darkness. Jack could hear Dwight yelling and firing his revolver as well. He stood, aimed in the direction he thought Vale was, and pulled the trigger. The blast kicked the shotgun back into his ribs.

It was over in seconds, and the rumble echoed off along the tunnel. They emerged from cover slowly, and Dwight swept the area with his light. They spotted one man — the big one — splayed across a rock. Rivulets of blood dripped down from his head into the mud. In front of him was Frank Carson lying on his back, staring up. His chest and shoulders were soaked with blood, his gun still clutched in his grasp. But there was no sign of Vale. Dwight moved his beam across the rocks and found a trail of blood leading back up the tunnel. But they couldn't see any movement.

"He's still alive," Jack said. "He got away!"

"He won't get too far." Dwight was staring at the ground a few feet away.

At his feet Jack saw a shattered glass jar. Its yellowish liquid contents were seeping into the mud.

Dwight bent down and lifted one of the pieces of dark glass. "This was a week's worth of perilium for all of us." He looked up at Jack. "What have I done?"

"We can find another way," Jack said. Though even as he heard his own words, he knew they rang hollow. "How much is left up at the lodge?"

"Vale keeps it under lock and key. Maybe a few vials. They always give us just enough to last until the next feeding time."

Jack took the flashlight and cringed as he inspected the bodies. "The big guy's dead.

Half his skull is gone." He came to Carson and saw him blink. His bloodied chest was moving. Perhaps already recovering from the wounds. "Let's just take his gun and get going."

Javier pried Carson's revolver out of his fingers and checked the bullets. Then he leaned over him. *"Cómo cambian las cosas en un par de semanas."*

Jack looked at Dwight. "What'd he say?"

Dwight just grimaced and shook his head.

They continued on. Jack had walked only a few paces when he noticed Javier was not with them. Suddenly a gunshot cracked the darkness behind him and Jack spun around. Dwight shone the light behind them, but all they saw was Javier walking toward them, sticking Carson's smoking revolver into his belt.

He didn't say a word.

Chapter 40

Elina was nearly faint with terror as Nun'dahbi finished marking her face with the black ink. She spread her hands over Elina's body, then took the staff and swept it across her again, rattling the beads and the round gourd affixed to the top.

After this she lowered her veil again and barked a few more commands to her men. They lifted Elina from the stone table and carried her toward the edge of the pit.

They looped additional ropes around her and tied them to another line connected to the log. Then one of the N'watu lifted Elina up and dropped her over the edge of the pit.

She screamed a muffled cry of terror as she felt herself fall away from the ledge over the open black maw. She swung out and then back, dangling from the log like a fishing lure.

She kicked frantically, trying to swing

herself back to the side, but another N'watu loosened the rope and began to lower her into the hole. Elina descended slowly into utter darkness. The smell of death and rot wafted up from below, a sickly sweet odor that filled her with fear. She could feel that her struggling was beginning to work the gag loose from her mouth.

Her heart pounded against her chest and she prayed desperately, wondering what was down here, what kind of horror she was about to encounter.

Then her toes scraped against something solid; she hoped it was a rock but couldn't be sure. They let her dangle there, twisting in the darkness. Waiting. She looked up and could see the black outline of the rim against the faint glow of the lanterns above her.

She hung in silence, weary from struggling. Yet her terror was like a noose, strangling her. She stared into the solid black void, waiting to die.

Suddenly a muffled clap of thunder echoed through the cavern. Elina looked up and heard some sort of commotion among the N'watu. Clearly whatever made the sound wasn't something they were expecting. She could hear them speaking to each other — arguing in their choppy, guttural language. Their sounds quickly receded, leaving her in silence again.

But now she felt a spark of hope kindle inside her. Maybe the others had gotten free somehow and were coming for her. Maybe someone had finally notified the FBI.

Or maybe . . .

Somewhere in the darkness in front of her came another sound. A low, erratic tapping, unlike anything she had ever heard before.

CHAPTER 41

The passage came to an abrupt halt, depositing Jack, Dwight, and Javier into a large, open chamber. Jack took one of the flares from his bag and snapped it open. The bright red-orange glow lit up the whole room.

Along the far wall was a large wooden gate of some kind. It stood over eight feet tall and at least six feet wide.

"Not another one," Jack groaned. He slid his hand along the wood. "So that's where they took her?"

They inspected the surface, looking for a way to open it. Jack told them about the first door he had encountered and how it opened upward. Yet this one was different. There was a clear crease running vertically up the center that seemed to indicate it opened from the middle. But there were no handles. They pushed against it to no avail, and there was clearly no way to pull it open either.

Dwight stepped back. "Looks like it only opens from the inside."

Jack sat down and rubbed his eyes. "Any suggestions?"

Javier reached into Jack's bag and pulled out one of the grenades they'd taken from the armory. *"Vamos a tocar a la puerta."*

Jack stood. "Is he going to try what I think . . . ?"

Javier scooped a bit of mud from under the middle of the door, pulled the pin out of the grenade, jammed it under the wood, and ran for cover.

Jack and Dwight scrambled back to the other side of the chamber and flung themselves behind a jutting rock formation. A few seconds later the ground shook as a clap of thunder erupted in the cavern. Jack felt his ribs jolt from the force of the blast. Rocks and debris scattered across the room, and when the air cleared, his ears were ringing from the explosion.

He stood and brushed off the mud. "Are you crazy? You could get us all killed! You don't just go setting off explosions inside caverns. You could bring the whole place down on top of us!"

But Javier was shining his flashlight at the doors. One side was cracked and splintered and had been torn off its hinge. And the other had swung wide open. He turned and grinned at Jack. "Good, yes?"

Dwight shrugged. "Well, now they know we're here."

Jack grabbed the flare and tossed it into the passage beyond the doorway. The place seemed deserted. At least for now. They got their weapons ready, Jack grabbed another couple flares, and they proceeded inside.

They spread out and moved along the passage quickly. Dwight held his flashlight out along with his gun. Jack snapped a second flare and tossed it farther ahead.

He looked into his bag and now wished desperately that he'd brought more of them with him. And to make matters worse, there was only one hand grenade left.

Dwight paused in the tunnel, his shoulders stiffening. Jack nudged him gently. "What's wrong?"

Dwight shook his head and shuddered. "Jack . . . I have to tell you something."

"What is it?"

Dwight flicked the light toward Jack's face. "We're probably not making it out of here alive."

"Come on, Dwight, don't talk like that. We're going to find her."

Dwight leaned close. Jack could see a

strange sort of resolve in his eyes. Or maybe it was resignation. "If you do — if you make it out of here — there's something in town you need to see."

"What?"

"In my office, in the back room, is a closet — a supply closet full of boxes. They're my journals. And there's something under the floor that you need to see."

"What? What is it?"

Dwight shook his head again. To Jack it looked like he was shaking himself out of a trance. "You have to make it out of here to find out."

He turned and continued through the tunnel. They walked on for several minutes before Jack could see a dim light ahead. The tunnel widened and he noticed a few side passages leading from the main tunnel. Jack saw that the passages here seemed larger and more evenly shaped, as if the N'watu had carved them right through the rock over the years.

One of the tunnels opened into a long, oval-shaped room with several small glass jars of the glowing slime scattered around the perimeter. In the middle were two long wooden tables and a large wooden chair. Dozens of pots and jars and other vessels of various sizes littered both of the tables. The whole scene reminded Jack of something out of the Dark Ages. Like an ancient alchemist's laboratory.

Jack noticed one bowl in particular looked similar to the one he had seen during the ceremony earlier. The interior appeared to have some sort of thick, dried residue on it. Jack also spotted several more glass jars of a milky, yellowish liquid stacked along the wall.

He pointed to the jars. "Is that . . . perilium?"

Dwight inspected one of them and nodded. "This must be where she prepares it."

"Who? The woman I saw? Who is she?"

"They call her Nun'dahbi. She's the matriarch of the tribe. Their queen."

Jack just shook his head as he looked through the objects in the room. "This is pretty incredible. These tables and chairs definitely show an outside influence on their culture. Maybe they're not as xenophobic as Vale says they are."

"Trust me," Dwight grunted. "They hate outsiders."

Javier had been waiting by the entrance and motioned for them to continue on. He was obviously anxious to find his cousin, and Jack quietly chided himself on getting distracted by this room. Elina was in serious peril.

They moved onward and soon emerged into another open cavern. Only this one was different from all the others. Jack could see that this one contained remnants of structures. Pillars and archways in varying states of decay. And all around them were glass lanterns similar to the one Jack had seen out in the bone pit. Clearly this was some sort of common area of the N'watu.

Jack shone his flashlight around, momentarily stunned by the discovery.

"Look at this place," he said softly. "My dad always said there was an underground city somewhere out here. This must be part of it."

Suddenly Javier grabbed Jack's shoulder as if trying to tell him something, but instead he seemed to be choking. His eyes bulged and blood dripped from between his lips as a serrated spear tip emerged from the middle of his chest and a skeletal face loomed up from behind him.

"No!" Jack shouted.

Javier slumped forward and Jack stood, stunned at the sight. The pale N'watu warrior yanked the bloody spear from Javier's back and now fixed his white eyes on Jack.

Jack could see the warrior towering over him, but he was frozen with shock. Paralyzed. He tried to will his arms to raise his weapon or his legs to run, but he felt like he was in a dream, unable to even control his limbs.

Then a gunshot rang out, snapping him out of his daze. The warrior lurched backward as a bullet tore into his chest. Jack glimpsed Dwight standing a few yards behind him, his revolver smoking. Jack spun back to see that the N'watu had quickly recovered his balance, his face contorted into a mask of fury. He raised his spear.

But now Jack lifted his shotgun and fired. White-hot pellets hit the N'watu's chest at close range, tearing through his flesh and ribs. The warrior stumbled back another few steps as Jack felt rage welling up inside him. He pumped the next shell into the chamber and fired again. This time the shot blasted directly into the warrior's face, lifting him off his feet and flat onto his back.

Before Jack could react or even check on Javier, another spear came whizzing out of the darkness and sliced across his upper arm. Jack ducked, clutching his tricep. He could feel warm blood on his fingers. He snapped another flare and tossed it out in front of him. Immediately the chamber lit up, overwhelming the soft glow of the lanterns. And Jack saw two of the warriors cringing from the light not more than fifty feet away. He strode forward, keeping his eyes fixed on the N'watu, and fired another shot. This time he was aiming high — straight for the head. One of them dropped like a sack of rocks. Jack pumped and fired at the second one, who dove behind a crumbled archway.

Jack snapped another flare and tossed it back in Dwight's direction. He could see that Dwight had both revolvers drawn and was keeping a couple more warriors at bay. One pale corpse lay at his feet.

Jack knelt next to Javier. He was coughing up blood and was barely coherent.

"Elina," he said, blood spattering from his lips. "Find . . . Elina."

Chapter 42

Elina could hear the tapping sounds echoing in the darkness, almost like someone hitting a pair of baseball bats together. Fast, then slow, changing timbre ever so slightly.

She struggled to free herself. Twisting her neck, she could feel the rope holding the rag in her mouth slide down farther.

Now off in the darkness, along with the tapping, came more noises — a series of thuds like a pickax jamming into rocky soil, and the sound of something heavy scraping along the ground.

From above she heard gunfire echoing across the cavern. Several shots were fired, and they sounded close by. Hope rose again in her, and as she twisted her head sideways, she could feel the rope slipping from her mouth.

She worked it down below her chin until at last she was able to spit out the rag, suck in a lungful of air, and scream. . . .

■ ■ ■ ■

Jack and Dwight moved back-to-back across the cavern, guns poised to fire. The flares seemed to be keeping the N'watu at bay, and they resorted to flinging their spears blindly from their positions of cover.

"Do you see her anywhere?" Jack said.

"No, I —"

Suddenly a terrified shriek echoed up from somewhere in the darkness. Jack snapped his head around and saw an open pit.

"Elina!" he cried out. "Where are you?"

"Down here!"

Jack rushed across the cavern with Dwight following close behind. Jack ignited another flare and flung it ahead of him. It hit the ground and the orange glow lit up more of the chamber. He could see several carved stone structures all situated around a central pit. A stone table stood off to one side and another structure — some sort of primitive altar — had been built right at the edge of the pit. A thick log had been mounted to the altar and extended out over the hole. Jack could see a rope hanging down from the end.

"There!" He leaned over the edge as Elina's frantic voice called up from below.

"Pull me up!"

Dwight climbed onto the wooden beam where the rope was fastened. "I'll pull the rope over."

Jack could hear the sheer terror in Elina's voice as she cried out, "Please hurry!"

Dwight scooted forward, stretching his hand out for the rope. The beam extended perhaps eight feet from the edge, and the rope was just out of his reach. He inched out a little farther, but the whole structure shifted under his weight.

Dwight slipped and plunged into the darkness.

"Dwight!" Jack screamed. Just then he saw movement from the corner of his eye. A shadow detached itself from behind one of the carved figures and shot toward him like a missile.

Jack leaped out of the way as the dark shape landed in the spot where he had been standing. In the flickering glow of the flare, he recognized the diminutive figure, the tribe's matriarch who seemed to be the leader. Dwight had called her Nun'dahbi.

She was cloaked in black veils and holding a long wooden shaft tipped with a jagged spearhead that looked like it had been fashioned from part of a kirac's foreleg. She shrugged off her outer cloak and crouched before Jack. Jack suppressed a gasp as he got his first good look at her.

Her skin was ghostly pale and her head was completely hairless. Beneath the veils she wore a snug jerkin made from some kind of animal skin, interwoven with beads and animal claws. And Jack could see she was also still wearing the amulet she'd had on earlier. The image from his father's papers.

Nun'dahbi glared at Jack with yellow eyes reflecting the light of the dying flare. The skin around her eyes was blackened, accenting the glow of her irises and giving her gaunt face a skull-like appearance. Her black lips peeled back and she hissed words Jack could not understand. Though one of them did register.

"Outsider!"

She spat the word with such contempt that Jack could almost feel her venom.

He swatted the spear away from his face and was reaching for his shotgun when something hard slammed into his ribs. He fell to his knees, gasping for breath. The woman's bare foot drew back as Jack blinked, wondering how she had struck him with such power for her size.

He rolled to the side as the spear flashed

out at him, slicing his shoulder. Jack sucked in painful gasps of air. He hadn't seen anyone move so fast in his life. The woman crouched low and moved sideways, circling him like a cat preparing to strike. Jack had never taken any formal hand-to-hand combat training, no martial arts, nothing. So reacting purely on instinct, he swept his leg back across the woman's feet, but she jumped easily out of the way.

Jack struggled to stand, dazed from the blow to his ribs. But before he could even straighten up, he felt another kick to his side and tumbled back to the ground. Nun'dahbi leaped in and out of the ring of light like a panther, striking hard and then jumping back into the darkness.

Jack had managed to stagger to his feet again when she drove a fist hard into his jaw and another one just under his sternum. He crumpled to the ground, gasping for breath. His mind wavered on the brink of consciousness and he reached blindly for his gun. Nun'dahbi leaped to the edge of the pit, raising her spear to finish him off.

But Jack rolled to the side and brought his shotgun up into her abdomen. His lips parted in a bloody grin.

"Not . . . so fast. . . ."

Her face twisted into a mask of hate as

Jack pulled the trigger. The blast launched her diminutive frame off the ground and out over the pit. She plunged, shrieking, down into the darkness.

"Jack!" Elina's terrified voice cried from the pit.

"I'm coming."

The wooden beam was tilted downward after Dwight's fall. Jack leaned against the altar, gasping for breath. He was stretching out for the rope when a deafening shriek echoed up from the pit. But Jack knew it had no human source; he had heard that sound once before, out in the caverns as he and Ben were escaping.

Elina screamed again.

Jack snapped another flare and dropped it into the pit. Now he could see the hole went down at least twenty feet. Dwight lay in the mud, and Nun'dahbi's twisted body was sprawled out on the rocks, covered in blood. Elina lay on the ground between them, wrapped tightly in ropes.

She looked up, wide-eyed. "Jack! Get me out of here!"

"I can't reach the rope!"

"Hurry; something's down here."

Jack secured his shotgun and the bag of flares around his back and leaped out for the rope. He felt it in his fingers and clutched it. The log shifted again, and he slid down several feet before managing to stop himself. The rope tore the skin off his palms as he lowered himself farther into the pit.

He reached the bottom and bent over Elina's quivering body. They had painted her face with what looked like the same type of marks that the warriors had covering their bodies.

"Are you hurt?" He fumbled with the ropes in his bloody hands. "Is anything broken?"

"No . . . I'm okay," Elina said. "You're bleeding."

Jack shook his head. His wounds throbbed and stung, but he couldn't afford the luxury of worrying about that now. "I'm okay."

Jack surveyed the elongated cavern that extended away into darkness. The flare lit the immediate area, and Jack could see numerous tunnels and side passages leading off the main chamber. Large rocks and bones cluttered the floor of the pit. The remnants, he guessed, from an untold number of human sacrifices to the Soul Eater.

Beside them, Dwight groaned.

Elina sat up. "He's alive?"

Jack moved to check him. "Dwight? Are

you okay?"

Dwight groaned again and rolled onto his side. He looked up at the top of the pit and rubbed his head. "What happened?"

"You fell," Jack said. "You should be dead."

"Yeah . . ." Dwight sat up gingerly. "I should've been dead a few times in my life."

Jack was still struggling with Elina's ropes. "I can't get them untied. I need to cut them."

"Hurry."

Jack turned to retrieve the spear wedged in the rocks beside Nun'dahbi's limp body when he saw the amulet glimmering in the light of the flare. His eyes widened. He'd lost his pack in the caves earlier and with it, all the evidence he and Rudy had collected. But this medallion would be even better. To come back with an actual N'watu artifact, a piece of their culture . . .

Momentarily forgetting everything else, Jack crawled over and reached out for the amulet.

A cold, bony grip clamped onto his arm. Nun'dahbi clutched his wrist and lifted her battered head. Blood gurgled though her clenched teeth as she grimaced, hissing with what seemed to be pure vitriol.

Jack let out a yelp. Obviously the perilium

made the N'watu as hard to kill as the kiracs.

Just then a second chilling shriek burst out of the darkness at the far end of the cavern, followed by a familiar tapping. Whatever was in the darkness was getting closer. Jack could hear a scraping sound — like something big being dragged across rocks.

Something very big.

"Hurry, Jack!" Elina's voice came from behind him.

Jack yanked his hand free from Nun'dahbi's grip. She immediately clutched the amulet in her broken, bloody fingers, still hissing curses at him and struggling to move. Jack picked up the spear instead and returned to Elina.

Dwight stumbled to his feet. "How do we get out of here?"

"I don't know. I've never been in this part of the caves." Jack sliced through the top rope and started on the bands around Elina's feet. Then the flare died out and darkness folded over them like a wave. Jack could hear Dwight digging through the bag for another one.

He snapped the cap off and ignited it.

Elina screamed.

Shadows fled away, partially revealing the

bulk of an enormous, armored beast looming directly over Dwight. It reared up, flexing its huge mandibles. The jaws opened to reveal a hideous mouthful of dripping fangs. It lifted one of its massive, spiked forelegs and stabbed at Dwight, who barely managed to duck out of the way. The pointed claw sank into the ground where he had been standing. Then it swiped sideways and flung him into the rocky wall of the chamber. Dwight fell back to the ground, groaning.

Jack found himself stunned by the sight. This thing — this *Soul Eater* — was more hideous than he could have imagined. Based on what he'd seen in Dwight's lab, he had expected the queen to be larger than the other kiracs . . . but not *this* big. Its long, bony forelegs looked like gnarled tree branches, and its jagged shell was the size of a large dining room table, ringed with hundreds of spiked protrusions.

Jack reached for his shotgun and fired directly into the beast's underside. It shrieked again — deafening at this close range. Jack pumped in another shell and fired once more. The Soul Eater lumbered backward, maneuvering its bulk with stilted, jerky movements.

Jack could sense great age in it. A twisted,

hulking beast that had been stalking these tunnels perhaps for centuries. The creature swatted at Jack with its other foreleg, sending him tumbling across the rocks. He felt like he'd been hit by a truck.

He looked back to see Elina kick her feet free of the ropes and scramble against the wall of the pit. The giant kirac swiveled its massive body around, clicking its palps as if in search of new prey. Suddenly the beast turned, raised itself off the ground, and lumbered away from Elina. Then Jack saw its new target.

Nun'dahbi was dragging herself with one arm toward the far side of the pit. Her other arm hung limp at her side and both of her legs were contorted, with a bone jutting through the flesh of one calf. Still, she struggled furiously toward one of the side tunnels. Jack spotted the amulet still in her grasp.

But the Soul Eater stalked hard after her, raising its foreleg and impaling Nun'dahbi through the back. She let out a horrifying scream and flailed her arm as the beast quickly pulled her writhing body under its bulk and sank its fangs into her neck. Nun'dahbi's cries were cut mercifully short as the Soul Eater sucked out what little life was left in her.

While the beast was occupied, Jack scrambled to his feet and rushed over to Elina. "Are you okay?" His voice was a hoarse whisper.

"I'm okay; I'm okay," Elina whispered back. "How do we get out of here?"

For a moment Jack thought they might be able to use the rope to climb out, but they'd never get up fast enough and would only be an easier target. He shrugged, keeping an eye on the giant kirac. He was quickly running out of time and his thoughts were scattered. But he couldn't let fear overwhelm him. This creature could probably smell fear from a mile away.

Just then the queen kirac lifted itself from its food and turned toward him.

Jack pulled Dwight to his feet and pointed toward one of the side passages. "Through there!"

Dwight nodded groggily as Jack pushed Elina down and into the tunnel first, then Dwight, and then . . .

Another high-pitched roar thundered through the chamber as the Soul Eater lumbered toward them.

Jack scooped up his gun and the bag of flares and dove into the dark tunnel, bashing his knees against the rocks as he scrambled forward. "Move, move!"

He turned to see the creature's bulk blocking the entrance to the tunnel. Its mouth filled the hole with a tangle of twisted fangs, hissing and snapping in a blind fury. The confined passage was filled with another piercing screech.

Jack crawled on, fumbling through the bag for another flare. He found one and ignited it. The light revealed a rather tight space, barely two feet high and curving out of sight ahead and behind. He looked into Elina's eyes and then Dwight's.

Fear was painted on both of their faces like the marks on Elina's skin. He could hear the beast still growling behind them, but they seemed out of reach and safe for the moment.

"What now?" Elina said.

Jack shook his head. "I don't know. I guess we keep going. See where this leads."

They continued on, following the narrow passage as it curved away from the sacrificial cavern. They crawled for several yards until it opened into a smaller chamber. Jack stood, thankful to at least be out of the cramped tunnel. As they ventured across the room, he could see that all over the floor were scattered curved, bony shells and fragments of appendages.

Then Elina pointed at something up

ahead. "What is *that?*"

Jack held the flare out and spotted what looked like a large rock of some kind, an unnaturally rounded boulder nearly two feet in diameter. He stood, frozen. He had seen this before. He raised the light and could see more of the objects scattered around the chamber.

Elina leaned toward Jack and whispered, "What are those things?"

But Jack stood still. Too frightened to respond.

"Jack?" Dwight whispered. "What is it?"

"I think . . ." Jack's throat was dry. "I think we're in some kind of . . . nest."

CHAPTER 43

George Wilcox sat in Thomas Vale's spacious office, behind Thomas Vale's burnished oak desk, in Thomas Vale's exquisite leather chair, with a shotgun across his lap.

Malcolm Browne — Thomas Vale's business manager — lay dead in the other room in front of Thomas Vale's massive stone fireplace. Loraine Browne, along with the Huxleys and the Dunhams, had already left for the evening and had probably gone to bed some time ago. George would deal with them later. In fact, he probably wouldn't need to do a thing.

But for the moment, all was quiet in Thomas Vale's mansion. So George sat there in the darkened office, waiting for Vale to return.

He felt little emotion, numbed by Miriam's death. Some part of him suspected he might soon join her, and that thought no longer filled him with apprehension. His wife had faced her end with courage. A courage born out of a faith that he now knew was more than empty religion. He would mourn for her when this was over. But for now he just needed to be patient.

He swiveled around and stared out the window into the night. The moon was nearly full and had already risen high into the night sky and lit up the whole countryside.

Shortly after midnight, the silence was broken by the sound of footsteps. George could hear them coming up the stairs. He listened closely. They were hurried and uneven. Someone was frightened and perhaps injured. And George could also hear the sound of labored breathing.

The footsteps reached the top and were now coming down the hall. George spun around to face the door. Moonlight streamed from behind him and lit the room with a dim but usable glow.

A silhouette appeared in the office doorway and stopped. George heard the breathing pause a moment and then resume.

Vale felt for the light switch and flipped it on. His shirt was drenched in blood, his face ashen with dark circles under his eyes. His hands were trembling, and he was sweating. Profusely. Yet he didn't look at all surprised to see George there.

George nodded toward Vale's bloodied shirt. "It looks like you ran into some trouble. It's a good thing you're immortal."

Vale scowled and lurched into the side room where he stored the perilium. George listened carefully for the sound of his reaction when he saw the refrigerators. The mangled, empty refrigerators.

A full twenty seconds later, Thomas Vale emerged from the room, his eyes looking glazed and unfocused. He clutched one trembling hand in the other. "What do you want?"

George's eyebrows went up. "Excuse me?"

"How much do you want? Ten million? Twenty?"

"Money? You think I want *money?*"

"What, then?"

George raised the shotgun and aimed it directly into Vale's face. "I want my wife back."

Vale's breathing grew more labored. "It wasn't . . . my fault. It was her . . . choice."

"Well, in that case, I'll settle for watching you die."

Vale glared at him. "What did you do . . . with it?"

George shrugged. "It's gone. Every last drop. I flushed it all down your own toilet."

George watched Vale's incredulity turn to hate. "You . . . have no idea what I was . . . offering you." He was sucking in air hard now. "The chance to be . . . young again."

George leaned back in the chair. Vale was no longer fearsome — now frail and thin, wrapping his arms around himself in an attempt to keep from trembling.

"When did you become so arrogant," George said, "to think you had the right to live off the deaths of innocent people like this? As if there would never come a reckoning."

"Off your . . . high horse, George," Vale said. "You know what you're capable of. We're . . . not so different . . . you and I."

"Tell me something, Mr. Vale," George said. "What are *you* afraid of? After all these years of cheating death, it's finally catching up with you. How does that feel?"

Vale opened his mouth, trying to respond, but his voice was already gone. He could no longer stop the tremors. Nor hide the symptoms of his impending fate. Both hands quivered violently. His arms began to tremble and then his legs.

He turned in a feeble attempt to leave. George imagined it was to find a place to hide. To keep George from witnessing the convulsions and so to rob him of that last bit of satisfaction. But his motor skills were negated now by the onslaught of his death.

George watched it spring upon him like some kind of predator as Vale crumpled to the floor — a trembling, contorted mass in its grip. His spine arched as his muscles contracted with violent spasms. His legs and arms stiffened at odd angles. Tremors racked his body and his head flung backward too, as far as his neck could bend. His jaw clenched tight as white foam frothed between his teeth. And George could see one of Vale's yellow eyes through the black snarls of hair, wide open in terror. His body flopped and jittered on the wooden floor, almost like a fish in the bottom of a boat or like some grotesque windup doll.

George drew long, slow breaths, fighting the urge to look away. It was a more gruesome spectacle than he had expected, and at length he could no longer stand to watch. His eyes moved to the clock on the wall.

Thirty seconds . . .

Forty-five seconds . . .

A full sixty seconds before the tremors finally abated and Thomas Vale lay still in a twisted heap.

But for the gagging rattle deep in his throat, it had been a silent, protracted death.

CHAPTER 44

Elina peered at the spherical objects in the light of the flare and could now see they weren't rocks at all. "What are they?"

"Egg sacs." Jack's voice grew shaky. "Like the one I saw before."

Dwight kicked the smaller shell fragments. "Then . . . I'm guessing these are bodies of the males. Maybe the ones who get eaten after mating or something."

Elina shuddered. "Mating?"

Then the flare went out and darkness fell around them. Elina reached out for Jack, but the only sound was their breathing, echoing through the chamber.

Complete, smothering darkness hung on them like a death shroud. Then out of the inky black void, Elina heard the tapping sound she'd heard in the other chamber, and it sent a shiver through her body.

Jack lit another flare, and the brightness of its orange light filled the nesting chamber . . . with the exception of a large shadow that emerged from a tunnel on the far side. An enormous black shape hauled itself into the room.

The beast paused just outside the circle of light, clicking its fangs together as if trying to get its bearings. Or trying to locate its prey.

Elina fought to keep still, remembering what Vale had said about the creature's being able to smell fear — sensing it somehow in its prey. She sucked a long, slow breath into her lungs and held it.

But at that moment the beast lurched toward them. Its armored legs pounded across the stones in great, jerky strides and its jaws opened in a deafening shriek.

Jack yelled, "Get back in the tunnel!"

They spun around and dashed the way they had come with the creature lumbering after them. Elina's foot twisted on the shell fragments littering the floor and she tumbled to the ground. She felt a hand on her arm and saw Jack leaning over her, holding the flare.

"Come on!"

He tugged at her arm, trying to help her up, but it was as if time had slowed down as a huge, twisted shadow appeared behind them.

Suddenly Dwight leaped into the kirac's path, holding another flare in one hand and a pistol in the other. He fired off several shots directly into the creature's mouth, but the bullets only served to enrage it further.

The beast lifted one of its forelegs to strike.

Jack pulled Elina to her feet just as the giant queen impaled Dwight through his chest and pinned him to the ground. It reared up and hissed. Dwight's limbs quivered as blood poured from his mouth. One arm reached frantically for his gun but instead found the canvas bag Jack had dropped in the scramble toward the tunnel. He clutched it as the beast wrenched him sideways with an angry growl.

"Jack!" Elina grabbed Jack's arm and pointed to Dwight.

"Get out," Dwight gasped, choking on his own blood. "Go!"

He lifted his hand and Elina spotted a round, metallic object in his grasp. She blinked. It looked for all the world like a . . .

Hand grenade.

She saw him pluck out the pin as the giant spider growled and pulled him into its embrace, sinking its fangs into his chest.

Jack darted forward to grab the bag, then took hold of Elina's wrist and yanked her back into the tunnel as the explosion shook the entire cavern.

The roar was deafening and followed by a loud, steady rumble. She could feel the ground vibrating beneath her. Her mind gave way to terror as she realized she had escaped this horrible beast only to be buried alive under tons of rock. The roar of the quake seemed to go on forever. Dust filled the passage, choking her and stinging her eyes. She squeezed them shut and prayed as a strange peace began to fill her mind. Her heart calmed; her breathing slowed. If this was the end, then she knew her life — her *soul* — was in God's hands.

Elina lay in complete darkness for what felt like several minutes, wondering if she was dead. She was cold and wet and every muscle ached from her ordeal, yet she knew they weren't safe yet. The explosion had collapsed the cavern behind them, sealing them inside the tunnel. Her ears still rang from the blast, and she lay in the cold mud. The vision of the enormous armored spider had been etched into her brain. That and her experience with the N'watu would certainly rob her of sleep for many weeks to come.

As her hearing returned, she could make out Jack's steady, rapid breathing next to her, and she knew at least they were alive.

"Jack," she whispered, "are you okay?"

She felt him stir beside her. "I . . . I think so. How about you?"

"I'm okay. Nothing broken."

She could hear Jack feeling around the passage.

"Well, I still have my shotgun," he said after a moment. "And the bag of flares. But I only have a few left and they won't last long."

"How . . . how did you even manage to find me?"

"It was Dwight," Jack said. "He came down after Vale took you away and let the rest of us out. Apparently something gave him a change of heart."

"He freed everyone?" Elina's hope rose. "What happened to Javier?"

Jack didn't answer right away. There was a muted pop as he lit one of the flares. Sparks flew all over in the cramped space and Elina's eyes ached from the light, but she could see that Jack's face looked grim.

"What's wrong?" she said. "Where *is* Javier?"

Jack shook his head. "He came with us to save you. But he didn't . . . I'm sorry. He was killed during the fighting."

Elina stared at him. "Dead?" She ached as though a weight were pressing down on her shoulders. She had come all this way to find him. Now all the emotions she had tried so hard to control over the last few days finally broke through. She began to sob even as she tried to tell herself this wasn't the time for crying.

After a minute she felt Jack's hand on her shoulder. "Look, I'm sorry. I know it's a shock — and I'm really sorry — but we have to get going; we're running out of flares."

Elina sucked in a deep breath and wiped her eyes, choking back her tears. She knew he was right. She could mourn for her cousin later. "What do we do now?"

They inspected the tunnel. The way behind them was thoroughly closed off. Several large boulders blocked the entrance, and they couldn't move them.

Finally Jack sighed. "I think there was a side passage up here."

They had to maneuver on their hands and knees, which was slow going, but after several dozen yards the tunnel split, and the secondary tunnel eventually opened into a larger chamber. They emerged and stood up. Jack held the flare aloft and looked around. Elina peered up at him. He wasn't what she had expected. He was taller than she had imagined, for one thing. Taller than her by several inches and slender with short-cropped black hair, large brown eyes, and . . .

"Listen, Jack . . . thank you for saving me." She looked down sheepishly. "But . . . why didn't you tell me you were black?"

Jack blinked and looked down at his arms. "I am?"

Elina couldn't help laughing. "I mean, after I said all those things?"

Jack raised an eyebrow and smiled. "I guess I didn't think it mattered at the time."

Elina shook her head. "It didn't. I just —"

"And for the record, technically you never told me you were Hispanic."

Elina laughed again. Despite all the horror she'd just been through, in her exhausted condition it felt good to laugh. "You mean my last name being Gutierrez didn't give it away, or . . ."

She stopped as she saw Jack's smile fade.

"What's wrong?" she said.

Jack shrugged. "This place . . . looks a little familiar."

Elina wasn't sure this was a hopeful sign. "So you know where we are?"

Jack tossed the flare ahead of them. It flew up in a long arch and bounced to a halt in front of another strange rock formation. Only as Elina looked closer, she could see it wasn't rock at all. It was a pile of white . . .

bones. A huge stack of bones piled high against the side of the cavern.

"Are those what I think they are?"

But Jack had fallen quiet.

"Jack?" she said again. "Please tell me those aren't human —"

"We need to get moving," Jack said as he ignited another flare. "I think I know the way."

Jack pointed in the direction opposite the pile of bones and moved quickly across the uneven floor. Elina hurried to keep up but could feel a presence somewhere off in the darkness. Some kind of impending menace, like an enormous shadow preparing to swoop down and swallow them.

After a moment Jack stopped, tilting his head.

"What is it?" Elina said.

At first the only sounds she could hear were her own breathing and the hiss of the flare. Then soon she heard something else. The eerie tapping sound she'd come to dread. But this time it was different. This time it sounded like more than one.

A lot more.

"Jack . . ."

But Jack grabbed her hand. *"Run!"*

He led her on a zigzag route across the cavern. The flare crackled and sputtered and

Elina thought she could see shadows scurrying along the ground just outside the ring of light. Jack pulled her behind him until they finally reached the other side. A black wall of rock loomed up in front of them. Jack looked like he was searching for something.

Maybe another tunnel. Hopefully the way out.

Something skittered along the rocks behind her and she screamed. A black shape raced toward her out of the darkness. It was a miniature version of the giant kirac, only the size of a dog. But it was faster and seemed far more aggressive.

Jack charged the creature, flare held out in front of him. He swung his leg and booted the beast back into the darkness. Then he turned and yanked her arm. "This way!"

They moved along the wall until they came to another opening. A passage leading up at an angle. Jack tossed the flare behind them and boosted Elina into the tunnel.

The flare landed a few yards away, where it illuminated a horde of the spider creatures — of all sizes — scurrying toward them.

Jack pumped his shotgun and blasted the closest one, flipping it backward into the pack. The others immediately converged on the wounded creature, tearing it to pieces. One of the bigger creatures launched itself toward them. Jack raised the shotgun and fired point-blank, blasting a hole right through it. It bounced off Jack, knocking him down, and landed on the ground, twitching in front of him.

Jack scrambled to his feet, covered in yellow guts, and pulled himself up into the tunnel. "Go, go, go!"

Elina turned and climbed up the angled passage, scraping her hands and cracking her head against the jagged walls.

"I can't see where I'm going!"

Jack lit a flare and handed it to her. "Last one," he said. "Now go — hurry!"

Elina held the crackling flare in one hand and climbed as fast as she could up the tunnel. Water trickled down past her and she had to keep the flare from getting wet. At length the passage widened out and came to a dead end.

She crouched in the space and turned around. "What now?"

Jack was clawing his way up just a few yards behind her. "Up. Climb straight up."

Elina could see a small opening above her, perhaps into another passage. Water was streaming down through it. She stood and tried to find a foothold but couldn't reach the opening.

In moments Jack had joined her in the cramped space. He took the flare and boosted her into the opening. Elina scrambled up and found herself in a wide, low passage, worn smooth by a constant flow of water. She could feel it angling the other way, sloping down into complete darkness.

Jack struggled to climb into the passage. "Pull me up!"

Elina reached down through the opening and clutched his arm. Suddenly she saw something moving in the passage behind him. One of the spiders, a big one, was coming up fast.

"Jack!"

"I know!"

He turned, pointed the shotgun down the tunnel, and pulled the trigger.

Click.

He pumped and tried again but was clearly out of ammo. He jammed the gun diagonally into the passage, wedging it tight between the walls just as the kirac slammed into it, hissing and growling. Elina could see its fangs twitching. Its forelegs reached through and clawed at Jack's feet, but the gun held fast.

Behind it, Elina saw movement. More

were coming.

Jack turned and jumped for Elina's hand. She caught hold and pulled while he scrambled up. "Don't let go!"

Elina pulled his arms and shoulders into the passage.

"Pull me up!" Jack said frantically. "Pull me up!"

Elina strained, her muscles burning. She leaned back into the tunnel as Jack clawed at the rocks, trying desperately to pull himself up. She could feel her hands slipping.

Jack shook his head, his eyes wide in terror. "Don't let go!"

Elina pulled with all her strength. But his hands slipped through her grasp and her momentum sent her sliding backward down the passage into the darkness.

CHAPTER 45

"Jack!"

Elina slid through total darkness, clawing at the sides of the tunnel but unable to stop. She slid down the passage until she felt herself falling through empty space and plunging into icy waters. She surfaced, gasping for air, and felt a current pulling her along, swirling and spinning until at last she felt solid ground again under her feet.

A rush of terror swept over her. She was lost in complete darkness, and now she was utterly alone.

And Jack was probably dead as well. He had risked his life to save her, but she hadn't been able to save him. Elina couldn't hold back her tears.

Then, above the sound of the waterfall, she thought she heard another sound.

It was soft but grew steadily louder until she finally recognized it. It was Jack's voice. She heard him emerge from the tunnel above her and splash down into the water.

Her hopes rose. “Jack!”

“Elina?” he called back.

She laughed as relief washed over her. They called out to each other in the pitch-blackness until at last she felt his hands. She threw her arms around him and hugged him tighter than she had ever hugged anyone in her life.

He was laughing. “I know where we are. There’s an underwater passage here that leads outside. All we have to do is wait until daylight.”

With Jack leading, they found the shoreline and collapsed on the soft, pebbled ground, flooded with relief.

Elina lay on her back, exhausted.

Jack woke up to a dim gray light filtering into the cave. His head was still buzzing from the horrors he’d seen back in the tunnels. And yet his chest ached at the thought of losing the amulet in the pit. He wondered what the artifact meant and what significance it held for the N’watu. He’d actually held it in his grasp for an instant, but now it was likely lost for good. His lips tightened. He’d come so close.

If only he’d had a few more seconds.

He touched Elina’s shoulder to wake her.

"I think the sun's up."

He helped her up and led her along the shoreline until he could see daylight through the underwater tunnel. They plunged one last time into the water and swam through to the other side, where they emerged in the small lake under a blue sky.

They swam to the shore and lay in the dirt, soaking in the sunlight. After a minute, Elina crawled back to the edge of the water. Jack could see she was staring at her reflection. Her face was covered with black marks, obviously something the N'watu had done as part of their ritual.

Elina stood up to face him. "All I can say is this stuff better not be permanent."

Jack looked her over now in the daylight. She had short black hair and beautiful brown eyes. But any other feminine softness her face might have held was tempered by a firm jawline and a two-inch scar that ran across her chin. She carried herself on a short athletic frame with a rugged sort of beauty. Jack could tell she had been a cop, and a tough one.

The black marks on her face had faded a bit from being in the water but were still fairly distinct. There was no telling what kind of substance the ink was made from. Jack grinned and tried to sound reassuring.

"Actually, it's kind of attractive."

"Said the guy with no funky marks on his face."

Jack laughed and pointed toward the trees. "C'mon. The road isn't too far." He led her through the woods, retracing the route he had taken only two days earlier.

"What day is it, anyway?" Elina asked.

"Uhh . . ." Jack rubbed his eyes, trying to calculate the number of days he'd spent in darkness and terror. "It's Saturday. Or, no . . . Sunday, I think."

At length they came to a highway. Jack explained that this was where he had first run into Malcolm Browne. He pointed up the road. "The town's just up that way."

Elina stopped. "We're not really going back there, are we?"

Jack thought about that for a moment. "Well, Carson and that big guy are both dead back in the tunnel. And I think Vale was injured pretty badly too, so I'm guessing he's either dead or will be soon." He shrugged, recalling Dwight's enigmatic message to him before he died. "Besides, Dwight said there was something in his office that I needed to see."

"What is it?"

"That's what I want to find out."

They walked through the morning, slogging along the pavement without seeing a single vehicle. They passed the time talking, sharing their respective histories. It felt strange to Jack, but there was something about Elina that made him feel as if he'd known her for years. He told her more about his own journey and his father's disappearance. Elina seemed fascinated by the mystery but stopped short of saying what Jack himself had been thinking all along, though his heart had not wanted to speak the words.

"I can't bring myself to think about how he might have died," Jack said finally. "That they would have sacrificed him to that —"

"But you don't know that for sure," Elina said.

Not knowing was of little comfort. Something inside Jack still yearned to find out exactly what had happened to his father. Despite how gruesome it might have been.

His thoughts drew back to the mysterious amulet. It had been the confirmation he'd been looking for, the evidence he had come all this way to find, and now it lay under a mountain of rock. Forever out of reach. He could have validated his father's theories, but now he was leaving empty-handed with so many questions unanswered. He still didn't know what the symbols meant, and now he feared he never would.

But even worse than that was what he had lost along the way. He'd come through his nightmare having left his best friend back in those caves.

It wasn't until the sun was directly above them that they finally reached Beckon once more. They walked through the middle of town, where everything seemed as quiet and as still as death.

They came to the old Saddleback Diner and peeked in the windows, but no one was around. Then they crossed the street to Dwight Henderson's office and went inside. The place was cluttered and musty, and Jack made his way down the hall to the back room.

The door was locked, but after a few attempts, Jack managed to kick it open. Inside stood an antique desk, a couple chairs, and some file cabinets. In the corner was a door to the supply closet that was stacked full of boxes.

Jack inspected the boxes as he pulled them out. Each one was packed with notebooks. He shuffled through the top box and grabbed one of the books. "Looks like Dwight had been keeping quite a few journals."

Elina peered over his shoulder for a better

view. "What do they say?"

"Whoa." Jack tapped the cover. "Look at the date on this one."

Elina took the book and frowned as she scanned the pages. "Nineteen *forty-seven?*"

Jack opened a second box and pulled out another leather-bound journal. "Nineteen twenty-one."

"These can't all be his," Elina said.

But Jack was busy digging through another box. "He must have wanted me to find them."

Elina began searching through the boxes as well. A moment later she pulled out a folder and showed it to Jack. Inside was a photograph. A very *old* photograph. In the picture, Dwight stood in front of what looked like a saloon. He was wearing a striped shirt with a vest and a bow tie. Beside him was an attractive Hispanic woman. And next to them stood Frank Carson and Malcolm Browne. The sign behind them read, *The Saddleback.*

Elina stared at Jack. "This can't be for real . . . can it?"

Jack shrugged. "He told me perilium not only enhances the body's immune system but also slows down or even reverses the aging process."

Elina gestured to all the boxes on the

floor. "Well, these dates would mean that Dwight was more than a hundred years old."

"At least," Jack said. His gaze beat a trail around the room. "I wonder how old the others were. For that matter, how old were those N'watu in the cave? They might have been down there for hundreds of years."

The thought was staggering to Jack. He shuddered when he considered the implications of such a miracle drug. And the cost for the people trapped in this town by it. No wonder Vale went to such lengths to protect his secret.

Elina lifted out another leather-bound journal, this one tattered, its pages yellowed and stained. She thumbed through the brittle pages. Coming to one passage in particular, she stopped and read the words aloud.

"I am finding that my great distaste for these activities has waned of late, as well as for Mr. Vale and that godforsaken town. Regardless of my part in the matter, I can no longer pity those souls I have sent to their destruction. I no longer have the room left in my heart for it, for I am driven too deeply by love for my dearest Julia and I am ever compelled to save her. I will not lose her. My soul be cursed, I will not lose her."

She paused before reading the date. "October 11 . . . 1899."

They looked at each other in silence. After a moment Elina said, "I wonder if he found it again. His conscience, I mean."

Jack had found a bitter reflection in Dwight Henderson's words, echoed by the stinging indictment he had received from Thomas Vale. He'd been driven here by his obsession to solve his father's mystery. And more than that, to validate his father's theories and perhaps thereby gain some of that legacy for himself. But at what expense? Jack wondered now if he had lost a portion of his own conscience somewhere along the way, buried deep beneath his ambitions.

Alongside the bones of his friend.

But more importantly, would he ever find it again?

He looked back at Elina and gave a faint smile. "I think maybe he did."

Then a thought struck him. "Wait a minute." He began to dig furiously through the boxes, searching the dates until he located the right one. He looked up at Elina. "Twelve years ago."

Elina's eyebrows went up. "You think

there's something about your dad in there?"

Jack flipped through the notebook, his hands nearly trembling, following the dates until he discovered the one he was looking for. Part of him hoped he would find something — some clue or mention to help him gain closure. To know at last what had happened. But part of him hoped he wouldn't.

Then Jack froze as his eyes fell across his father's name. His heart was beating so fast he could barely read it.

"He *was* here," Jack said. "Vale lied to me."

"Of course he lied," Elina said. "He wanted to keep his little operation here a secret."

Jack scanned the pages. They had indeed captured his father. He had come upon the town and was asking questions. Asking for directions to the nearby Caieche reservation. Not suspecting a thing.

Jack fought back his emotions. "He . . . he never even made it to the reservation."

He read further as Dwight detailed how they had held his father captive in Vale's compound on the hill. Vale had hoped to utilize his knowledge to study the N'watu for his own advantage. Vale was, after all, a prisoner of the lost tribe like everyone else. And he was searching desperately for some clue to the secret of the perilium. A way to concoct it for himself. They held Jack's father there for several months, giving him limited access to part of the caves and allowing him to study the tribe at some length. Even to meet Nun'dahbi herself. No doubt his father had seen the woman's amulet even as Jack had. The artifact that appeared to have been so important in his father's other notes. Jack read until he came to a section that sent chills down his back.

One day his father had attempted an escape and fled into the woods. Dwight detailed how Carson and the others had tracked him down. They used dogs and hunted him. Cornered him like an animal. But his father was not going to give up easily. There was a struggle, and . . . And shots were fired.

> Carson acknowledged that Kendrick had left him little choice. In the end, the man was simply not willing to cooperate, and while his elimination was regrettable, he was too great a risk to keep alive any longer. And Vale has never been one to risk much.

Jack stared at the words on the page. The account had been written with such clinical detachment. Almost as if they had put down a rabid dog and not a human being.

He wept as Dwight described how they had hauled his father's dead body into the cave to be fed to the kiracs.

But there was something else.

Dwight also indicated that he had retained the research journal Jack's father had kept in hopes of eventually finding something useful. He wrote that he had hidden it under the floorboards inside the closet.

Jack went back to the closet and knelt down to inspect the floor. One of the boards was indeed loose and rattled beneath Jack's hand.

His heart was pounding as he pried it up, surging with the same emotions he'd felt when he first discovered the hidden compartment in his father's desk.

Under the floorboard was a thick notebook covered in dust. Jack lifted it out and blew the dirt off. He opened it and felt as if his heart would burst through his ribs. On the inside cover, written in faded ink, was a name.

David C. Kendrick

He held up the book. "It's his journal!"

Jack thumbed through the pages and

found that the entries went back several years before his father's disappearance. They appeared to chronicle most of his expeditions. Some of it was written in English, but other parts were in Latin. Some in Greek and even some in what looked like Hebrew. But parts of the last several pages were written in . . .

Jack peered closer. The writing used the same characters he had seen inside the caves. He looked up at Elina, not knowing whether to scream or laugh or cry. A thousand emotions clamored for dominance. He couldn't wait to pore over the pages of the book. To find out what secrets it might hold. And what answers. He rocked back on his knees, clutching the journal to his chest as though it were his father himself.

They left the office and stepped out onto the street. Jack held the old journal tight under his arm. Down the street he saw Malcolm's rust-colored pickup parked at the filling station on the edge of town. George Wilcox stood beside it, pumping gas.

Elina waved and shouted, "George!"

"So you made it out of there," George said as they ran up.

"Barely." Jack looked up at the shadowy lodge perched at the top of the bluff. "What about the others?"

"Most of them are dead. Or dying. I watched Vale die myself. Just after I told him I had flushed the last of his precious perilium down the toilet."

Elina peered into the garage windows. "They've got my car almost completely disassembled in there."

"Yeah, mine too," George said.

Elina shook her head. "They had their own chop shop set up to hide the evidence."

George pointed to the fenced-in yard behind the station, overgrown with weeds. "They must turn them into scrap metal and stick them out back."

Jack noticed a large bundle of linen lying in the bed of the pickup. It looked like a body wrapped in sheets.

"Is . . . is this your . . . ?"

"My wife, Miriam," George said, putting his hand on the sheet. "I brought her here to try to save her life, but she . . ." His voice cracked with emotion. "But she ended up saving mine. I'm going to bring her home for a decent burial."

"Would you mind giving us a ride?" Jack said. "I have an old RV that should still be parked a few miles away."

George gestured to the cab. "Hop in."

They climbed into the truck, and as George pulled back onto the road, Jack noticed the old wooden sign at the edge of town.

Welcome to Beckon. You're not here by chance.

And it struck him just then how true it was.

ABOUT THE AUTHOR

Jump in. Hang on.

Tom Pawlik is the highly imaginative, Christy Award–winning author of *Vanish, Valley of the Shadow,* and *Beckon.* His thought-provoking, edge-of-your-seat thrillers are infused with nonstop suspense that grabs you on the first page and won't let go until the last.

Tom's fascination with the weird, the creepy, and the unknown began at a very early age when he was introduced to a nineteenth-century storybook called *Der Struwwelpeter* — a collection of nightmarish morality tales by a German physician who obviously had too much time on his hands. The Mother Goose–meets–Stephen King nursery rhymes included "Daumenlutscher" ("Thumbsucker"), a disturbing yarn about a young boy who was warned that if he continued to suck his thumbs, the local tailor would chop them off with his sewing shears. Other macabre tales warned against playing with matches and being overly messy. Needless to say, Tom never played with matches, generally kept his room clean, and to this day retains the use of both his thumbs.

But the psychological damage was already done, and Tom's warped imagination turned him to writing his own creepy stories at a rather young age. Alas, no publishers were brave enough to bring them to print, so Tom would not realize his lifelong dream of becoming a published author until the ripe old age of forty-two. Today, Tom lives in Ohio and is happily married with five children of his own . . . who, oddly enough, never sucked their thumbs.

Visit Tom's website at www.tompawlik.com.

The employees of Thorndike Press hope you have enjoyed this Large Print book. All our Thorndike, Wheeler, and Kennebec Large Print titles are designed for easy reading, and all our books are made to last. Other Thorndike Press Large Print books are available at your library, through selected bookstores, or directly from us.

For information about titles, please call:
(800) 223-1244

or visit our Web site at:
http://gale.cengage.com/thorndike

To share your comments, please write:

Publisher
Thorndike Press
10 Water St., Suite 310
Waterville, ME 04901